"How Do You Like the Art Business?"

"I'm not sure it's what I expected," she said. "All the money! I thought it would be art for art's sake and all that, but it really is a business, isn't it..."

She leaned back and, for the first time, savored the pure physical intimacy of a kiss. Greedy for more, she put her free hand on David's shoulder, holding him there until, breathless, he was released.

"I never kissed anyone before quite like that," she said. "It's nice. Are you going to take me to bed?"

THE BIDDERS

John Baxter

THE BIDDERS

JOHN BAXTER

BERKLEY BOOKS, NEW YORK

This Berkley book contains the complete
text of the original hardcover edition.
It has been completely reset in a type face
designed for easy reading, and was printed
from new film.

THE BIDDERS

A Berkley Book / published by arrangement with
the author

PRINTING HISTORY
J. P. Lippincott Company edition published 1979
Berkley edition / September 1980

ISBN: 0-425-04604-4

A BERKLEY BOOK ® TM 757,375
Berkley Books are published by Berkley Publishing Corporation,
200 Madison Avenue, New York, New York 10016.
PRINTED IN THE UNITED STATES OF AMERICA

**For
HARRY LINNEY
Book-man under-ground**

The highest bidder shall be the buyer. If any dispute arises the auctioneer shall have the absolute discretion to settle it and to put any disputed lot up again....

They have full discretion to refuse any bidding, to divide any lot, to combine any two or more lots and to withdraw any lot or lots from the sale without in any case giving any reason....

Any statement as to authorship, attribution, origin, date, age, provenance and condition is a statement of opinion and is not to be taken as a statement or representation of fact.

From the "Standard Conditions of Sale" of Sotheby Parke Bernet and Co.

THE BIDDERS

PROLOGUE

The present

Loneliness is a winter in the heart.

Sara Hershman felt its chill as she wandered through the old building on 11th Street, searching for some fragment of the happiness she had once felt there.

No warmth remained in the cavernous spaces of the auction house, once so full of people and life. But as she gathered around her the shell of fur, of wool and silk, finally of flesh, she recognized that the real cold lay inside—under the ribs, around the heart.

Once, it had been her greatest happiness to play here, climbing the mountains of furniture stored in the warehouse, dodging the feet of customers as she crept into the auction rooms, huddling under the rostrum from which her father and grandfather ruled like prophets, the thunder of authority in the gavels that smacked down with a crash to signal a sale.

A similar sharp sound echoed through the building and she looked up, half expecting to see the room crowded again, and those lost men grinning down at her. But the room remained empty, and as a dozen more similar crashes followed, she knew the sound came from outside, where they were impatient to begin. As if to underline the point, the shadow of a machine glided across the grimy front window, tall, angular and predatory.

It was getting late. She would have to leave soon, with nothing found.

Little remained of the old interior. After the House of
Hershman moved uptown, a succession of lessees had occupied
the place on 11th Street. Of the offices at the front of the
building, once partitioned off from the main warehouse space,
only two remained, their wooden walls splintered by forklifts,
the windows caked with notices, posters, pinups. Even the locks
no longer functioned. One push of her gloved hand opened a
squealing door on a dark littered space....

"Lady?"

A man stood uncertainly behind her in the main door, a
hardhat silhouette against the yellow streetlight.

"Is it time?"

"Yeah. You'd better get-out."

"I'm coming."

She took a tentative step into the office and her foot kicked
something, sending it slithering across the floor.

"Have you got a flashlight?"

Uncertainly, he unhooked one from his belt. "There ain't
nothing here. We checked."

"I said I was coming." She still had the knack of giving
orders; ten years of retirement had not changed that. Even in the
dim light, her face showed the familiar defiance, her eyes the
same flashing black arrogance. Grudgingly he stepped back,
leaving her in darkness again.

The flashlight beam showed he had told the truth. Everything
was gone: desks, carpets, telephones, even the light fittings. A
single calendar, two years old, decorated the bare walls.

But she had kicked something. What? It had slid to the far
corner, into a heap of debris: dust, papers, broken glass.

It was a photographic frame, the gilt tarnished, the glass
broken, only the cardboard backing still intact. But she knew the
photograph that belonged here. Ignoring the shards of glass, she
scrabbled in the rubbish for it.

It was there—crumpled, edged with mold, but miraculously
intact. A stern bearded face under a flat black hat; a man
fashionably dressed in the double-breasted style of the 1930s;
another man beside him, his gray beard combed out over a silk
tie....

Sara brought the flashlight close to the picture, probing
through the dust for a flash of recognition. But more than dust
separated her from these men. Years lay between them—years of
blood and hate and a little love.

Dust clung to the sleeves of her coat as she straightened up and, with the photograph under her arm, walked toward the main door. As her hand moved to open it, a blaze of light flared through the windows, lancing through cracks in the wood; needles of light seemed to pierce her like knives.

She stepped out into a blinding glare. Across the street, floodlights sizzled in the light rain.

"OK," the foreman said impatiently, waving the crews forward. They converged on the building, dragging cables behind them over the wet street. "You'd better get back behind the barrier, lady."

Eleventh Street had been cordoned off to hold back the crowds. She took a few steps into the darkness beyond the machines, then paused, ignoring her resolution not to watch.

The cables were soon fastened. A winch whined, the wires tightened, and with a screech of rusted metal the ancient fire escape peeled off the front of the building like a dead vine, to fall with a roar into the gutter.

Before the red cloud of rust had settled, the first blow of the wrecking crane swung against the high brick frontage. Old and tired, the building offered no resistance. Almost without slowing, the metal hammer broke through and an avalanche of debris cascaded into the street.

Clutching the photograph, Sara pushed through the crowd of onlookers, searching for the car. She wondered if he could see her. Then he flashed the lights. Gratefully she climbed inside. People were rushing by, scarves of breath trailing over their shoulders.

"All finished?"

"No. But I didn't want to watch any more."

Snow had begun to fall. Wet flakes clung to the windshield, and the street beyond became less distinct as they backed into the darkness.

"You must be cold."

She gathered her coat around her, feeling the photograph press into her breasts.

It was ten years since she had turned her back on the world represented by the ruined shell of Hershman's—ten happy years, with no need to consider each part of her life in terms of its value on the auction block.

"No, I'm not cold."

She snuggled down, letting the smell of fur and dust carry her back to the days before it had all gone so frighteningly wrong.

BOOK ONE

1934

1

Sara loved the smells of her childhood best of all.

Fur. And dust. And the piney pungency of wood, overlaid with the tickling bite of the linseed oil her grandfather used to smarten up his stock.

Choosing some vast Victorian wardrobe in mahogany or walnut, she would slip inside and, crouching in the corner, reach out with her senses into the welcoming dark for hints of the people who had owned it.

That was in the thirties, so there was always silk and fur; sometimes she almost heard the rustle of gowns and suits swaying on their hangers, whispering together.

Occasionally, more than shadows remained in the abandoned furniture. Groping once toward something caught on a hook at the back of a wardrobe, she pulled back her hand with a squeal as it touched hard dry skin and mangy fur. In the slit of light from the almost closed door, an eye glittered glassily from an abandoned fur piece, too raddled to salvage.

Silk, fur—and perfume.

Heavy, cheap scent from the five-and-dime; the dusty tang of sandalwood; choking patchouli; and, sometimes, a softer, heavier musk, almost rotten, like overripe peaches.

Sara remembered vividly the first time that scent caught at her throat. Wrinkling her nose against it, she curled deeper into her warm corner—then, almost against her will, sniffed again, cautiously, hungrily. Sensation shivered through her. She felt dizzy and strange....

Then a voice boomed through the warehouse; a hand pounded on cupboards and tables; dust cloths were whisked aside, drawers pulled out and thrust back with a slam.

"Where's that girl of mine? I know she's around here someplace. I wonder if I can find her."

Stiffling a giggle, Sara snuggled into the deepest corner of the wardrobe until the doors were flung open and her father swooped to carry her in his arms out into the front of the store.

She must have been three or four then, which would make it 1934. In those days, the warehouse on 11th Street was still the second-hand furniture store it had been for twenty years, ever since her grandfather set it up after coming from Russia. The House of Hershman came later.

But forty years later, a picture of the old place hung in the boardroom of the House of Hershman, its bleak brick front and grimy windows a permanent reminder that buying and selling never changed—only the things you sold and the people who bought them.

In the photograph, her father and grandfather stood proudly on the sidewalk, flanking the large wooden double doors: young Nat, smart in a double-breasted pinstripe and a new homburg, his face with its thin mustache lit with a matinee-idol smile; and Jake, his beard only touched with white in those days, and not the tangled mat of hair, yellow-streaked and untrimmed, that it was to become in later years—the later years when her father—

But she tried not to think about what came after. Better to remember Father and Grandpa as they were that summer's day in 1934 when Nat carried her effortlessly in his arms out into the sun. Grandpa, sleeves rolled up, handkerchief mopping his face, was bargaining for a cartload of furniture with one of his oldest customers.

"Twenty dollars! Twenty?" Hymie Feinstein shouted. "You think maybe I'm in the gift business? Santa Claus, maybe?"

Jake tucked his thumb into his waistband and stared across 11th Street at the warehousemen spilling out at the end of their shift. "You know something, Hymie? I remember when that place was just a field. A field, would you believe? With cows already. This whole street"—he waved his hand to where 11th Street receded in the thick yellow haze of August—"all farms when I first came here," he said—inaccurately.

"The philosophy I can do without, Jake. We're doing *business* here."

"So let's do business," Jake said briskly, as if it was not his intransigence that held matters up. For the fiftieth time he strolled around the loaded cart, testing the plush on a chair with his thumb, rapping a bedhead with a knuckle, tugging on the web of ropes that kept the towering heap in precarious equilibrium.

Finally, standing in front of the aged horse between the shafts, he contemplated the animal with more enthusiasm than he had shown for the furniture.

"Hymie, you should do something for this horse. A sadder one I've never seen. Nathan—" He turned to look for Nat and saw him leaning against the door of the showroom with Sara clinging to his hand. "Go get some oats for Mr. Feinstein's horse."

"Jake, forget the horse! Forget the oats! The furniture, Jake! The furniture!" Hymie Feinstein yanked at the ropes so that the load trembled alarmingly. "You want to buy it or not?"

"Hymie, I'd like to help you. I can see you need the money, with your horse in this state, but . . . look, just wait. I'll go look in the cashbox."

He strolled into the shop, with Nat on his heels. Sara tagged along on short fat legs.

"Pop, that's good stuff," Nat said. "There's a mahogany bed, and the commode looks like maple."

"Yeah, it's maple." Opening the door of the tiny office, Jake flopped into his swivel chair and folded his hands over his stomach. Nat fidgeted, staring out through the showroom to where Feinstein stood in the sun, directing an angry tirade at his horse.

"Pop?"

Odd how like his mother the boy looked, Jake thought. Not much of me there at all. The Hershmans were stocky, with thick bodies and slightly bowed legs. Little Sara had the same build. If Nat's wife kept feeding her like she did, she'd grow up fat.

But Rachel, his wife, had come from the Polish tribes, thin, dark, and graceful. He had a brief vision of their wedding night, the shift slipping from that body, as white as porcelain except for— He dragged himself away from forty years ago, another country, and a woman already dead ten years, unlocked the heavy green iron safe, took out the cashbox, and counted twenty-five dollars in greasy bills. Shoving them in his pocket, he carefully relocked the safe and stood up.

"Let's go buy some furniture."

"At last," Feinstein said sarcastically, raising his hands to heaven in thanks as the Hershmans emerged. "I thought you'd gone out for lunch, or maybe to take steam at the Jockey Club."

"Hymie, good news." Jake extracted the bills and waved them. "I guess I can go higher, seeing we're old friends. Twenty-five dollars, Hymie. *Cash.*"

Grabbing the man's hand, he slapped the notes in his palm and curled the fingers around them.

Nodding with the weary acceptance of a man who has put his arm in a lion's mouth and had it bitten off for his trouble, Feinstein stared at the bills, glared at the Hershmans, and put the money in his pocket.

"Take it." He waved bitterly at the load. "I should know better than to come to a thief like you." He saw Sara staring up curiously at him, thumb in mouth. "And in front of the child too. Ashamed you should be." He turned and walked down the street. "I'm gonna go eat. Unload it yourself."

Jake watched him go, grinning. He loved this business. A little acting, a little theft, a lot of chutzpah. It stirred up his blood like a woman did.

"OK. Let's get it down." As they unknotted the ropes, he heard the horse give a contented shiver. A heap of manure steamed under its hindquarters. "And go get a bucket and shovel." Everyone knew Jake Hershman wasted nothing.

An hour later, sweating pleasantly from the exertion of unloading the furniture and adding it to the maze that filled the store, Jake sat in his office laboriously listing it in the inventory.

With care, he would turn eighty or a hundred dollars on the load. But then Hymie had obviously picked it up at one of the big houses uptown, probably convincing some old lady the things were worthless, maybe even charging her to cart them away. That was the fun of it. You didn't really sell the thing itself; you sold what people thought it was, what they wanted it to be.

Nat was chatting with a young couple who had come into the shop a moment before, after browsing among the bureaus and chairs carefully arranged on the sidewalk. Not too carefully arranged, of course; if you lined them up like in the windows of the big stores on Madison or Fifth, they looked expensive, and people didn't come down here to spend money.

As Jake had taught him, Nat took it slowly, talking about the weather, the heat, flirting a little with the girl as an implied compliment to her husband. The chat was restful, like music, and Jake listened with sleepy satisfaction as it diminished, Nat leading them into the storeroom where they kept the wardrobes and beds, all of them mantled in the dust without which nobody believes he has found a bargain.

Nat still worked in the store, even though Jake knew his heart was not in it. The boy had ambitions. Lately, he'd pestered Jake to turn the store into an auction room, selling not only furniture but carpets, silver, paintings even. It made sense; Jake had to admit that. In the last year, the European Jewish community had been shaken, and the emigrants coming to America brought with them valuables they preferred to sell through their own people. So far, Jake had turned down the offers from these new arrivals, but sooner or later he would have to take Nat's suggestion.

But he remained nervous still. Something in the scheme promised trouble.

Sara wandered in, and Jake took his granddaughter on his knee. No grandsons yet to carry on the family, but Nat was young. There would be time.

Even as he entertained the thought, some premonition of what was to come shadowed it. He looked speculatively at the little girl on his lap and put her down again on the floor. Sara stared up in surprise. Her face wrinkled with tears as she felt herself excluded from the warmth and affection rightly hers, and her fingers dug into Jake's thigh as she tried to climb back—angry hands, eager with need.

2

Hunched against the wind, David Moore searched for pockets of warmth in his secondhand army greatcoat, heavy as a horse blanket but thin where his growing body flexed against the thick khaki cloth. A replacement was needed, desperately. Maybe he'd find one today, as he had discovered some weeks before the workman's boots that kept his feet from the cobbles of the road, and the week before that the balaclava (knitted in what felt like furry string for some long-dead soldier in the trenches) that wrapped his ears, face and chin.

The year 1934 was no time to be eighteen in London. With millions unemployed and the government promising worse, one took work where one found it. Putting aside his ambition to work in the National Gallery, young David had traded on his discovered skill for selling other people's castoffs by dealing in junk.

Every Friday morning, after a week spent scouring the suburbs, he took his accumulated profits to the Caledonian Road Market, hoping to stumble on a find rich enough to buy his freedom.

Once or twice lately, on icy mornings like this, he felt, rising at 3 A.M. to get in with the first dealers, that it was not worth the effort. But something drove him out into the cold and dark, some need he never troubled to analyze. At least he wasn't alone. Threading his way through the dark streets around King's Cross, he was soon part of a steady trickle of men and women

dressed much like him. By the time he glimpsed the kerosene
lamps of the market, the trickle had swelled to a crowd.

The market had begun on the cobbles of the Caledonian
Road but spread into empty lots on both sides of the street, a
congregation of more than a hundred wooden tables and carts
piled high with merchandise. After two years, David knew every
twist of the narrow lanes between the stalls, every detail of each
pitch.

Some boasted a canvas awning to keep off the frost, others
just a few scarecrow shreds of cloth clinging to rusted uprights.
Everywhere, lamps shed yellow light over heaps of crumpled
newspaper, corners of porcelain, the gray gleam of silver, the
glint of crystal. In the soft sidelight, the rough faces patched with
beard, the eyes masked carefully with greed begged to be
painted. David imagined Rembrandt finding biblical characters
here as he had in the streets of Leyden and Amsterdam: a Judas
sorting suspiciously through old prints, or Moses with a drip on
the end of his nose and tobacco stains on his white beard
feigning indifference as dealers scrabbled among his knives and
forks.

"Morning, your 'ighness."

David looked over his shoulder at the gap-toothed old
woman who sold worn and usually unmatched shoes. "Hello,
love."

He'd wondered about the "'ighness" for a while until
someone jokingly pointed out his general resemblance to
Edward, Prince of Wales—the same slight build, the forelock of
sandy hair falling perpetually over his eyes, the air of gentility
that he owed to his mother's frustrated ambitions for her boy.

At the center of the market, early arrivals who had pushed
their handcarts from the suburbs around midnight dominated
the biggest and driest pitches, though people continued to
dribble in off the first trains and buses, swelling the market at its
edges like a living organism. Soon it filled every vacant space for
a quarter of a mile around, confined only by the blank walls of
the warehouses that loomed out of the dark.

They called the Caledonian Market "The Stones," perhaps in
tribute to the cobbles underfoot, and for London it was the
clearing-house for a thousand auctions, jumble sales, house
clearances, and thefts. By tradition, sales here were not
examined too closely by the police, who in any case would have

been lost within five minutes among the maze of stalls. It took years to memorize their patterns and to distinguish the dealers who carried only junk from others who, however untidy their displays, always had some treasure tucked away for the serious buyer.

Walking down the aisles at the center of the market, brilliantly lit by a forest of lamps, David knew he was out of his class. The big dealers came here, aware that they had a good chance of finding a Roman bronze, a small Flemish landscape, some jewelry good enough to clean and reset. David watched as a fat dealer in a sealskin coat counted out ten five-pound notes for a silver tureen and handed it to his chauffeur to carry; then, reluctantly, he turned down into the shadows where he could do business on his own level.

Seeing a familiar face, thin, predatory and sly, he paused. "Morning, Arnold. Anything for me?"

"Dunno whatcha want, do I?"

"Cuppa would be nice." The man nodded sourly. Visions of hot sweet tea and a good breakfast sustained them through the worst of the morning when the wind was as cold and the night as dark as this. "Any bits of china?"

The man gestured with shoulder and chin, unwilling to take his hands from his pockets. Grudgingly removing one mitten, David let it dangle from the string sewn to his cuff and picked up the pile of plates.

"What's your best?" The formula came automatically.

"Have the lot for a tanner."

Shuffling through them, David recognized scraps of a dismembered ducal dinner service. "Give you threepence." They settled on fivepence and, slipping the plates carefully into the canvas bag he carried rolled in his pocket, David shouldered deeper into the crowd.

By five thirty his bag was almost full with a nice Crown Derby teapot, slightly chipped; a brass figure of a girl that might be eighteenth century; some bits of silver that would improve with cleaning: all for less than five shillings. You could spend a whole week knocking in the suburbs and find less.

Knockers went from door to door, asking housewives if they had anything to sell. Half the time you just got the door slammed in your face. If they did let you in, it was generally to unearth some Toby Jug they claimed had been in the family for a century and demand ten times its worth. No wonder knockers regarded the house owners as fair game and conned them whenever they could.

Greed made people eager and careless, so David often played on it by picking out some quite worthless item—a picture, a cut-glass bowl—and admiring it extravagantly. Surely, he would suggest, this piece is very valuable. Of course pictures (or glass, or silver) were not really in his field, but this looked much like an item that had fetched more than a hundred pounds at Christie's a few weeks before. He urged them to take it down for valuation immediately, and the house owner, so deeply impressed by the honesty and integrity of this young man, gladly sold for a few shillings the genuinely valuable side table or rug on which he had had his eye all the time.

Occasionally, of course, knocking was a pleasanter occupation, and one got something for one's trouble—not always antiques. A bored housewife welcomed the diversion of a personable young tradesman knocking politely on the back door. One such lady supervised David's sexual initiation a few weeks after his seventeenth birthday, matter-of-factly leading him upstairs to the big bedroom with its pair of men's carpet slippers peering dauntingly from under the draped bedspread.

Not that these were the biggest thrills. Once or twice in his career as a knocker—soon to end forever, though he had no idea of it then—an old lady had brought out a bowl or a piece of silver that shrieked quality and asked diffidently, "Is this worth sixpence to you?" That was the true excitement of the business, more satisfying by far than servicing some young woman on her couch with your trousers around your ankles and your eyes carefully surveying the contents of the mantelpiece.

David knew the contempt with which he was viewed by his colleagues in the antiques trade. Knockers occupied a low rung on the ladder, only one step above the totters, who cruised the streets in their horse-drawn carts, shouting the traditional "Any rags? Any bones? Any old iron?" Both groups were regarded with equal contempt by the dealers who owned their own shops or stalls, by the runners who scouted material for them, and, naturally, by the smart salerooms of the West End—Sotheby's, Christie's, Carthew's, Snow's.

But David had his eye on that narrow space at the top of the ladder. The Stones was a kind of casino where luck or a moment's carelessness on the part of a dealer could mean a fortune. All David needed was just one killing. Then he had planned exactly what to do.

Around six, as dawn smeared blue-gray smudges of cloud across the sky, he reached the farthest edge of the market, where latecomers spread their stock against a warehouse wall, squatting uneasily themselves among the scavenged vegetable boxes and cabbage stalks. So stiff with cold that he could hardly bend, David nearly skipped one haphazard heap of items on a blanket guarded by a man he'd not seen before: a tough-looking chap, face masked by the scarf wrapped around his neck and chin.

But his interest quickened as he noticed a copper warming pan and four wineglasses, the delicate "air twist" stems betraying them as Georgian and valuable. Some books were piled by them—heavy volumes, bound in Tree Calf, a rare, expensive, and fragile system where the leather binding was treated with acid to imitate the grain of wood. Casually picking one up, he opened it and ran a finger down the ragged edge where a flyleaf had been ripped out—to remove an incriminating bookplate?

And at the edge of the blanket, half hidden by some clothes, were six bowls.

Only one interested him, but he took each in turn, holding it up as if looking for cracks. The texture, the weight, the sheen of the fourth was unmistakable.

"What's your best on these?" he asked.

"Two quid for the lot."

"Fair enough." Pulling off his mitten, David dug deep inside his coat, feeling for the roll accumulated shilling by shilling against just such a moment. Merely by touch, he separated the notes, taking two from the five rolled there, and handed them to the man.

As he did so, he knew he'd been too eager. The man was doubtful. The thin fingers with their blackened nails hovered ... then snatched the money. David thrust the bowls under his coat.

At that instant, the man realized his mistake. "Give 'em 'ere and I'll wrap 'em for you."

"No need." Turning on his heel, David pushed through the crowd, protecting the fragile bundle inside his coat with a bent arm.

"Come back! I changed me mind!" But David ignored the shout. Two minutes later he slipped into a tiny café squeezed between two rows of warehouses; only a regular would know to look for him at Edna's.

Its warmth was paradise after the chill outside, the air a broth of steam from a bubbling tea urn and smoke from the kitchen, where three clattering cooks labored to feed fifty men crowded three to a side at the narrow tables.

"The usual?" Edna, red-faced and square as a boiler, hardly paused in her expert filling of thick chipped cups from the steaming urn.

"Thanks, love. And give me some tea now, will you? And a bit of paper."

Handing him the next cup off the assembly line, she dragged an old newspaper from under the counter, slapped it down, and yelled into the kitchen, "Egg, bacon and bubble."

David put his bowls on the counter, pushed aside the five worthless ones, and carefully wrapped the last in five thicknesses of newspaper. Half a minute later, his breakfast slid out from the kitchen: a fried egg, a slab of bacon a quarter of an inch thick, and heaps of "bubble and squeak"—last night's boiled cabbage and potatoes fried with onions and bacon fat. He realized suddenly that he was starving, mostly from excitement.

He hung around the café for an hour, joking with the other knockers. Purchases made by lamplight were unwrapped, to be revealed either as bargains or trash, and there was much casual buying and selling. Dealers from the West End often dropped around on Friday morning with wallets full of new notes to see what was for sale at Edna's besides tea, bacon and eggs.

The streets outside were busy with horse-drawn vans and office people on their way to work when David stepped out of the café. If the man who sold him the bowl wanted to make trouble, he would hardly do so now, in broad daylight, but nevertheless David kept one eye over his shoulder as he walked to the corner and caught a bus to Piccadilly Circus.

He was out of place here, in the commercial heart of London; people stared at his enveloping coat and the dirty canvas bag hanging from his shoulder, and David felt himself begin to cringe from their looks. Then he remembered the newspaper-wrapped bundle in that bag. He could buy and sell them all now.

The clock on the Ritz Hotel in Piccadilly said seven forty-five, too early for Snow's. Turning off the street, he walked down through Green Park to the little fountain where he sometimes ate his sandwiches on days in town. Sitting on the stone balustrade, he carefully washed the bowl in the icy water.

As soon as he had touched it, he knew the bowl was Chinese and very old. Now, as the accumulation of grime from centuries of coal fires and cigarette smoke thinned under his careful rubbing, he recognized the delicate green, yellow, blue, and gold foliage of famille verte. Porcelain makers abandoned this style about 1720 for the more common famille rose, so this piece could not possibly be less than two centuries old.

With a moist corner of his handkerchief he cleaned a spot high on the rim. A crisply enameled blue petal stood out sharply against the white background, exposing a faint halo of iridescence around the blue, the infallible sign of authentic famille verte. Gingerly David put the bowl back inside his bag and relaxed, looking around for the first time.

A long cliff of luxury apartment buildings ran down the hill along the margin of the park. On a terrace on top of the closest building, a couple were being served breakfast. Silver glinted in the soft morning sun and he heard the woman laugh, a sound as crisp as a shaving of brass.

3

Five miles away, on the hills north of London where the large houses clustered along the edge of Hampstead Heath, Simon Snow, for three weeks chairman of Snow and Son, rang for his car.

Putting down the phone, he stared at it, as if expecting it to clang again with the news that this would not be possible—that he would have to walk into town for what promised to be the most momentous morning of his life.

When nothing happened, he left the study and walked upstairs, stooping a little as if curving his shoulders and arms around his chest. Tall, slightly potbellied, with receding hair and round rimless glasses, Simon looked older than his thirty-five years, an owlish young man poised indeterminately between schooldays and premature middle age.

The house was quieter than on any day since the funeral. Even the occasional creak of a stair tread under his foot or a door slamming belowstairs seemed muffled. Once, as a child, he held a firework too close to his ear and the crack left him almost deaf for a day. The same sensation dogged him now.

While his parents lived, the whole place quivered with energy. Phones rang, the doorbell shrilled with new guests, and the Victrola played incessantly the light opera his mother loved—Gounod, Offenbach, Meyerbeer: bonbons of music, crisp outside but soft and syrupy at the heart.

Her records still lay scattered around the bedroom, disks of

23

black on the beige carpet, waiting for her to wander in, pick one up, and put it on the turntable, humming the melody in a thin soprano as she dressed for dinner. His father's papers were just as he had left them in the study: Sheafs of assessors' reports, letters from clients, the proofs of Snow's next catalogue, now never to be corrected.

That they should both be dead, and in the same trivial accident—the car seemed barely dented—was incredible. The company, the house, the records and files lingered, disbelieving. Even the friends who had made the house famous for its parties waited by proxy in the hall downstairs in heaps of black-edged cards.

For the first few afternoons, he found himself listening for their return. In a minute they would burst in, faces flushed from driving with the top down, tossing their coats and hats at the maid and demanding tea and toast in the morning room. But then there was the funeral, mourners slogging through the mud of Highgate Cemetery to lay them at rest with five generations of Snows. He stood with the crowd, knees braced awkwardly against the steep hill, and watched the coffins carried into the dank cell. Then he believed.

The memory brought on a mild attack. Hurriedly, as his throat tightened, he sprayed it from the small atomizer. Asthma, his lifelong affliction, was also his salvation. Unaggressive by nature, he developed a sense of purpose that made indecision unnecessary, since worry and tension were sure to trigger a choking fit. All his life he had known what he wanted to do. Now he was free to do it. But, at thirty-five, he had too little time. His parents had lived too long.

Wheezing a little still, he left the house. Across the road, the chestnut trees were almost bare, their pulped leaves clogging the gutter. In the wedge of sky at the end of the road he glimpsed the city. It seemed to gleam, its buildings swept clean by salt breeze.

"The rooms, Spencer," he said to the chauffeur, unconsciously imitating his father's tone, and settled down with *The Times*.

Anyone strolling along Albermarle Street, on the edge of Mayfair, might have taken Snow and Son for a discreet backwater of the financial world: a private bank, or a brokerage catering to those few remaining rich who preferred to keep their wealth a secret.

A narrow entrance, flanked by sandstone columns in

impeccable Doric, and a bland stone facade resisted even polite interest, while the heavy glass of the swinging double doors had the daunting glint of a headmaster's spectacles. After peering into the gloom, the tourist moved on, not even noticing the brass plate, so polished over the years that the words SNOW AND SON, VALUERS AND AUCTIONEERS were mere hollows in the metal.

Since 1739, when an ambitious young dealer in furniture and objets d'art noticed that his aristocratic customers, though often in need of ready money, disliked approaching a dealer directly, Snow and Son had dominated fine art sales in England. The greatest names in Debrett's and *Burke's Peerage* (and even some members of the royal family itself) rountinely brought their surplus treasures to Snow's salerooms, confident of anonymity and quick payment in cash immediately after the sale—services for which a five percent commission seemed not unreasonable.

In the middle 1800s, the first Snow's great grandson, Bowker, bought two houses in Albemarle Street as headquarters for the firm. In the search for space, successive generations had burrowed into the cellars and bought the buildings opposite, but in most respects Snow's remained a small concern, little changed from the aristocrats' convenience of a hundred years before, although the commission on sales was now seven and a half percent and would soon rise to ten. Of newer firms like Christie's and Sotheby's, whose salerooms lay less than a quarter of a mile from Albemarle Street, along with half a dozen lesser imitators, it was said they were either gentlemen trying to be businessmen or businessmen trying to be gentlemen. Snow's tried to be neither. It merely existed—infuriatingly conservative, undeniably supreme.

Casual visitors drawn by this reputation seldom got farther than the foyer of the main saleroom. Bussell, the porter, a fierce broad figure with the bristling mustache and harsh manner of a sergeant major, had been known to eject interlopers at the toe of his boot. Through the second set of doors they might just glimpse the elegant Nash staircase twining toward the oval skylight two stories above before they found themselves escorted firmly back to the street.

But to the elite, Snow's offered the subtlest of welcomes—a calculated indifference. A regular customer received a cool "Good morning" from Bussell when he strolled in, took a catalogue from the table, and ascended the staircase to the rooms where next week's lots were laid out for examination, unprotected and unguarded. Technically, a customer *might* slip a silver snuffbox or a small book into his pocket and walk off with it, but this happened so seldom that Snow's saw no need to employ a porter on guard duties when his time could be better used elsewhere.

On warm afternoons, a churchlike quiet pervaded the building, the only sound a distant rattle of teacup on saucer, or the murmur of voices as a Snow's expert strolled with some colleague down the long shadowy saleroom hung with pictures, the walkers barely disturbing the motes of dust that drifted in shafts of sun.

A visitor with business on his mind would be shown by one of Snow's young men into a small drawing room where a decanter of dry sherry stood on a Chippendale side table, and sooner or later someone would drop in for a conversation that might take in the week's hunting, the cost of property in Wiltshire, and the state of South African gold shares before arriving at the picture, silver collection or library to be disposed of.

Such rituals encouraged Snow's staff to see themselves as more than mere tradesmen. No Snow ever thought of the saleroom as a business; like a lawyer, priest or doctor, he existed to maintain a tradition of service. To change that would be as disastrous as to tear down the Nash staircase in the hall. It would bring the whole edifice of Snow and Son crashing around their ears.

This was just what Simon Snow had in mind to do as he climbed the staircase to the boardroom.

They were three old, rich, comfortable men.

One was fat, with quivering chins, his watch chain draped over an ample breakfast; the second, thinner, wore a military mustache which gave his unremarkable face some character, the receding chin, popeyes, and drawling voice exactly fitting the music hall stereotype of the dim-witted aristocrat; while the third, with his monocle, slicked-down hair and slightly sporty suit, played comic foil to the other two.

Oliver Turnbull, the fat one, took out a leather cigar case and asked perfunctorily, "Anyone mind if I smoke?"

"One day, Turnbull," Lord David DeMarney said through his mustache, "I shall say yes, just to see what happens." Cecil Taylor-Windus grinned awkwardly, unsure whether his cousin had been snubbed or not. Ignoring them both, Turnbull lit his

Corona Corona as if alone in the room.

None of the three took much notice of the two other men at the table. Harley Debenham, treasurer of Snow and Son, was in his early fifties, thin to the point of gauntness, crowded into a suit that hung on arms that seemed to have one joint too many. His stoop and guarded eyes betrayed a long and intimate association with money.

Simon, the fifth man, had taken his seat next to Debenham, opposite the other three. Years of watching him grow from a sickly child to a self-effacing and undramatic adult had reduced him in their eyes; they barely acknowledged his presence as agendas were passed around and sherry glasses filled.

Polishing his already gleaming glasses, Simon surveyed his adversaries. The next few minutes would settle the fate not only of his career but of Snow's itself.

They chatted among themselves, unworried, unsuspecting. They could afford to be. Between them they owned a controlling interest in the company.

Lord David's holding was a token, voted in return for his usefulness as an aristocratic figurehead, but Turnbull and Taylor-Windus, by virtue of the fact that their family had gone into partnership with Bowker Snow's son, Humphrey, half a century before, had every reason to think of themselves as the real owners of the firm, despite the holdings distributed among various members of the Snow family.

Debenham cleared his throat and examined the sheet of paper on the table before him as if for signs and portents.

"I think we might begin, gentlemen, if you're agreeable." He looked around the table. "Let me just emphasize that this is not a formal board meeting, even though all members are present. It was felt, you'll remember, that some ceremony was in order to welcome our newest member, Mr. Snow"—he smiled thinly at Simon—"and acquaint him with our current situation."

There was a murmur of agreement. "Welcome to the firm, Simon," Oliver Turnbull said. The others muttered, "Hear, hear!" Simon nodded silently.

"You have the financial report before you," Debenham continued. "I believe it's self-explanatory, but if you have any questions, Mr. Snow...?"

Simon studied the sheet as if every figure was not engraved on his brain.

"There *is* one point I'd like to clarify." His smile was

disarming, ingenuous. Years of practice with his parents had perfected it as a tool of social ease. "The actual value of each capital sum on deposit is given: Mr. Turnbull, nine thousand pounds; Mr. Taylor-Windus, seven thousand pounds; His Lordship, one thousand pounds; and of course my own holdings—that left me by my parents, plus my grandfather's trust shares that I come into automatically on their deaths. But I don't see any unit value for each share."

Lord David leaned back and stared at the ceiling. This was all over his head.

"We aren't quite like a public company, Mr. Snow," Debenham said. "Under the articles of agreement, the partners are required to meet once a year and divide the accumulated profits according to their holdings. Of course, expenses are deducted automatically and we keep a fund for emergencies."

"What about property? This building, for instance?"

"Technically, it belongs to you—or, to be precise, the Snow family, since you can't actually sell it as long as there is a direct heir. It's leased from you by the company, which pays a ground rent. I could show you the papers if you're interested."

"So Snow and Son isn't a company at all," Simon persisted. "More like a partnership. A syndicate, in fact." He said this as if it had just occurred to him.

"Quite." Turnbull was bored with the discussion. "Surprised your father didn't explain all this to you, young Snow. Back before the war, he and I used to get together at my place in Berkshire round the start of the grouse season and split the cash in a couple of hours. All a bit more businesslike now, of course. Financial board meetings and so on. Same principle, though. Same principle exactly."

Simon looked ingenuously around the table. "That being the case, it is simply to you gentlemen that I would have to apply to buy you out?"

It took some seconds for the remark to sink in. Then Taylor-Windus turned in his chair, screwed the monocle more tightly into his eye, and stared at Simon with icy curiosity. Even DeMarney came down to earth. "Upon my soul," he said wonderingly. Turnbull was incapable of speech.

Debenham, who had anticipated something like this from Simon's detailed examination of the books during the previous few days, spoke up quickly.

"Perhaps it would be...er, more suitable, Mr. Snow, if I answered on behalf of your colleagues. The rules of agreement are quite clear. Partners may not sell their shares to anyone outside the company but are free to dispose of their holdings to other partners or to their close relatives. So all share dealings must take place among the people in this room."

"What about decisions on the running of the company? Are they made on the basis of ownership? I mean, does my holding give me a larger say than Mr. Turnbull, for instance?"

"Of course not!" Turnbull's baby pink had warmed to a mottled rose. "Damned cheek!"

Debenham cleared his throat judiciously. "I'm afraid, Mr. Turnbull, that in theory it does."

"Nonsense. His father and I settled what business there was like gentlemen, at his home or our clubs."

"With respect," Debenham said tersely, "that was merely the method most convenient for the outgoing board." He used the term carefully, now that the wind was clearly blowing in a new direction. "Under the agreement, each board member may nominate a director for every ten percent of stock or fraction thereof which he holds. Thus Mr. Turnbull with twenty-four percent could nominate three members, Mr Taylor-Windus two, His Lordship one, and Mr. Snow with, I believe, fifty-eight percent—"

"*Six* directors?" Turnbull said incredulously.

"Including himself, yes."

"All with equal voting powers?"

"Indeed."

Turnbull drew on his cigar but, finding it had gone out, ground it into the ashtray as if he wished it were Simon's face.

Turning to Simon, Debenham said, "May I ask if it is your intention to exercise this provision in the agreement, Mr. Snow?"

"That depends."

"On what, dammit?" Turnbull snapped.

"On whether my plans for the company meet with everyone's approval."

"What plans?"

Simon took a bundle of papers from his inside pocket and gave them to Debenham to pass around.

Except for an occasional expostulation as they read his

suggestions, the next three minutes were silent. Then Turnbull
leaned over toward Taylor-Windus. There was a brief whispered
conversation in which DeMarney joined. Turnbull stood up,
and the others with him.

"Snow, we're making no response to these proposals at this
time except to deplore the manner in which they were presented
and the contempt for this firm that they represent." A finger
stabbed at Debenham. "I want that in the minutes."

"And when can I expect your reaction?" Simon asked calmly.

"You won't hear it from us," Taylor-Windus said. "From
now on, I suggest we communicate through our respective legal
advisers." They filed out stiffly.

Squaring up his papers, Debenham took a slim gold pencil
from his pocket and made some notes in the margin.

Simon stood at the window, looking down Albermarle
Street to the green slice of the park. "What do you think,
Debenham?"

"Frankly?"

He turned from the window with a smile. "Of course."

"I like a lot of what you suggest. It'll be good for the
company. But you may have bitten off more than you can chew.
You have less power than you imagine."

Simon's smile suggested none of his inner qualms. Debenham was very likely right. But if they gave him a year, he might
do it.

They left the boardroom and walked to the top of the spiral
staircase.

There were few people about this morning. Hardly anyone
came in before noon, since Snow's, like most of the older
salerooms, held sales only once a week—on Saturday at 2 P.M., a
reminder of the tradition that buying and selling were pastimes
for men busy with more important matters during the week. The
place, Simon thought, was like a tomb.

"Do you think you could find me an office?"

"I daresay, Mr. Snow. Of course your father and the other
partners always preferred to work from home."

"I know." Something else to change.

As they descended, Simon ran his hand along the worn
banister he had so often longed to slide down as a child. Once, he
tried, but his mother hauled him back. He always remembered
the hissed and angry words. "Simon, have some respect!" As if

the building were a church, not a place of business.

The commotion in the foyer stopped them halfway down. Bussell, maintaining a tight grip on the collar of a young man, was propelling him toward the door.

"Stop that!" Simon said sharply.

Astonished, Bussell reluctantly placed the boy's feet back on the floor. "Just a lad who's come to the wrong place, sir."

Despite his drab clothes, there was something about the boy's manner, an imperious quality; arrogance, even. He shook himself back into his ridiculous greatcoat as if it were made at Gieves in Savile Row.

"Can I help you?"

"Who are you?" The question wasn't insolent, just curious.

"Simon Snow." He looked around the foyer, realizing for the first time that it was truly his. "I own the place."

"Then you can." The boy hauled something wrapped in newspaper from inside his coat. "I want you to sell this."

Simon took the bowl, rubbed his finger across the grimy base to look for marks, then held it up to the light. It glowed with the faint translucency of fine porcelain.

"Where did you get it?"

"Why? Do you think it's stolen?"

"No," Simon said mildly. "I'm just interested."

"Caledonian Market," David said reluctantly. "That's famille verte. You sold one just like it a few months ago for a hundred pounds."

Simon wondered about a young man who knew Snow's catalogues that well—or had the nerve to bluff so firmly if he didn't.

"Totter, are you?"

David bridled. "No! I deal a bit. And I do some knocking."

Simon turned the bowl around in his hands.

"I think we can sell this for you, Mr.—er—"

"David Moore."

"All right, Mr. Moore. We'll be happy to put it in the next suitable sale." He handed the bowl to Debenham. "You'll get a receipt. And if you have anything else of this quality, please bring it in."

Studying the boy, Simon had an idea. Unlike most runners and dealers, he looked neither furtive nor dishonest. There was an air of well-bred gentility. Suddenly the resemblance hit him.

Good grief, he looked just like—

"Is porcelain the extent of your expertise, Mr. Moore?" he asked suddenly.

David shrugged. "I can spot gold and silver. I know a bit about furniture. And pictures."

"Would you like a job?"

For the first time, the boy's confidence seemed shaken. He blinked in surprise.

"I don't know. What sort of job?"

"Oh, general things." Having made the gesture, Simon found himself at a loss to back it up.

"Not sweeping up, or portering. I'd rather stay on the street than do that."

"I'm sure we can find something more useful for a man who can spot porcelain in that condition." He'd been thinking of someone to go around to the country sales, keeping an eye on business out of London, picking up news of anything Snow's might be able to handle more effectively than the small country auctioneers. Moore might do very well.

"Can you drive?"

"I can learn."

"What do you think, Debenham?" Simon glanced at the accountant, wondering if employing this street Arab would turn even him against his employer.

Debenham paused, as if weighing a crucial decision, "Certainly," he said at last, with an unaccustomed, crooked grin. "As the Americans say, you're the boss."

That night, Simon dreamed again—the same dream he had suffered since early childhood, a phantasm so familiar that he wondered it didn't seem friendly by now, like an old scar. But it still had the power to bring him bolt upright and wide awake from the deepest sleep, his throat choked by an invisible hand.

Always, in the dream, people knocked at the door. Always they took him to a deserted and miserable place—sometimes a copse choked with bracken, at other times an abandoned house with the floorboards torn up in one room. There they showed him the corpse of a child, blue-white, puffy, and asked him to identify it. As he searched for something familiar in the slack, smudged features, the dream ended and he woke, sweating.

As usual, there was no baby, no inquisitors. Sitting up in bed, he waited for his pulse to slow, then went to the window. Beyond the foot of his garden, London sprawled under the blue-white glare of the full moon. Pulling the curtains and switching on the desk lamp, he opened the heavy brown cover of Frits Lugt's *Repertoire de Catalogue des Ventes*. There was comfort in the long columns of figures, the listings of every major art sale in Europe for the last two centuries, and he read and took notes until the maid came with his tea at eight.

4

Sara Hershman, six years old, bored and dressed in her Sunday best, kicked her feet under the dinner table, testing with stretching toes the distance to the floor and escape. The bow of her pink dress cut into her waist, but each struggle only rustled the taffeta and drew a warning glance from her mother.

Nobody else seemed aware of her boredom. Almost from the moment they sat down, the tall thin lady with the white beads looped around her skinny neck dominated the conversation, pausing only to heap her plate with more pot roast and potatoes. In these occasional silences, her husband, as round and tubby as she was tall and thin, chimed in with more comments Sara didn't understand.

The idea of a foreign language, alien to her six months ago, was now a familiar part of her life. Half the people who visited them talked in words Sara didn't understand, and the first time Grandpa had replied in the same jumbled way, she'd gaped at him and reached instinctively to cling to her father's leg.

There had been a lot of laughter. "They don't learn the old language over here," Grandpa said at the time ot one of the visitors, whose black beard and heavy brows left only a slice of frowning face visible.

"Even a girl should learn," he said shortly.

"This is America," Nat said defensively. He seemed embarrassed, but his hand on her head was a comforting reassurance of his love, ever-present, ever-reliable. "Why bother? I want her to grow up an American."

"And not a Jew?"

"Yes. Sure. Of course, a Jew. But American. Maybe if you hadn't been quite so strict back in Germany—"

The voices became angry after that, and Momma led Sara off to her bedroom and told her to play until dinnertime. She listened to the distant murmur of argument for a long while. What had made them so annoyed?

She learned to watch, listen and say nothing—harder and harder to do as the foreign visitors increased, until a new couple came to dinner every week, always with a wrapped parcel or a small suitcase which was placed discreetly by the hatstand in the hall.

After dinner, Poppa, Grandpa and the visitors disappeared into the front room while Sara helped her mother clear the table and stack the dishes for Mrs. Klein, who came in every morning to tidy up.

Sara knew this night would be the same. When the fat man came in, he had carried something square, wrapped in cloth. Sara stole a peek under the wrapping while he went to the bathroom.

It was a picture of a lady with no clothes on. She was still peering at it in fascination when the tall lady with the beads snatched it away and shoved it into the soft white hands of her husband as he emerged from the bathroom. Sara met his eyes and found them solemnly sympathetic.

Feeling a proprietary interest in the painting, Sara slipped away from the kitchen and crept along the hall. Like most doors in the apartment, that to the front room closed inefficiently, and even her fat little fingers were strong enough to ease it open an inch.

Her father and Grandpa sat on one side of the parlor table, cigars in their hands. On the other side, the little man smoked a cigarette through a white tube ringed with gold. Apparently uninterested in the conversation, his wife prowled along the walls, examining the pictures hanging there. Sara came so seldom into this room that she noticed for the first time that their numbers had increased; some walls were almost crowded with paintings, framed heavily in gold. She connected them at last with the suitcases of earlier guests.

"It's very fine," Jake said, holding up the painting of the naked lady. "Very fine."

"Of course, there's a number of them about." Sara hardly recognised the tone in her father's voice, a cold, uninterested note. He never spoke like that to her. Never.

"Even zo," the woman said from the shadows. "You can zell it?"

"We'll try. Had you thought of a price?"

"In former times," the little man said cautiously, "such a work fetched twenty thousand of your dollars."

Nat shrugged off the figure. "In former times, perhaps. Now—"

"We'll try," Jake broke in, with a glance at his son. "Who can say more than that? If you don't like the price, we'll talk again. You don't mind to leave the painting with us for a day or two? For the catalogue?"

The little man glanced over his shoulder toward his wife. "There will be a receipt, of course?"

Nat bowed in her direction. "I'll write it immediately." He reached the door before Sara could scamper more than a few feet from it.

"You listening, Sara? Go and help your momma. Your grandpa and I got business."

Reluctantly, Sara let herself be shooed back to the kitchen. She was so clumsy with the plates, almost breaking one of them, that her mother gave her a glass of milk and a cookie. She sat at the table, nibbling, until Momma put her to bed. Even under the covers, she lay awake, listening to the buzz of talk, puzzling out this new thing and her beloved father's involvement in it.

5

Two years to the day after he took over the firm, Simon Snow sat in his new office and ticked off the items on his mental list of necessities.

The schedule presented to the other partners at his first board meeting spelled them out in greater detail, but he could reduce most of them to one word apiece.

The first was "Board."

A few days after that meeting, Oliver Turnbull, in an act that reminded Simon of a big frog gobbling up the smaller fry in his private pool, bought out both Taylor-Windus and DeMarney, then announced, through his solicitors, that at the next meeting he would nominate five board members of his own selection.

Simon promptly co-opted Debenham onto the board—part reward for long service, part a move to guarantee his loyalty before Turnbull tried to buy it—and set the accountant canvasing the City for suitable people to represent his interests in the fight to come. He needed men who knew boardroom tactics, who could temporize and delay, giving him the time he needed to bring Snow's back to life—if that was possible after the years of neglect.

"Buildings," the second category, showed less progress; here the neglect had been almost fatal.

His first tour through the rooms had been a shock. Behind the elegant facade, conditions ranged from untidiness to crumbling decay.

"I dunno 'ow it's stood up as long as it 'as," the foreman said as he guided Simon into the catacombs under the buildings. Sniffing the musty tang of rot and damp, Simon felt his throat catch, but forced out of his mind the sense of a thousand tons of brick and masonry hovering above him.

"Look at this 'ere." Contemptuously the workman poked at a whitewashed wall. A shower of rotted fragments clattered to the floor, exposing brickwork from which mortar trickled like sand.

It was worse upstairs. Most of the roof timbers were rotten, the roof tiles cracked, the glass loose in the skylight frames. Even more disasters came to light when they ripped up floorboards and carpets. Woodworm, dry rot, poor construction, hasty repairs over the last half century had left the building little more than a shell.

Simon recognized the hopelessness of either approaching the board for money or going to ordinary financial sources for a loan. In the depressed money market of 1936, Snow and Son was a poor investment. At least one bank told him frankly that they regarded saleroom business as finished—a vestige of the old aristocratic days, soon to be swept away in a wave of austerity and revolution. But by scraping the contingency fund, enough cash was found to shore up the worst spots and prevent Snow's from collapsing into the street. For weeks, periodic thumps and a steady sifting of dust from the roof had indicated that work was in progress.

"Staff." A line under that one.

Like other salerooms, Snow's had relied on outsiders to put together its catalogues, recruiting experts from the museums for a few guineas a time. They got what they paid for: skimpy and ill-researched work, full of errors that too often favored the sellers, who were not above greasing a few palms in return for an inflated estimate of value or a flagrantly favorable description of the piece being sold.

Simon's decision to increase the number of sales from one to four a week merely increased the problem, which came to a head a few months after he took over. The porter on duty in the main saleroom rang urgently to request his immediate presence.

On his way in, Simon had seen a small crowd of dealers browsing among the fifty pieces of furniture to go on sale the following day. As usual, the promise of a big sale of classic pieces lured out a whole range of auction types—collectors, dealers, browsers, furniture makers and restorers, and even the professional commission buyers, not often seen in the Mayfair rooms but drawn to Snow's by the accelerated sale schedule.

The furniture belonged to a big dealer in Sheffield, an old customer whose descriptions were so detailed that, in Simon's father's day, they were reproduced in the catalogue without alteration.

Furniture experts reminded Simon of horse traders. Each piece to them was an almost animate creature with a personality of its own, and they peered and prodded as assiduously as buyers at Newmarket. When he came into the room, three men were on their knees, peering at hidden undersides with the aid of pocket flashlights. Others had bureau drawers piled beside them as they ferreted for signs of damp or woodworm in the skeleton of the chest itself, while a trio with flashlights and jeweler's loupes examined the depth and condition of lacquers on the two exquisite French cabinets that were the stars of the sale.

The man standing next to the porter was an exception to this active prowling and peering. Tall and thin, in a dropping tweed suit, he kept his eyes averted from the bureau beside him as if the mere sight of it offended him.

"Gentlemen here has a problem, sir," the porter said and disappeared, scared of being held accountable.

"Mr. Cantaloe, isn't it?" Simon said. He remembered the man from other sales: an expert in Regency furniture. "I enjoyed your article in *The Apollo* last month."

"Very kind. Look, Snow, I don't want to tell you your business, but this piece—" He tapped the bureau sharply with a knuckle, then opened the catalogue and read the description with ill-concealed sarcasm. "An important Queen Anne Walnut wood bureau, c. 1710."

"Yes?"

"It's a fake, my dear chap!"

"Are you sure?"

"Plain as a pikestaff." Pulling out a drawer, he thrust it under Simon's nose. "Look at those dovetails."

"I'm sorry," Simon said helplessly. "Furniture isn't really my field."

"Pieces this old weren't made with *machines*. All hand done, so the work isn't smooth. Should be a little irregular, the dovetails slightly different sizes. Not like this. And here." He ran his finger along the inside edge of the drawer. "Oak: that's right enough. But sharp edges, notice? On these pieces, the drawers are always rounded. And look at this!"

He crouched, and the beam of his flashlight picked up a pattern of tiny holes near the ground.

"Surely you'd expect some worm damage on a piece this old?" Simon said.

"Perhaps. But this isn't worm." Taking a pin from his lapel he poked it into the hole. "Dead straight. Woodworm don't eat in straight lines. Means only one thing."

Simon knew that forgers of furniture sometimes simulated wormholes by peppering a piece with small-bore bird shot, but he'd never seen it in real life. He straightened up. "Have you had a chance to look at the other pieces in the sale?"

"Most of them."

"And?"

Cantaloe lowered his voice. "Some are good. A few. The others... well, to be frank, I don't believe 'em. A lot are restorations. Some original material, but rebuilt. Others aren't even that. It's the cabinetmakers, you see. There's so much unemployment that they knock up imitation antique pieces and sell them in the street markets. A dealer comes along, buys 'em for a pound or two, adds a few scratches and some fake worm damage, then ships them down to London where nobody knows the difference." Realizing the insult to Simon, he said, "Sorry, Snow. No reason you should know all this. But it's my business, do y'see?"

Simon sighed. "Mr. Cantaloe, if you have a moment, I'd be glad if you marked in the catalogue those pieces you ... uh, don't believe, and I'll make the necessary announcement tomorrow. And if you're interested, we might discuss the possibility of retaining you to catalogue any future sales of this kind."

Cantaloe now looked like becoming head of Snow's Furniture Department, to join Piper in Old Masters and Gideon in Silver. But he needed more people he could rely on.

"Scout." Another problem that was on the way to being solved. David Moore might be young and a little too aggressive, but his eye was unerring and he had the right personality to travel around the country, sniffing out possible commissions and keeping an eye on prices. Already two sales had been made up from his discoveries, culminating in a superb Romney found abandoned in a potting shed in Dorset. Knoedler's had asked Simon to earmark it for one of that gallery's tame millionaires.

He put down his pen and stared out the window. A late May

storm was rolling in from the south, lining the sky with bruised blue-gray clouds that promised rain.

It did not minimize David Moore's effectiveness to admit that he was a problem. Not everyone on the staff liked him, and among the older people there was positive enmity. "He isn't a gentleman," Piper sniffed, perhaps upset at David's coups.

"I don't want a gentleman," Simon had replied. "You don't find business in Mayfair drawing rooms any more—not the kind of business we want, anyway."

A saleroom couldn't depend these days on the small profit from the sale of a single picture or a few pieces of silver culled from a collection when its owner needed ready cash. Simon had his eye on whole houses, rooms of furniture rather than the occasional castoff.

Simon knew it was right to erode the aristocratic image of the saleroom. Sales by auction would boom as the Depression evaporated and its defeatist mentality with it. People would have money, and they would want to spend it on the luxuries denied them since 1929. A new society was growing all around them, its tastes fed by the movies and dance halls, the popular music and advertising of America, with its brash ability to publicize and exploit.

David Moore belonged to that generation and shared its acquisitiveness. That he was also personally devoted to Simon increased his usefulness; after some thought, Simon had actually encouraged the younger man's hero worship. He had inherited too little loyalty from his father's staff to throw away that so generously offered.

Lately, however, there were tensions. He dated them from an evening almost exactly twelve months before.

Working late, he noticed a light still burning in the cubbyhole used by David as an office in the corner of the Old Masters department. He opened the door, unprepared to find David, vest and collar unbuttoned, immersed in a pile of reference books from which he had scribbled pages of notes.

"Oh, sorry. I didn't know you were here."

"I was just finishing up." He closed the heavy book—the catalogue of the large Bleymuller collection, broken up at the end of the Napoleonic wars but until then the largest in Europe. "I was trying to identify some of those drawings I found."

"You really think it's worth it?" Good drawings of the kind they often found in old houses would sell to Bond Street dealers whether they were signed by the artist or not. A year or two after the sale, the best of them always turned up on the market, with either a spurious new signature or an expert's opinion "definitely attributing" the work to some expensive master.

"I enjoy it, actually," David said, a little crestfallen.

Embarrassed at having dampened his enthusiasm, Simon said hurriedly, "Would you like to have a quick supper? Then, if you like, we can work on them for an hour or two. Two heads and all that. We might turn up something."

His awkwardness made him realize how seldom he made social overtures of any kind. But if David noticed the strain, he was too pleased to find it offensive. Grabbing his coat from the back of the chair, he shrugged into it. "That's fine. I was going to take a break myself."

At the bottom of Albemarle Street they paused, watching the theater traffic inch down Piccadilly. "I hadn't thought where we should eat," Simon said. "There's the Ritz, of course...."

Across the tops of the cars, they could see the hotel's columned facade, with men in top hats and women in evening gowns milling on their way to the bar and dining room. "Looks crowded," David said diplomatically, not mentioning that their business suits would get them politely turned away at the door.

"Where were you thinking of going?" Simon asked.

"Uh, well, there's a little pub around the corner, but I don't suppose—"

"No. That's splendid. I only want a sandwich."

The Cock and Feathers occupied a narrow corner just off Berkeley Square. Simon remembered passing it a hundred times in the car.

The barman smiled at David's obviously familiar face. "Evening, Mr. Moore. Usual?"

"Please, Arthur. And a couple of rounds of sandwiches." He turned to Simon, who was staring around at the plush seats, stuffed birds, and cheerful red-faced drinkers. "Beef and ham all right?"

Simon tore himself away from the surroundings. "Oh, yes. Very nice."

"And what to drink?"

The barman had filled David's glass with something dark and frothy. "I'll join you, I think."

"Right. Another half, please, Arthur."

They took their meal into the Snug, a cubicle at the end of the bar whose half-glassed door offered peace and quiet away from the noisy society of the main bar.

Simon drank gingerly. "This is rather nice. What is it?"

David paused with a sandwich halfway to his mouth. "Guinness. Haven't you ever drunk stout?"

"Never. To tell you the truth, I've never even been in one of these places before." He took another sip to hide his embarrassment at David's obvious surprise.

"Well," David said, watching the stout disappear, "you'd better have the other half of that, just in case you don't have another chance."

Midway through his second glass, Simon felt at ease for the first time in weeks. A ridiculous bonhomie filled him, extending even to men like Turnbull and Piper. They weren't too bad. Just misguided. Maybe a glass of Guinness would do them some good. Noticing that David had loosened his tie, he itched to do the same.

"Do you come here a lot?" he asked, looking around.

Momentarily cautious, David wondered whether to tell him that juniors from all the Mayfair salerooms used the Cock and Feathers as an informal club.

Information was exchanged, opinions canvassed on difficult sales, the idiosyncrasies of the saleroom hierarchy mercilessly pilloried. News that David Moore had been drinking here with Simon Snow would be all over town tomorrow, which would do him no harm at all professionally.

"Sometimes I look in for lunch, and a lot of my friends drink here."

"That must be nice." For a moment, Simon glimpsed a world in which one could relax with friends, get a little drunk, take off one's tie—even harmonize on some old music-hall song to an out-of-tune piano like the noisy crowd next door. Then the censor in his mind flicked it away into a storeroom already crowded with such vain hopes. Putting down his glass firmly, he stood up. "If we're going to look at those drawings, we'd better get back."

Weaving slightly from the alcohol, Simon stepped out into the dark street; he had taken a deep breath of the cold night air before the familiar hated smell registered in his nostrils. There was a fog. During the half hour they had spent inside, London's damp spring air and the smoke of soft coal fires had come together in a choking yellow cloud that cloaked the city.

As the fumes reached his bronchial tubes, Simon felt them shrink. His lungs labored. He lurched back, groping for the door, but already the fog turned every light a murky yellow. His fingers rapped painfully against a frosted window through which he glimpsed a startled flushed face.

David grabbed his arm. "What's wrong? Are you ill?"

"No, it's . . . just get me a cab."

"Look, I'm sure there's a doctor around here. Or a brandy—what about a brandy?"

"A cab, damn you!" He had no breath left for talk. The longer he stayed in the fog, the harder it would be to take control again. Like a drowning man shrugging off the help of another swimmer, he stumbled toward Berkeley Square. Almost immediately the pumpkin yellow lamp of a taxi loomed out of the fog. He flagged it down and slumped into the damp, blessedly fog-free interior.

"Highgate. An extra half a crown if you get there in a hurry."

As they clattered away, he belatedly remembered David and, looking through the back window, saw him standing at the curb, his face expressionless. Then the fog came between them like a curtain.

That was a year ago, and they had never spoken so intimately again. Only one legacy remained from that night, a guarded recognition that each had seen the other's secret and now had a hold on the other. Their relationship changed, became more formal. Like kings of adjoining countries, they watched one another warily over a contested border, recognizing the desirability of an alliance but never forgetting the possibility of war.

Instinctively, David saw the risks of this new situation and spent more time than ever away from London. Simon checked his diary. He was in Somerset this week.

He remembered Somerset. It was years since he'd been there, but one warm night he danced with a girl in a long green dress, and after . . .

Then his eyes focused on the scene beyond his window. It might be May but it looked like March, with the rainstorm he had glimpsed earlier sweeping down the streets, coaxing a gray sheen from the vista of slate and chimney pots. Dust sifted from the ceiling at a particularly loud thump from the man working on the foundations, and he went back to his list.

6

Sometime in every childhood, a door opens and lets the future in.

Sara found her door in the spring of 1937, on her birthday. As a treat, she was allowed her father all to herself for an entire luxurious afternoon.

It was rare to see him for so long a period; some nights he didn't come home at all, but slept at something called a club which Momma didn't like, and about which she and Mrs. Klein talked darkly over cups of coffee in the kitchen, always stopping pointedly when Sara came within earshot.

They had moved out of Manhattan to a new house in New Jersey, with a garden and trees everywhere. Poppa had a new place to work as well, in a tall building with windows looking down on an expanse of green, though Grandpa still liked to stay in the old building on 11th Street.

A pretty lady with gold hair sat in the outer room of her father's office and used a typewriter. Poppa called her Patricia, and on special occasions, like today, she was allowed by Patricia to play with the typewriter keys and finger the buttons on the dictaphone that brought her father's voice magically from the other room, so loudly and sharply that she pulled back her hand in surprise.

She had lunch with her father in the park, sitting under a big colored umbrella.

"What would you like to do now?" Nat asked as she finished her ice cream sundae.

"I don't know." Her range of experiences was limited. "Go to a movie maybe?"

"If you like. Or I could show you something better than any movie you ever saw." He pointed behind them to a huge stone building that seemed to take up a whole block. "In there."

Until then, Sara had seen no public building larger than Radio City Music Hall, and as they climbed the steps she prepared herself for the same interior gloom.

But instead of figured carpet, looped golden cords, and uniformed ushers, a lake of polished marble stretched away to infinity, washed with white light from an impossibly high ceiling. The cozy mustiness of cinema was replaced by a tang she remembered from her earliest years: old wood and canvas, wax and oil.

Most of the people who entered the building with them walked straight through a turnstile and up the broad marble steps, but Nat paused at the desk of the doorman, who made a brief phone call. A few minutes later, a young man in a blue suit and shiny collar slipped out of a tiny door and came over to them.

"Mr. Hershman, good to see you. Something I can do for you?"

"Not really. I just looked in with my daughter here, and I thought you might have a minute to show her around. It's her birthday."

"Well, of course." The young man looked down on Sara with considerable seriousness. "Happy birthday, young lady."

Sara stared, wondering how to talk to a man too distant for family but too close for a stranger. Remembering the manners taught by her mother for the benefit of foreign visitors, she curtsied with a quick bob. The man grinned.

"What would she enjoy, do you think?"

"We're in your hands entirely."

"Well, let's begin with the Old Masters."

With their looming figures on each side, Sara was shepherded up the stairs, her plump hand in her father's.

"Have you had a chance to work on the Renoir?" she heard her father say.

"They've got it in the lab now. I'm fairly sure we'll say yes. Anything else we might be interested in?"

"Well, we were offered some miniatures last week. . . ."

Sara let the talk pass over her head. She was used to it. And when they entered the first gallery, she no longer listened. Her eyes were entirely on the pictures.

She had seen paintings before, but never like this: so huge, so vivid, so close at hand. Close enough to touch, though as she tried to do so, her father pulled her back and shook his head.

For the first time, she realized paintings were not seamless, smooth creations like dress fabric or the illustrations on a magazine.

From a few feet away, the portrait of a smiling man with a beard seemed as real as Grandpa's reflection in a mirror. But if she moved closer, the face dissolved, swimming into smears, dabs, squiggles, until she saw only a landscape of paint, ridged and cracked, with grime caked in the fissures.

The game never lost its attraction as they moved from room to room. Sara was adrift in a world of people larger than life, animals never seen by mortal eyes; the inhabitants of her childhood fantasies had faces, shapes, and names now, and she would never be free of them.

"Well, we've seen almost everything," the young man said after an hour. "But perhaps you'd like to see what we're doing to that Renoir."

Another small door like the one from which he had first emerged led to steep concrete staircases with iron railings, and long halls whispering with the subdued roar of air conditioning. Following two men in dust coats who carefully edged a huge painting through a door marked RESTORATION, they came into a long brightly lit room more like a laboratory than an adjunct to an art gallery.

Awed, Sara watched the men place the painting reverently on a wide wooden table, draw lights from the roof to within a few inches of the surface, and pore over it, inch by inch, with black lenses screwed into their eyes.

At other tables, colleagues dabbed and patted at paintings, their tiny brushes and blades repairing the damage of centuries. Near the door, a minor Renaissance portrait, half cleaned, rested on an easel. One half of the Venetian grandee's face glared at her, the eye clear above a cheek so pocked and bristly that it seemed alive. Yet the rest remained in slaty shadow, numb and dead.

Sara left the room shaken and excited, aware of having

glimpsed a mystery that only a lifetime would unravel.

For weeks, memories of that birthday treat blinded her to the changes going on in her family. Poppa went away now for long trips, and though he explained to her carefully that they were essential, to buy things for them to sell, she felt subtly betrayed.

And then there was school: alien intelligences crowding in on her, new facts obscuring the things she most wanted to know. The ruthless injustice of the schoolyard placed her, unattractive, insecure, and confused, low in the pecking order, the butt of every malicious joke and prank. Often, through the years, she thought of that visit to the Metropolitan as the last happy day of her life.

7

A wind born somewhere near the South Pole whistled across the English Channel and flung icy spray onto the tight-shut frontages of Brighton's holiday hotels. From a congenial pub, David watched holidaymakers dart from doorway to doorway, as if stalking a summer always out of sight around the next corner.

He'd come down early to check the antique shops of Brighton, but the rain had soon driven him off the streets. The auction he was there to attend didn't begin for another hour, but he was content to sit here, savoring his hot toddy and taking stock of his life.

Three years with Snow's had changed him. Little remained of the argumentative young junk dealer. He had adopted the tweed and gray flannel of his older colleagues and even cultivated a small mustache. In bright sunlight it became alarmingly transparent, but others took it as an earnest of age and privately placed him at least five years older than his twenty-one.

He was well known around the rural sales now, a useful source of gossip and free drinks; grateful auctioneers and real estate agents often slipped him tips about a wealthy family anxious to sell off some treasure or a big house about to go on the market. It was not the work on which he expected to spend the rest of his life, but for the moment the salary, the car, the apartment, and the chance to learn his trade made it worthwhile. Sooner or later, he would pull off a coup which Simon Snow must recognize.

His contemporaries, the clerks and trainee auctioneers of the big salerooms, envied him. They couldn't know the frustrations of being an outsider in the firm, distrusted by the old hands, who saw him as a symbol of Simon Snow's regime, and resented by the rest for the ambition that made him a constant irritant with his suggestions, and growing knowledge.

Then there was Simon. Were they enemies or friends? A little of both, David supposed, knowing that sooner or later he, as the weaker of the two, must opt for one role alone in order to survive. The auction trade encouraged the belief that everything could be categorized, evaluated, and then bought or sold—even friendship and loyalty. What price, David wondered, did Simon put on him? Eventually there must be a confrontation: perhaps natural, perhaps engineered.

He realized the gloomy weather was affecting his state of mind. And it was nearly sale time. Downing the last of his drink, he struggled into his coat and battled through the empty streets to the saleroom.

An echoing warehouse with bare cement floors, the building chilled its occupants as effectively as any icehouse. David felt the warmth drain from his feet the moment he stepped through the door, but resignedly he joined the other dealers huddled at the back around a feeble one-bar electric radiator.

One glance at the catalogue had told David there was nothing here for him, though a chat with the locals afterward might elicit some useful information about future sales.

The few people in the room seemed to share his lack of interest. Of the fifty pieces of furniture on sale, less than half a dozen were worth bidding on, and even those—solid country-made chests and sideboards, devoid of ornament—were too plain to have much market value in London. The rest, mostly bureaus and tables in the softwoods that collectors disdained, weren't worth the cost of buying as firewood.

Only one buyer showed any interest in this rubbish. A smart young man only a few years older than David and dressed with snappy elegance, he squeezed determinedly between the piles of furniture, scribbling constantly in his catalogue. When bidding began, he was waving his pencil aggressively before the auctioneer had time to reach the reserve. Within half an hour, he'd bought almost everything in the place.

David nudged the dealer next to him. "What does he want with all that stuff?"

Had he been a spitting man, the dealer would have

expectorated for effect. Instead he sniffed wetly. "American," he said, as if that explained everything.

The British antiques trade was almost used to Americans now, though for ten years after the First World War a new kind of conflict seemed about to erupt as young American ex-officers arrived in Europe, pockets full of cash, with the expressed determination to corner the antiques market.

Dealers cursed as they erupted into the country sales long regarded as their exclusive territory and paid top prices for whatever took their fancy, some of it exquisite but most, by English standards, junk. Shrewder and better financed dealers from New York and Boston followed, often hiring the young amateurs as runners to scout out material. Georgian silver, eighteenth-century pictures, and a good deal of fine porcelain flowed to the United States as they combed the country, always paying top prices but demanding the best.

Britain also had its first experience of the gentleman collector with the bottomless pocketbook, a type through which Joseph Duveen and the other big American dealers had made their fortunes. One such millionaire in the twenties hired a British scholar to accumulate a collection for his local museum, to be bequeathed to it on his death. But since the millionaire's special interest was doors, it was these the scholar had to buy, and he haunted sales, often purchasing the whole house just for its front portico, which was shipped back to America at enormous expense.

Another collector, the director of a large American food company, conscripted his British managers into the hunt for antiques, sending them across the country with orders to hand out hampers of his fifty-seven varieties of food products in return for tips on collectible glass and silver. In the Depression, when the antiques trade suffered worse than most, he was a welcome visitor to many small businesses.

These days, however, Americans were rarely seen at country sales, preferring to stick with the big London firms. Drawn by curiosity, David followed the young man into the lane behind the saleroom, where he was supervising two workmen as they loaded his purchases into a large van.

"Looks like you had a good day."

"Pretty fair."

For a few seconds they sized one another up. Then David gave him his card.

"Snow's!" the young American said in surprise. "Hell, I

bought some pictures from you two weeks ago. A Gainsborough and some great Dutch drawings."

Groping in his own wallet, he took out his own card.

Nathan Hershman
House of Hershman
224 Central Park West
New York

West 11th Street
New York

Jacob Hershman
Proprietor

"I'm Nat Hershman. My father runs the firm. Pictures are my specialty, really, but since I was over here on my own account, I picked up some stock for him."

David looked along the rain-drenched alley with its debris and dead cats. "Looks like you got the dirty end of the stick, Mr. Hershman. Could I buy you a drink?"

"Sure. Love one. Just let me get this sorted out." Handing the driver of the truck a slip of paper, he watched the van sway out of the lane toward the coast road. "I just hope he makes it to Southampton without losing that load."

David steered Hershman toward the Ship, the nearest pub where they could be sure of privacy from the eyes of other dealers.

"This weather of yours has just about done me in," Hershman said as they hurried, heads down, across the rain-swept Esplanade. For the first time, David realized that the other's smart black overcoat and shiny Oxfords did nothing to keep out either cold or wet. "Can you really get a decent drink in this town? All they've got at my hotel is beer or sherry, and I can't take either."

"We'll find you something better than that." David led him into the Ship and ordered two hot toddies.

As they waited, Hershman took out his wallet and slipped David's card into it. Behind a celluloid window, David saw the picture of a plump little girl, staring at the camera with an expression of polite disbelief, as if daring the promised birdie to appear.

"My daughter," Hershman said. He seemed about to add something more, but instead flipped through the remaining pictures in the wallet: a smart house, presumably modest by American standards but luxurious to David's eyes; the frontage of an office building with one window crossed in ink to indicate Hershman's headquarters; the sleazy premises of the actual saleroom, a picture glossed over swiftly as the barman put two tankards down on the bar in front of them.

Disconcerted by this naïve capsule autobiography offered to a man he had just met and might never see again, David covered his embarrassment by grabbing his drink. "Well, happy days."

Hershman came spectacularly alive after the first few sips of hot whisky, water and lemon, sneezing explosively. "Hey, this is some drink! And boy, do I need it. I haven't been warm since I got here. How do you stand the place?"

"You get used to it. Long underwear helps."

"You mean a union suit?" He shook his head wryly. "I never thought of that. Maybe my father has one he can lend me. Or better still, next time *he* can come."

"That brings me to something I wanted to ask you."

Hershman grinned. "The furniture? I guess you think we're crazy."

"I'm not after trade secrets...."

"No, no. Glad to tell you. I don't guess Snow and Son would want to go into the furniture business." He took another sip of the toddy. "Mmmm, that's going right where it's needed. Well, when it comes to furniture, English makers are strong on hardwoods. All the good men worked in sycamore, oak, ash, mahogany. It's very nice stuff, of course. But America doesn't have much hardwood, and all *our* old furniture—the stuff that's really collected; what we call Colonial—is softwood. Pine and deal." He grinned. "You follow me, Mr. Moore?"

David had suspected something like this. Only a real expert could tell the difference between a genuine American-made Colonial piece and the cheap nineteenth-century English rubbish on its way to Hershman's warehouse. He would probably make thousands of pounds on the lots he picked up that morning for less than a hundred. Dishonest? Probably— though if American dealers were anything like the English, a plain statement that something was faked would not deter them from buying, providing it remained a secret between dealer and buyer.

They talked until the pub closed, Hershman pouring out stories about the American art scene. David had heard most of them before, but in Nat Hershman's New York accent and liberally lubricated by half a dozen hot toddies they came new-minted. He could smell the money, the blood.

Before 1900, there was not one fine art auction house in the whole of North America. Today, there were hundreds, led by New York's American Art Association and Anderson Galleries—both, oddly, owned by the same eccentric millionaire, who chose, for reasons of his own, to play one against the other. Hershman confirmed the rumors then circulating in London that the ablest men from these two companies, Hiram Parke and Otto Bernet, were planning to leave and start their own firm.

The big salerooms warred openly with the major dealers—Knoedler, Wildenstein, and especially Duveen—for the patronage of the oil, steel, and coal barons who alone had the cash to buy a Rubens, a Velásquez, a Rembrandt, though it was obvious that the great days of the millionaire collectors were over. As they died and their collections passed into the hands of the trusts set up to exhibit them, museums became the new powers in art buying.

Now civic pride was making a belated appearance in the prospering industrial towns of the Midwest, and each local museum wanted its own Rembrandt, some of them not caring how much it cost or where it came from. As a result, the art business in American hovered uneasily between trade and outright brigandage. Listening to Nat Hershman describe the coups of his father in the furniture market and his own ambitions to exploit the vogue for Old Masters, David realized this young man was best handled with care.

They parted at dusk, with mutual promises to keep in touch.

On the road back to town, David's head buzzed with Hershman's stories. Turning into the small square behind Victoria Station where he lived, he parked the car, sat in it for ten minutes, then abruptly drove off again toward the West End, knowing the hopelessness of trying to concentrate on catalogue copy tonight. He needed company.

It was early for the Cock and Feathers, but he recognized a few familiar faces at the bar. One of them, the pudgy moon face of Michael Gothard, a clerk at Carthew's, lit up as he saw David.

Before he'd reached the bar, Gothard had him by his sleeve.

"Moore! Just the chap. What are you drinking?"

"A Guinness, thanks. What have I done to deserve this?"

"Nothing, yet. Come into the Snug."

Out of sight of the other customers, Gothard took a folded sheet of paper from his pocket. "This came in last week. Our guv'nor turned it down; says it's too much trouble. But it's just the kind of thing you people specialize in."

David read the letter, written on heavy linen paper, with an indecipherable crest embossed at the top. Briefly, with the brusque offhandedness of the very wealthy, the writer asked Messrs. Carthew's and Co. to undertake the sale of the goods presently contained in St. Anselm's Hall, near Cardiff, terms to be discussed at a later date. It was signed with the single scrawled surname that indicated a peer of the realm: "Alderney."

David knew about Lord Alderney, had seen his square red face glaring from every magazine dealing with hunting and shooting in the British Isles. He was the sort of man who looked undressed without a shotgun in the crook of his arm and a dead stag under his foot.

"What's this St. Anselm's? I thought he lived in Yorkshire."

"He does. Apparently the place belongs—belonged, actually—to a younger brother, who died a while back. Since then it's been empty. He probably wants it cleared out for the next cousin in line."

It was a familiar pattern. Old families like the Alderneys had property all over the country: town houses in London, beach houses in Lyme Regis and Brighton, country seats in almost every county, shooting boxes in Scotland, fishing cottages with ten bedrooms on the best trout streams. As the clans intermarried, so their holdings increased—a convenience, since the number of relatives unlikely ever to inherit a title or the family fortune grew at the same rate.

By tradition, a family member too young or too remote from the succession to qualify for the title received a house and land as a sort of consolation prize. He could hunt, farm, fornicate, or drink away his disappointment and enjoy—if the farms on his land were reasonably fertile—a degree of financial comfort.

David weighed the letter. "Presumably you're not doing this out of the goodness of your heart."

Gothard looked sheepish. "Well, there's a bundle of drawings just come in. They look like Romneys to me, but I can't find anything on them. You handled some Romneys recently, didn't you?"

"We had a few. Bring them over, if you like, and I'll check them."

Gothard beamed in gratitude. "Look, is tomorrow too soon?"

"Make it after lunch. About two?"

After Gothard left, David read the letter again. He had a shrewd idea of what he was being thanked for. Gothard, like all clerks and young auctioneers in the larger salerooms, was eager for a higher job, but too often nepotism jammed the upper levels with young aristocrats or the sons of board members. To earn promotion, a junior had to prove his skill at researching difficult works, then defend his attributions at the weekly meetings of experts where his colleagues would try their hardest to prove him in error; each ambitious newcomer put in his place made their own jobs that much more secure.

Carthew's own experts could have checked the alleged Romneys and given an opinion at least as good as David's, but that would destroy Gothard's chances of a coup and possible promotion.

He stuffed the Alderney letter into his pocket, unaware that it would change his life and career completely and sever him finally from Snow's, from Simon, and from England itself.

8

"School of Giotto."

"Of course."

"Veronese."

D. Clement Parker bent his leonine head close to the tiny picture. "Really?"

Nat swallowed and passed to the next canvas in the gallery.

"Rembrandt."

"Hmmmmm. Very interesting." Taking out a gold watch that might have been made by Cellini, he studied the dial with a wrinkling of the famous eyebrows. "I wonder if we might talk now, Mr. Hershman. I have an appointment at twelve."

"Of course. Come back to the office."

Nat congratulated himself once more on opening the Fine Art Annex of the House of Hershman up here on Central Park West, rather than taking his father's advice and buying the empty warehouse opposite their place on 11th. How could you invite a man like Parker, one of the great dealers and connoisseurs of the century, down among the cut-rate furniture stores and two-bit barbers? Up here, with the rich green tapestry of the park fifteen floors below and the solidity of brass and mahogany all around, they felt at home. And a man who feels at home is one who spends money.

Nat pressed the buzzer on his desk. "Coffee?"

"By all means."

Patricia slipped in. "Coffee, please, dear."

As she closed the door, Nat caught the gleam of her wide blue eyes, and re-experienced in a flash of pure lust the moment that morning when he pulled up her skirt to show those long slim shiksa legs. He could still feel her fine blond hair and the long lazy body. . . . Feeling himself begin to color, he hastily switched to a new subject.

"You mentioned an 'opportunity' on the phone, Mr. Parker."

Parker drew one more time on his cigar and placed the remaining three inches in the ashtray. He was all business now.

"You might call it that, Mr. Hershman. My colleagues in the venture share with me an inclination to rate it somewhat higher. A challenge, certainly. A mission. One might, with justice, even describe it as a crusade."

"I didn't realize others were involved." Hershman's had succeeded mainly at the expense of other older firms, and any group rounded up by Parker was bound to include enemies.

"Some of our most important dealers, Mr. Hershman, have been concerned at the degree to which sales of important works are concentrated in the hands of a few individuals."

Nat knew who he meant. Joseph Duveen had tied up all the big buyers, and scores of dealers had broken their heads against his egotism and business genius.

"You're not alone in that belief, Mr. Parker, but what can we do? Duveen—"

Parker held up a hand as if warding off a blow.

"Please. If names are to be bandied about, let me mention a few. Samson? Alvery? Loutain *et cie?*"

Nat's surprise diverted him even from Patricia's return with the coffee. "You're right. Those are impressive."

"And they're not the only ones, Mr. Hershman; as I told you, this is no mere business deal. One would have to go back centuries for a comparison—the sale of the Duke of Mantua's collection to Charles the First of England, perhaps."

Baffled, Nat asked, "What exactly are we selling? And to whom?"

"Griffith." Parker exhaled the name like a cloud of smoke.

"Cyrus Griffith? The automobile man?"

"Indeed."

"But . . . I don't recall him ever buying a work of art in his life."

Parker frowned at this negative intrusion on his confidence.

"It's true Mr. Griffith is a man of . . . well, simple tastes. But all the more need for him to be exposed to the work of the Great Masters. I'm sure I don't have to remind you that Griffith's resources are greater than those of Mellon or Widener, almost of Rockefeller. We happen to know that Mr. and Mrs. Griffith are leaving Chicago for the first time to take a house on Long Island for the coming-out of their daughter. The house will need decoration commensurate with one of the great fortunes of the United States. We expect to provide that." He glanced at his watch again. "Good heavens, is that the time?"

He stood up and took his pearl gray fedora and cane from the hatstand.

"I'll be frank with you, Mr. Hershman. The work you've shown me is not of the superlative standard contributed by some members of the consortium, but time is of the essence and conditions in Europe at present militate against obtaining any better. Your stock is available, and the price is right. I hope I don't offend you by speaking so bluntly. One of our people will call on you in a day or two with concrete proposals. Good day."

After Parker had gone, Nat collapsed in his chair. This was the break for which he had prayed. His father would shy away from the heavy investment, at least until Nat explained the obvious advantages. Head spinning with excitement, he thumbed the buzzer.

"Patricia, come in here, please. *Now*."

"Pop, it's the opportunity of a lifetime!"

"So? Opportunities we got, Nat." From the catwalk high above the warehouse, Jake waved at the gang struggling to find space for a van load of heavy furniture. Nat flinched from the vulgarity of the heavy mahogany dining-room suites, the tables big enough for banquets. The few pictures mixed in with them were horrors, vast canvases of lowing herds and country race meetings, cherished in the nineteenth century but now dumped on the market in their hundreds.

"There seems to be more of this stuff than last week."

"Most of this we got at the Rentslaer place. The silver did good, but we had to buy in the furniture. We'll sell it, sometime. I've got more than a hundred thousand bucks tied up in this place alone, and ten percent is ours. You don't call that an opportunity?"

"*If* you can sell it. Listen, Pop, ten thousand is peanuts. I'm talking about millions."

"From Griffith? Never. That skinflint's got the first dollar he ever made. The first *dime!* What would he want with paintings anyway?"

"You *make* him want them, Pop. You create a taste. That's how Duveen works, and look at him. Do you think Frick was born liking Rembrandt?"

"Maybe, maybe. But how are you going to make Griffith want pictures? A grease monkey out of Nebraska who never saw anything closer to art than a chromo on a calendar from Sears Roebuck."

"Parker's figured it out. I told you: the books—"

"Oh, sure. The books." Leaning over the railings he bawled at the workmen struggling with a huge sideboard. "Look out, idiots! That's French Polish. Wrap it up, wrap it up!"

The veins stood out on his temples, and for the first time Nat realized his father was no longer a young or even middle-aged man.

He came back, mopping his forehead. "How's Ruth?"

Nat blinked. "Ruth? Fine. Why?"

"When are you two gonna have some more kids? You think one daughter's enough?"

"Pop, the paintings. . . ." Nat sighed.

"We'll see, we'll see." Someone let go of a corner and a table crashed to the floor. Turning again, Jake yelled at the workmen. "Klutz! Any damage, you pay for it." Peeling off his coat, he scrambled down the steps into the warehouse. Once a furniture dealer, always a furniture dealer.

In his father's office, Nat slumped in the creaky leather chair.

All around the walls hung the family portraits. Nat's own fourteen-year-old face beamed from a bar mitzvah photo hung next to pictures of his mother and father at their wedding and Nat at his own beside a plump, complacent Ruth—inevitably his father's choice.

Elsewhere, faces stared at him from the years before he was born. His mother as a girl, dark-eyed and solemn; a bearded patriarch—he assumed his grandfather—in some forgotten town.

Across the room, a blank wall waited for generations as yet unborn. Well, if a son was his father's price. . . . Staring at the empty plaster, Nat reached for the phone.

"Mr. Parker, I've talked to my father. We'll be delighted to join you."

* * *

Griffith had taken the most lavish mansion on the crescent of Long Island, an ocean liner of a house, stranded in its grounds as if on a sandbar. As the three limousines rolled up the wide drive, the barbered lawns and the crisp elegance of shrubs and hedges chided the low ambitions of the passengers in them. Money may have made this perfection possible but, like the army of gardeners and groundsmen who labored to achieve the effect, it was invisible.

The dealers waited for ten minutes in an echoing hall of ballroom dimensions, its walls lined with slim gilt chairs as fragile as Meissen china. While Parker chatted in murmurs with the other five members of the delegation, Nat occupied himself counting the chairs. He had reached fifty-three and still had two walls to go when the double doors opened and a bored maid announced them.

As familiar as he was from photos in the papers, Griffith managed to appear even more bean-pole and hangdog than they expected.

"Mr. Parker?" he said uncertainly.

Parker wrung the long hand with warmth. "A pleasure, sir. May I introduce my associates?"

What Griffith called the parlor was as sparsely furnished as the reception hall. Nobody was cheaper than a millionaire, and Nat guessed the one who leased Griffith this house had removed everything but the light bulbs when he left. Griffith seemed not to mind—perhaps he was used to such spartan surroundings.

"I'm very glad to see you gentlemen." He smiled around the group, a little uncertainly. "What exactly can I do for you?"

"Mr. Griffith," Parker said softly, as if correcting a childish error in grammar, "Rather ask, 'What can we do for *you?*'"

For the next half hour, Nat watched in admiration as a great salesman went to work. Parker's rich fruity voice rolled over Griffith like a tide of honey, seducing and immobilizing.

The old man listened with polite but—Nat thought—slightly baffled interest. Were they any different in his eyes from the drummers who visited his Nebraska garage selling a new kind of spark plug?

Sensing that his customer's interest was wavering, Parker reached for the black kid case and laid it reverently on the table. Untying the silk ribbon, he took out the two books.

A lot of time, not to mention money, had been spent on these books, as Nat had reason to know. His own share came to something over a thousand dollars. Not that they were worth less. Any bibliophile would have gladly paid that.

For one thing, they were unique. Only one copy of each had been printed, and the plates then destroyed. Each was bound in the finest calf, printed on handmade paper, assembled by hand. The text would never be published elsewhere, each section having been commissioned from an expert in his field for this use alone.

But the pictures made the books. Page after page of glossy plates illustrated one hundred great works of art, as the gold-embossed title on the cover of each book suggested, "The Greatest Paintings in the World."

For months, Parker and his partners had scoured the collections of the world for major works available for sale, then added the cream of their own stock. The result represented a potential expenditure of more than fourteen million dollars.

Griffith pored over them in awe. Finally, after running his fingers over the page on which Rembrandt's last self-portrait was reproduced, he closed them reverently.

"These are certainly very fine books, Mr. Parker!"

"They are indeed, Mr. Griffith. And they are yours!"

"Mine?" Griffith looked around with puzzled eyes. "Well, gentlemen. I don't think ... why, books like these—they must cost a great deal."

The silence stretched. Then Nat said helpfully, "They're a gift, sir. We had them made up for you."

"A gift?" Apparently beyond speech, Griffith rose from his desk, went to the door, and called quietly.

A thin woman came in, wearing a plain old-fashioned morning dress that reached her ankles. Gray hair was pulled sharply back from a thin face and tied with black ribbon.

"Gentlemen, this is Mrs. Griffith." Dramatically, he handed her one of the books. "Ella, can you believe this? These gentlemen have given us these books."

She opened the volume nervously, blinking at the blaze of color.

"I don't know how to thank you, Mr. Parker—gentlemen. My wife and I will treasure these. You've sure done a lot to make us feel welcome in the East."

For the first time, Nat saw Parker lost for words. After an agonized glance at the others, he swallowed and said, "Well, Mr. Griffith, we didn't actually get them up only as a gift. We hoped you might be interested in buying some of the paintings. The *originals*."

The idea took almost ten seconds to sink in, but when it did Griffith blinked with complete surprise. His wife was clearly just as astonished. They were not offended; merely bewildered, as if, on boarding a streetcar, someone had suggested they purchase the whole vehicle rather than simply pay their fares.

"But gentlemen," Griffith said helplessly, "why would we want them when we have the pictures right here in front of us?"

As the meeting broke up in confusion, Nat quietly asked the maid for directions to the bathroom.

As he might have expected, it was built on the grand scale, with a nice view of the Sound from a window conveniently placed by the lavatory. Even the plumbing was heroic: chunky taps of cast brass and a shower whose curving network of pipes washed everything from underneath and above at the touch of a foot pedal.

Nat washed his hands, looked at his reflection in the mirror, and began to giggle uncontrollably. Tears ran down his cheeks. He tried to suppress his hilarity, but hoots of laughter echoed around the room.

Then, mopping his eyes, he went back to the others.

Jake looked up incuriously as Nat came into the office and collapsed in the visitor's chair.

"Sell any pictures to Griffith?"

"Pop—"

"You work in this business as long as I have, you get to know people. Frick, Mellon, Rockefeller—they're old money. They're used to pictures. Had 'em on the wall as kids, probably had their portraits painted. But Griffith's a hayseed. He'll spend money on a horse, a tractor, even a house, but pictures? Never."

"What about furniture?"

"Yes, sure. Furniture. He'd spend—" Jake's eyes narrowed. "Say, does he need furniture?"

"Not any more. I sold him a van load. You should see that house. Hardly anything to sit on. After the others left, we made a deal."

Jake took out his special cigar box and handed Nat a Romeo y Julietta. "I always said you had a future in this business," he said.

Nat sighed. He felt the familiar sensation that the walls were closing in.

9

Driving across Dorset on his way to Wales, David watched the landscape change subtly as the rich counties of the landed gentry gave way to those slipping daily deeper into industrialization.

Increasingly, railways crossed the road or ran parallel with it, and macadam replaced the old road surface of gravel or clay. Once, the only delays on these roads had been caused by farm trucks carrying high loads of hay. Now David found himself crawling behind motor lorries jammed with Boothroyd's Patent Boots from the factory that defaced the landscape a few miles away, polluting the river and the air with the stink of tanning hides.

Beyond the Welsh border, it was all coal country, with gallowslike pithead machinery looming over the hills and spoil heaps swelling like boils. Coal towns had a disturbing sameness, with the mineowners' complacent mansions commanding the high ground while the workers' cottages clung to the slopes below in long uniform lines. Once these houses must have looked like the dutiful employees themselves, calmly awaiting their orders. Today, they seemed more like an army in siege.

The few privately held pockets of land had a choked, deserted look. David passed in a few seconds from an airy industrial landscape, its pale blue sky streaked with plumes of smoke, into the Wales of five centuries before, overgrown and dark.

It was almost two o'clock before he glided to a stop at the

gatehouse of St. Anselm's. He'd had a frustrating hunt for the
place down a dozen unsignposted lanes, some so clogged with
greenery that branches met over the road and he drove in a
tunnel of deep gloom. Weeds and twigs from the untrimmed
hedges flicked at his windshield, and the few people he met
plodding along the side seemed equally anxious to bar his
progress with contradictory and inaccurate directions.

The sagging, unpainted wooden gate by the tumbledown
gatehouse suited the area. Since the gate threatened to crumble
entirely if he shook it, David parked under a drooping elm and
cautiously walked toward the house, avoiding the potholes filled
with scummed water.

Once, an avenue of huge oaks had lined the drive, the last pair
framing the house. Now two were gone altogether, leaving
stumps the size of dinner tables, and of the others at least one
had recently been struck by lightning, its burned and shattered
trunk adding to the eeriness and air of decay. Pushing through
the branches that blocked the drive, David had his first view of
St. Anselm's.

An oblong mansion four stories high, it was topped by a
forest of roofs which, like the facade itself, combined half a
dozen architectural styles. Built of bright red sandstone carted
from God knows what distant quarry, it sat like a squalling
red-faced baby in the discreet Welsh landscape of gray and
green. False columns and capitals in a style the ancient world
lacked both the energy and the poor taste to perpetrate lined the
ground floor, flanking bay windows that bulged like popeyes.

Precisely centered over the entrance was a three-foot red
sandstone owl, presumably a family emblem. Above it, the
house rioted in a medley of roofs, turrets, bay windows,
verandas, skylights, crenellations, and spires.

David pounded on the main doors at the top of the steps for a
full ten seconds before noticing a seam of gray putty bulging
from between them. They were sealed shut, and from the look of
the wood had been so for years. Through the grimy glass he
made out piles of books in what had been the main hall.

Backing off, he stared up at the frontage, puzzled. Had they
sent him to an empty ruin? Then, high above, a window flew up
and a girl looked out.

"They've all gone!"

"What?"

"They've all gone. To Pendine. Are you Gwennie Frame's
friend?"

"No. I'm David Moore. From Snow's."

"Who?"

"From Snow and Son. Lord Alderney asked me to come down and look over the house. For the auction."

"Go round to the side and I'll come down." A white arm waved vaguely, and David caught a glimpse of shoulders wrapped in what looked like a blanket. He plowed through the knee-high grass to the east frontage.

This side of the house was even more fanciful, a colonnade of gray Carrara marble shading a terra-cotta paved terrace and half a dozen large windows. The rooms behind them were as disordered as the hall, full of more books and furniture shrouded in dust sheets. Everywhere, the symbol of the owl spread minatory wings, over vast fireplaces, dark wood staircases big enough to hold four people abreast, and vistas of dusty corridors and locked rooms.

A lawn had once sloped down to a line of elms two hundred yards away, but it was some time since the grass had been mown. It was two feet high except where a small area had been trampled flat. A dozen tables were scattered across this patch, some still set with the remains of a picnic: chicken bones, sandwiches sodden with dew, a looted hamper from Fortnum and Mason's. The plates were beautiful: Royal Doulton and Crown Derby, parts of two or three services jumbled together. On one table sat a phonograph, felt pad soaked. Records were littered in the grass.

"Who did you say?"

She stood on the colonnade, shaded by a column, and the open window behind her flared briefly in the sun so that she seemed not one person but a group, the glass infinitely replicating her small alert figure.

"I'm David Moore, from Snow's. Lord Alderney sent me to appraise the house. Surely he wrote you?"

"Probably, but the postman doesn't come here much now. Anyway, I'm glad someone's come at last. I've been waiting for simply ages."

She was short, hardly more than five feet, with a squirrelly eagerness and chunky softness that reminded him of nurseries and stuffed bears. He guessed at her age and decided she might be two or three years younger. Like most redheads she had green eyes and white, almost porcelain skin. What set her apart from the ordinary was her smile, so memorable that in years to come he could recreate her merely by remembering her mouth and eyes. Gradually she would reconstruct herself around that smile, materializing like the Cheshire cat in *Alice*. Even in tears she would grin, as if in bemused resentment, clinging to the one feature she knew made her unforgettable.

"I'm Cicely Blandford." She took his hand lightly. "Do come in."

Little sunlight penetrated the house except through the dusky skylights four stories above the main staircases. She receded ahead of him in the watery gloom like a ghost, her dress a blur of white muslin.

There were signs of habitation on the western side of the house. The room they entered had a small table, a few chairs, a chaise, and a floor covered deep in carpets—contemporary horrors from the northern mills jumbled willy-nilly with priceless Kelims and intricate symphonies of red and green silk from the Second Empire. The room's confusion was aptly echoed by the view through the French windows of a rampant kitchen garden, seeded cabbages fountaining four feet in the air and nettles struggling with crimson poppies for space to breathe. Among the profusion of blooms, butterflies reeled in a delirium of greed.

She waved to a chair and flopped down on the chaise, reclining with complete animal comfort, unconcerned that her skirt showed pale silk stocking almost to the thigh.

"I thought you were one of the people my cousin invited down for the weekend. They went off this morning to the races. I didn't think I'd ever get rid of them. We were dancing till three. But I expect you'd like a drink."

Leaping up, she rummaged in a cupboard among dozens of bottles, lifting each and holding it to the light, all the while keeping up a running commentary.

"Gin, gin...must be some gin somewhere. What's this? Good God, brandy. Must be *eons* old. Vermouth. Awful stuff, I've always thought, haven't you? Ah, gin...empty, of course. No, wait on; there's some in this one. But nothing to mix it with. If we had some bitters we could have pink gins. Or a gin rickey. Have you had those? The Americans drink them all the time. Quite nice, actually."

"Americans or gin rickeys?"

"Both. Paris is full of them these days." With a half-full bottle of gin in her hand, she dug for glasses on the crowded sideboard.

"Is that where you've been living—Paris?"

"Switzerland, actually. And Vienna for a bit. I was in school—finishing school, really. Then Daddy died and it wasn't easy to get back. Not that I wanted to. Do you know Switzerland?"

"No."

"It can be rather boring." She seemed to be formulating the opinion for the first time. "A bit like Bournemouth in the winter, all invalids and old ladies. But the school was fun. They used to have a dance every Saturday night, and all the young men would come up from the hospital. I did the maxixe once with a man who only had one arm. He lost the other in the war in Spain. It was rather sweet." She offered him neat gin in a dusty glass and asked brightly, "Are you supposed to look over the whole house?"

"Well, get a general idea. Is there much?"

"My dear, tons! You could spend a year at it. I haven't looked in some of the rooms since I was a child. And these books!" She waved to indicate unseen libraries lurking in other rooms. "Daddy went rather strange at the end, I'm afraid. Of course I was away, but I used to hear things."

"Was he collecting something in particular?"

"He used to buy *everything*. I went with him once in the Rolls and we just loaded up in every town. Once he bought the whole library of a bishop. Thousands of books about God." She smiled at the absurdity. "I don't read a lot. Do you? It always seems such a waste of time. I do love to dance, though. Have you ever heard of Josephine Baker?"

"Yes." This was shaky ground. The black American dancer's exploits in Parisian cabarets were the stuff of smoking room stories.

"I saw her once. At the Bal Tabarin. She danced quite naked."

David blinked. "Naked?"

"Oh, well. . . ." She fluttered a hand in front of her thighs. "A bunch of bananas, but—"

A vestigial puritanism stirred him. "I'm surprised the school let you go to something like that."

She looked annoyed. "It wasn't the Presbyterian Ladies' College, you know. They're very advanced in Europe." She stood up abruptly. "I suppose you had better start looking."

The tour began in stiff courtesy, but before they had pored over the first room Cicely was giggling at newly discovered bits

of bric-a-brac and telling stories of her childhood in this
rambling ruin.

They browsed deeper into the house until David was quite
lost. The gin in his empty stomach made him vague and dizzy.
Occasionally their bodies collided softly in the gloom, and once
she grabbed his hand to steady herself as she tripped over a
rolled-up rug.

He lost track of time, ceased even to jot down in his notebook
details of the treasures he found. Elizabethan coffers, a portrait
that looked like Van Dyck but was mantled in varnish and dust,
priceless silver jumbled in boxes, bedrooms in the servants'
quarters furnished with Spode and Sèvres toilet sets, the water in
them long dried to puddles of dust, Sheraton and Hepplewhite
furniture, some splintered and worm-eaten but the bulk
recoverable. The value was incalculable.

High in the upper story, he paused as Cicely led the way along
a corridor and pushed at a door standing half open. The
bedroom inside was better kept than most, with oil lamps set
about and linen on the big bed. The books were not piled in
columns, as elsewhere, but scattered in ones and twos, as if
meant to be read. The side table held medicine bottles and an
odd domestic detail, a box of lemon acid drops from a shop in
Poole. He stirred them with a finger and found the sugar grains
that coated them still crisp and white.

Cicely appeared at the door, dwarfed by its huge frame.
Something in the room seemed to daunt her.

"Some of this stuff is wonderful," David said. "The table
must be Jacobean, and a few of the paintings—" He put down
his lamp to peer at the portrait of a horse-faced woman over the
bed. "Good grief, this is a Gainsborough!"

"It's my great grandmother," she said quietly. "I think it came
from the house where he was born."

"Your father? Oh, you mean—" He looked around the room.
"Oh."

"He died in that bed. I haven't been up here since."

David grabbed the lamp. "I'm sorry."

She shook her head and came diffidently into the room. "I
don't know why I should be nervous. Let's look around while
we're here."

They began poking in corners, turning small pieces of
furniture to the light. David pulled the bedside table out from
the wall and dislodged a pile of books at the back. Something

about their unconventional binding and dimensions caught his eye. A few were covered in what felt like vellum, others in cheap wrapping paper. He opened one in the light of the lamp.

Ralph the Rover, or the Cocksman's Art. By a Gentleman.

Fascinated, he leafed through it, read a few lines, and closed it hurriedly. Feeling his face flush, he opened the next one. It was illustrated.

"Not *more* books," Cicely said from behind him. "I don't know where he found the time."

With a start David tried to shove the bundle back into place, but she had already picked one up. Saying nothing, she began to read. After the first page, she turned over and began the second.

"They were at the back of the shelf," David said lamely. "I suppose one of the servants—"

"What's a scrotum?" she asked.

"Uh ... well—"

"It says here, 'Enter the Brothers Bollocks, a merry pair....' Well, I get that. Then it says, 'and Scrotum, their wrinkled old retainer.' Unless ... oh, *I* see." She beamed at him. "My dear, you're red as a beetroot."

Taking the other books from his hands she scattered them on the bed, flopped face down, ankles neatly crossed, and opened the first of them. "I could do with some light relief."

Sitting down on the edge of the bed to read over her shoulder, David reached out to touch her hair, gleaming an almost coppery red in the lamplight. Instead of recoiling, she pushed her head up against his hand, like a cat being stroked.

One finger touched her ear, her cheek. She took no notice.

"This one's not very interesting." She tossed it aside and reached for another. "Who'd have thought Daddy read this kind of thing?"

The new book was thicker, and in French, though most of it was illustrations, lovingly engraved and colored by hand. He heard her breathe more heavily as image followed image. Bewigged courtiers from the golden days of Versailles disported themselves in its lofty damasked bedrooms, pink buttocks and breasts drooping from unlaced gowns, swollen phalluses peeping from tight breeches.

David's hand gently explored the shape of her back, feeling the delicate ridges of buttons and tapes. It slipped down the back of her thighs and under her skirt. He felt the slick silk of her stockings, then warm flesh.

Lazily she shifted her weight, resting on elbows and knees to spread her legs, sprawling on the broad hummock her movement had thrown up in the feather mattress. His fingers found soft crevices, a welcoming wetness...recoiled as she gasped...then touched again. Touched and slowly penetrated.

"Look at *this*," she whispered.

The picture showed two couples in a huge bed, wigs obscenely at odds with their naked and intricately depicted bodies. David's hand toyed and fondled, feeling her body subtly taut, the muscles tense in belly and thighs, like a rider urging its mount toward a jump. With one careful finger he probed deeper. She sighed with utter abandon and slumped forward.

Her face toward him now on the pillow, flushed and smiling, her lips half open and wet, she looked at him for the first time since they sat down. Her eyes were green with delight.

"Isn't this *wicked*," she whispered.

Cicely heard the car start up, out of sight behind the trees. Then David tooted the horn twice and accelerated down the invisible lane. She listened until there was no more sound, only the cawing of rooks in the elms and the distant drone of a tractor, and went back into the house.

It didn't seem five days since he came to St. Anselm's. Perhaps it wasn't; she had lost track of time since returning to England. Drowsing through the long afternoons, the blinds drawn against the sun, she had succumbed to her own internal rhythms, letting the clock of her body decide when to eat, sleep, bathe.

Flopping down on the chaise, she picked up the list David had left behind. Somehow, sense had been made of the jumble inside the house. Anything salable now bore a small white cross of chalk, with an additional circle in blue if the item needed restoration or repair. There were a lot of those blue circles; years of neglect had not been kind to the treasures dumped here by the Alderneys.

Cicely skimmed down the columns. Pages and pages. "Bureau (Chippendale?). Chestnut, inlaid rosewood, satin-wood...Etching. Madonna and Child. Sgd. A. Durer (copy?)" She dropped the sheaf of papers lazily onto the floor, unable to interest herself in the dull recital of facts.

Already, the memory of David was receding, carried off like the whole experience of the last five days into that limbo where

Cicely stored her different lives, like bottles in a wine cellar. She might open this one again in a few weeks, when she went to London. She knew nobody in the city, and David could be a pleasant companion, perhaps a useful protector. Or perhaps she wouldn't bother, letting Snow's sell everything and send her the money—in Paris or Switzerland. She knew the Baron would be glad to see her again, despite the abruptness with which she left Zurich, and René would, as ever, welcome her back with passion and generosity. They understood her.

But David Moore did not. She sensed that from the first day, but nothing could dispel the romantic mood he insisted on creating around them. Finally, she gave in and let him carry her along with his schemes and whispered endearments, closing her eyes so that his voice became the murmur of many, blurring like the rush of blood through her own ears.

She drifted off to sleep in the sun, light from the cracked window laying a faint web of gold over her forearm's white skin.

As much as this house with its crazed mirrors and anonymous portraits, she belonged here. Both were scraps of flotsam cast aside by the broad slow stream of European aristocracy. Genes from five royal families were tangled in her, each at war with the next. She had inherited the subtle perceptions of that inbred and incestuous society, and more than a little of its madness.

10

"Any other business?" Simon looked around the table at his heads of department, hoping none of them would speak. The congestion in his chest, merely irritating when the meeting began just after lunch, now felt like a brick lodged just below his breastbone.

"There *is* one small thing." Piper spoke up with creditable diffidence, aware that Simon wanted the meeting over as soon as possible. But as head of Old Masters, he felt a responsibility that transcended Simon's comfort.

"Yes?" He tried to make his irritation apparent in the curt monosyllable.

"All these German and Austrian items. At the last meeting, we agreed to put the matter off until some pattern emerged. Well, I really don't see one, and it's frankly become a major problem."

There was a murmur of agreement around the table. Gideon, who headed Silver, said, "The vaults are overflowing, and I can't sell even a fraction of it."

For five years, European refugees had been trickling into London. The smartest, seeing the writing on the wall, arrived in 1933, immediately after Hitler became chancellor, many shipping their entire collections to Switzerland after paying off the right Nazi with a Cranach or a Rembrandt.

By 1935, the trickle was a flood and the prevailing air of those who arrived in Britain a weary desperation. No more collections got through. These people carried only the jewelry they had been able to snatch up as the Gestapo pounded on the door. Some of the luckier ones saved larger items: silver boxes, small ivories, jade, a single tiny oil, the pathetic remnants of a life-style they would never regain.

Public opinion in Britain, initially warm toward the refugees, cooled noticeably as the numbers swelled. Now passport officials often refused entry to fugitives who lacked a fat bank account or British relatives to guarantee their support. Occasionally, one was rash enough to try smuggling valuables into the country; confiscation and savage customs duties inevitably followed.

The desperate owners arrived on the doorsteps of all the London salerooms, pleading for money to tide them over until their valuables could go on the market. Many were old customers, and for a while the salerooms obliged them, until what looked like a promisingly profitable situation became a burden as the objects piled up, threatening to flood the market.

As a matter of policy, Simon did what he could, offering advances in the most desperate cases, squeezing even more items into already crowded sales. If he did not, unscrupulous smaller companies and dealers were always ready to snap up the treasures at a tenth of their value. But it wasn't enough. There were always more refugees, more things to sell.

"I can't go into this now," Simon said. "We all know the problem. I think it's insoluble, unless we reduce our acquisitions altogether. I don't feel we can do that. Are there any alternative suggestions?"

He listened with only half an ear to the usual ideas: consigning some of the items to American salerooms, offering sellers a lower commission in return for delaying their sales. At the back of his mind, though he never dared acknowledge it fully, was the conviction that this year, 1939, would see Britain itself engulfed in the tide of fascism. Then he might be smuggling his own valuables off the boat at New York or Buenos Aires, praying that the customs officials would be kind.

The block in his chest had become intolerable. He cut off discussion with a curt slap of his hand on the table. Look at them stare, he thought. Like fish in an aquarium.

"I'm sorry. We'll have to stop here. Let's look at the problem at the next meeting."

He barely made it back to his office before the wheezing

began. Pulling the inhaler from the drawer, he pushed his face into the mask and breathed deeply until the fumes cleared his chest. The asthma seemed to get worse each week, triggered by the damp of this soggy autumn but aggravated still further by a sense of doom that rose like a fog from every evening paper. Chamberlain's pathetic attempts at conciliation with Hitler looked more and more like the gestures of a modern Canute against the tidal wave in which all were fated to drown.

He pushed the inhaler aside and went through the papers on his desk, brightening slightly as he came to the proofs of the Blandford Catalogue.

David had turned up a treasure there. Even old Piper had been silenced, reluctantly admitting that it was "a damn fine piece of work" to locate such a collection and ensure that Snow's had exclusive rights.

Looking around the faces at that meeting, three months before, he'd realized that each man knew David and Cicely Blandford were lovers. Perhaps they could even give, as he could, the address of the flat in Lancaster Gate where they met. Undoubtedly they disapproved as much as Simon did. Equally, they realized that the relationship protected Snow's investment. Lately, he saw most situations in this light. The company, which he had grasped so eagerly four years earlier, now clasped him in an unshakable embrace. It was like a sick relative whom one could neither abandon nor endure.

Occasionally, in moments of depression, he toyed with the idea of handing the company to Turnbull and his group, who waited for the slightest excuse to move in and regain control. Capitulation would be simple, since he had already, by a decision taken months before, placed himself in their power.

Any hopes of getting the building back into shape with a few repairs had faded the previous spring when the firm of engineers presented him with a lengthy report along with their even lengthier account. If Snow and Son didn't fall down within two years, it would be, in their considered professional opinion, a miracle.

Reluctantly, Simon put the problem to Harley Debenham, knowing Turnbull would block any large expenditure even on something as essential as repairs. The accountant offered a drastic set of money-raising methods: a mortgage on the buildings, which Simon, as owner of title, had the legal (if not the moral) right to raise; personal loans on his own house and

collection; some shady manipulation of the trust under which he
inherited the firm. Simon read the list with raised eyebrows, then
signed without argument.

"Let's get this over with before they throw us in jail."

In four hectic months, they all but gutted the building,
rebuilding totally inside the shell. Of the old fittings, only the
spiral staircase remained, and even it now rested on a renewed
steel structure. Rotted plasterwork and paneling were recon-
structed from old sketches, the gilding painstakingly restored by
the few craftsmen in England who still understood Georgian
decoration.

Snow's reopened as London's most beautiful saleroom—but
also the deepest in debt. If the Blandford sale did not pay off,
they were finished, and Oliver Turnbull would have his excuse to
move in.

Yet Simon found himself almost resenting both David and
the sale. An encounter with David and Cicely, heads together
over a table at the Ritz, or giggling in Bond Street, loaded down
with parcels from the latest shopping spree, could leave him
tense, sometimes trembling. To make amends for his irrational
animosity, he forced himself to see them often, socially. They
were dining together that evening, in fact. Could *that* explain his
short temper, the asthma attack? Irritated with the thought, he
buzzed his secretary.

"Elizabeth, did you make those reservations for this
evening?"

"Yes. Table for three, Savoy Grill, eight. Was that right?"

"Yes. Thanks." He flipped up the key, conscious of being
committed, but aware as well of a familiar discomfort at the
thought of the evening, of Cicely—playful, flirtatious, attractive—and of David—too young, too enthusiastic, too ambitious. Too close for comfort.

"Come away from the window!"

"Why?"

"Someone will see."

"Oh, sucks to them." Cicely, naked, pulled back the curtain a
few more inches and peered down into the street, three floors
below. "They don't care what happens up here."

"What about the house opposite?" From the bed, David
could see its windows quite clearly, though Cicely, half wrapped

in the white net curtain and silhouetted against the afternoon light, was a phantom shadow.

"There's nobody home." She paused, staring, then squealed and threw herself back into bed beside him. "There *was* someone! A man with a mustache."

"Cicely, I told you...." He was blushing.

"Prude." She giggled at his discomfort. "There wasn't anyone. You're so silly sometimes."

Putting his arm around her, David drew her to him, wedging the curly-haired head onto his shoulder. No matter how much time they spent in bed, he never tired of her. Even when, as now, he lacked the energy for more sex, there were the peripheral satisfactions of watching, feeling, touching.

"What time is it?" he asked presently.

"Nearly five." From the corner of his eye he caught the glint of her new wristwatch from Cartier. She spent money like water. Eighty guineas for that watch alone. Then there were the clothes, this flat, and the seemingly bottomless pit of her requirements for meals, cosmetics, taxis.... His advice urging caution, at least until after the sale, was met with laughter.

"Don't forget dinner with Simon tonight," he said. At least someone else was picking up that bill.

"No, I haven't. What will I wear?" She was out of bed again, pulling open the wardrobe to confront the scores of dresses, almost all of them new. "Do you like this?"

She held a peach gown in front of her, swirling the pleated skirt, then dropped it to the carpet carelessly in favor of a black one, a beige.... Soon the floor was littered ankle-deep in clothes.

"Oh, I don't know." For a moment, she contemplated the still half-filled wardrobe, then turned and glanced coquettishly across the room at him. "Of course, I could go like this." Shyly she laid one hand on the tiny triangle of red hair, the other across her small breasts, and smiled invitingly. "Do you think Simon would like that?"

David, to his astonishment, found himself excited again. Scrambling out of bed, he grabbed her around the waist and they fell to the floor among the scattered gowns. Making love on the frail colored fabrics was delicious. He crushed her down on them, the rustle of silk joined with her murmured obscenities like the soft crackle of flames.

*   *   *

Dinner began badly. There had been no time to bathe before they met Simon, and David knew he must smell on them the musk of the afternoon's lovemaking. Cicely was pettish, irritable, claiming to find a scrap of shell in her oyster cocktail and sending it back, then pushing the replacement aside, barely touched.

But the wine softened all of them. Cicely, for a change, made an effort to draw out Simon, even prodding him into the occasional smile. After little food but three bottles of wine and a number of brandies, they reeled slightly as the revolving doors thrust them into the noisy London night.

The forecourt of the Savoy accommodated a theater as well as the frontage of the hotel and its Grill Room. A few yards away, a street musician coaxed coins from the homegoing theater crowd with the "Merry Widow Waltz" played on a wheezy harmonica. Still dizzy, Cicely began a solo waltz, then grabbed Simon's arm and made him her initially unwilling, then complaisant partner. David grinned drunkenly as they danced gravely up toward the Strand.

"Will Mr. Snow be wanting his car, sir?"

David tried to focus on the doorman. "I daresay. Yes. And we'll need a cab ourselves."

Snapping his finger for a page to run to the corner and hail a taxi, the doorman signaled for Simon's car. It cruised calmly down to the door, with Cicely running after it, dragging Simon by the hand.

She was panting and grinning with the fun of it. "You're not a bad dancer, Simon. We could go on the halls. 'Simon and Cicely—Fantasies in Dance.' Think you could carry me over your head with one hand?"

"Only if I get to swing you by the ankles as a finale."

They leaned on one another, giggling, as the doorman, Simon's chauffeur, and a slightly irritated David looked on. Cicely's face suddenly became strained.

"I think I've had too much wine," she said. "I would really like to lie down." Still clinging to Simon's arm, she sank slowly toward the ground. He hauled her upright again.

"Perhaps I'd better take her home," Simon said diplomatically. "It wouldn't do to have her—" He glanced at the curious stares of the guests emerging from the hotel.

"I've asked for a cab," David said, but the doorman shook his head pessimistically. "Well, I suppose, if you don't mind. Sweetheart, I'll come round when I get a taxi."

"Thass all right. Quite all right." She looked half asleep as Simon bundled her into the back seat of the Rolls. The door was closed before David remembered to call "Good night; thanks for dinner." But then, the large car had already slid away from the curb. Glumly he walked after it toward the Strand to join the boy in his vigil for a cab.

As the Rolls turned through Trafalgar Square and headed up the Mall, Simon glanced at Cicely's head resting on his arm. Her eyes were open.

"Feeling better now?"

"Oh, much." She straightened up, rummaged through her purse, and corrected her makeup. The reflection of her face in the tiny mirror was as crisp and bright as a miniature.

"I don't know your address," Simon lied.

She closed the purse with a snap and smiled up at him. For the first time he saw in her eyes the hint of some hovering devilry. "I know yours. Seventeen East Heath Road. You might ask me up for a nightcap. I've never seen your house."

After a long pause, Simon leaned forward. "Home, please, Spencer."

As they drove through the park, Cicely put her small warm hand on Simon's thigh. He made no attempt to remove it.

11

"Old Lady Cuthbertson," Simon observed quietly as one of London's most distinguished collectors tottered up the staircase on the arm of her newest young male "secretary." "Flat broke, I hear." More loudly, as she reached the top of the stairs, he said, "So glad you could come, my lady. David, show Lady Cuthbertson to her seat, won't you?"

Not sorry to leave his post by the stairs, where under the guise of carrying on a casual conversation he and Simon were counting the house, David steered the old lady and her companion into the already crowded main saleroom, almost all its seats occupied except for those reserved in the two front rows for the most important guests—the big dealers, traditionally the last to arrive.

A few last-minute browsers studied the paintings which, until a few months before, had hung on the walls of St. Anselm's. Glimpsing the placid Gainsborough lady who had stared down complacently as they made love in that upstairs bedroom, David looked away, understanding why Cicely was not coming to the sale. It would be like watching one's life parceled up and sold.

Simon was deep in conversation with a newspaperman when he returned. For the past few weeks, most of his lunches had been spent with these people, to the improvement of the firm's press but the decline of Simon's prestige inside the company. Piper put it concisely over a half-dozen oysters and a bottle of Chablis in Wheeler's when he dined there with his cronies from

Christie's. "A gentlemen from *The Times*—that I can understand. But *reporters!*"

For once, David agreed with him. Cicely's coverage in the
tabloids, with the usual yellow-press emphasis on cliché—lone
heiress, crumbling mansion, priceless treasures—offended him
as much as it delighted her. But if it meant a better turnout at the
sale and higher prices as well, he'd be a fool to protest, especially
since, on careful analysis, many of St. Anselm's "treasures"
showed alarming evidence of their long neglect. Piper's staff had
achieved prodigies of emergency restoration, but both David
and Simon knew everything depended on the sale's hitting its
stride from the beginning, creating a momentum in which
defects were forgotten in the collective fever to buy.

Returning to the top of the stairs, David saw a familiar face
below him—Michael Gothard, his fat friend from Carthew's,
whose tip brought the St. Anselm's sale about. The anguish on
his face as he glimpsed David was so surprising that David
hardly noticed his companion. But Simon's mouth straightened
into a thin line of irritation, instantly smoothed out as the pair
came into view.

Charles Carthew seemed to belong on a cricket field rather
than in the cranky untidiness of a saleroom. The fair curly hair
and youthful complexion, the air of faint disdain, all better
suited the head boy at some smart public school than the
chairman of a major auction house.

"Morning, Snow." The drawl suggested a singular lack of
interest in Simon and anything he might have to say.

"Glad you could come, Charles." Simon could afford to be
affable. It was the joke of the year inside the business that
Carthew's turned down the Blandford sale as "too much
trouble." Wondering if Gothard's anguished look implied that
Carthew knew of their deal months before, David tried to catch
his eye again, but the crowd carried his friend into the confusion
of the main saleroom.

"Good turnout," Carthew remarked.

Simon glanced over his shoulder. "Not bad, I suppose." He
might have been seeing his audience for the first time.

"Think you'll get rid of everything?"

"Oh, I imagine so. Don't you?"

"Never can tell, old boy. Never can tell." Staring around the
domed hall, he nodded in approval. "The old place looks quite
smart."

"Thanks. A lick of paint, you know."

As Carthew sauntered off, David asked quietly, "What was all *that* about? Sour grapes?"

"Let's hope so." Simon didn't mention that there had been a look in Carthew's eye he did not like.

Only a trickle of people came up the stairs now, and David checked his watch. Still ten minutes to go. Like most salerooms, Snow's stuck rigidly to the tradition that sales always began exactly at the advertised time, whether before a large crowd or in a nearly empty room. He wondered if he could stand the tension for that long.

The late arrival who hurried up the stairs was a godsend. His subtly too-formal suit, too tight and too noisily checked, and the air he exuded of aggressive but unfelt good humor didn't matter. He was obviously disoriented and in need of guidance, and David descended on him, delighted to have something to occupy himself. (Later, reviewing the effect Carl Bleigen had on his life, he wondered at its course had he ignored the man, or followed Gothard into the saleroom a few minutes earlier. But by then the damage was thoroughly done.)

"Can I help you?"

The man turned on him a wider version of an undertaker's ingratiating grin.

"Yeah, you sure could." David instantly recognized the New York twang. "Am I too late for the sale?"

"You've got a few minutes. Did you reserve a seat?"

"Uh, no. Should I have?"

"It's advisable." Precisely on time, the big dealers were arriving, strolling up the staircase to greet Simon with casual nods or, in some cases, frosty indifference. This was no place for David. "Shall I see if anything's left? It's Mr., er...?"

"Bleigen." The offered palm was moist, slightly clammy. "Carl W. Bleigen." His pronunciation of the initial—"double-yer"—put the seal on his phoniness. David thought of George Bancroft playing the small-time gangster in a Warner Brothers melodrama.

"Your first visit here, Mr. Bleigen?" (A small businessman, in London on his first foreign trip for the firm and anxious to see all the sights, including a real fine-art auction sale?)

"It sure is. And I want to tell you, it's quite a thrill."

David felt expansive, in spite of Bleigen's oily manner. "Like to look around? We don't get many visitors from the States."

Remembering young Nat Hershman and their meeting in Brighton, he decided two Americans less like one another could hardly be imagined.

"Well, I don't want to take you away from your work. . . ."

"It's no trouble. We still have a few minutes."

Despite the sale in the main room, work went on in other departments; as they paused at the door of the jewel and porcelain room, one of the half dozen dealers tapped on the glass of the new display cases and a porter hurried with a key to unlock the armored glass cabinet. The system lacked the casual freedom of the old days when items were kept in open boxes, wrapped in newspaper, but damage and theft were almost impossible.

At the saleroom door, David slipped in and returned with a numbered slip of paper. "I've found you a seat. It's on the side, but we're very full, as you see."

"I really want to thank you, sir. I do indeed." Again that oily smile. Though his enthusiasm for Mr. Carl W. Bleigen was waning, David finished the thumbnail tour. They looked in on the book room and the small salon kept for silver, its floor and walls glowing with Persian carpets—one of Simon's ideas to display goods and improve the atmosphere at the same time.

Their last call was at the newest innovation. At the rear of the building, near what had been the delivery entrance, two counters had been installed, and a score of people stood waiting patiently, each clutching a parcel or shopping bag.

"We encourage the public to bring in things for valuation," David explained. He didn't add that small dealers, runners, and knockers also used the service—one reason why he encouraged Simon to set it up. Had the big salerooms been this accessible when he worked the markets, his life would have been considerably easier.

Three busy appraisers at each counter sorted through the potential treasures.

"You ever find anything?" Bleigen asked as a woman dumped down a stuffed turtle that dribbled sawdust all over the floor.

"Only about two percent is salable," David admitted. "But last month, someone brought in a Goya. It'd been hanging over the fireplace for years and you could hardly recognize it for soot." Glancing at his watch, he said, "I think perhaps. . ." His mouth was suddenly dry with the familiar pre-sale tension.

"Sure, sure. I really appreciate you showing me around, Mr., er . . . ?"

"Oh, David Moore." Odd how he hesitated to give his name to this man. Something about Bleigen put him on his guard. As the American squeezed to his seat—one of the few left vacant in the room—David spotted Simon at the back and joined him.

Beck, the auctioneer, was already on the rostrum, unhurriedly going through his catalogue while the three clerks at the lower desk beside him sorted through the commission bids handed to them by clients not able to attend the sale in person.

Around the walls, a few people still peered at the paintings, grabbing a last look before the sale, though viewing had officially finished half an hour before. Nobody took these men seriously. They were amateurs or tourists, using the saleroom as an informal art gallery or as shelter from the rain. A serious dealer went to often absurd lengths to hide his interest in an item, sending emissaries to bid on his behalf or tipping a clerk or saleroom porter to do so.

If they actually turned up in person, it was often only after arranging an elaborate code with the auctioneer to disguise the fact that they were bidding; the interest of a major dealer or expert in a cheap picture could send its value soaring as his competitors jostled to grab what might be an unrecognized masterpiece.

In the secret world of the fine art auction, a wink could be a bid. So could the raising of a little finger, the waggle of an ear. The dealer might be bidding as long as he held a pencil in his hand and *not* bidding when it was in his pocket. Some warned the auctioneer that they would top every bid as long as they were on their feet, but would show lack of interest by sitting down. (On one famous occasion, a dealer working such a system forgot it altogether on seeing an old friend across the room. He hurried to join him, then returned to his seat and the alarming news that he had just bought three lots he didn't want.)

Tourists at a sale cringed if the auctioneer looked in their direction, fearful that a sqeeze or a chance movement would be interpreted as a bid. Few realized how hard it was to bid unless you were known as a serious buyer. Almost every bid at a large auction was made by someone the auctioneer knew. The usual collection of interested bystanders hardly registered as his trained eyes scanned the room for the eight or ten people who really mattered.

Precisely at ten thirty, two porters placed the first lot on the easel to Beck's left. He glanced down at the small painting with the cool indifference that is the mark of a good auctioneer.

"Good morning, my lords, my lady, ladies and gentlemen. The first lot is *Landscape with Horsemen* by Ruysdael, showing on my left. Shall we start at five hundred pounds?"

David held his breath. It had begun.

It seemed, at the beginning, that they had nothing to worry about.

The Ruysdael went quickly, for twelve hundred—about their estimate. A small Constable followed, generally agreed to be second-rate (and suspected by David to have been painted in part by John Constable's son Lionel). But a prominent collector of English pictures snapped it up for two hundred more than they hoped. A Lawrence portrait went to another private collection at a good price.

But the real hurdle still remained. Like most auctions, this one had its plums—a dozen important works which must fetch top prices if the sale were to go into the black. The art of planning an auction lay in placing these so that they not only sold well but also encouraged high bidding on lesser items.

Every big sale had its element of theater, and the best a symphonic progression. High prices could fan an audience to fever heat; slow bidding could have them fidgeting, riffling through their catalogues. So far, everything had gone to the small collectors. The big dealers, whose interest could bring the sale to the boil, were holding back.

Another minor English painting, a John Sell Cotman, completed the overture to the sale, and David felt the tension rise as the first of the major works was carefully placed on the easel. Beck, handling the moment well, paused like an actor about to deliver a soliloquy.

"*Portrait of a Nobleman*, by Sir Anthony Van Dyck. This, as you know, is believed to be the sole surviving picture of Sir Peregrine Granvier, created first Lord Alderney for his services to Charles the Second. Nothing I can say will add luster to this superb work. I must begin the bidding at ten thousand pounds."

A catalogue waved in the first row. David recognized the almost deformed figure of von Elstring, the diminutive and stooped front man for one of the large Bond Street galleries with a clientele spread over three continents.

"Ten is bid," Beck's voice showed neither surprise nor enthusiasm. "Do I hear twelve?" Another nod from the front row. "Twelve, then. Thirteen.... Fourteen...."

Beck was taking bids off the wall now, imaginary bids that merely reflected the general enthusiasm of the crowd. The rhythm of his chant should catch the crowd's interest, forcing up the price.

Someone at the back waved on fourteen thousand and he said confidently, "Fourteen thousand is bid. Do I hear fifteen?"

There was a sudden silence. People craned around, looking for a new leader in the bidding, and saw only other curious faces.

"Fifteen thousand," Beck repeated, puzzled by the check. "Will someone say fifteen?"

A soft murmur shimmered within the crowd. David and Simon watched the small group of big dealers in the front row. They were not looking around, since it was obvious they expected no other bids. A common purpose welded them into a single unit, all attention pointedly concentrated in the middle distance behind the rostrum. Only one face was visible to them from the back—Charles Carthew's profile, showing the faintest trace of a superior smile.

Suddenly David understood Gothard's distraught expression and Carthew's sarcastic air. "They're ringing it," he said quietly. Beside him, Simon nodded.

The ring was one of the simplest and most pernicious tools of the art dealers' trade.

Buyers at a sale merely agreed among themselves not to bid against one another. One member of the group, chosen beforehand, bought everything of value, knowing that, without competition, prices would be rock bottom. Later, the syndicate met privately for a "knockout," when the day's spoils were auctioned off among the ring's members, with the profits shared equally among them. Everyone profited except the seller, who had to be content with a fraction of his goods' real value.

Parliament formally outlawed the ring in 1927 with the Auctions (Bidding Agreements) Act, but nobody had ever been convicted for running or participating in a ring. Nobody ever would, unless a member informed on his colleagues, unthinkable in the claustrophobic fine art trade, despite its vicious internal feuds.

The face of Peregrine Granvier looked out dourly over the assembled dealers with an expression of glum helplessness exactly echoing the mood of everyone in the room, with the exception of the front row of collaborators. The smaller buyers remained silent, cowed by the naked show of force and the thin smile of triumph on Carthew's face.

"Gentlemen, I can't believe that this masterpiece will fetch only fifteen thousand pounds! Will nobody say seventeen?" Beck look appealingly along the front row. "Gentlemen!" But their eyes were everywhere but on the painting. David felt furious, sick, helpless.

In a normal sale, the house would buy in such a picture if the bidding halted at this low price, in effect taking it out of the auction with a false bid in a code name. But Cecily had specified that the St. Anselm's goods be sold without reserves, for whatever they would fetch. Simon, desperately needing the commission, had agreed.

Intent on the tiny group of ring members, Beck at first didn't glimpse the movement on the far side of the room. One of the clerks caught it, however, and snapped his fingers to attract the auctioneer's attention. With a grin of delight, Beck swooped on the bid.

"Are you bidding, sir? Seventeen thousand pounds?" He turned in triumph to the ring. "Seventeen is bid. Do I hear eighteen?"

The murmur rose in pitch. Two dealers stood up to stare openly at the man rash enough to oppose them. David too craned, trying to see over Simon's shoulder.

"Who is it?"

Puzzled and amused, Simon said, "Your friend. The American."

"Bleigen?" He could just glimpse his brilliantined head at the edge of the room where he'd found him a seat.

In the front rows, a hurried conference took place. Bond Street needed these paintings. In some cases, they would already have been committed to clients who would be furious not to get them. Reluctantly, von Elstring waved his catalogue to attract Beck's attention and nodded significantly.

"Eighteen?" The dealer's look would have turned any normal person to stone, but Beck was impervious. "Eighteen is bid."

Beck turned quickly to Bleigen as if afraid he might have evaporated. The American had a small book in his hand from which he appeared to be making calculations. Putting it back inside his coat, he said clearly, "Twenty thousand."

The rest of the sale was a sensation. Routed, the ring's individual dealers scrabbled for the Van Dyck, their careful scheme reduced to shreds. But Bleigen took it at thirty-five thousand pounds, five thousand more than Simon's estimate. When he also bought the next two major paintings, the ring collapsed entirely. Bids were shouted into astonished faces, catalogues waved as much in fury as to attract attention. Caught up in the madness, lesser buyers bid high for the least remarkable works. David watched in awe as tiny daubs by the School of Paris went for five times their estimate, and a dowager duchess and a prominent theatrical producer all but came to blows over an indifferent Canaletto.

But even with the ring broken, its members got little. Bleigen bought almost everything of importance, bidding well over the estimate for the remaining big pictures as well as a dozen smaller works. There would be red faces that night in Bond Street as dealers tried to explain to customers why the promised bargains had not materialized.

At the end of the sale, as the dealers gathered in an angry group to argue sotto voce about the debacle, Simon threaded his way through the chairs to where Bleigen sat, writing in his notebook, and introduced himself.

"Gave you a bit of a start, did I, Mr. Snow?"

"You did, rather." He watched a knot of dealers turn to bear down on them. "Um, perhaps you'll take a glass of sherry in my office?" They left hurriedly as David moved to head off the angry deputation.

"They seem a bit riled," Bleigen said, settling himself into Simon's best armchair. He glanced around the office with a look of calm appraisal that Simon found slightly insulting. One had the feeling he was planning its redecoration.

"It's not unknown for unscrupulous salerooms to plant a confederate in the audience to push up the prices."

Bleigen nodded. Simon surmised he was no stranger to this chicanery or worse. "A shill. Yeah; well, in case you're suspicious, take a look at that." He pushed a slip of pink paper across the desk. It was a certified bank draft for two hundred thousand pounds.

Simon waited for his heart to stop thumping. "I'm not sure what to say. Except thanks, of course. It'll take a few hours to change this, I'm afraid."

"Don't bother. Take that as a credit to my account."

While Simon digested this, David slipped in. "We have some ruffled clients out there."

"It'll do them good," Simon said. "Watch them come

flocking back next week." Without comment, he held out the draft for David to read. Noting the figures and watching Bleigen's calculating gaze as he looked around the office, David wondered if Snow and Son would ever be the same again.

12

The day after the Blandford sale, David bounded into the rooms in wild high spirits, tipped Bussell's cap over his eyes as he studied his morning paper, and ran up the stairs with a vigor that set even the new steel skeleton vibrating.

Elizabeth, Simon's secretary, received a dazzling grin. "Is the great man in?"

"If you mean Mr. Snow, he won't be in today," she said severely. "Nor for the rest of the week."

"Is he sick?" Simon was *always* in, weekends included.

"That's none of my business. Nor yours, if you'll excuse me saying so, Mr. Moore."

David retreated, confused. All night, he'd contemplated the final satisfaction of his coup in finding the Blandford collection: the meeting with Simon at which he would wring from him an acknowledgment that he deserved a higher place in the firm, if not beside its proprietor then at least close to the seat of power. His plans, hatched over the last four years, for Snow's improvement and expansion were carefully rehearsed, ready for presentation. They lacked only an audience.

On the way to his office, he pondered the significance of Simon's disappearance, but recognized that it suited the mood of the place today. The building felt abandoned, stunned by the magnitude of yesterday's drama. He was almost surprised on entering the main saleroom to find someone there, and doubly so when that person proved to be Carl Bleigen.

"Hi." Again the sweaty handshake. Of all people, Bleigen was the least welcome. David was busy fabricating an excuse to avoid him when Bleigen added to his astonishment by saying, "You're just the man I wanted to see."

"Oh? Well, come on through to my office."

Bleigen's frank glance around the clutter of David's tiny room was eloquent with distaste.

"They expect you to *work* in here?"

"I'm sorry you don't like my office," David said shortly. "If you'd care to leave—"

Bleigen held up a calming hand. "Sorry, sorry. I keep forgetting how touchy you English are. New York's kind of a different environment, know what I mean?"

"I've heard that. Mr. Bleigen, I don't mean to be rude. I'm glad you bought so much yesterday. It's no secret that you saved us from an awkward situation. Anything I can do, please ask. I mean it." He tried to sound sincere.

"Well, there is one thing," Bleigen said, opening his briefcase and taking out a file of papers.

Astonished at being taken up on what was meant as a polite gesture, David took the folder and opened it. There were a half dozen black-and-white photographs of a painting and a sheaf of papers that he recognized as a provenance—the pedigree of a work of art, listing its characteristics, distinguishing marks, past owners, and general condition.

"I'm an agent by trade, Mr. Moore," Bleigen said. "For the last ten years, I've specialized in purchasing art for various clients who don't want their names in the papers. The guy I bought most of those things for yesterday, he's one of my biggest customers, You'd know the name if I told you."

"We assumed you were representing someone. I thought one of the New York galleries. Not that it matters, of course. It's entirely your own affair."

"Yeah, well, I tell you"—he leaned back expansively, then straightened up in a hurry as David's only chair creaked under the strain—"I got to thinking I was crazy to work for a percentage when I could be cashing in on this game myself. So I started doing a little buying and selling. Nothing big. Just things I knew I could get cheap and sell at a profit. A few friends came in with capital, and we formed something called Fine Art Holdings."

"Your group bought the rest of the paintings from the Blandford sale?"

"Yeah. It's our stock. Some we'll sell right away, others we'll hang onto, let the price rise."

David fought back a smile. "Well, I hope you aren't disappointed."

"Why should we be? Do you know the sort of profits the big stateside salerooms turn over in a year? It isn't peanuts. And it's gonna get better. All this stuff coming out of Europe with these refugees. You can pick it up for a song. We figure to double our money in the first two years, triple it if there's a war."

Bleigen's blunt effectiveness impressed David, despite the man's vulgarity. London's dealers were no different, although they cloaked their greed in the rituals of politeness.

"Why I mention all this . . . er, David, is, I wonder if you'd like to do a job for us."

Hefting the folder in his hand, David asked, "Something to do with this?"

"Yeah. That mean anything to you?"

Though he didn't care for Renaissance painting, David recognized the work easily—or at least its style. The madonna and child was a perennial seventeenth-century favorite, every chapel, schoolroom, and, in the case of particularly pious citizens, bedchamber demanding its copy. Many, like the one illustrated in the photographs, were round and painted on panels of wood, designed to be carried from country house to city palace as the family moved between seasons.

By modern standards, subject and style were ridiculously unrealistic. The oval-faced Virgin complacently clutched a white, angry-looking baby, as stiff in its mother's arms as a celluloid doll. Behind the couple, cherubs cooed on a clump of cloud, while, lower, a landscape that looked like Tuscany rolled in a patchwork of vineyards and cypress groves to a sky of almost oceanic blue.

"Bellini?" David guessed.

"So they say. I can't tell Bellini from Buck Rogers, but one of my clients wants to borrow money on it and I need an expert opinion. Is it worth a hundred thousand dollars?"

"Probably, if it's genuine."

"Can you tell that, from those papers?"

"Perhaps." Researching a provenance normally posed no

problems, though in this case some of the papers were in German. He had, he supposed, a moral duty to help out such an important client. And it might impress Simon with his devotion to the good of Snow's.

Taking his hesitation at a different valuation, Bleigen said, "We'd pay a fee, of course. For your opinion. Say—a hundred pounds?" Mistaking David's surprise once more for greed, he hurriedly amended the offer. "Er, guineas, I mean."

It was too easy a job to turn down. "All right, Mr. Bleigen, I'll check up on it. Who has the painting now?"

"Well, we have, back in New York. The outfit that wants the money handed it over as security." David could imagine how much choice Bleigen gave them. "They're just a little kike auction house. Did a lot of business but got ahead of themselves, buying all this refugee stuff. They got this from some German, I hear."

David gathered up the papers. "Let's hope it's genuine, then."

An unreadable expression crossed Bleigen's face. "Just give me the facts, David, whichever way they go." He stood up and again offered his clammy hand. "Say, if this works out, we might find a place for you in Fine Art Holdings. Always looking for bright guys, The outfit's on the way up. We can use a man with your get-up-and-go."

The resemblance to Simon's words of four years earlier was too close for him to keep a straight face. For an instant Bleigen's smile was wiped away, revealing something far less pleasant.

"I'm sorry, Mr. Bleigen. You just reminded me of something that happened years back. Nothing to do with you, believe me. Look, I'll be happy to look into the painting for you. As soon as I have something, I'll call you at your hotel."

With Bleigen gone, David checked his watch. Almost one. He didn't feel like lunch, and besides he had a dinner date with Cicely that evening. Might as well get it over with. Checking again that Simon had not come in, he walked across Piccadilly into St. James's Square, where the London Library, one of the city's few private subscription libraries, offered the best collection of art reference books in the area.

Few people came in on these rainy afternoons, and the art room was empty. Spreading the photographs across the table, David studied them, wondering why the painting looked familiar. Well, not *really* familiar.... He tried to put his finger on the element of strangeness, and within half an hour of puzzling through the bills of sale and catalogue listings in his halting German he had developed a suspicion.

He showed the pictures to Ted, the art librarian, a south Londoner like himself and an old friend.

"I've seen this somewhere before, but I can't remember where. It might have been a book in some eastern European language. Russian? Not German, though."

"Hang about." Ted disappeared, to return with the first of many piles of catalogues, scholarly studies, and indexes. Time faded as they dug together through the yellowing pages, their fingers at first powdered, then grimy with dust.

Finally, in the catalogue of a large Czech collection broken up more than a hundred years ago, David saw the familiar oval face, the same stiff child. He read the caption underneath with astonishment.

When he stood up, an hour later, his head and back ached appallingly. Collecting the twenty or thirty close-written pages of notes, he shoved them in his pocket and went downstairs, waving to Ted as he left.

"Find what you were after?"

"Yes. Thanks." He'd gone in at high noon, but it was dark now, and a veil of rain touched his face. He hailed a cab.

Had he found what he was after? If he simply rang Bleigen and told him the painting was a Bellini, his life would have taken an entirely different turn. At least one man might not have died; others might have saved their reputations and peace of mind.

It was late and his head ached. The thought of Cicely pushed all others from his mind. He gave the driver her address and leaned back.

"I'm sorry, sir. I really don't know."

David stood irresolute in the doorway, peering past the maid. "She told me she'd be in. I rang earlier to tell her I might be late. You took the message."

The girl looked embarrassed. "I'm really sorry, Mr. Moore."

Her eyes pleaded with him but, too angry to take the hint, he shouldered past and walked down the corridor toward Cicely's bedroom.

He hoped...what did he hope? To find her in the arms of someone else? To catch her curled on the bed, giggling in that silly titter that often tipped over into the frenzy of sex, her kittenish playfulness turning feline and voracious?

The room was empty.

Her bedroom always irritated him, but everything in it matched her personality. The thick white carpet, the only soft thing in the room, seemed to crawl around his ankles. Everything else dissolved in a cascade of reflections. Her dressing table, taking up half one wall, was a shrine of mirrors that threw back images of the cream walls, the satin bedspread swimming with twisted whirlpools in the soft light of a dozen hidden lamps. Her scent, a musky amalgam of Circo's Surrender and the unforgettable odor of her body, thickened the air.

Feeling like an intruder, David prowled around the room, as if its furnishings could provide a clue. Picking up one of the expensive perfume bottles littering the mirrored glass of the dressing table, he turned it over in a professional reflex and read *René Lalique France* engraved in flowing script on the base. Yellow as pus, the perfume swirled around the tiny spherical cell in the glass.

A scrap of underwear hung over the edge of the basket she used for soiled linen. As he picked it up, the beige silk slipped between his fingers as if alive. There were other things in the basket: camisoles and brassieres and pants fringed with lace. Her smell permeated them. He longed to take a handful and bury his face there.

Crumpling the garment back into the basket, he hurried from the flat.

Rain and smoke had brought another fog down on London. Damp and cold, the few pedestrians ignored one another, and even the buses ground by in half-seen silhouette, their windows like the luminous markings of deep-sea fish.

Without knowing why, he walked back toward Albemarle Street and the saleroom; it was too soon to go home, and he felt utterly unprepared for the society of the Cock and Feathers.

On the corner of Piccadilly, the banked fire of a chestnut seller's brazier glowed in the fog. He bought a bag and picked at the hot shells as he waited for the night porter to open the main door. They burned his fingers, but there was a masochistic pleasure in the sharp sensation.

His office felt like a coffin. As soon as he opened the door he knew it had been a mistake to return, but as he turned to leave, the white oblong on the desk caught his eye.

Simon had addressed the envelope in his own hand; the short

sharp upstrokes and tight curves told you everything you needed to know about Simon Snow.

Slitting the envelope, he took out the two closely written sheets.

"My dear David...."

Minutes later, he put the letter down beside the little heap of roasted chestnuts, the ruptured shells cool now. Automatically peeling one, he put it in his mouth. The mealy flesh was warm and sweet, like sugared potato, and quite impossible to eat. Bending over the wastepaper basket he spat it out, then hung above the bin, trying not to retch.

Joints creaked somewhere in the depths of the building. For the first time since joining Snow's he felt the accumulation of years that lay on the place like grime on an undusted cornice, the inherited tiredness of centuries spent in the pursuit of *things*. He was as empty and desolate as the split chestnut shells scattered over the desk.

He had no trouble finding a cab in Piccadilly, though the driver grumbled as he turned along the winding roads into the suburbs north of the city, old villages, crusted over with cheap terrace housing and corner shops, their names—Kentish Town, Camden Town—the only remnants of a lost past. Somewhere in this maze was the Caledonian Market where all this began; the cold of the stones and the smell of kerosene, newspaper, and frying onions came to him from centuries away.

The moon when he glimpsed it through the fog was soft and swollen as a breast. Then the fog thickened as they climbed Archway Road toward Highgate.

One light showed in the house. David pounded on the door until Simon opened it, staring down at him through his spectacles, slippers on his feet, a dressing gown worn over shirt sleeves and trousers.

"Is this a good idea, David?"

"I think so."

He sighed. "Come in, then."

The study at the back of the house overlooked a lawn silvered in moonlight. Clear of the fog, the moon was no longer orange, but hard as a wet sixpence.

"Is she here?"

"No. Staying with friends. We thought that would be better."

"For whom?"

"Everyone. She left you a letter."

"Where?"

"At her flat."

David shook his head.

"Oh." The news produced Simon's first reaction: embarrassed irritation. "She promised she would."

"You don't know her very well yet."

"I suppose not."

"Well enough, however." His voice was sarcastic, but he felt on the verge of tears. The refrain of childhood dinned in his ears: *It isn't fair, it isn't fair....*

"David, look. Cicely and I . . . well, I need a wife. You've said so yourself. And she needs . . . well, a protector, if you like. It makes sense. Don't you see that?"

"Does love come into this neat equation?"

"I'm not sure either of us is capable of what you call love." This was ground mentally prepared well in advance; David recognized the formal perfection of self-justification and rationalization. "I can imagine loving something beautiful—a painting, for instance. Something that never changes. The Elgin marbles will be as beautiful when I'm dead a hundred years as they are now. But how can you love people? They change, grow old, die. No, marrying Cicely is"—he mulled over the correct word—"expedient."

"Just another business transaction," David said sarcastically.

"If you like."

"But if you can buy her, so can someone else. Doesn't that disturb you?"

"No, I'm sorry. Truly." There was nothing more to be said.

The cab had waited, knowing the unlikelihood of getting another fare this late from so remote a corner of the city. David was halfway back to town before he remembered the notes in his inside pocket and Carl Bleigen's offer. He had meant to mention them to Simon, but it hardly seemed to matter now.

The chestnut man still stood on the corner, the brazier so clogged with ash that it gave only a fitful glow. He moved slowly from foot to foot, moisture frosting his muffler and mustache. "Chestnuts. All 'ot, all 'ot." The weary mumble expected no response.

Across the road, outside the Ritz, two couples waited for a cab, the women gathering furs around their shoulders, the men helping one another into overcoats, courteously holding the awkward top hats out of harm's way. Sensing a good tip, the hotel porter had darted for David's cab as soon as it stopped opposite. Halfway across Piccadilly, he hovered uncertainly between the streams of cars, looking like a flat cardboard cutout in the lights.

"Want to come home with me, dear?"

Watching the porter, David hadn't noticed the girl come out of the shadows. She had the familiar city face: thin, pinched nose and mouth, tiny eyes like punctures, outlined in mascara and eye shadow. Her hat was slanted over one eye in nervous imitation of Bette Davis, and she pulled a raddled fur tippet around her shoulders with automatic coquetry.

"How much?"

Professionally gauging the worth of his suit, coat, hat, she said, "Two pounds for all night?"

The porter was still stranded in the center of the street. David climbed back into the cab he had just left, the girl following him. They trundled toward Victoria, sitting a foot apart on the cold leather seat. The air soon filled with the smell of her cheap scent.

London lay becalmed around them in a fog, not only of rain and smoke but of cold, poverty, and fear. On the Thames Embankment men lined up by the dark river for a bowl of soup and a piece of bread, wandering off to sleep under the rumbling railway arches of Charing Cross. Elsewhere, children dozed, hungry, and mothers lay awake, wondering about the next day.

He was sorting through the contents of his desk the next morning when someone knocked diffidently on the door.

Trying to decide which, if any, of his catalogue copies to retain, David didn't look up for a few seconds. When he did, it was to see Cicely standing in the doorway, lively as a daffodil in a new dress of spring green linen. His heart lurched.

"Cleaning up?"

For the first time, he saw the room's full disorder. Deep under the papers in the overflowing wastebasket, the kernels of last night's chestnuts lay buried, like evidence of guilt.

"I'm leaving," he said stiffly.

She smiled, as if he had made a joke. "Oh, *really*, David." He felt suddenly adolescent.

Pertly dropping into his swivel chair, she revolved experimentally.

"I always wanted one of these at home, you know. So that I

could just whiz round if I wanted to turn on the radio or pick up the phone or read a magazine. Just sit in the center and whiz round." She stopped turning to take in the office. "This is really a very dull room, darling. Why not ask Simon for one of those nice offices on the street side?"

Her fixed smile, familiar enough to be disconcerting, resolved his suspicions about her reason for being here. "You've seen Simon this morning, haven't you."

"Why?" He knew that stock ingenuous stare by heart.

"He told you to come and see me, didn't he?"

"No!" As always, she lied poorly. "Oh, well, yes. He was cross about me not leaving you a note."

"Didn't you think I deserved at least a note?"

"Of *course*, sweetheart." She got up quickly and hurried to him, leaning her head on his arm. "But there would have been such a scene and . . . well, in the end, what difference will it make?"

The note? Or the marriage to Simon?

"Darling, just let it blow over, and it'll be the same again, I promise."

"What do you mean 'the same again'?"

Coquettish now, aware of her advantage, she went back to his chair and whirled carelessly. "Simon just wants someone to live in that dreary house and have his children. *We* can still be friends. Like before."

For a moment, the urge to hit her was almost overpowering, like a stab of desire. Yet in his anger was the sneaking vision of a discreet little flat and Cicely available when he needed her, with no strings, no responsibilities. . . .

More tired than angry, he dumped all the catalogues into the wastebasket, where they flowed onto the floor.

"After I saw Simon last night," he said, "I picked up a girl in Piccadilly. A whore. We went back to my place."

"David!" Her smile was fading.

He pressed on, determined to hurt. "She needed a bath, of course, so I gave her one. Just the way you like it, sweetheart. Then we went to bed. She did all the things we do—used her mouth on me, and I had her from behind, and then I did that other thing—you know, tied to the bed. Of course, I had to pay more; she said it hurt. I hadn't ever realized that. You should have told me. I would have given you an extra dress, or some more perfume."

Except for the blotches of color high on her cheekbones, Cicely's face was white.

"It was marvelous," he said softly. "A lot better than you, darling. I suppose she gets more practice."

He left her sitting in the swivel chair, small and cold.

Bleigen was at the Dorchester. One of the cheaper rooms, David noted, as the desk clerk rang up to announce him.

The American was in shirt sleeves and still had a patch of lather behind his ear from shaving. On a tray were the remains of some rolls. Bleigen gulped at a cup of coffee as they talked.

"So, how did it go?" he asked. "Oh, say, would you like some coffee? I could send down for another cup."

"No, thanks. Before we talk about the Bellini, I wondered if that offer of yours is still open."

"Which offer is that?"

"A job in New York, with your company."

"Well, I tell you . . . er, David, after I mentioned that, I kinda gave it some more thought. We've got a tight operation over there. I know you'd fit in fine, but we're moving fast. There isn't a lot of time to brief a new man."

"I can move as fast as you like." He tossed his notes on the Bellini on the coffee table.

Putting down his cup, Bleigen read through the summary of his findings. "It's fake, then?"

"More like an honest copy. The collector saw the painting, needed a madonna for his house, and commissioned this one. While the painter was at it, he made a few . . . improvements."

"So it's worthless, right?"

"Not totally. I could research it some more. The copier might have been a known artist. That would increase the value."

"No, that's OK. You've given me all I need." Apparently unmoved by the bad news, he took a well-filled wallet from his back pocket and counted eleven ten pound notes onto the table. "A hundred guineas."

David didn't pick up the money. "And New York?"

Bleigen looked pained. "I told you, pal. I don't think it'd work out."

"How much did you pay for the paintings you bought at Snow's on Tuesday?"

"Hell, you know as well as I do—eighty-some thousand dollars."

"You overpaid."

There was a long pause. Bleigen looked narrowly at David. "How come?"

"The Van Dyck is good. So are the Vermeer and the Tintoretto. But that Guardi's been heavily restored. No gallery would look at it. The same goes for some of the others."

"How many?"

"Four or five."

"I like your timing, Moore. You coulda told me this before the sale."

"I would have, if I'd been working for you."

Bleigen chewed this over. "Yeah, I see what you're driving at. Maybe I could use you in New York after all."

"You needn't lose out," David went on. With the image of Simon and Cicely in his mind, he found betrayal easy. "If you send the pictures back, Snow's will have to refund your money."

"Can I do that?" Bleigen brightened considerably. "It's not illegal?"

"The pictures aren't as described in the catalogue. If there are defects, they should be listed, or a phrase like 'Condition Noted' or 'Sold Not Subject to Return' added to the description."

David actually overstated the case. A court would probably demand that Bleigen pay, with perhaps a discount for the damage. But Simon was desperate for money and too conscious of Snow's good reputation to want it dragged through the courts. He would take the paintings back or revise the cost to whatever Bleigen suggested.

"I guess you know your job," Bleigen said. "Just why are you doing this?"

"I want to get out of England." He left Bleigen to guess at the rest.

"Can you be ready to leave by Friday?"

"I'm ready to leave now."

"Friday will be soon enough. Get a booking on the clipper." He took another hundred pounds from his wallet and put it on top of the rest, then gathered up David's report on the Bellini.

"Do you mind telling me what you're going to do with that?" David asked.

"Since you're in the firm now, I don't care." Bleigen's face assumed the oily smile he had seen and disliked on their first meeting. It was the look of a predator about to descend on its prey. "I'm going to put that uppity little Jew Hershman outa business."

"Hershman?" David's stomach lurched.

"Yeah. 'House of Hershman' they call themselves. You ever hear anything like it? A couple of furniture dealers trying to be uptown. Selling pictures on Central Park West. Makes me sick." He stood up quickly and held out his hand. "You did a good job, David. See you on Friday."

Downstairs, David grabbed a passing waiter and pressed a pound note into his hand. "Brandy." His hand was shaking but he got most of it down.

13

"I don't believe it!"

Nat Hershman stared defiantly around the room, challenging the others to meet his gaze. Bleigen's secretary kept her eyes glued to the pad on her knee, pencil point moving infinitesimally across the page. Jake Hershman, head sunk on his chest, beard crushed into his shirtfront, said nothing. In the corner, David felt ill.

"I'm sorry," Bleigen said. His voice lacked conviction. By now, David knew him well enough to see the triumph behind his smile.

"There really isn't any doubt about it, I'm afraid," he said. "The painting you have was in the Czerny collection for more than two hundred years. It was his mark on the panel, as I've pointed out. The real Bellini is still in Italy, in private hands; the man who painted this made it larger by adding more clouds and the landscape in the background. The photographs—"

"It's just your opinion!" Nat snapped. "We've got our own experts over here. They say it's genuine." Realizing his voice had become shrill, Hershman smiled nervously. "Sorry. But you can imagine the effect of what you're saying."

"Nobody's stopping you from getting your own appraisal," Bleigen said.

Jake Hershman raised his head and looked straight at Bleigen. The contrast between father and son was striking—Nat suave, dapper, like a movie star in his sharp double-breasted suit and impeccable silk shirt; Jake a biblical patriarch in a rumpled blue serge that would not have been out of fashion thirty years before. "Where do we stand right now with you people?"

Bleigen fidgeted. "What can I tell you, Jake? Do you have any more collateral?"

"You've already got our note covering the warehouse, the annex and our stock. What else is there?"

"Hell, Jake, you don't leave me any alternative. I'll have to foreclose."

"That would ruin us."

"I know. I'd do anything for it to be otherwise, but we can't leave that much paper outstanding without security."

David had to admire the bald-faced nerve of the man. To fill the awkward pause, he said to Jake Hershman, "I didn't realize you'd actually paid for the painting."

"If we hadn't, we wouldn't be in this spot."

Nat avoided his father's eyes. "It looked good," he said, defensively. "A runner came to us with the story that an old family in Germany wanted to sell the Bellini for cash. Hitler was cracking down on Catholics, and they needed to get out of the country fast. The deal they offered . . . well, we felt we should take it, so we liquidated some other holdings. I hear this is illegal in England."

David nodded. Auctioneers in Britain could not buy items to sell on their own behalf, but the law was broken so frequently that it now lacked almost all force.

"The Metropolitan was interested," Nat went on. "We just needed a little money to cover the loans, so we came to Carl."

"Have you tried to contact your runner? Or the people who sold it to him?"

"For the last two months, I haven't done much else. But Mr. Greenbaum—not a fashionable name in Germany today—has disappeared. We're still trying." He looked at Bleigen. "How long do we have?"

"I can hold off for another week. Get your own appraisal. Send someone to Germany if you want. We're as anxious to clear this up as you are."

"I doubt that," Jake Hershman said, standing up. He shook hands with Bleigen and with David. "I'm sure we'll meet again, Mr. Moore. Enjoy your visit to New York."

McGarritty, the man from the Metropolitan Museum of Art, looked more like a medical intern than an art expert. He had the sandy-haired geniality of a student and a voice to match, snappy and brash.

"What's it supposed to be? Bellini?" He flipped the panel expertly, studying the back.

"That's what it *is*," Nat said acidly.

Examining the surface, McGarrity grunted. "Paint looks too smooth. But we'll see." With a scalpel he flaked off a fraction of the pigment at the edge of the panel where the clouds were at their whitest.

"Back when this is *supposed* to have been done"—Nat flinched at the emphasis—"painters got white pigment by putting a sheet of lead over a beaker of vinegar for a few hours. White lead salts formed on the underside of the plate. But that stuff's poisonous and it doesn't always stay stable, which is why they developed zinc-based white in the nineteenth century."

Poking among the bottles on his bench, he carefully dotted a drop from one of them on the white paint. "Nitric acid. If it dissolves..." He peered at the spot.

Nat leaned over his shoulder. "It's not dissolving," he said hopefully.

"White lead would have," McGarrity said. "I'd say this was zinc." He replaced the bottle. "Sorry."

"You mean—that's it?"

"Look, Mr. Hershman, I can test the thing for a month if you like. We could try plain alcohol on the surface. That dissolves new pigment. We can X-ray it to see if there's underpainting. I'm fairly sure we'll find some old seventeenth-century picture that this artist has used as a base; it gives body to the painting and the cracks show through; makes the copy look more authentic."

He held up the panel and looked at it critically. "But you just have to feel the thing to know it's wrong. The panel should be poplar, but it feels like pine to me. And Renaissance artists tended to frame their pictures before they painted them, to make the frame part of the composition. There should be a ridge of paint around the edge where the frame was removed. They also used to bevel the wood, shaving it down at the edge. It made the picture lighter, easier to carry."

He handed it back to Nat.

"It's up to you, Mr. Hershman but, frankly, I wouldn't bother."

Back in his office on Central Park West, Nat propped the panel on a chair and looked around the room.

There was an air of decay about the place now. What had

been a sanctum was now a cell, with this cool young virgin as his jailer.

He lifted the phone. "Patricia, get my home, please. And come in when I've finished."

Ruth answered. She had never gotten used to having a maid. Most of the time they sat in the kitchen together, playing pinochle.

"Nat? What's wrong?"

"Nothing's wrong. Can't I ring my own family?"

"We're packing Sara's things for camp. She has to get the bus in an hour."

"Is Sara there? Let me talk to her."

"Nat, I told you, we're packing." Then, sensing his anger, "All right, I'll call her."

A few seconds later, Sara came on the phone.

"Poppa?"

"How are you, sweetie?"

"I'm fine, Poppa. Momma says what do you want?"

"Just wanted to talk to you, sweetheart, before you go off to camp."

"Do I have to go, Poppa?"

"You'll love it, darling. I promise."

He paused, unwilling to break the connection. "You still my best girl, Sara?"

"Oh, Poppa, you know I am." She might have been talking to her lover.

"That's my Sara. You take care of Momma now."

The tone of his voice puzzled her. "When will I see you?" She sounded afraid.

"We'll drive up on the weekend. Say good night to Momma for me." He hung up, drew a sheet of paper toward him, and started to write. Ten minutes later, he buzzed for Patricia.

When she came in, he already had his tie off. Without comment, she pulled the blinds and reached for her earrings.

"No, leave them. Just the dress." He changed his mind. "No. Everything."

Patricia was as surprised as anyone.

Mr. Hershman (she never got used to calling him Nat though he often asked her to) didn't look like that sort of man. I mean, a bit moody...well, everyone got moody, didn't they? Even Patricia had her bad days, especially when she was out of work.

Which was why she never minded . . . you know, *doing* it with Mr. Hershman. Right from the start, he made it very clear what he expected. Very nicely—a glass of champagne in his office, the phone off the hook, and a nice quiet chat. A girl likes to be asked. It was romantic, kind of.

So it got to be a routine. He would say, "Come in, Patricia, and hold all the calls," and she knew that was an hour less typing and probably another five dollars in her pay envelope at the end of the week.

Not that he was hard to please, either. Mostly Patricia just took off her underwear and stood by his chair, looking down at the park while his fingers . . . *you* know. Then he undid his buttons, and after a few seconds she had to grab the handkerchief from the pocket of his coat to stop the suit from being ruined. (Once, she wasn't quick enough. There was a crowd in the park where they were shooting a movie and she got sort of distracted. They poured a cup of coffee over the stain and sent down to the valet service in the lobby. Mr. Hershman had to sit there in his shorts and suspenders for half an hour, but he never complained once. Such a nice man.)

But now *this*. He'd called her in and right off she could see he was upset. So when he wanted her to take off everything, she didn't mind too much. And then he really wanted to do it! I mean, do *it*. She'd even agreed to that, though if her boyfriend ever found out he'd be furious.

Afterward, she went down the corridor to wash up, and when she came back the office door was open and there was a draft through the window in his office that was wide open, and she heard screams coming from the street far below.

14

The phone rang deafeningly. At first, David refused to believe it was happening to him. Then, reluctantly, he lurched from bed.

"Well, who'da believed it, eh?" It was Carl Bleigen.

"Believed what?"

"Haven't you seen the papers?"

David glanced over to the table where his paper lay beside a chill pot of coffee and a plate of rubbery toast. "No, I slept in. Why?"

"Take a look. Front page."

He shook open the paper. Its report was brief and graphic, like the illustrating photograph. The crash of 1929 was far enough in the past for New Yorkers to be surprised when someone jumped from a fifteenth-story office to a smeared death on the sidewalk.

"God!" The phone amplified his choked voice.

"Yeah. Young Nat. Who'd have thought it." Then Bleigen's familiar snappiness returned. "But listen, Dave. This puts us into kind of a corner. Can you get over here?"

"Now?"

"Sure. You want me to send a car?"

"No. That's all right." He stared at the photo of the oozing lump under the tarpaulin. "I never thought—"

"You've got no reason to blame yourself. The Metropolitan backed you up all the way. Sure you don't want a car?"

"I'll take a cab." He put down the phone sharply. He was

learning about America: the sudden meeting, the overnight debauch, the one-week friend. Grief seldom outlasted the newspaper that printed the obituary. He had not known Nat Hershman well, but well enough for Nat to expect more from him than yesterday's betrayal.

The city looked different. Waiting at the door of the Algonquin for the doorman to call a cab, he put it down to his own fatigue after a heavy night of talking and drinking in the bar until the odd color of the light drew his attention to the sky. Its bronze glow hurt his eyes. As the cab took him to Bleigen's office, he could hardly make out the Chrysler Building's silver pinnacle through the gray-yellow haze.

"Dust," Bleigen explained, tracing a line on his desk. "Half of Oklahoma is blowing about out there. Look, Dave, I called you up here so that we can sort out this Hershman thing."

"How do you mean 'sort it out'?"

"Well, we foreclosed, of course. As of now, we own the place."

David frowned. "Wasn't that a trifle sudden?"

"What else could we do? House of Hershman isn't a public company, but it's got staff, goodwill, customers, creditors. They'll all suffer for what Nat's done. Leave things go for a week and the place would never recover. Now, with good management, we can move in and keep it afloat. That's why I wanted to talk to you. Are you interested in running Hershman's for us?"

"Run it?" It was too early for such decisions. His mind refused to function. "You mean, be manager?"

"Manager, director, chairman. Whatever you like to call it. We're not in the auction business. We need an expert."

His own company. In New York. David could imagine the effect of this news on Simon and Cicely.

"I'm interested," he said shortly.

"Fine." Beaming, Bleigen held out his had. "Shake on it." This time the clammy palm carried traces of grit, as if the undertaker had turned gravedigger. "I'll draw up the papers."

Bleigen's alacrity rang a warning bell. "Papers? Do we need papers?"

"Well, sure, Dave. You'll be acting as our representative. A handshake's good enough for me, but you know lawyers."

Reluctantly, David let the subject drop. "What about Jake Hershman?"

"Don't worry about old Jake. I'll have a talk with him. He'll play ball. Hell, what else can he do? I could throw him out on the street if I wanted. If he stays with the business, he gets a salary and his name stays on the door. Just keep things ticking over for us until we figure out what to do with it. Hell, we might be in a war next week."

"Well, I imagine Jake will mostly be concerned with the downtown saleroom. I'll want to spend most of my time at the Central Park West annex. That's a marvelous location."

"Yeah, too marvelous. We're selling the lease."

David blinked in astonishment. "But—"

"You gotta understand, property is booming in this town. The way we're set up, we can't handle two places."

"But we agreed that the pictures you bought at the Blandford sale would be the nucleus of your first sale over here! That's my primary interest, you know that."

"We'll get around to it, don't worry." Bleigen's voice was soothing. "We just feel it'd be better to put the pictures on ice for a while. They won't depreciate. When we've got a good collection together, we can make a splash. You said yourself that stuff wasn't top grade. That sound sensible to you?"

"I suppose so," David said reluctantly. "Just how long do you think it'll take to get this sale together?"

"Oh, a few months. By the time you have things sorted out down there on Eleventh Street, we'll be ready to go." He was stirred by a vestigial sense of propriety. "Uh, better not move in down there right away, Dave. Leave it a day or two."

As he left the office, the suspicion David had felt earlier returned to trouble him, but a breeze had cleared the air over Manhattan and the sun put him in good spirits again. His own saleroom, he thought as he walked down the sunny street. It was easy, at twenty-three, to think one owned the world.

"Greenbaum, Hoppel, Heifetz, Hershman...." The swimming instructor looked up from her clipboard. "Where's Hershman?"

The front row of girls looked at each other and stifled their giggles. Knowing the signs, the instructor, a veteran of ten years in summer camps, tapped the board absently on her thigh and said, "Where's she hiding?"

Someone always snitched. You could feel their eagerness. A girl at the end of the row put up her hand.

"Please, Miss Jacobs, she's in the bathroom."

Glancing over her shoulder at the restrooms half hidden behind a stand of pine trees, she said, "Go and get her, please. No, not all of you," she went on sharply, to stem a general stampede. "Two girls. You two."

As Sara heard the feet approaching, she wedged herself deeper into the toilet stall, hoping that this time she might get away with it. They wouldn't see her, so far back, behind the pedestal. They'd look, then give up and leave....

"Hey, Hershman!" A pounding on the door. Hands over her ears, she tried to push the sound out. Then fingers hooked over the top of the door and a face peered down at her.

"Miss Jacobs wants you."

The walk back, with her captors on each side, felt endless. Sara dragged her feet in the dust, spinning out every second. Behind the ranks of smug, superior girls, she could see the river, its gray-green water barely moving.

"What were you doing, Sara? Didn't you know it was time for swimming class?"

"No, Miss Jacobs," she lied.

"I'm sure it's not because you don't like swimming. It isn't, is it?"

Sara shook her head. The instructor felt a pang of sympathy for the child, bulging out of her tight pink bathing suit, but you couldn't have favorites in a place like this.

"No, of course not. We all enjoy a swim on a hot day like this. Don't we, girls?"

The others shouted their agreement, not out of any love of swimming—for most of them, the murky river represented an ordeal to be endured like everything else in camp from the food to the mosquitoes—but in satisfaction at the discomfort of someone weaker and uglier than themselves.

Sara's eyes swept along the rows with a fury that cowed half of them, but the chorus of shouts continued until Miss Jacobs stemmed it with a sharp clap of her hand on the clipboard.

"That's enough. Everyone take a tube and go down to the bank. Not into the water yet. Just to the edge."

As they scrambled down the crumbling bank, she looked at Sara. "You learned to swim last year, didn't you? In the tadpole classes?"

Sara nodded mutely.

"Well, what's wrong with the river?"

Useless to put into words the fantasies that filled her

nightmares: the groping hands from underneath, the clinging ooze of the bottom mud, the brackish, bitter taste of the water itself. She shook her head.

"If you don't have a reason, then you'll just have to join the others. Miss Fineman and I will be watching you from the other side, and you'll have your float like the others—" She looked over her shoulder. "Now here's Mr. Hart. I'm sure you don't want the camp director to hear about this. Just run along and we won't mention it."

Sara shuffled toward the group dancing at the water's edge, pounding one another playfully with the inflated inner tubes provided by the camp as a primitive safety measure.

"Is that the Hershman girl?" Hart asked. Like most directors of children's camps, he had a look of permanent abstraction, as if a record of parents' complaints and orders murmured in his ear every moment of the day.

"Yes. She doesn't like swimming. If I looked that way in a suit, maybe I'd feel the same."

"Well, let her off for today and send her over to the office." As he explained why, he became even more despondent.

An incredulous and delighted Sara was led back from the water's edge. As she trotted toward the office, the remaining girls, feeling themselves cheated, watched her receding back in sullen resentment.

Her ecstasy lasted right to the director's room, only to fade as she saw her mother sitting by his desk, a handkerchief crushed in her hand.

"Momma?" she said questioningly. But already she knew.

Ten minutes later, the class had already paddled to the far side of the river and back again. A few, draped like sunning seals over the black rubber tubes, continued to circle near the bank, while Miss Jacobs marshaled the rest into groups to shower before lunch. Quietly, under a tree, three girls were plotting to get Sara Hershman by herself in the showers and administer an appropriate punishment for her escape.

Only the instructor heard the distant slam of the office door. Looking around, she saw Sara running toward her—running headlong, her body thrust before her feet. so that only her momentum kept her from tumbling in the dust.

Reaching the top of the riverbank, she stared at the water,

eyes so filled with a chillingly adult loathing that the woman
automatically put out a hand to restrain her. Sara brushed it
aside.

Floundering down the bank, she careened into the group of
silent, staring girls, sending half of them reeling into the mud
and the others into the water, and dived wildly into the stream.
The impact wrenched from her a cry of animal pain, as if she had
impaled herself on a stake hidden beneath the surface.

The child swam with a thrashing fury, her arms slapping
flatly on the surface, her legs churning a yellow wake through
the green water.

It took her only a minute to reach the far bank, but even in
the shallows she continued to thrash and squirm, her hands
tearing up mud that showered down on her back.

From the girls, there was absolute silence. Even from across
the river, Sara's sobs were clearly audible. Peeling off her jacket,
the instructor waded into the river and swam toward her.

15

Eleventh Street hovered uncertainly between residential gentility and brash commercialism. A few large houses still retained their air of Edwardian luxury, but within a block the brownstones took over. Women sat gossiping on the front steps, trying to restrain the children who grabbed for David's legs with sticky fingers, while from the windows above a cacophony of music, argument, and the rattle of machines poured into the street. He wondered about the last sound until a painted sign on one front door announced APEX SHIRTS TWO FLIGHTS UP. Most of the lofts and attics of these buildings housed small factories or sweatshops.

Beyond the brownstones the warehouses began, block after block of them, running all the way to the East River. The House of Hershman was indistinguishable from its neighbors except for the smarter coat of brown paint on its double doors and the large sign that spanned the frontage. Rattling the small door set into the larger one, David found it open and stepped inside.

It wasn't Snow's, Sotheby's, or Christie's—that much was clear from the smell alone, a blend of dust, damp, and long-term occupation by humans, cats, and other less identifiable creatures. Peering down the long central corridor with its bare cement floor, he was reminded of a railway station after the last train of the night, when the place is abandoned to the cleaners and the rats. As if to endorse this comparison, a cat glided along the floor a few yards in front of him, clinging to the shadows until it faded in the watery gray light of the huge storeroom that took up most of the building. He made out the shapes of furniture piled twenty feet high, but despite the bright sun outside only the palest shadow of its light penetrated the grimy skylights.

Wooden partitions divided the front half of the building into offices (on his right) and auction rooms (to his left). Both were deserted. He peered into the first room to find untidy rows of chairs and a rostrum above which a stuffed moose head looked down eerily in the half-light. The offices seemed equally deserted. Opening the door marked *Mr. N. Hershman*, he found the first trace of any modern improvement: a smart desk with a gooseneck lamp and, on the floor, a square of carpet in bold modern motifs. The paintings looked like originals, but the place had an air of disuse; Nat, he assumed, had spent most of his time in the uptown annex David was destined never to see.

A sudden block of blinding sunlight fell into the corridor. Turning quickly, David saw a silhouetted shape stepping awkwardly through the tiny door.

"Who's that?" he asked, squinting against the glare.

Jake Hershman carefully closed the door behind him before identifying his visitor. He grunted, a flat, discouraging sound. "Oh. Moore. I thought maybe it was a burglar." His tone showed which he would have preferred.

"I'm sorry. The door was open...."

"Yeah, yeah. That's OK." There was an awkward silence. "I hear I work for *you* now."

Discussion was clearly pointless. David saw he would have to establish his authority from the start or not at all. "That's about it, I'm afraid. If you want to stay on."

"In my own place?" David could feel the contained anger in his voice. "Where else would I go?"

"I was hoping you would stay. I'll need your help. We do things differently in England."

"Yeah," Hershman said sourly. "Over here, a man who's got his own business that he's built up over the years, you leave him to enjoy it in his old age."

David let the comment pass. For a few seconds, Hershman stood in the gloom, looking past him into the depths of the warehouse. Then he sighed. "I guess you aren't to blame, Mr. Moore. Come on up into the office."

Hershman's office, directly above his son's, was well placed to look down over the partitions into the two salesrooms. From here, he could keep an eye on everything that happened below. Switching on the light, the old man gestured to the visitor's chair.

"Take a seat. I just went out for some lunch." Carefully he removed two sandwiches and a large pickled cucumber from a brown paper bag. Recognizing the sparseness of the meal, he added, "The girl used to make coffee. I never got the knack."

"We'll fix that," David said, looking around the office, which was more like a museum than a place of business. Framed photographs covered every wall—glum family groups against a harsh flat landscape that he took to be Russia, formal studio pictures of a recognizable Jake Hershman in his early twenties, black-haired and slim, standing stiffly beside a seated woman whose long hair coiled to frame an exquisite oval face. The same woman featured in the next picture, this time nursing a white bundle, the shawl obscuring all but a pair of buttonlike black eyes.

"You've got it all up there, Mr. Moore," Hershman said, following David's eyes. "The House of Hershman." He pointed to a stern bearded man in a long black coat. "My father. A rabbi. Never left our village except to go to Moscow for a meeting of the learned college. He didn't like Moscow. Too much traffic, he said."

Rising, he went to the wall as if to see the pictures more clearly, and tapped the portrait of his younger self and the dark girl. "He never understood why we wanted to leave, Rachel and me. Crazy, he thought. But we came to America. Three months, it took. Trains, boats, more trains." He glanced at David. "I guess you never had to go through that in England, Mr. Moore."

David shook his head, recognizing that Hershman was coming to an acceptance of the situation in his own way. The ritual recitation of family history was like the telling of beads.

He peered at the picture of his wife with the baby for a long time. "We had three babies before Nat. They all died. The East Side was tough then. But we got by. People always need furniture, so I bought a cart, went buying around town, set up a shop." He waved his hand around to indicate the building. "Not bad for someone who got off the boat with nothing."

The pictures on the last wall were all of Nat, stiff and eager in his early teens, presumably at his bar mitzvah, then slick and sharply dressed as David had first met him, posing beside a pretty but plump and characterless young woman. "You knew Nat had a family?" Hershman said.

"Yes," Brighton. . . .The photograph of a plump little girl. It seemed centuries ago. Hershman was staring at what looked like an enlargement of the same picture. Carefully he took it down. Slowly he went around the walls, removing each photograph from its hook while David looked on in embarrassment.

"You'll be more comfortable in this office. I'll take Nat's old room. You thinking of opening up soon?"

"I don't know. What do you think?"

Hershman shrugged. "You're the boss."

"Next week then," David said. "We'd better talk about getting the staff back."

Obviously surprised, the old man paused in his collection of the pictures. "You want to take on *our* people?"

"Why not? They know the business, I don't. Do you think they'll come back?"

"Maybe. I'll make a few calls." For the first time, he seemed to look on David as something less than an enemy. "Mr. Moore, let me ask you a question. How come you got mixed up with a shmuck like Bleigen?"

David didn't recognize the word, but the tone was eloquent. "I'm not mixed up with him. He offered me a job and I took it."

Hershman seemed to be weighing up how much he could safely say. "You know I didn't want Nat to take that painting—the fake thing?"

"I gathered that."

"It didn't smell right—the owner not answering letters—but all those papers . . . it was too easy. Almost as if they were setting it up."

Feeling uneasy, David said, "Who were?"

"Bleigen and his backers."

"Why should he?" David asked, guiltily. "Did he really want this place that much?"

"*This* place?" Hershman looked around, grinning ruefully. "He could have it, and welcome. No, Nat was doing pretty good up there on Central Park West. He sold stuff to people who had only bought from the big dealers before. Did you know we even won a judgment against Duveen a couple of years ago?"

"No." The idea of the Hershmans defeating Joseph Duveen, the most prestigious salesman of fine art in the world, was so extraordinary he knew it could not be an invention.

"Sure. The old crook told one of our customers that a

painting we offered her was fake. She pulled out of the deal. Then he sent one of his clerks around to buy it cheap. Only the clerk talked and we took Duveen to court. Got seventy-five thousand and costs. Anyway, Nat had his eye on a couple of Bleigen's customers too. Ever hear of a man named Sklar?"

"Arthur Sklar? Of course." In a community of collectors noted for their flamboyance and delight in display, Sklar was the exception. He seldom loaned pictures to galleries or exhibitions, and his holdings had never been photographed or even described in print. A millionaire who made his money in wildcatting for copper and other minerals in South America, he lived in isolation with his collection—reputedly containing some of the greatest masterpieces to pass through the market during the previous twenty years.

"Bleigen is Sklar's agent. Some of those pictures he bought from Snow's were for him."

A suspicion stirred in David's mind. It was an old trick to cover up a major deception by admitting to a minor one. Faced with the danger of losing an important client, Bleigen was capable of going to any lengths. He had admitted to David that he hoped the Bellini was a fake, so that he could foreclose on the Hershmans. What if *he* had been behind the offer of the painting to Nat Hershman in the first place? With the market flooded by refugee treasures, it would be simple to steer this skillful copy with its equally clever forged provenance to the eager young Hershman. And no doubt Bleigen had been more than cooperative when Nat approached him with the request for a loan to cover the purchase.

Meeting Hershman's gaze, David could almost imagine that those cool gray eyes looked straight into his mind. "Do you really think..." he began, but the old man had levered himself out of his chair and picked up the pile of pictures. Pausing at the door he looked back at his desk, frowning at the waste of his lunch.

"My eyes are bigger than my stomach, Mr. Moore," he said. "Why don't you finish up those sandwiches?"

David sat in the office for a long time, thinking about Carl Bleigen and wondering what he had committed himself to in allying himself with his shadowy operation.

Three days later, he learned the full extent of his blunder.

The call from the Metropolitan Museum of Art came out of the blue. Could he find time to see the head of the Paintings

Department? Since an invitation from Barrett Wyndham amounted in the art world to a summons, he made time.

An imposing man in his late fifties, with a shock of almost pure white hair shooting out of his scalp as if in surprise at the ideas within, Wyndham greeted David with a slight frown.

"I must admit I expected someone older, Mr. Moore."

Unable to frame a suitable response, David said nothing.

Wyndham went on. "But clearly you know your business." (This was an obvious reference to the Hershman tragedy. He could have no better advertisement for his expertise than the death of another dealer on its account.) "I wonder if you'd consider doing some consultant work for us."

David couldn't entirely contain his surprise and interest. Belatedly stifling the impulse to grin, he asked, "What sort of consultancy?"

"Our English collection has frankly never been very good. A lot of it came through bequest, and we sometimes have no idea where the donors obtained their pictures. Someone with your background could sift through them, give us an expert opinion. Interested?"

"I think so," David said cautiously. "It would depend on the pictures, of course. I might have to go back to London for background on some of them."

"That would be up to you. The budget could run to a few trips—though with the news the way it is, I suggest you take them quickly."

David's visions of a triumphant return to London as both the director of his own saleroom and a representative of the Met were interrupted by a niggling worry at the back of his mind. A few days ago, he'd signed an agreement with Bleigen, the terms of which were fairly sweeping.

"I'd have to consider some commitments. Can I let you know?"

"Certainly. Any time before the end of the week."

Bleigen listened solemnly to David's description of the meeting with Wyndham. The absence of his familiar ingratiating half smile should have been a warning.

"So you see it wouldn't interfere with Hershman's. I could do the work for the Met on my own time."

"I see that, Dave. I really do. And I hate you to miss out on a great opportunity like this."

"Miss out?"

"Well, it's impossible. Your deal with us specifies 'all personal services.' That cuts out work for any other organization. Even the Met."

"But you hired me to run Hershman's, not for research work!"

Bleigen's smile was returning as he recognized his power. "We might want you to do some research for us—when we get ready to sell off our Old Masters maybe. Say, just a few days ago you were telling me how keen you were to begin that. You lost your enthusiasm?"

"No, of course not. But you said—" He recognized it was hopeless.

"I'm really sorry about this, Dave, but you're a valuable asset to the firm." (And a dangerous potential competitor, David thought bitterly.) Bleigen stood up behind the desk and held out his hand. "If you've ever got anything else to discuss, just drop in."

Ignoring the hand, David stormed out.

A lawyer did nothing to contradict Bleigen's view of the contract. He offered to fight it, but pointed out that Bleigen could place David on unpaid suspension until the case came to court, which might be years from now. Better to work it out and learn the hard lesson that only a fool signs contracts in a hurry.

He had sentenced himself to a three year term of imprisonment, with Carl Bleigen as his jailer and the House of Hershman his prison. There was a special irony in the fact that today, May 25, 1939, was his birthday. He was twenty-four. For him, the world seemed to have come to an end.

Standing in the front window of his office, David looked down into the salerooms of the House of Hershman. About fifty people wandered noisily among the day's items, mostly junk that would hardly draw enough commission to pay the heating bill on this cavernous building.

Though a week had passed since his meeting with Wyndham, the gloom and self-pity of that day persisted. He could feel them eating at the roots of his ambition and resolve; soon the damage would be permanent.

On impulse, he hurried downstairs to Nat's old office, where Jake sat incongruously among the ultra-modern furnishings, an old dog in a debutante's parlor.

"Jake, do you have any objection to teaching me the auction business?"

Hershman raised his thick white eyebrows. "I thought you were the expert. Isn't Snow's an auction room?"

"Not like this." He nodded over his shoulder at the confusion in the saleroom, the milling crowds, the kids clambering over the day's lots, the sustained roar of conversation and argument.

For the first time since they had met, Jake Hershman smiled. "Yeah, I guess it isn't much like Bond Street." Putting on a black homburg, he got up from the desk. "C'mon, I'll show you how we do it on the East Side."

Jake's appearance downstairs evoked shouts of greeting, ribald remarks in Yiddish, and an eruption from among the people in the front rows whose goods were obviously in today's sale. They plucked at his sleeve, urging him to get the best price possible, since the baby was sick, the son's bar mitzvah was coming up, the wife was pregnant....

Stopping short, Jake wheeled on the tiny man who made this claim. "Your wife pregnant *again*, Fink? How many's that?"

The little man grinned. "Nine."

"And you want me to finance it? You think maybe you're Rothschild?"

A roar of laughter and applause greeted this, and Jake climbed onto the high rostrum, took up a gavel as large as a mallet, and pounded for silence; the genteel tap of the ivory disk used in London salerooms would have been lost in the background roar of Hershman's.

"OK, OK. Enough fun. We're here to sell . . . hey, what are we selling?" A clerk hurried up with a sheaf of dog-eared papers, which Hershman flattened on the rostrum in front of him. "Oh, yeah. I see we got some furniture, a few paintings, some china and glassware, a few books"—looking up, he stared pointedly at the line of silent men, uniformly dressed in dark coats and homburgs at the back of the room—"and from you schnorrers back there, I don't want no four-bit bids. House of Hershman sells quality merchandise only; anything you buy here, you can take back uptown to your shops and sell for a good profit."

Turning back to the front page of his list, he said, "OK. Lot One. A wardrobe. That's it, over in the corner. C'mon, Fink. Just the thing for your wife's maternity clothes. You want to say two dollars?"

David emerged from the saleroom two hours later with his

head ringing. He had never seen an auction like this one, not even in the remotest corners of the English counties, where manners left a lot to be desired. Acting more like a circus ringmaster than an auctioneer, Jake kept the proceedings from slipping over into anarchy, though this sometimes meant shouting at the top of his voice to make himself heard over an argument between two rival bidders, throwing his gavel at a dilatory clerk who failed to come forward with the lot when called for, and indulging in backchat with members of his audience which ranged from the amiably insulting to the specifically obscene.

Jake joined him. Sweat beaded his face and soaked his old-fashioned striped shirt; he might have just run a mile instead of managed a simple commercial transaction.

"Well, Moore, you think you can handle our kind of selling?"

"I can learn. I was thinking, Jake; if you'd like to take the sales for the next few weeks, I'll clerk for you. That way I can see how it's done from the rostrum."

Jake looked at him keenly. "You're sure?"

"Yes."

Shaking his head, Hershman went back into his office. David could imagine his confusion; it was echoed by his own. But he was stuck in this place, and if it was not to destroy him he must master it.

A man walked diffidently through the front door and coughed to attract David's attention.

"Hey, mister, is that right you sell things for people?"

"Yes. Can I help you?"

Pushing his hat to the back of his head, the man said, "Well, I don't know. You want to come and have a look?"

For a moment, David thought the man's car was crammed with a number of passengers unseasonably dressed in heavy fur coats. But as he came closer, glazed eyes, shining horns, and clawed paws appeared in the confusion.

"My mother-in-law just died and left these to me and the wife. I guess the old man did some hunting in his day."

"Are they all bears?" David asked.

"Hell, no! I just put the bears on top, because they were biggest. No, down there he's got a couple of raccoons, a fox, and some birds. The stuffing's coming out of some of them, but I guess you can fix that. You think you can sell these for me, mister?"

David sighed. If he was to cut his ties with Snow's, this was the time to do it. "We sell anything at Hershman's,"he said, opening the door. A large snouted head lurched at him and a stuffed arm reached out as if in a posthumous embrace. "Let's get them inside before we're arrested."

16

It took more than three years to put the House of Hershman back on its feet; during that time, first Britain and then the United States went to war. Swept along by events, David concentrated on the daily problems of the business, refusing to think about the country with which he had severed all ties.

With Jake, he retained an uneasy relationship that teetered between resentment and grudging admiration. Through his growing ability to handle the madhouse of the main saleroom, David earned the old man's acceptance, but always the shadow of the dead son stood between them. Not that there was time for recrimination. War brought staff shortages, as the best young men were taken by the draft, and equally difficult shortages of material; the essential equipment to keep Hershman's running soon dwindled as rationing took hold.

But after the first two years, David could look back with some satisfaction. They were getting somewhere with the place, especially since the war began. The English salerooms might have gone back to their Red Cross charity sales, a patriotic gesture that had kept the British auction business frozen throughout the First World War as well, but David did not intend to make that mistake, any more than did Parke-Bernet, who advertised pointedly in the trade press that business boomed during the First War and would do so again, whatever Hitler chose to do.

Their advertisements in the New York papers brought in a steady stream of commissions.

Turn your grandmother's junk into CASH. Get rid of your old clothes, your old furniture, your old books and pictures. Let the House of Hershman give you a free valuation. Our commissions are the lowest in town. We Sell Everything But Your Grandmother.

The war changed living patterns. As the draft took hold and families, having lost a father to the Army, moved to a smaller house or shared a home with relatives, their household goods came on the market. Hershman's offered free pickup service, a quick sale, and cash on the line. The same attractions also lured the carriage trade, who at one time would never have considered approaching any saleroom but the fine art houses above 60th Street. Fuel shortages closed down some of New York's oldest homes, and the owners, squeezing into apartments on the ground floor or moving out of the city entirely, let David loose on the contents of the abandoned rooms rather than see heirlooms deteriorate in the cold and damp.

Before each sale, whether of antiques or junk, David scanned the list for anything out of the ordinary and made a private deal with the owner, placing the item in a personal stock kept at the back of the warehouse. He benefited especially from a series of scares in late 1941 that threw New York's art world into total confusion.

In December, 288 fighters left Mitchell Field to defend New York against a German air raid that turned out happily to be a false alarm, but when Goering announced his plans for a long-range bomber capable of carrying five-ton bombs across the Atlantic, the Metropolitan Museum decided to follow the example of the National Gallery in London and move its paintings to a country retreat.

In February 1942 they began shifting all the museum's treasures to Whitemarsh Hall, a sprawling mansion near Philadelphia. The sight of large sealed trucks leaving the Metropolitan night after night, rumbling down the empty streets with the nation's treasures inside, precipitated a wave of panic selling among private collectors convinced their canvases would soon face incineration. Many of their better pieces found their way into David's private hoard.

Having reluctantly turned his back on the big money of the international salerooms, David was surprised to find that even the House of Hershman could make a respectable profit if handled correctly. And the difference in overheads was fantastic. The man selling old furniture at Hershman's would never demand a discount on the commission, or load down the accountants with elaborate payment schemes involving cash transfers at dead of night, or pettishly withdraw an item at the last moment if he disliked the catalogue copy. He just wanted his money, as fast and as liberally as the House of Hershman could provide it. Even without Rembrandts, the company was a gold mine.

"You never told me," David said as he and Jake added up the week's takings after a particularly busy series of sales.

"A pro I don't have to tell," Jake said dryly. "Bleigen knew. Only Nat had to get ambitious."

The reference to Nat chilled the conversation. By common consent, they went back to silent calculation.

Toward the end of 1943, David arrived early at Hershman's to find the place oddly silent.

Jake was always there before him, often sleeping on a cot in his office ("We should pay a night watchman when I can do it myself?"). Though he lived with Nat's widow and daughter in New Jersey, he often came in at six to open up and take coffee just inside the main door with whichever of his cronies happened by on the way to a sale uptown. Diplomatically clearing this noisy and argumentative group of Jewish businessmen from the step constituted David's first job for any day. But he found the door still closed.

Inside, a soft pressure against his calf and an imperious miaow indicated that Mischa had not been let out last night—Jake's last job before he left the building. His spine prickling with apprehension, David half ran up the stairs and found Jake crumpled on the first landing.

"You never can tell with strokes," the medical orderly said as they lifted the stretcher into the ambulance. "Sometimes they're as good as new in a few weeks. Other times—" He shrugged.

"Get him a private room if you can," David said. The orderly laughed.

"Mister, there's a war on, remember?"

"Well, see what you can do." He looked down at Jake's

unseeing eyes and vacuous smile, on lips from the corner of which spit dribbled thinly, and stepped back. With a wail, the ambulance raced off toward Broadway.

The rest of the staff had arrived by now, and the doors were open. The familiar smells of hot tar, exhaust fumes, and the stink from the tannery two blocks away amalgamated to give 11th Street its characteristic aroma, now so familiar to David that he hardly noticed it. People were already wandering in for the first sale of the day.

"We gonna stay open, Mr. Moore?" The old man who swept up the back room and made the coffee leaned on his broom just inside the door.

"Sure, Mr. Levenson, Why not?"

"Well, I thought—Mr. Hershman and all. . . ."

"Do you suppose he'd want us to close just because he's ill?"

"I guess not." He pushed his broom philosophically toward the warehouse, picking up little dust but disturbing what there was so that it hung in his wake like a cloud. Jake would have greeted such lackadaisical work with a shout and the threat of a boot in the rump, but David lacked that mule-driving energy. He had adjusted to Jake's world, but it would never adjust to him, and with the old man gone, perhaps for good, it was time seriously to consider his next move.

But before that, he had one more duty.

"He gonna live?" Bleigen asked shortly when David telephoned him.

"They don't know. He's in Mount Sinai. I asked them to see if he could have a private room."

"Well, that's his problem. His family know yet?"

"*I* didn't tell them." David flinched from having to relay the news. "Shouldn't you call?"

"I've got a pretty heavy morning, Dave. Why don't you? Susie'll give you the number." And abruptly he was speaking to Bleigen's secretary.

Fortifying himself with a strong cup of coffee, David called the New Jersey number.

"Hershman residence." It was a girl's voice. Nat's daughter.

"Could I speak to Mrs. Hershman, please?"

"Who shall I say is calling?"

"David Moore."

There was an involuntary "Oh!" on the line. Then the phone was banged down abruptly in his ear.

It took half a minute for his next call to be answered. This time it was Ruth Hershman.

"It's David Moore. At the saleroom?"

"What can I do for you, Mr. Moore?" The voice lacked warmth, but he had no right to expect any. The image of Nat's shrouded body flashed through his mind.

"Look, Mrs. Hershman, I'm afraid it's bad news. Your father-in-law...well, he's been taken ill. A stroke."

There was no emotion in the silence that followed. Just when David expected another peremptory click, she said, "Where is he?"

"Mount Sinai. I asked for a private room."

"That was kind of you."

"I hope he's all right.'

"Yes. Thank you."

Recognizing the futility of further conversation, David carefully replaced the phone.

He never forgot the first answer to his call: the girl's gasp and the phone slammed suddenly down. It was his first encounter with Sara Hershman, and a characteristic one.

17

An afterglow from the new moon guided Simon as he turned into Albemarle Street, the sound of his footsteps echoing flatly off the stone walls—a sound increasingly typical of London now that the blackout and gas rationing made cars rare in the city after dark. Ed Murrow, the American journalist, compared the sound of London's pedestrians to "ghosts creeping by in steel shoes." Simon recognized the accuracy of his image. Too often, London seemed a city of the dead.

The policeman on the beat, his face oddly square under the flat steel helmet, nodded as Simon put his key in the door of Snow and Son. Instinctively, both looked up at the sky, the faint shimmer of moonlight visible as it had never been when neon signs and street lamps filled it with a yellow glare.

"What do you think, constable?"

"Wouldn't be surprised if they came over tonight, Mr. Snow. 'Bomber's moon,' they call it."

"Thank God for our cellars, then."

The policeman nodded. "Even so, sir, I'd try to get down into the underground if there's an alert. Safer there, believe me."

"I'll do that." The thought of the underground railway tunnels, with their ranks of bunk beds and whole families settled in for the night and perhaps the duration of the war, brought the familiar tightness to Simon's chest. He'd take his chances here; his own cellars were so deep he sometimes never even heard the sirens.

Inside, there was little evidence of the war. Regulars noticed fewer (and dimmer) light bulbs and the absence of some valued paintings, sent away to the country for safekeeping, but by comparison with the National Gallery, its empty halls piled with sandbags to protect the few remaining second-rate pictures, Snow's looked prosperous.

Simon knew that this prosperity was barely skin deep. The decision to commit Snow's to a series of Red Cross sales seemed inevitable at the time, since the rest of London's salerooms were following suit, but reading the trade press, especially from New York, made him itch for the opportunity to reopen general sales again. Parke-Bernet had not let the war cramp their style, nor had the House of Hershman. David Moore—

The name knotted his stomach in the familiar cramp. He had just come from an argument about David—not the first and by no means the last time he expected to plow the old contested ground with Cicely. He had wearied of the fight years ago. Now, when her vituperation became too shrill, he merely called for the car and came down to the peace and quiet of the office.

He could still hear that grating contempt. "You're really going to let him get away with it, aren't you? Robbing me—robbing *us*—of thousands of pounds. As cool as you please, he hands it over to that toad Bleigen and you just sit there!"

Useless to point out that the fancied robbery took place almost five years ago; she had long since gone beyond logic into a world of fancied hurt and injured pride where he could not follow her. His own resentment of David's defection was less deep, and in calmer moments he could see the irony of their situation. If only he had stayed away from Cicely, let David endure her pettiness, her tantrums, her undisguised infidelities! David must be laughing now, if the gossip about her had spread to New York and not just all over the London art world.

He should, he supposed, be philosophical about his marriage. There had been happy times. But pregnancy changed Cicely. The thought of an interloper in the body on which she lavished so much care and from which she derived so much pleasure was horrifying to her. The miscarriage, blandly announced when he returned from a business trip, occurred too conveniently to be accidental, but he never pressed her about it. Shortly after, she moved into one of the spare bedrooms, her halfway house to another existence in which he had no place.

Unlocking a small door behind the porter's table, Simon went downstairs into the cellars. Few of the objects offered for sale on behalf of the Red Cross were worth putting in a strongroom, so Simon had taken over one of the smaller vaults for a personal hobby that occupied an increasing portion of his time. The room, marked CATALOGUE: PRIVATE, was an escape hatch from the depressing and insoluble problems of his life. It contained all Snow's records of sales, some of them going back two hundred years, as well as the basic record books that allowed an art historian to trace the provenance of any work.

For the last month a medieval altarpiece, probably by Duccio, had occupied most of his time. Following a chain of long-forgotten sales and exchanges, he tracked it from Renaissance pope to Bourbon nobleman, a trail that led further and further from the reality of war, Cicely, and his own failing health.

Occasionally, taking down a new reference book, he found a scrap of paper with notes in David Moore's unmistakable hand. Stirred by such a phantom encounter, he had begun a letter to David, spelling out his regrets, wishes, and hopes, but after a few lines he tore it up. Their personal history could not be rewritten; the transaction, recorded and confirmed, had the irrevocable force of a sale in his own auction room.

His own? That too might be open to interpretation. Oliver Turnbull's attacks had become more vigorous, his pressure less polite. Simon even suspected that Turnbull might be cultivating Cicely in expectation of his eventual collapse through ill health. At the occasional social functions Simon felt obliged to hold as evidence of solidarity within the firm, the two seemed friendly, sometimes even conspiratorial. . . .

With a grimace, Simon put the idea out of his mind. Pure paranoia. The cold, his asthma, the reminders of David were luring him into depression. He bent once more over his books.

The planes came over so quietly that the whole building was throbbing with their engines before he realized it. Almost instantly after that realization, the first bombs shook the stone floor.

Slamming shut the catalogue he was studying, Simon went to the door and looked out into the corridor. Dust sifted from the ceiling. Another thud followed, heavier than the first, and high above he heard wood and glass splinter.

The incendiaries burst easily through the roof and ignited the upper floors. Glass and porcelain softened in the heat, melting to milky puddles. Silver bent and sagged. The surface of a painting blistered, fumed, then ignited in a sheet of flame.

As the first wisps of smoke eddied into the cellars, Simon darted for the stairs, then paused, returned to the catalogue room, and unhurriedly shoveled the books and records into the huge fireproof safe originally placed there for jewelry.

The upper floors were well alight when he returned to the main foyer. Scraps of burning debris pattered on the marble floor, and a bloody light rippled on the white balustrade of the Nash staircase as if it already burned. The space was filled with a warm golden radiance in which he seemed to see the heart of Snow's for the first time. It flooded from above, that rich yellow light, pouring down from the central skylight. Walking to the foot of the staircase, he looked up, transfixed by the beauty that made every cornice, every carving, a thing of intricate beauty.

He was still standing there when the joists gave and the whole building fell on top of him.

BOOK TWO

1950

18

"Hey, Hersh, you coming to the game?"

Sara looked up from her desk to her roommate in the doorway.

"No, I guess not, Sue. Robert's coming over. We've got some work to do."

Sue raised her eyebrows. The announcement by any other student that she proposed to spend Saturday afternoon with a man would have brought a variety of ribald suggestions, but Sara Hershman—Hershman the Horse, Hershman the Hog— had long ago exempted herself from that.

"Well, have fun," she said.

"You too." Sara was already reaching for her pen to make another note.

But as the door closed and Sue's footsteps disappeared down the hall, she put down the pen and closed the book. They were just protective camouflage, useful whenever she might be forced into any college social activity or conversation she didn't relish. Camp and then high school had taught her that rudeness brought only resentment and inevitable retaliation. Bookishness, an acceptable trait in a recluse, earned, at worst, an envious derision. At eighteen, she had been hiding behind books almost half her life.

Sue must have been the last to leave for the game. Except for a few latecomers running by, feet ringing on the frozen concrete paths, the quad below her window was silent. An occasional

143

roar carried from the stadium, half a mile away, as the crowd kept itself warm with chants and war cries, waiting for the game to start.

Half the crowd had driven more than a hundred miles from the nearest all-male college just for the game and the strictly monitored socializing that followed. It said a great deal for the power of sex. But Sara never regretted the circumstances that cut her off from that pleasure, that release; she had her own satisfactions. The dreams of retribution against David Moore, the fantasies of violent death, of humiliation, of her triumph over him, seethed at the back of her mind with all the vividness of adolescent eroticism. Locked in a bottom drawer of her bureau, she kept a dossier in which his every activity was detailed with the obsessive interest of a lover.

The college clock struck three in its flat clanking tone. Robert was late, not for the first time in their relationship. When she met him, his thin, acned face and stooped shoulders first irritated, then fascinated her. A physical specimen as ill-favored as she was would make an ideal partner, she decided, and Robert, in this as in all things, meekly followed her directions.

Robert offered her an experimental animal on whom she could test her will, her ideas, and whose body could satisfy her curiosity about herself. They had even made love—twice, once in the back of his car, and a second time, more comfortably if with no greater satisfaction, in his parents' bed during vacation. Both incidents moved her so little that she barely remembered the details. As Robert's skinny body labored on top of hers, her eyes wandered to the plaster moldings on the ceiling. Fretted ogee, egg and dart. Art History was her major.

"Was that OK?" he had asked afterward.

"Wonderful." And, after a decent interval, "Say, let's raid the icebox. I'm starving."

With her mind on these events, she missed his arrival, and only his diffident call from the quad caught her attention. Gathering up her books, she went downstairs, signed out with the housemother—even though she was only going across campus—and plunged out into the icy November air. Robert tagged along dutifully.

"How have you been, Sara?" he asked as they reached the lobby of the Art Annex and shed their coats.

"Why?"

"Just asking."

"Well . . . fine, I suppose. How about you?"

"Not so bad." She knew him well enough to sense that he was nursing a revelation. "I got the scholarship."

"To the Courtauld?" Something inside her felt crushed, but she stifled the impulse to show it. "That's tremendous. When are you going?"

"February. I don't suppose that you—"

"You know I can't. Momma would die." No use telling him the real reason, though her limited wardrobe, her lack of a car, her part-time job in the school canteen, her problems with textbooks that forced her to line up for the dog-eared library copies must have made it clear.

The collapse of the House of Hershman after her father's death left the family almost bankrupt, though as long as the old place on 11th Street remained open under the management of Carl Bleigen and David Moore, there was some income— enough to keep up the New Jersey house and put Sara through a college education of sorts.

"I wish you could come, Sara." Robert's thin face looked even more pathetic than usual. "You know I only applied because you told me to."

"Robert, the Courtauld has the best Art History course in the world. Don't be a dope. Maybe I can make it next year."

"I hope so. Hey, I got a present for you."

She unwrapped it; a book—Antonio Valerii's *Artists of the Renaissance*—so crisp and new as to be almost unrecognizable as a copy of the worn and mutilated library book she had used all year.

"Robert, it's beautiful." Impulsively, she kissed him on the cheek. "It's very kind of you." She put her arm through his. "But if you're going to the Courtauld, you need to do more work on Bernini and Pisano. Go get the slides. I'll set up the projector."

As she plugged in the ancient projector and pulled the black felt curtains over the windows, she wondered about Robert and London. His family was rich. If they got married . . .

But she shuddered at the thought. He would make as good a husband as any, given her limited needs in a man, but a partner would clutter her life, divert her from the aim that mattered more than any other. To do what had to be done, she needed to travel alone.

Most people ate off campus on Saturdays, so she had little to do in the canteen. The other girls had by now ceased to relate Sara in an apron dispensing hash and hamburgers to the plump girl at the back of their classes. She took orders phlegmatically, ignored even by Sue, who went on chattering with her date about the game even as Sara filled her plate with pork chops and gravy.

Sara found she didn't mind their contempt. It merely fueled her anger, adding to the reservoir of hate. It was generosity like Robert's that she had to guard against.

Back in her room, she opened the Valerii book again, leafing through the pages. At the foot of the acknowledgments, as she expected, Valerii had noted "the assistance of Mr. David Lawrence Moore." Carefully, she ripped out the page and crumpled it into the wastebasket.

From the bottom drawer of her desk, she took a small locked cashbox. The clippings inside were yellow and brittle, and the letter in its long white envelope showed the wear of countless readings. Holding it under the light, she went through the words yet again, like a prayer. *My dearest Sara. When you read this, I will be dead. . . .*

Afterward, she went to bed and slept deeply, hugging her hate to her like a soft toy.

19

"I don't see your problem. You're doing all right, aren't you?"

David fidgeted in his chair, wondering whether it was plastic or real leather. Looking around the lush new premises of Fine Art Holdings, he decided leather was more likely. It might even be human skin.

"It depends on what you mean by 'all right.' I can't complain about the money—"

"You sure can't! Don't think I haven't heard about your little deals. You must have made a fortune outta Hershman's." He grinned as he said this, and though Bleigen's smile seldom meant anything, it was clear he respected David's ability to turn the original situation to his advantage.

It was true he had done well out of Hershman's, especially since Jake became an invalid and the management had been placed entirely in his hands. He'd seen the market and exploited it shrewdly, buying low and selling high. Through a chance meeting with Tonino Valerii, the art historian, he'd made valuable contacts with the European market. Big buyers from the Continent routinely called on him during their New York visits, and he'd been able to make some spectacular coups.

But now the saleroom, which had been a useful base, was becoming a hindrance. He needed freedom, a place of his own, but Bleigen found him too useful to let go without a struggle.

"Listen, if it's money, Dave, maybe we could talk about a bigger slice of the action."

"No, Carl. The money's irrelevant. I want out—it's as simple as that." He stood up. "You'll have my resignation in the morning."

"I'm sorry to hear you talk like that, Dave. Real sorry." Carl's expression showed little compassion, and David waited for the familiar oily smile of self-satisfaction. "Maybe you don't realize it, but things are different out there." He nodded toward the New York skyline, soft in the haze of summer smog. "There's a whole new world, and it doesn't enjoy competition. Some people might not like someone muscling in on their territory."

David recognized the implied threat and knew its force. It was one thing to be a private dealer in paintings with a discreet circle of clients, another to launch the kind of enterprise he had in mind. Parke-Bernet and the other auction houses had expanded vastly in their power and influence since the war, and Madison Avenue was lined with lush galleries whose expensive decor disguised big money and even bigger greed. His capital, though substantial by his standards, would hardly pay the decorators' bills for these palatial establishments.

Perhaps it would be better to stay with Hershman's....

But the thought of 11th Street with its noises and smells flooded over him with the vividness of a nightmare. He was almost thirty-five. More than fifteen years of his life had been spent in the auction trade, and he was tired of it. If he didn't move now to do the things in which he believed, it would be too late.

"I'm quitting, Carl. I'll have that letter on your desk first thing tomorrow."

Leaving the office, he felt a curious lightness of spirit. In the lobby, one of Bleigen's comments came back with a false ring. The old toad had given him an idea.

Standing on the front step of the modest brownstone house, David wondered if anything about the man he was visiting would disconcert him as much as his home.

He had expected an office in some skyscraper, a chrome and glass eyrie guarded by secretaries as shrill as birds of prey. Suspecting he had come to the wrong place, he rang the bell.

But there was no mistake. "If you'll wait in the library," the young black butler said, "Mr. Sklar will be right down." David settled down to admire the paintings.

The walls were hung with half a million dollars' worth of Impressionists, most of them glowing Bonnards of Provence, with three or four blue-period Picassos and an exquisite Seurat mixed in. He was puzzling over the last, a confetti storm of blues, purples, and reds that miraculously became a quiet Paris suburban street as one backed away a foot or two, when Sklar bounded into the room.

About sixty, David decided. Crinkly hair, slightly graying, steady blue eyes, a handshake as quick and informal as the bite of a friendly dog.

"Drink, Mr. Moore?" He opened what had looked like a Boule cabinet to reveal bottles and glasses.

"I could use some coffee, if that's possible." Their appointment was for 8:30 A.M.

"I see you haven't picked up our bad habits yet. Myself, I need a pickup before breakfast. You won't mind if I have a Fernet Branca." He poured a tiny measure of thick black liqueur and tossed it down, grimacing. "Wormwood. Tastes foul, but my system seems to need it." He rang a bell and the young black returned. "Bernard, coffee for Mr. Moore. Actually, I think I'll join him." As the man left, he waved at the walls of his library. "What about my paintings, Moore? See any fakes up there?"

"I'm sure Carl's too good a partner to buy anything for you that isn't impeccable."

Sklar's eyes swung from the painting he had been admiring. "How do you mean 'partner'?"

"You put up seventy-five percent of the capital for Fine Art Holdings, didn't you?"

"Did *he* tell you that?"

David smiled. "Hardly. No, I've been keeping my ear to the ground. I got that piece of information the same way I found your address and arranged this appointment."

"The person who recommended you doesn't know about my deal with Bleigen."

"I didn't say that he did. I have other sources. Don't think that I bring this up to embarrass you, Mr. Sklar, just to establish that I know my business."

Bernard brought in the coffee and set it at the table by the bay window which looked out on Sklar's garden. Through the rippled glass, David saw a lawn dotted with statuary, the bronze and stone glistening and dark with dew. An Egyptian torso, splintered at the waist, the face disfigured but proud still; a rearing horse that might be Leonardo; a Rodin; the leaping spindle of a Brancusi.

Sklar watched him narrowly. "Brandy with that?"

"I don't think so, thanks. Let me come to my reason for wanting to see you. Frankly, I need a backer for a project I'm starting."

"What about Bleigen? Won't he help?"

"He doesn't know anything about it. Nor does he know I've come to see you."

"Go on."

"I walked up here," David said, "past all those galleries on the fifties and sixties: Knoedler, Duveen, Wildenstein, Durand-Ruel. It struck me that they're the last gasp of an art business that's fading away."

"They do good business."

"Yes, but always with the same people, and more often than not with other galleries. Duveen scooped up almost all the great pictures in the twenties, and now they're in galleries, donated by the collectors to escape death duties. Millionaires don't invest in art any more. These days, it's colleges, foundations, charities. They're afraid to have valuable paintings on the walls—the insurance is too high, and so is the risk of theft. From now on, a large proportion of the paintings sold by big galleries and auction rooms will go straight into bank vaults. And they'll stay there."

Sklar seemed to be enjoying David's argument. Perhaps he knew parts of it already. Why else would he keep only these relatively inexpensive modern paintings in his home? Where were his Rembrandts, the Van Dyck that Bleigen had bought for him at Snow's?

"What sort of people would lock up paintings like that?"

"Speculators. Investors. People who treat art works as a commodity. I see them all the time, the new big buyers: a slippery property dealer from the Netherlands who only wants something small enough to fit in the bottom of a suitcase if he had to leave the country in a hurry. The mayors of large towns who need something big and prestigious for the town hall or the new art gallery. A nice fat nude, after Rubens, that they could admire on wet days.

"But the men who interest me," he went on, "are a few French and Swiss dealers who like paintings but buy for investment, not admiration. They expect to hold onto something for ten or fifteen years, keeping it in a vault in Zurich or Basle, then sell it for ten times what they paid."

"And that's what you want to do—speculate on the art

market?" Sklar's tone made it clear that he regarded the idea without enthusiasm.

"No. I want to start a company that *advises* speculators, that builds up artists for the market. You could call it a gallery, but it wouldn't be just that. More like a stockbroker or an investment counselor. I know the art market, and I know painting." He leaned forward eagerly, nearly upsetting his coffee cup. "I can make it work."

Sklar seemed to find the suggestion intriguing. "Who would use a service like that? You said the millionaires don't buy art these days, and that's true enough. The government makes sure you don't have the cash."

"Things are changing," David said. "The average price of the art sold at auction goes down every year, even if the peaks are higher. More people are buying art, even people with average incomes. If a man will buy savings bonds or an insurance policy as a safeguard against inflation, he'll buy a painting or a sculpture for the same reason. It's like land—an investment that can't depreciate, providing you wait long enough and buy with good advice. One of these days, pension funds will buy art the way they buy real estate. It's the one area of investment where you can't lose."

For more than a minute, Sklar stared out into the garden. David wondered whether his presentation had offended him; was this a pointed suggestion that he was no longer welcome? But when Sklar looked round again, he seemed amiable, if a little sly.

"I'll tell you a better investment, Mr. Moore. That's people. A good judge of people can make a fortune. I think you might be worth investing in. Put these ideas on paper and I'll give them some thought." He stood up and shook hands. "You might be looking around for premises as well. It's a good time to buy, but I can't speak for the spring; I have a feeling prices will rise."

Outside, David walked along the street with its line of tiny beeches inside their cylinders of wire and wondered why Sklar left him confused rather than elated. He had sensed interest there, but something else as well. Sklar was too broad a thinker to be bothered with stealing David's idea; one coup on the futures market could net him more than David expected to make in his first five years. A secret enjoyment, that was it. Sklar had seen the scheme not only as a chance to make money but as an opportunity for ... could it be amusement?

Three weeks later, David found out something else about Arthur Sklar. He had a well-developed sense of humor.

The lawyer from the uptown firm with fifty partners patiently explained twice, to make sure David understood. Mr. Sklar, after serious consideration, had decided not to invest directly in Mr. Moore's project, since he already had, in Fine Art Holdings, a similar enterprise over which he enjoyed majority control. However—and here the lawyer fixed David with a penetrating stare, as if mere concentration could force the information through his uncomprehending frown—however, Mr. Sklar was making over to Mr. Moore a fifty percent share in Fine Art Holdings, the book value of which—estimated at $78,000 —could be repaid by Mr. Moore over a ten-year period.

"I know you'll think me obtuse, Mr.—er, Singleton, but I want to get it straight in my mind. Sklar is making *me* a majority stockholder in Fine Art Holdings?"

"Uh, no, not quite, Mr. Moore. At the same time as the transfer of this stock to you, his remaining holdings will be sold to the other principal in the business. Mr. Carl Bleigen."

The full extent of Sklar's sense of humor began to dawn on David. "So Carl and I will be equal partners in the company. Fifty-fifty."

"Quite!" Singleton nearly babbled in his delight at having made it clear at last. "You've summed it up admirably. Fifty-fifty."

"Have you spoken to Carl about this?"

"I believe Mr. Sklar conveyed the essence of the arrangement to him in person this morning."

"That must have been quite a conversation. Mr. Singleton, I appreciate you coming down to explain all this to me. Forgive me if I've appeared slow; it's all been rather a surprise."

The phone rang. Picking it up, David heard the first familiar syllables and put his hand over the mouthpiece. "I wonder if you'll excuse me," he said with a grin. "It's my new partner. I think he has a few confidential observations on our future working relationship."

He waited for the lawyer to leave before he allowed himself the luxury of slightly hysterical laughter, then picked up the phone again.

"Carl," he said amiably. "How are you?" It was time to start turning the knife. "How's business—*our* business?"

20

On August 17, 1955, Sara Hershman got up at 8 A.M.

It was a hot, still morning in New Jersey, with the sun already shining through the grove of birches at the back of the house and glinting on the pond. Even before her shower, she sat down at her desk and meticulously wrote in her diary "The day." Then, almost as an afterthought, "My birthday." She was twenty-four.

The phrase gave shape to the morning. Although she had until ten thirty (a time strictly laid down, part of a schedule detailed by hour, week, and month on another page of the diary almost a year earlier), the setting down of those words put the whole scheme in motion. With them, she was committed.

Downstairs, the house was deserted, though a pan on the stove showed that Grandpa was up, as usual, and huddled on the back porch with the cup of bitter coffee that he hardly ever remembered to drink. She visualized him there, beard on his chest, chin bent on it, eyes distant and veiled, his mind in the wordless limbo where he had lived for the years since his stroke. Confirming her vision, his rocker creaked thinly and she heard him mutter, a terse nugget of consonants, meaningless.

At the Short Hills railroad station the lady at the newspaper stand sold her the *New York Times* and half a dozen candy bars. The front page of the paper hardly interested her—Eisenhower was still talking about his "summit conference" of the month before and there was a war in Goa, wherever that was. Turning to the arts pages, Sara read through the saleroom news and a

long article about new American artists. Her heart jumped
when, halfway down the page, she read, "Of the newer New
Yorkers, Manuel Arcalo, with the backing of the prestigious
Atropos organization, seems most likely to exploit the coming
boom in abstract expressionism."

Reading her way through the paper, she absently consumed
three Hershey Bars and a Baby Ruth. In a peasant society, her
wide hips, short legs and strong back would have been the height
of functional beauty. But in the America of 1955, with Grace
Kelly about to marry Prince Rainier of Monaco and Marilyn
Monroe the reigning sex symbol (her fifty-foot silhouette
perched high over Times Square, skirt blown high on slim white
legs in advertisement of *The Seven Year Itch*), Sara was out of
place.

Sara had learned to ignore the gibes of her friends, with their
matador pants and stiletto heels, and to accept the indifference
of the boys whose ducktail pompadours imitated the current
rock favorites. The past was her refuge. The Rubenses in the
Metropolitan—plump women, naked and pink, hustled through
antique landscapes by muscled warriors—gave her the stuff of
her fantasies.

It took almost an hour for the commuter special to reach
Manhattan, and she left the station with a wave of preoccupied
businessmen. She enjoyed crowds, and let this one carry her,
ignored and anonymous, up the concourse. At ten twenty-eight
she stood in front of the gallery on Madison Avenue, reading
carefully—though she knew every detail from long and
persistent scrutiny over the years—the words lettered on its two
windows.

Along the top, in discreet sans serif lettering, ran the words
DAVID LAWRENCE MOORE: OLD MASTERS AND TWENTIETH
CENTURY WORKS OF ART. Lower down, it merely said ATROPOS:
A DIVISION OF FINE ART HOLDINGS.

The other window was blank and empty except for a small
painting, set so far back that the sun could never reach it. An
abstract of reds and blue-blacks, it was signed with a sprawling
Arcalo.

Sara pushed through the heavy bronze glass door. It was just
ten thirty.

Instantly she felt the presence of money. No single feature
trumpeted it; the Moore gallery lacked the taped Mozart, the
indirect lighting, the plastic-covered album of reviews from past

shows that one found automatically in other Manhattan art showrooms. At first glance, it even lacked pictures. The four canvases hung in the main gallery were so discreetly lit that the delicate rose and gray brocade wallpaper appeared to swallow them up.

An acre of dove-gray carpet, unmarked even by a single footprint, stretched to the far end of the room, where a woman sat at a small desk, carefully examining her nails. Conscious more than ever of her weight and ungainliness, Sara walked to the desk.

"Can I help you?" The receptionist looked up dubiously at the moon-faced girl in the unbecoming pink shift.

"Is Mr. Moore in?"

"Do you have an appointment?"

"No, but I think he'll see me. Will you tell him it's Sara Hershman."

"I can't do that, Miss Hershman. If you'd like to leave your name—"

"Please." Sara's voice was so insistent that the girl hesitated.

"Wait over there for a minute," she said at last, pointing to the far side of the gallery. Fingering the tiny intercom on her desk, she murmured a few words into it.

Sara looked at the painting nearest to her, a Boucher she remembered seeing in the *New York Times* six months ago when Moore bought it for a quarter of a million dollars. The plump, giggling courtesans tumbling from their swing reassured her with their pink disorder. Not everybody could be the birdlike creature who watched her narrowly across the room.

A motor whirred somewhere in the quiet and a door behind the receptionist's desk which Sara had taken for an office opened on a tiny personal elevator.

David Moore stepped out, said a few words to the girl, then walked across the carpet toward Sara. She felt her stomach clench.

She knew what he looked like, of course. Her scrapbook bulged with clippings. Moore at the Met—museum and opera—and at sales; Moore standing in front of the Van Gogh he'd bought for Arthur Sklar, beating all the big dealers; Moore displaying two Rodin bronzes spotted at a small sale in Connecticut and picked up for a song; Moore on the arm of a succession of beautiful girls.

The pictures made him look tall but he was only average in

height, and slim—more Montgomery Clift than Marlon
Brando, Sara decided, though as movie-star material he was
improbable. His face kept too much back, and he had a general
air of watchfulness. The gray suit and silk handkerchief in the
top pocket might have indicated a banker or a broker, though
nobody in the money market would have risked the vivid blue tie
or striped shirt.

"You wanted to see me?" There was still a trace of English
accent; she was to find that in moments of stress it returned far
more strongly.

"I'm Sara Hershman. Nat Hershman was my father."

"I know."

She hadn't realized he would be gray at the temples, even
though he was around forty. He looked and acted much
younger.

"You'd better come into the office," he said at last.

The office was decorated by a single Monet of water lilies, a
swimming window of purple, red, and blue which the room
showed off to perfection. How many visitors, stepping into the
office "for a chat," emerged with a new addition to their
collections? Everything about David Moore, she began to see,
worked by misdirection.

"What can I do for you?"

"You could give me a job."

"What sort of job?"

"I don't mind. I want to learn the art business."

He seemed to find this amusing. "Is that what you're
interested in?"

"Yes."

"How old are you?"

"Twenty-four. Today."

"Happy birthday. What have you been doing lately?"

"I graduated from Isherwood with an Art History major.
Then I did two years postgraduate work on the Impressionists."

"You mightn't like the art business, you know. It can be
difficult. Painful sometimes. It isn't all cocktail parties and
gallery first nights."

"I didn't think it was."

"Sometimes you have to be cruel, hurt people. That doesn't
worry you?"

"No."

He frowned. "It should. But I'll assume you're just trying to make a good impression. My capacity for ruthlessness is considerably overstated. When you have to do it, you'll find it harder than you imagine. Why did you come to me, incidentally?"

"I thought you might feel guilty—about my father, I mean." Long ago, she had decided only brutal honesty would get what she wanted from David Moore.

He paused so long she wondered if his silence was a pointed indication that the interview was over. "That's a reasonable assumption," he said at last, "but then you don't know me very well. One of these days we must have a talk about your father. Incidentally, how is Jake?"

"OK, I guess. He doesn't say much."

For a long time, Moore looked at the bare top of his desk, fingers rapping quietly on its edge. Then he said, "When can you start?"

"Now!"

"You don't mind cleaning up, unpacking things, taking inventory?"

"Not if I'm learning."

He smiled for the first time, his face suddenly flashing the charm that collectors loved and other dealers talked of with distaste. "Oh, you'll learn, if that's what you want."

David sat at his desk for a while after Fran Pellegrino had taken Sara away to show her around the gallery. He had thought himself free of the Hershmans, but clearly they were to be his cross, a permanent reminder of evanescence, like the slave who stood behind Caesar as he paraded through Rome and whispered repeatedly, "Remember, you are but a man."

After the interview with David Moore, Sara wandered into the street with a sense of unreality.

In high school and college, nursing her grudge against the man who caused her father's death, the prospect of ever achieving a concrete revenge had been so remote that, even in her wildest fits of resentment, she never took it seriously.

Only in her last two years of postgraduate research in pursuit of an as yet unachieved doctorate (the Hershman fortunes still would not run to the essential year's work in Europe) had the dream approached the possibility of fulfillment.

Meeting and interviewing professional critics and dealers had also given her access to their gossip, much of it centering on

David Moore and Atropos. Jealousy, misinformation, or spite made up most of the stories, but through them wove a strand of obvious truth. Moore *did* operate on the fringe of the law; many of his deals *did* transgress either minor laws or the unwritten rules of the art business. And those transgressions made him vulnerable.

Sara was determined to track down his offenses and turn them against him. Now, with such miraculous simplicity that she hardly dared believe her luck, the means to do so were in her hands.

As Moore had warned, the art business did not live up to her expectations.

For the first month, under the eye of Fran, the suave receptionist, she spent her time shifting paintings from room to room.

At first, there was a Christmas excitement in unpacking each new arrival, watching ornate frames and exquisite canvases emerge from mountains of excelsior and splintered wooden cartons. She noted their arrival in the records, filed away the sheafs of provenances, then hauled the paintings to their eventual home in the long air-conditioned vault that ran along the back of the main gallery.

But gradually it became tedious. Occasionally she glimpsed Moore in conversation with customers who strolled in to look over the newest show, or saw Fran usher others discreetly into the office.

Watching these circumspect, almost secret comings and goings, Sara wondered how Atropos had earned its reputation as one of the most powerful art-dealing organizations in the world. According to the trade press, it was regularly approached by galleries and collectors in every country, and increasingly by investment bodies anxious to hedge their holdings against inflation. Atropos, it was said, created taste as well by adopting promising artists and coaxing them into top sellers. But as to where and how this was done, she had as little idea after eight weeks in the company as she had when she began.

Sara and Fran Pellegrino found themselves drawn together by mutual boredom, and on long summer afternoons when the door to the gallery hardly opened she often joined the receptionist at her desk to talk and probe quietly for more information.

"I don't understand," she said on a particularly quiet day. "Is business always this bad?"

Fran stopped buffing her nails to stare at Sara in amused astonishment. This look was her stock in trade and, Sara suspected, the main reason for her job with Atropos. A combination of slightly receding chin and hair gathered high on the back of her head in what the fashion magazines called a chignon but would soon name the beehive gave her a chilly hauteur that could reduce the strongest to stammering inarticulateness. This camel stare and a remarkable set of talonlike nails which she groomed perpetually with a variety of surgical instruments gave her a head start in her battle with the world.

"Business bad?" she drawled, eyebrow raised. Then her voice slipped into her native Brooklynese. "Honey, this place is a gold mine. You know what he took last year? Mr. Humboldt, the accountant, is a ... well, a close personal friend, and he told me. Three hundred thousand dollars! *After* taxes."

"But who buys? We haven't sold a picture since I've been here."

"Not in here, dearie. But up at Parke-Bernet we sold five. And Mr. Herzberg—you know, with the department store?—he bought two of those Augustus things. But with a man like that, you take the pictures to *him*."

The door opened and a woman elegantly dressed in slacks and a silk shirt strolled in, smiled vaguely toward the two girls, and wandered into the smaller back gallery with its mixed show of abstracts from the gallery's stock.

"Maybe we'll sell something," Sara said, watching her. "She looks rich."

Fran shook her head. "Women in trousers never buy anything," she said with finality.

"You're not serious!"

Fran stopped buffing her nails, a sign that she was about to say something of importance. "Listen, honey, let me tell you about buying from art galleries. You don't buy a painting as if it was a cantaloupe; it's an event—you think about it, you come in maybe three or four times to look at the thing, you bring in your friends to get their opinion. And when you finally decide, you don't wear slacks for the big day. It's your best clothes, and *all* your jewelry. Some of them come in looking like Christmas trees."

Sara reviewed the people she'd seen come into the gallery since she'd worked there—pairs of matrons, obviously in Manhattan for their weekly day in the stores; men and women, most of them well dressed and obviously wealthy, who strolled around the gallery with every sign of interest, then looked at their watches and left—and understood why Fran paid so little attention to them. To many people, an art gallery, like a bookstore, was a place to browse and kill time rather than buy. But there had been others. . . .

"What about that couple who came in last week? You said he'd inherited a whole office building, and they'd just got married. Wouldn't they be likely to buy something?"

"Oh, sure, if *he* was the one who looked interested. But he didn't; she brought him in."

"So?"

"Sara, something you've got to understand about people with money. No matter who they're with or who they're married to, spending is *their* business. You won't find anyone cheaper than a millionaire, and if he doesn't want something, he won't buy it, no matter who pushes him. Now if a rich man comes in with that buying look in his eye, jump on him, even if his wife is trying to drag him out of the place. . . . Oh, good afternoon, Mr. Moore."

David came in with a beautiful woman. She wore a pencil-thin black suit, a scrap of a hat hardly larger than a fluttering sparrow, and carried a swordlike umbrella that had clearly been pressed into service as a parasol to protect a china-white complexion.

"Go on through, dear," he said quietly. Obviously knowing her way, she strolled toward the elevator, stepped in, and rose, Sara had no doubt, to Moore's apartment on the building's tenth floor.

"Hello, Fran. Anyone come in?"

"No, it's been very quiet, Mr. Moore."

"Very well. I don't expect anyone, but if there are calls, take a message, please. And Fran." He didn't look at Sara. "I'd rather you didn't have other members of the staff up here for conversations."

"Yes, Mr. Moore."

As he walked to the elevator, Sara felt a blush of shame and anger rise from her breasts and flow over her face.

"You heard what he said," Fran remarked quietly. "Sorry, honey."

Storming back to the stockroom in a rage, tears of fury on her cheeks, Sara vented her frustration on a heap of wooden crates. They were largely matchwood when she was done kicking them.

For the rest of the day, her temper remained at a slow boil. Glimpsing herself briefly in the mirror of the ladies' room, she was surprised at how much a high color became her. With cheeks flushed and eyes blazing, her face seemed transformed. The insight prompted a general physical reappraisal.

Traveling between New Jersey and Manhattan every day left her perpetually tired, a fact which, in combination with skipped lunches and hard physical exercise, had reduced her figure. She was still fat, but there was the beginning of a waist and of more shapely arms.

Obviously this change had not gone unnoticed. Later that afternoon, as she worked on the shelves of paintings, her anger still simmering, Danny, a gawky adolescent with an Adam's apple so prominent it was almost a deformity, grabbed her from behind and groped her breasts. Instinctively her elbow came back sharply and she heard a satisfying *whoosh* of expelled breath. When she turned, Danny was sitting on the floor, clutching his stomach.

"Whatcha do that for? I was only fooling."

"Go fool with someone else!" she said hotly, secretly alarmed and delighted. As he grabbed her, she had felt a surge of pure erotic sensation that left her trembling.

"Jesus, what a place," Danny said, getting up painfully. "I s'pose you're gonna turn out like that freak Sascha." He slunk off.

"Who's Sascha?" Sara asked Fran the next day at lunch. (They had assumed David's rule did not extend as far as the Automat.)

Fran stopped with a forkful of chicken pot pie halfway to her mouth. "Sascha," she said distastefully, "is Mr. Sascha Beauclair, Mr. Moore's assistant. He spends a lot of time in Europe. Who told you about him?"

"Danny."

"Oh." She smiled thinly. "He and Danny don't get along."

"Why?"

"You'll see."

In September, the gallery closed down for inventory, and for the second time in her three months there, Sara removed the paintings from the vault and checked them against the files. Many of them were old friends by now, and she renewed their acquaintance with affection. Grudgingly, she had to acknowledge Moore had been right to put her in the stockroom. Almost by accident, she learned her trade through the need to dust, stack, file, label, and pamper these masterpieces. Understanding art, she realized, had less to do with degrees in Art History and newspaper reviews than with an instinctive feel for what a painting had to say.

Every great work had a voice, and the best of them spoke clearly, without equivocation. She had come to know the process connoisseurs call "a work going dead on you." Before buying any major piece, a dealer or collector always left it hanging in a place where he would see it a dozen or more times each day. The weak painting or the clever fake might look superb on first viewing, but after a week, drained of its novelty, the thinness of the underlying intelligence and skill were glaringly apparent.

It happened to Sara early in November when, reaching the end of the racks, she brought out four paintings she especially enjoyed. All were Impressionists: a Bonnard of a Provençal hillside, two tiny Sisleys of the Seine in high summer, and a Renoir of a girl bathing by a window. In moments of depression she often took one of them out of the rack, propped it against the wall, and let its color and vitality light the room.

Today it was the turn of Renoir's plump pink bather. Carefully choosing an empty space where she could see the painting from the corner of her eye, she went on with her checking. An hour later she took a closer look, wondering why the painting no longer had the familiar effect of freedom and comfort. After another closer look, she decided something was wrong.

In the middle of the afternoon, Moore glanced into the room to find her staring at the Renoir yet again.

"Mr. Moore, does this look right to you?"

He came in and stood beside her. "Right? How do you mean?"

"It's just... I don't know. I wondered if it was... well, a fake."

"What's on the card?"

"*Young Bather*. Renoir. 1896. But there doesn't seem to be a provenance on file."

"That doesn't mean a lot. With Impressionists, they've sometimes been in the same collection ever since they were acquired from the artist."

"I know. All the same...."

She leaned the painting on a chair and looked at it again. The girl was too pink, the impasto not giving a three-dimensional quality as it usually did with Renoir but clogging and choking the subject. And there was, Sara saw now, an uncharacteristic stiffness about the pose of the girl leaning over the basin, breasts drooping, hair glowing with the light from the window.

"It just *feels* wrong. Look at her back, and that color."

"What would you say this painting is worth?" David asked slowly.

"The insurance valuation's sixty thousand dollars."

"Hmmmm." He considered the picture critically. "You're right about the back. You really think it's a fake—not just Renoir on a bad day?"

"I don't know. But there's *something* wrong with it." She made a sudden decision. "Yes, I *do* think it's phoney. I've never seen a Renoir that didn't have something good in it."

Picking up a knife from a crate, he handed it to her. "Better stick this through it, then. We don't deal in fakes here."

"You mean it?"

"If it's wrong, it isn't worth anything. Might as well cut it up." He wasn't smiling.

"But if it's real—"

"You just said it wasn't. You're *sure*, aren't you?"

Sara took the knife, feeling ill. Could it be a Renoir? No—that back; clumsy, ugly. In a sudden burst of conviction she slashed at the canvas.

Stiff with paint and taut on its stretchers, the canvas resisted, the point hardly scraping the thick paint. *A sign*, she thought desperately. *I've been given a second chance.*

But something made her bear down on the blade. With a rip that sounded deafening in the little room, she slit the canvas right down the center, through the wide pink back.

David took the knife from her trembling hand.

"I'd forgotten this thing," he said. "It shouldn't have got into the inventory at all. I suppose Danny did it before you came. The Cleveland Museum sent it in for appraisal a year ago, when they got it in a bequest. Since it was obviously a copy, they said they never wanted to see it again." He contemplated the gutted painting. "We seem to have looked after that."

Sara wept—tears of relief, and of hatred at the game he had played with her. It was all she could do to restrain herself from throwing herself at his throat.

Just after Christmas, David offered her a permanent job.

"Doing what?" she asked, trying to keep the excitement out of her voice.

"Deal with clients, attend sales, work on catalogues. You'd work under Sascha Beauclair. Interested?"

"Sure!"

"Good. Consider yourself on the staff. From now on, you earn one twenty-five a week. And don't think you won't earn it."

Sara wandered out of his office and, in the privacy of the empty back gallery, tried an awkward pirouette.

21

Also at Christmas, Sascha Beauclair returned to New York.

He was a walking advertisement for everything one had ever heard about the decadent South. His manners were impeccable, his clothing exquisite, his voice a New Orleans drawl so affected that listeners relaxed visibly as he spoke and women reached out a hand as if to trail it in the waters of the Mississippi. In his late twenties, he still had the sensual blond looks of a Renaissance David, and piercing eyes with which he could fix a victim with a hypnotic stare or sum up the wealth, social prospects, and sexual predilections of a crowd in one quick glance. Like many people in the art business, he was aggressively and lasciviously homosexual.

These sexual tastes contributed to a repertoire of behavioral oddities, most of them linguistic. At various times, Sara found herself addressed as "Petal," "Flower," "Sweetie," and, at moments of particular enthusiasm, "Heart."

When David Moore introduced them, Sascha extended a limp hand. "Pleasure," he said wearily.

"I want you to show Sara the ropes. Take her around. Introduce her to the clients."

"Yes." His expression as he examined her appearance and clothing was eloquent of his misgivings.

"Now tell me about the trip." As Sara turned to leave, David said, "No, better listen to this, Sara."

"Well, the usual love and kisses from Valerii, of course."

165

Sascha smiled, the grin of a satyr in some Grecian frieze. "And Paola."

"Spare me the sarcasm."

"Just my little joke. Valerii gave me various papers." Opening his attaché case, he placed a carefully wrapped bundle on the desk.

Antonio Valerii—generally known as Tonino—ranked high among the world's art experts. A major art historian in his twenties before the First World War, he had known (and understood) Renoir, Seurat, and even the younger Fauvists long before their worldwide acceptance. As a dealer after the war, he supported Picasso, while dealing at the same time in Old Masters, particularly Italian paintings of the fifteenth century, on which he was the greatest living expert.

The breadth of his interest and knowledge made him the most sought-after of authorities, rivaled only by Bernard Berenson, who had done so much to establish Joseph Duveen as the premier dealer of the early twentieth century. Recognizing, like Duveen, the value of having such an expert always on call, David Moore followed his lead in placing Valerii on a retainer, allowing him to move from Paris to Italy and settle down in Tuscan comfort during his old age. An invitation to his villa Zurlini was as coveted a mark of acceptance in the close-knit art world as a similar summons to Berenson's "I Tatti," outside Florence.

Moore weighed the bundle. "What's in here?"

"Various. A report on that Soutine you sent him. He doesn't believe it. 'Poor Chaim was mad but not *that* mad.'" Sara recognized a parody of a low-pitched, heavily accented English, somewhere between Charles Boyer and a harassed wine waiter. From David Moore's grin, she guessed it was accurate.

"Toledo won't be happy about that. Did he find anything on that Tiepolo?"

"Some sort of drawing, I think. It's all in here."

"I'll read it later. What else? How is London? Did you see Gothard?"

"Yes, of course. The new offices look fine. Was he always that fat, even when you were clerks together?"

David frowned. "I wasn't a clerk. But Michael's never been exactly slim, no."

"Anyway, he said to tell you that Impressionists still look soft. He's against our buying."

"We'll see."

"Well, I certainly hope so, David. There are a lot of them out back, and no buyers in sight."

"Not again, Sascha. Tell me about London."

"Quite a nice sale of silver and porcelain at Christie's," he said, sulking slightly. "And I went to Snow's a couple of times."

"Oh?" David was noncommittal, but Sara felt the tension. Exacting his personal revenge, Sascha bored in. "They're thriving. The fabulous Cicely is still in charge, though Oliver Turnbull runs the place, of course. His nephew, Mark, is very much in evidence." He allowed himself a feral smile. "Very attractive."

"I'm not interested in your bedroom activities."

"Neither was he, sad to say, but I did elicit the interesting information that they're selling the Thornhill collection soon. It might be your chance to pick up the Bonnard Sklar set his heart on. How is he, by the way?"

"Dying. It could be any time now."

"Then we might as well forget it, I suppose."

Moore shrugged. Sara knew that Arthur Sklar had backed Moore, helping him to set up Atropos, the investment counseling department of the Moore enterprises. It was a standing joke in the trade how Sklar, to test the young newcomer, had pitted him against his former employer, Carl Bleigen, by forcing them to share the management of the company—a scheme familiar to the New York art world from the antics of Cortlandt Field Bishop, who, during the twenties, had bought New York's two main salerooms, the American Art Association and the Anderson Galleries, then set them against one another, to disastrous effect.

Since then, Bleigen and Moore had existed in uneasy partnership, with Moore gradually edging out his colleague and establishing himself more firmly in Sklar's confidence as his genius for the art business became apparent. Before Sklar was immobilized by the cancer that was slowly killing him, the two men were often seen together—at sales, at the racetrack, at house parties in Sklar's various homes.

His shrug, then, was puzzling. Indifference? Or feeling too deep to express? Marking it as a potential weak point in the Moore armor, she promised herself a deeper investigation.

Abruptly, David changed the subject. "I think it's time to launch Ted Augustus. Do you think Sara would do?"

Sascha looked her over dubiously. "Do they know her at Parke-Bernet?"

"I've kept her out of sight, just in case."

Under their critical gaze, Sara felt like a heifer at market. "A little dressing-up is called for, I fancy," Sascha said at last.

"Fran can see to that. Ever bought anything at auction, Sara?"

"No."

"Well, now's your chance. We'll even give you the money."

Early in February, Sara walked into Parke-Bernet's palatial Madison Avenue saleroom and looked around, trying not to appear uncertain.

She was helped by her clothes. After a depressing tour of the larger stores, many of which could only produce tentlike shifts or maternity dresses, Fran, in a flash of genius, steered her into the fur department of Bergdorf-Goodman.

Sara now sweated grandly in a full-length mutation mink coat. With a tiny veiled pillbox hat and patent leather pumps it created an effect of unalloyed opulence. Even Fran was impressed. "Honey," she said, "you look *filthy* with the stuff."

The doorman at Parke-Bernet all but fell over himself to help her through the entrance, and a passing staff member bowed as he directed her to the main second-floor saleroom. All her fears evaporated.

Although this was her first sale, Sara felt she knew more than enough about how they worked. Before he lapsed completely into senility, Grandpa loved to talk about the great coups of the House of Hershman. She even wrote a term paper once about the auction trade, with his copious guidance and illustration.

Nevertheless, she felt a quiver of nerves as she took her seat unobtrusively at the side of the room.

Although just ten minutes remained until the advertised starting time, only a few seats were filled. But behind the rostrum, things were already humming. Two of the clerks who would assist at today's sale sorted through piles of forms, conferring in whispers and writing busily in their specially prepared catalogues, the pages interleaved with large blank sheets on which would be written a full account of every purchase at today's sale. In separate books, they recorded the day's mail and phone bids and any commission bids they may have been asked to make for dealers or collectors not able to attend.

Glancing through her glossy catalogue, with its color photographs and neat, precise descriptions of the pictures on sale, Sara realized it contained only a fraction of the information one needed in order to buy intelligently at auction.

Today's sale was classified merely as "Modern and Impressionist Pictures," which indicated to any expert that it contained little of major interest. A few valuable items, up to two or three thousand dollars, would have justified adding the adjective "Good" to the title, while slightly higher prices earned "Important" and a sharp increase in interest throughout the trade. Above "Important" lay only "Major," reserved for the two or three big sales of each year—set pieces with fifty-dollar catalogues, guests in evening dress, flashbulbs flaring as prices crept into the millions.

Precisely at ten thirty the auctioneer ascended the rostrum and bent over his catalogue like a priest over a breviary.

"Good morning, ladies and gentlemen. The following lots have been withdrawn: three, seventeen, two twenty-four, and three oh one. Lot One, a pair of watercolors by Whistler." He glanced to his left to be sure that the porters had located the pictures from among the hundreds crowded along the walls and placed them on the easel. "I'll have to start at"—he checked his notes—"one hundred dollars."

Sara could afford to enjoy the auction for itself. Even at the rate of three lots a minute—the international average—it would be half an hour before it became personally interesting to her.

Fascinated, she watched the drama of buying and selling play like electricity under the apparent tranquillity of the room, almost silent except for the call of bids and the clatter as pictures were lifted from the walls and placed on show.

From the auctioneer's face, she could tell when a lot failed to reach the minimum reserve price placed on it by the seller and had to be bought in by the company, using a fake name, half a dozen of which were listed in the auctioneer's private catalogue for this purpose. Later, the owner would have the chance to offer it in another sale or sell it to the highest bidder in a private deal; among the clerk's most important jobs was the recording of the name of the closest underbidder in each sale, in case either the seller or Parke-Bernet needed to contact him later.

The buy-in figure on any sale was the most closely guarded of all auction secrets, showing as it did the company's efficiency in disposing of goods. An indifferent crowd and a poor auctioneer could push the B. I. figure as high as two thirds, though most companies maintained the fiction that only about five percent of the lots did not find a buyer.

Sara soon spotted the amateurs in this largely professional crowd. A young couple in front of her erupted in nervous enthusiasm as a tiny Frederic Remington sketch came up, the man waving his catalogue as soon as the auctioneer said, "Can we begin at fifty dollars?"

The picture was newly and professionally framed, a sure sign that some gallery was disposing of its excess stock, and a man at the back, obviously sent by the owner for just this purpose, calmly ran the couple up to $350 before sensing their flagging interest and dropping out. By contrast, a far more valuable sketch by Sargent went for half this figure to a sleepy-looking gentleman who let the bidding wander on, then topped the last bid by five dollars just as the hammer came down.

Finally, the porters hauled out Lot 114 and propped the huge abstract on the easel. Under the unflattering overhead light it looked shopworn, the frame scuffed by careless handling.

"Lot One fourteen. *America the Beautiful* by T. Augustus. Can we start at ... two hundred dollars?"

Someone bid at the back, a skeptical, probing offer, to test the crowd's interest. Everyone knew David Moore was promoting Augustus as an important painter; was Augustus destined to make big money in the saleroom or remain a dilettantes' interest? In sales like this, dealers read the signs.

Sara waited for the price to reach five hundred, where it stuck. Then she waved her catalogue.

"Six hundred?" The auctioneer raised an eyebrow in inquiry. "Thank you, madam. Six hundred in a new place. Six hundred with a lady." He looked toward the back of the room. "Against you, sir, at six hundred."

A new bidder with six hundred dollars to spend on a minor modern painter caused a perceptible increase in interest. Her opponent at the back went to six fifty, and Sara countered with seven hundred. At fifty-dollar rises it went to eight fifty, where the man dropped out. With a rap of the ivory disk the auctioneer used as a hammer, it was knocked down to Sara.

"Name, madam?" It was unusual for an auctioneer to have to

ask—most of the people in the room would be regular buyers, even friends.

Surprised to find her throat dry, Sara croaked "Woolrich," her chosen pseudonym. A clerk came down the aisle with a card on which she wrote her name, a fake address—Fran's apartment—and the number of the lot she'd bought. She had just spent eight hundred and fifty dollars of someone else's money. It was exhilarating; she felt like giggling.

The second Augustus painting came up half an hour later; a more popular artist's works were generally lumped together in an auction, since specialist dealers liked to buy all at once and then leave, but the shrewd auctioneer scattered the products of a minor painter right through a sale or series of sales, so as not to flood what little market existed.

Sara bid this time with more assurance, starting at four hundred and taking it finally for more than a thousand against two interested opponents. A man in the front row turned to stare in curiosity at someone with this kind of money to spend. Ten minutes later, when the third and last Augustus came up, there was audible excitement in the room.

All auctions are theater, and bidders respond to the tingle of excitement. The puzzling vertical panel of green, yellow, and red Augustus called *Fruili 1949* was suddenly intriguing, perhaps valuable. Before she had time to bid, others had raised the price to fifteen hundred dollars. Remembering David Moore's injunction to push as hard as she liked, Sara competed vigorously, waving her catalogue and once shouting "Seventeen hundred!" when other bids seemed likely to drown her out. The final price of twenty-nine hundred dollars was the most ever paid for an Augustus at auction, and the next day's papers and, later, the trade press would announce this fact with interest.

Out on the sidewalk half an hour later, her receipt for $4,800 in her bag, Sara felt wafted on a new sense of confidence and self-satisfaction. It was better than the champagne she had tested only once, on her sixteenth birthday; better even than the furtive sexual experiences of her lonelier nights. With the mink clutched around her, she drifted down Madison Avenue imagining herself Anna Karenina, Camille....

The elation lasted only as long as the coat. Handing it over to Fran to be returned to the store, she climbed the stairs to Sascha's office with a feeling of anticlimax.

"Take a chair, dear heart," he said absently, adding up figures. His taste in decor, except for the smart new electric adding machine, ran to the bizarre—onyx and ivory skulls, lifelike alabaster models of babies' hands and forearms (a Victorian affection that always made Sara feel ill), and a set of tortured modern lithographs whose half-glimpsed subject matter evoked even more uneasiness than the rest.

"How was it this morning?" he asked at last.

"Wonderful!" She sounded rhapsodic.

"God, the girl's caught the bug. We won't be able to get you out of the place. Next thing, it'll be spending your savings on El Grecos. How much did we drop this morning, by the way?"

Sara handed over the receipt.

Sascha looked sour. "Well, I suppose our leader knows what he's up to." Taking a large buff card from the filing cabinet, he fitted it into the adding machine and punched out figures. Looking over his shoulder, Sara saw that the card itemized two years of transactions between Atropos and Ted Augustus. In a few places, figures appeared on the credit side: a few paintings sold for low prices, never more than five hundred dollars, and the occasional few dollars for permission to use a painting in some reference work or exhibition.

But on the debit side marched figures totaling thousands of dollars, paintings bought at auction sales, as this morning, or from private collectors. And each month, Augustus apparently received $200 from Atropos, under the laconic heading *Advance*.

"Advance on what?"

"Future sales, of course. We put Augustus on a monthly salary, if you like, in return for exclusive rights to merchandise his work. We keep up the price of his paintings by buying them in, we publicize him, put on shows if there seems to be enough interest; we also wipe his nose and arrange for his more . . . specialized needs. All part of the care and feeding of the modern artist."

"It hardly seems worth it. I mean, you'll have to sell an awful lot of his paintings to make back all this money on commissions."

"Not if the commission's fifty percent."

Sara gaped. "You don't really take fifty percent! I thought ten at the most."

"We'd starve. So would any gallery. Only one painter in ten

thousand is worth taking up, and of that handful, maybe two or three in a generation become big sellers. Who have they got now? Pollock, Rothko, Motherwell...and that's the lot. Augustus is lucky we don't take seventy-five; some galleries do."

"That's awful," Sara said. Sascha's matter-of-fact commercial view of the art business struck directly at her illusions about the heroes who sustained her through her adolescence.

"Not if you think about it. We keep these deadbeats alive for years on advances. We nurse them through divorces, breakdowns, drinking bouts. We earn it, believe me." His bored tone returned. Like most people in the art world, he found money a distasteful subject for discussion. "Do you like our Ted's work?"

"Augustus? Some of it, I suppose."

"Want to meet him?" He took an envelope out of his drawer. "He prefers his monthly money in cash, but I'd just as soon not enter that zoo he lives in. Why don't you take it down? I'm sure he'll appreciate your sympathy."

Sara took the envelope almost gratefully. Perhaps meeting a real artist would restore her illusions.

But Greenwich Village didn't help. It was too close to the memory of her father's downfall. The House of Hershman, which, since David Moore's foundation of Atropos, had degenerated into an outlet for bankrupt stock in the clothing and rug trade, still operated in the old building on 11th Street, its profits, filtered through Carl Bleigen's holding company, keeping her mother content in the New Jersey house, one of the few pieces of property wrested from the receivers after House of Hershman collapsed.

In the years since her last visit, lower Manhattan had changed radically, and the Village especially so. Families from across Broadway who used to regard it as their shopping and social center were driven from the streets by a new and puzzling breed of New Yorker. Young for the most part, they affected bizarre clothing, ranging from tattered ponchos to the ragged remains of blue serge suits, worn incongruously with T-shirts and sneakers. The beards she saw on every corner would have flattered a student of the Torah, but the new Villagers were not Hassidim—just products of an equally uncertain society.

The little neighborhood delicatessens she remembered were new, fancifully renamed meeting places for the new people. There was jazz in the air, and a new poetry, a ranting demagogic chant mad with suppressed fury. Street painters panhandled at corners; guitarists strummed inaccurately and sang wheedling, angry songs of frustration.

At first, skirting the central Village between Sixth and Seventh Avenues, Sara lost her way entirely. Then the maze of streets led her down toward the docks on the Hudson and she found 225 West Houston, a warehouse like most other buildings on the street. A roughly assembled directory announced that the E-Z Fit Shoe Co., Finberg Modes, and Pandemic Press shared space here; only a spidery arrow and the word "Augustus" pointing up the splintered wooden stairs showed the location of the painter's studio. She started to climb.

There was no bell on the blank wooden door five flights up. She knocked.

As the door opened, Sara felt a blush billow up from her stomach in a tide of heat. The tall bony man with the stringy beard and lank hair was quite naked.

"Yeah?"

"Uh...are you...um...?"

Sara had seen so few naked men in the flesh that his body held a grisly fascination. His genitals, so small, shriveled...and why was one lower than the other?

Tearing her eyes away, she thrust the envelope at him and turned to flee.

"Oh, right. Hey, listen, don't go! I've got to...like, sign."

Reluctantly, Sara stepped into the loft where Augustus lived—a space as vast as a car barn which the few pieces of furniture did nothing to soften. From the scores of paintings leaning against every wall, it was clear he had used the place as a studio for some time.

"Who is it, honey?" A girl pulled back the curtain from a corner used as a kitchen. She looked about Sara's age, but there was a baby on her hip, complacently sucking at a heavy breast.

"Hi." She had a companionable smile. Catching Sara's stare, she glanced at Augustus and sighed. "Ted...."

As if noticing for the first time that he was naked, Augustus put down the Atropos money and wandered off, returning, to Sara's relief, in a pair of jeans.

"Like some coffee?" the girl asked kindly.

"Yes, please." Anything to hang onto.

Augustus handed her the signed receipt. "Jenny getting you some coffee?"

"Yes, thanks." To make conversation, she said, "I bought

three of your paintings at Parke-Bernet today. For the firm."

"Oh? Right." He seemed little interested. Taking a flat tobacco tin from his back pocket, he expertly rolled a cigarette and lit it. The smoke, heavy and sweet, caught in Sara's throat.

"I like those," she said, pointing to the nearest paintings, poorly lit by the grimy skylights.

Augustus worked on the limits of the visible and familiar. Images of flags and signs, isolated words, and even photographs were all dissolved in fields of color. With her training of the last year, Sara had begun to understand what painters like Augustus were saying, and found in his best work the sunny optimism of Renoir, allied to a sense of approaching dissolution and decay.

One painting in particular held this vision better than most. Hardly larger than a TV screen, it crawled with disciplined movement. She leaned over it, holding her coffee at arm's length to avoid dripping on the paint.

"Macy's parade?"

For the first time, Augustus came out of his torpor. "Yeah. Sure. Some other things there, but . . . yeah, the parade." He handed her the half-finished cigarette. "Like a taste?"

Sara took it gingerly, puzzled, but recognizing a compliment. She had never smoked, except for one school experiment that left her tongue dry and a taste of burning leaves in her mouth that lingered for hours. This one, however, was sweet and soft. She felt a slight singing in her ears as she sucked smoke into her lungs.

For the next ten minutes, she wandered around the loft, unselfconsciously admiring the paintings, the baby lying in a patch of sun on the bed, the sparse furniture and bare wood that no longer looked threatening or strange. When Augustus rolled another of his cigarettes, the three of them shared it automatically. Sara found herself in a confiding mood.

"It's not fair," she said, waving at the paintings. "I just bought some of your pictures at Parke-Bernet for thousands of dollars to push up the price. But if the others sell, you get hardly any of it. Why do you let him do that to you?"

Augustus stared at her, then got off the bed and wandered away. She had the feeling something had offended him.

The girl, quietly playing with the baby, said, "It's not like that, you know."

"Not like what?"

She looked after the figure of Augustus, wandering, gaunt

and pale, in the shadows at the other end of the loft. "Ted wouldn't be alive but for David Moore. He's sick. He's been sick for almost all his life. A blood thing. He won't live for more than another five years or so." She said it without any sense of tragedy. It was a fact they had obviously learned to accept long ago. "David makes him take the money. He says it's for me and the baby."

She poked the child in the stomach. It gurgled happily. "I was there when they first met. Two years ago. Ted had a couple of drawings in a shop over in the Village. Just student things. David saw them and said he wanted to meet Ted. Ted didn't want to: galleries and all that. But they did meet, and . . . I don't know. Guess they understand one another. David used to come down here a lot to see us. He wanted to give Ted a lot of money, to buy some of the paintings outright, as an investment. Ted wouldn't let him. Just enough cash for me and the baby, he said, and when he's gone they all go to me and the worm here. In trust."

Sara frowned, trying to integrate what she had been told with her own vision of David Moore. It was harder and harder to bring the two images together. Sometimes they coincided; at other times, she seemed to see two men.

Awkwardly, she struggled off the bed. "I've really got to go," she said, wondering why her lips refused to form words properly. "It's been great."

Augustus wandered out of the shadows with a small painting. "Hey, you like this thing?" It was the picture of the parade. "Take it."

"I couldn't."

The girl nodded. "Sure, we'd like that. You've got nice eyes."

Sara felt an overwhelming urge to beam. The world had taken on a new sunniness. She was billowing with warmth, floating on a purple tide, with tiny pillows bound under her feet. Clutching the canvas to her chest, she pressed her face on impulse against Ted Augustus's bony ribs, hearing his heart beating nervously in there, like a bird in a cage.

"I love it," she murmured to his skin. "Love it, love it." Recoiling, she stared around, then oriented herself on the door. "Got to go. Thanks for the . . . the . . ." Thoughts wouldn't form. Halfway through a sentence, she no longer remembered having spoken the first words.

She fell rather than walked down the stairs, bouncing from

wall to wall. Even the cold air of the street did nothing to alleviate the sensation of a head filled with cotton wool.

Some time later, she found herself on a bench in a frozen park, squinting at a shadow across the sun. An arch. Washington Square. The painting lay on her lap and next to her a bum in an army-surplus overcoat bound at the waist with rope was nipping on a bottle wrapped in a paper bag.

Suddenly, the whole world was Sara's friend.

"Hey, you know, when I was just a kid, my daddy telephoned me?"

"Yeah?" The bum was used to nut cases.

"He said I was his best girl. Then he jumped out the window of his office." There were suddenly tears in her eyes, icy on her cheeks. She wiped them angrily away.

"Jumped out the winda?" This detail briefly intrigued her companion.

"Uh-huh. And right then I promised myself I'd get the man who made him do that."

Revenge and retribution were shopworn topics for the bum, who returned to his bottle. Sara stared across the square, where mothers pushed their baby carriages stolidly along frozen paths, administering sunlight and air like medicine to the muzzled offspring.

"I'm going to do it too. Somehow." But the words lacked conviction. When she first came to work for David Moore, these assertions had made her cheerful, providing comfort in the night, so that she drifted off to sleep cuddling her hate. Why was it harder now?

Cold began to seep in. Standing, she swayed for a moment on unsteady feet. Odd images festered in her muzzy head. Two kids ran by, feet pounding on the frozen ground, and she moved to follow them, breaking into a clumsy trot as she thought she heard behind her the answering thud of a heavier tread. The warriors were coming, thighs thick and terrible, their heavy legs weighed with greaves of brass. A delicious terror possessed Sara. She ran in exaltation, the wind burning along her nerves.

Two months later, as Sascha had predicted, all New York was talking about Ted Augustus. Sara was given her first creative work at Atropos when, with Sascha, she helped choose the sixteen paintings that would make up the new show of his work.

Waving around the crowded studio, she said, "Why only sixteen? We could fit in fifty."

Sascha looked pained. "And who would buy them? There's about fifty people who might take an Augustus at our prices. Hang fifty pictures and we might sell ten. Hang sixteen and we'll sell the lot—and have them clamoring for more."

Another illusion expired on the eve of the show opening, as Sara saw David Moore and Sascha in whispered consultation with a stout, dapper, bald, and somehow familiar little man as they browsed through the gallery. After a long colloquy before one of the best pictures in the show, a subtle autumnal abstract, Sascha stuck a tiny red disk on the frame, indicating that it was sold.

"Wasn't that Martin Grossman?" Sara asked them as he left.

"None other," Sascha said. "If he is to be believed, his column next week will hail Augustus as the new Rothko. Apparently his work embodies a new conception of topological space, whatever that is."

"And he bought a painting? I didn't think art critics had that kind of money."

David and Sascha exchanged an amused glance.

"Oh." Obviously Grossman didn't discover new concepts in the work of artists whose galleries did not offer a little souvenir.

For more than two years, Sara worked for David Moore. She moved away from New Jersey, rented an apartment—and watched. In the process, emotions she had sought to clarify merely became more confused.

Sometimes, his distance, his irritation at an error, his impatience with those who could not anticipate the twists of the art market with his instinctive skill brought back her earlier hatred.

But the next day he would come down from his apartment with a flower in his buttonhole, joking and flirting with Fran and Sara, and dislike became impossible.

On one such morning, in the spring, he took Sara, Sascha, and Fran to lunch at 21, where she stuffed herself on venison, squab, pears in red wine, and a succession of burgundies, liqueurs, and brandies that left her reeling. Their table became the object of visits from a score of celebrities. Sara emerged from her bemused state at one point to find herself clinging to the hand of a baffled Cary Grant and from there drifted into a reverie so profound she didn't wake from it until three hours later, to find herself in David's apartment.

She was never in any doubt as to where he had brought her; the bare, almost ascetic decor agreed precisely with her expectations of his home. The floor was polished planks, with a few heavy rugs scattered around. The gas fire threw a warm glow over the waxed wood.

"How are you feeling?"

In the shadow of the evening, she hardly saw him, sitting across the room. Had he been watching her sleep? Oddly, the idea didn't alarm her; it was as if she had slept protected, guarded by a friend.

She sat up with surprisingly little nausea. "Not bad, really. I guess the food soaks up the alcohol."

"I guess. Can I get you something?"

"A glass of water maybe."

The light went on in the kitchen, divided from the living room by a low counter. With its glinting range and ranked stainless steel implements, it had a look of quiet efficiency.

"You do your own cooking?"

"It's my hobby. You get sick of restaurants sometimes." He came back with a flask of mineral water and a glass. "Cheers."

"Oh, right. Cheers." She drank the glass dry in nervousness. Paradoxically, the water just brought back the symptoms of the afternoon. A growing warmth filled her stomach and seeped quickly into her arms and legs.

For the first time, she realized a record was playing softly from hidden speakers—modern jazz, a diaphanous web of piano, chiming vibraphone, and a hush of brushes on drums. Records covered one wall in neat lines, and books two more. Slipping off her shoes, she tucked her feet under her on the couch, feeling completely at home.

"How do you like the art business, now that you've had a year or two?"

"I'm not sure it's what I expected." The alcohol had made her confident. The words came easily, as if spoken by someone else—the secret sister who made all her important decisions. "All the money. I thought it would be art for art's sake and all that. But it really *is* a business, isn't it? We might as well be bankers. But I don't mind that so much any more. I want to learn about how it all works; how to make it work...."

Dizzy with a sudden whirling in her head, she leaned back. Moore disappeared.

"You're a long way away over there. Why don't you come over here?"

She stared at the gas fire, watching the blue flames float on their skirts of orange, until David's weight depressed the cushion beside her. As she leaned back, she saw, out of the corner of her eye, his head bend forward.

Her college lovemaking had prepared her for the physical reality of sex, but not for what followed. Champagne, excitement, the ambivalence of her feelings about David Moore combined in a heady swirl of emotion in which she felt helpless and yet, paradoxically, more in control of herself than ever before.

For the first time, she savored the pure physical intimacy of a kiss, the blur of lip and spit and tongue, a sensation as private and satisfying as relieving oneself. Never with Robert had she felt the combination of sacrifice and conquest within the act. Greedy for more, she put her free hand on David's shoulder, holding him there until, breathless, he was released.

"I seem to have struck a nerve," he said.

"I never kissed anyone before quite like that. It's nice. Are you going to take me to bed?"

He laughed for the first time in her hearing. It was dry but appealing.

"It had occurred to me. But wouldn't it be a shame to waste this fire? The couch is quite large enough."

"The bedroom would be better. It's darker. I know what I look like with no clothes on."

"I'm sure you're beautiful."

"Not really. But in the dark it doesn't matter. Is that the bedroom?"

Unsteadily, she marched through the door and pulled her dress over her head. By the time he came in, after switching off all the lights, leaving the other room bathed in firelight, she was naked and under the covers.

She closed her eyes as he moved around in the darkness, then turned her head away as he slipped in beside her, skin purring on the cool sheets. The scenario from now on was one with which she was familiar. If only she could carry it off with a semblance of adult skill, David Moore would be even more thoroughly within her power. Nervously she opened her thighs, her mind reaching for the images of rape and violence that always produced in her the proper physiological conditions for sex. Then, gently, his lips touched her ear.

She jumped, giggling at the sudden shiver of pleasure running across her scalp, down her arm.

"Don't you like that?"

"It tickles!"

"So I've heard. What about this?"

Delicately, his fingers probed through her hair, touching the nerves that ran down the nape of her neck. A delicious weakness swept over her, her eyelids drooping at the sensation in her shoulders, almost down to her breasts.

"Does that tickle too?"

"Uh . . . no, it . . ."

Now his fingers ran down her shoulders, arms, paused at her elbows, and delicately stroked the soft inside of the joint where the blood ran close to the skin. In the flood of new feelings, she barely felt the hand drifting softly over her stomach, brushing the hair between her thighs, not touching the flesh beneath but setting up a tickling zone of pleasure that cried out for more brutal satisfaction.

She seemed to be melting. And as the nervousness flowed away from her, a new intelligence took over, drawing on memories buried so deep she had never before known of their existence.

Her hands, suddenly deft and sure, teased and aroused him to straining firmness, then guided him between her thighs with easy movements.

Almost before her legs closed on his, the first orgasm surged through her, an uncontrollable rush of pleasure that shook her like a tiny animal in the jaws of a dog. Her head thrashed wildly on the pillow, her hands clawed his back, digging through muscle to the bones of the rib cage. He cringed and shrank inside her.

"I'm sorry!"

She was crying with hysterical excitement and remorse. "I didn't mean . . . oh, please, please. . . ." She stroked, caressed, petted him like a doll. There was no act she would have refused at that moment. "Do it again. I love it so much. Please." She had no shame, only a desire to be engulfed in pleasure, to give herself up to the night.

The next morning, David took her to meet Arthur Sklar. As they walked up Fifth Avenue, Sara watched her new lover covertly from the corner of her eye. A relationship that had seemed credible, even inevitable the previous night, was bizarre in the extreme by the light of a bright morning sun. Could it continue? What would the clients feel about such a liaison? (She imagined Fran Pellegrino's amused derision and shuddered inwardly.) The etiquette of casual fornication demanded a far more detached and distant treatment than David had offered this morning; expecting a quiet but firm ejection from the apartment, perhaps with an avuncular peck on the cheek and a light breakfast, Sara had been surprised and warmed by his affection, his apparent willingness to let their affair go beyond the expected one-night stand.

They had even made love again, languorously and with an intimate attention to detail, David pulling back the covers and lavishing the touch of his fingers and tongue on her eager body. Unself-conscious for the first time in her life, Sara responded with a lasciviousness that, even after the frenzy of last night, surprised her. There were in sex, as in art, some things one knew instinctively and that no teacher, whatever his skill, could inculcate.

And now, this visit to Sklar, whom even Sascha had never met. As they paused at a streetlight, Sara moved as close to David as she thought wise without telegraphing their new intimacy and asked herself why the whole adventure had an air of slightly threatening incongruity.

The house on 85th Street was identical with the dozen brownstones that flanked and faced it. David pulled the bell with authority.

"Don't be too surprised at Arthur. He's been ill for years—almost as long as I've known him."

A black servant opened the door. "Good morning, Mr. Moore." Sara, expecting a southern drawl, was surprised at his flat Boston twang, a cousin to David's transatlantic accent.

"Hello, Bernard. This is Miss Hershman, an associate of mine." He handed him his coat and Sara peeled off her own, wondering how he would view her slightly rumpled dress, a relic of yesterday's lunch.

"A pleasure, miss. Why don't you go right in, Mr. Moore. He's in the study. Not too cheerful this morning. I'll bring coffee in a little while."

Sara followed David across the intricately inlaid marble floor and stopped short at the door of the library.

She knew of Sklar's collection and, accustomed to Impressionists, thought herself beyond surprise at their vividness. But this room leaped with light. There were no pictures here, just windows that opened on a dozen landscapes: purple Provençal hillsides, cornfields in the Midi, the Brittany seacoast. For the first time, Sara felt the full impact of the Impressionist vision.

The little man in the wheelchair seemed to bask in their heat. What was once a solid and compact frame had collapsed like a mummy whose flesh had dried and desiccated to half its volume. The hands lying on the lap robe might have been wax, and she saw every ridge of bone where skin stretched tight across the knuckles.

"Arthur." Moore took the man's hand carefully, as if handling a delicate ivory.

"Hi, David." Sklar's voice was surprisingly energetic, the only remnant of a once-active man. "If you've come huckstering, forget it; the Dow-Jones is down five points. I'm a pauper."

"Then we're both in big trouble. That Xerox stock you made me buy hasn't moved in months."

"Don't worry about that. It'll make you rich one day." He looked at Sara with bright birdlike eyes.

"Oh, I'd like you to meet Sara Hershman. She's just joined the firm."

Sklar glanced at David in surprise, then turned his chair to look closely at Sara. "Yes, you're Nat Hershman's girl all right. I knew your daddy well. We did some business in the old days. I hear your grandfather's still alive."

"Yes. He lives with my mother over in Jersey."

"Give him my regards. He was an old bandit, Jake, but I guess that gave us something in common."

Bernard brought in a silver coffee service and laid it by the big bay window looking out over the sculpture garden.

"What do you think of my collection, Sara?" Sklar asked as she turned back to the room. "I should tell you right away that most of it came from your boss. And it's *his* idea to keep the best things locked away in a vault somewhere."

"I can't begin," Sara said helplessly, waving at the wall of Bonnards, the still-lifes of melons and oranges, the palm-enclosed villas and hills clothed in dusty wild thyme and mesquite. "They're the most beautiful things I've ever seen."

"Not as beautiful as the place itself. I'd trade all of them for just a year of that sun. Hell, a week! Ever been to the south of France? No?" He turned to David, who was stirring his coffee and watching both of them. "Dave, you're depriving this girl of her rightful artistic education!"

"I'm thinking of correcting that. Snow's are selling the Thornhill pictures. We could get the other Bonnard you want so much. Would you feel safe having her bid for it?"

"With a name like hers? Who better? But David, do you really think...?" Anxiety mixed with the pain in his face.

"You can afford one more. In a year's time I can sell it for five times what we pay. That goes for all your paintings. I've told you before."

"I trust you." He held up a waxy hand. "But this damn canker doesn't have much more of me to eat. After that, my family's in your hands."

"If you don't think I appreciate that responsibility, you don't know me very well." Sara could see the bond between the two men.

"Prices haven't been good," Sklar fretted. "That Dufy at Parke-Bernet last month—I suppose you heard."

"I know about the Dufy—also the two Picassos at Christie's and the Matisse in Washington. Trust me. In another twelve months, those prices will look like bargain basement throwouts. Your pictures will clear two million at least. Maybe three."

Sklar stared at him keenly. "You know something I don't?"

"The British are removing their currency restrictions."

"David!" Sklar's face glowed with a hint of the old vitality. For a moment, money made him young again. "If that's true—"

"It's true. Michael Gothard, my man in London, spent a lot of money to make sure."

"David, I thank you. My family thanks you. My *accountants* thank you. What can I do?"

Moore's face flickered with an emotion Sara could not grasp. "You did it already, Arthur. I'm just returning the favor."

For the first time since meeting him, Sara thought Sklar looked truly at a loss for words. "It didn't seem like a favor at the time, you know. The joke of it appealed to mē more than anything else."

"Well, it worked out better than either of us expected. I guess Carl keeps it interesting."

"How is that old crook anyway?"

David shrugged. "I see him about twice a year. But I guess

he's still scheming, waiting for me to blow it. In a strange way, he helps me. With a partner like that, you always have to stay one jump ahead." They shook hands again. "Arthur, I'll bet you your Bonnard. And don't worry about the money."

They walked back to the gallery, enjoying the crowds on Fifth Avenue brought out by the first touch of spring. The season's new clothes ran to pony tails and skirts with layers of petticoats frothing around the calves. Sara could admire the couples with less envy than a year before. Her weight was down by twenty pounds and with Fran's help she dressed more intelligently, exploiting her rich figure and often startling eyes.

"I didn't understand that business about the currency," she said as they paused for the traffic at an intersection.

"Since the war, the British government has frozen most of its financial traffic," David explained. "You couldn't take English money out of the country, and all the foreign currency, especially dollars, were kept by the government to pay for the imports they needed to keep going. Anyone selling a work of art in London could only be paid in pounds sterling, and he couldn't take that out of the country. Now that things are better, they're removing restrictions on dollars coming in and sterling going out."

The light changed and they crossed the road. Sara didn't need to hear any more. She could see the explosive effect this would have on the art market. European collectors and dealers could now send their pictures to English salerooms, confident that American dealers would arrive in droves, leaving behind large amounts of foreign currency which the sellers could take back with them to the Continent.

The market was bound to boom, especially in Impressionists, which in David Moore's view, now that most Old Masters were out of circulation in the big public collections, would be the next category of art to skyrocket in price. After that, contemporary art would have its turn, when all the good Impressionist paintings had been snapped up.

Sara was beginning to understand the way his mind worked. Moore traded on instinct, but it was the instinct of a seasoned hunter, built up by trial and error over a decade, the distillation of a thousand skirmishes.

"You really mean that about London?" They were at the gallery.

He turned to look at her, and for a moment she felt he was about to withdraw the offer. Then his face relaxed in the accustomed slight smile. "Of course, if you'd like to go."

"When?"

"In June. The sale's on the twentieth. You might go on to Italy and see Valerii afterward. Sascha will have plenty to do here, preparing the Sklar pictures. Arthur won't last more than another month or two at most."

He paused just inside the gallery door, watching Fran passing out catalogues and rare smiles to a couple she obviously decided were wealthy enough to be worth cultivating. "You know, Arthur gave me this business. Bankrolled me when I didn't have anything but a lucky break and a good idea. I owe him everything." His voice took on a special intensity. "Remember that, Sara, when you're inclined to make judgments."

22

Cursing under their breath, the three workmen strained on the rope as the black metal cabinet swayed precariously over their heads, climbing toward the two metal braces set high under the skylight of Snow's new showroom.

"Bit more," yelled the man clinging to the braces like a monkey. With a squeal from the block and tackle it rose another foot, and he hastily slipped bolts through the two holes and tightened them with a wrench. The electronic currency conversion board, the first in the world, hung there as if it had been in place for centuries.

"Looks safe enough," Mark Turnbull said.

"Safe as 'ouses, guv'nor," the foreman agreed confidently. "Do you want it 'ooked up now?"

Mark checked his watch: 3 P.M. Another five hours until the sale. "We'd better try it out again, just in case something got jolted loose. I'll be in my office."

But instead of returning to his office on the third floor, Mark went down the spiral staircase to the foyer of Snow's new rooms.

From the street, little seemed to have changed. The sandstone facade and the florentine metalwork over the windows had survived the bombing. But little else had remained to salvage.

Mark remembered coming here with his uncle for the first time. That was in 1946, the year he went up to Oxford. A policeman let them in through the wooden fence that

187

surrounded the gutted building. They walked across a narrow lobby floored with cracked and blackened marble. A light snow made everything smell of wet burned wood.

But it was a new Snow's now, rebuilt and improved with the healthy injection of Turnbull money made possible when Simon Snow's widow placed her seats on the company board in the hands of his uncle. A visitor from the old days would see little that he remembered except the Nash staircase—or at least its facsimile, refashioned from the original drawings. With it, Snow's acknowledged the importance of its traditions, but the rest of the building honored the present and the future.

At the bottom of the stairs, a new larger main foyer stretched right to the front door in a sea of moss green carpet, its color echoing the enameling that edged the oak wall panels.

Two large square counters dominated the foyer. Behind the smaller of them, two girls sold catalogues for sales to come and handed out free copies of the company's Monthly Review, a sumptuous brochure actually produced at little cost by printing a few thousand extra copies of the advertisements and schedule of sales prepared for trade magazines like *The Apollo* and *The Connoisseur*. Stapled inside a glossy color cover, it was one of the firm's most powerful weapons in the fight with Sotheby's, Christie's, and Carthew's for London saleroom supremacy; unfortunately, since it could be so easily copied, Snow's competitors were already producing their own versions.

The catalogues came in all sizes from the most common, a slim paper-covered pamphlet in the familiar "Snow green," by now a trademark, to hefty volumes with color plates which detailed an entire collection. Only the public and a few amateur collectors regularly bought their catalogues at the saleroom; serious buyers subscribed on an annual basis and received every catalogue in their chosen area by mail at a reduced price, a calculatedly subtle appeal to a buyer's greed being far more effective than blatant advertisement.

The other counter in Snow's foyer, a square island that accommodated eight people and a bank of telephones, was the company's front line, its public face. Half its business began here, with the young trainees who manned the desk from nine thirty in the morning to six at night. Mark, at his uncle's insistence, had spent his first six months in the firm at the desk, a galling sentence at the time but valuable in retrospect. On the counter, one learned the auction business the hard way, by bitter experience.

"I don't understand," the dowager whined. "You did *sell* the service, didn't you?"

"Yes, it did sell, madam," the girl said patiently, "but it may take a week for the dealer who bought it to pay us, and of course we can't pay you until then. Look, I'll ask Mr. Arbuthnot of the Silver Department to come down and explain this to you."

Elsewhere along the counter, young men and women picked up house phones to announce visitors, directed puzzled buyers to the galleries where next week's sales were on view, indicated the location of the paying desk, the restrooms, the catalogue shop, the restrooms, the delivery bay in the alley at the rear of the building, the restrooms. . . .

Slipping through the flip-up entrance to what they called the Foxhole, Mark buttonholed a harassed Charles Asprey-Norton, the Reception Manager.

"Who's come in for tonight?"

Asprey-Norton handed him a sheaf of cards. "Quite a crowd." Snow's first big sale of the season always drew a number of international buyers, most of whom routinely advised the company so that seats could be reserved. Those not known to the saleroom would also have sent banker's references or drafts to avoid delays in paying for and collecting what they bought.

"Does Jarvis know to reserve the chairs?" Mark asked.

Asprey-Norton looked at him bleakly over his glasses. "My dear chap."

"Sorry." After five years in the Foxhole, Charles ran it like a watch.

Mark's arrival inside the counter heralded a new assault from the public, always two deep even on average days. As one girl fell back to call upstairs, a middle-aged couple clutching a large parcel fixed him with an unavoidable stare. Reluctantly he stepped into the vacant spot.

"Can I help you?"

"We wondered if someone could look at this for us." The man started to pick at the knots.

"What is it exactly?" Mark asked quickly, before the desk became covered in brown paper. He peered at an exposed corner. "Porcelain? Well, if you'll come with me. . . ."

Slipping out of the counter, he steered them toward the six

numbered doors along the wall. Lights showed over 1, 2, and 4, indicating they were occupied. He ushered them into 5.

"Just unwrap the piece. There'll be someone here in a moment." He dialed the Porcelain Department as the couple looked nervously around the room. He could hardly blame them—the resemblance to a doctor's surgery was inescapable.

Unwrapping did nothing to enhance the object in the parcel. An extremely unattractive example of old china, about three feet high and studded with knobby extrusions, it was crudely painted with figures engaged in obscure rural activities. At the end of each extrusion was an eggcup-like hollow with a hole in the bottom.

"Ah," Mark said noncommittally. "Yes. Indeed."

Balfour of Porcelain hustled in, looking like a radiologist at the end of a long shift. Nodding to Mark, he turned his attention to the object on the table.

"Well, this is it, eh?" Turning it expertly, he looked at the marks on the base, the signature of any piece of china, ran his hands over the surface, and put it down. "Quite nice."

"A quite nice *what?*" Mark asked curiously.

Balfour looked surprised. "Oh, vàse, of course. Eighteenth century. English." Seeing some explanation was called for, he said, "Around that time, everyone had heard of Chinese porcelain but there wasn't much of it about. English potters produced their own copies from drawings and descriptions. This would have been for flowers." He poked a finger into one of the holes. "Tulips, most likely."

"Is it valuable?" the man asked anxiously.

"Oh, fairly. I'd suggest a reserve of, say"—he checked the marks again—"a thousand?"

"In other words, we wouldn't be able to sell it for less than that," Mark explained.

The man looked astonished. "Pounds?" he said uncertainly.

"You might get twelve hundred," Balfour said. "One of these went through Sotheby's last year for fifteen hundred, but it was in better condition. There's a lot of damage on the base."

"Couldn't you just give us the money?" the woman asked greedily.

Her husband nodded. "We'd take"—he calculated quickly— "eight hundred?"

"Can't be done, I'm afraid," Mark said, so used to this that the reply came automatically. "We're just a saleroom. We act as your agents to sell things. Ten percent of the price is deducted as our fee. By law, auctioneers can't buy for resale, but if you just wait a few months, I'm sure we can get a good price for this."

"A few *months?*"

Checking his notebook, Balfour said, "Best I could do is July twenty-third. We've got a major china sale then. There's nothing in it quite like this, so you should get some interest. Would you like an illustration in the catalogue?"

"Is that a good idea?"

"Well, yes, I think so, in this case. Of course you have to pay the cost of the photograph...."

Mark slipped out as Balfour led them through the intricacies of putting a piece up for sale.

In a few minutes, with the vase no longer carelessly wrapped in paper but carried in both arms like a baby, he would conduct them to the glassed-in booths where four typists worked all day, recording items brought or sent in for sale and typing details on the huge E7 forms.

He would explain in simple terms the conditions of sale, drawing their attention to the small print that absolved the company from blame for anything less than theft or willful destruction on the premises. Once signed, one copy of the E7 was given to the owners, a second went to the Porcelain section, a third accompanied the vase to the storage room at the back of the building, while another went to the office which now kept a file on everything sold by Snow's.

What Mark had just seen was, he knew, incredibly rare.

Art objects are fragile. Only a fraction of them survive the destruction of war, earthquake, fire, and simple accident. Those that do are usually well known to collectors and experts, illustrated in reference books, recorded in sale catalogues, and, if paintings or important drawings, stamped with the emblems of the collections through which they have passed. For this reason, auction rooms do business almost entirely with people "on the inside"—dealers, serious collectors and experts. For a member of the public to bring in an unknown piece of any value was exceptional.

With the cards for tonight's sale in his hand, Mark went back up to the main saleroom. The conversion board was flashing satisfactorily, reeling off multiples of a thousand pounds which he hoped augured well for the evening. Elsewhere, in a side room, technicians set up the closed-circuit TV that would relay the sale to overflow audiences; banks of telephones waited for the bids expected from overseas. At the height of the sale, half a dozen clerks could be hanging on those phones, shouting bids against those made by people actually present at the auction. He found himself looking forward to tonight with an almost sexual excitement.

As he came back into his office, the phone was ringing. He picked it up. "Is that contraption of yours up yet?" his uncle barked; anything new was always Mark's.

"They're trying it out now. Looks very good." Riffling through the cards, he said, "Does the name 'Hershman' mean anything to you?"

"Why?"

"A Sara Hershman's reserved a seat for tonight. From New York. Brought quite a bit of money with her, apparently."

"That's interesting." He didn't elaborate. "Cicely's coming with you tonight, I take it?"

Mark frowned. He'd forgotten. "Yes."

"Good. She might be on time for a change. See you at seven then."

After Oliver hung up, Mark glanced at the picture over his desk. Few good likenesses existed of Simon Snow, but this speedily executed head and shoulders by Graham Sutherland, whom Snow had championed before the war, was the best of them. Mark kept it there, pointedly, to the specific displeasure of his uncle and Cicely.

Looking up now at the round, faintly anxious face, almost cherubic in some lights, the fine hair, inclined to balding, the pinched nose, a reminder of the asthma that plagued him all his life, he wondered again about the truth of those stories—that Snow, protected by the heavy concrete of the vaults, could easily have escaped from the collapsing building had he wanted to. It did not surprise him that Cicely had driven one man to his death; she was capable of far worse.

It was almost 5 P.M. Not much time to get to Highgate and back, allowing for Cicely's notorious slowness at dressing. Reluctantly he put the cards aside. She hated people to be late.

Simon Snow would not have recognized the Highgate house, now that Cicely had divided it into apartments, keeping only the top floor with its spectacular views of London for herself. Thumbing the button on the Entryphone, Mark noticed a new name beside the bell for Flat 1—presumably another wealthy American lured in by Cicely's undoubted charm as a saleswoman.

"Yes?" The phone did nothing for her already abrasive voice. "Mark."

A buzzer opened the door and he went up the now familiar stairs with their framed lithographs—Ben Shahn, Henry Moore, even a small Matisse, all technically the property of a Snow's client who went bankrupt before collecting his purchases. Until the receivers resolved the financial tangle of his affairs, they should have reposed in the NSV—No Salable Value—room at the saleroom, but Cicely, like most saleroom executives in the big firms, regularly looted this accumulation of clever fakes, forgotten commissions, and rejected purchases to furnish her own home.

At the door of her flat, Cicely laid cool lips on his cheek with a rustle of silk from her gray dressing gown.

"Make some drinks, there's a dear. I'm just putting on my face."

Obediently pouring her favorite gin and tonic and a small malt whisky for himself, Mark carried them into the bedroom. If Cicely noticed the glass beside her, she made no sign, too absorbed in her appearance to see anything beyond the mirror.

No longer preoccupied with the problems of tonight's sale, Mark found time to look objectively at his mistress.

He saw a small, neat woman of forty, fighting a shrewd but expensive rear-guard action against middle age. Anyone poorer or less jealous of her looks would have surrendered long ago, but Cicely attacked every wrinkle and incipient gray hair as if time had directed its barbs exclusively at her.

As a result, she looked twenty on her good days, thirty-five on the worst. Superbly casual French clothes disguised the slight thickness of waist and thigh, and careful tinting the few flecks of gray in her fox-red hair. It would be twenty years before Cicely looked her age, and Mark could already anticipate the gold chokers and roll-necked sweaters of future seasons that would disguise the crepe skin of her neck, the birdlike thinness of her wrists. In hiding her age she merely made it, to Mark at least, more apparent.

She caught him studying her, and her reflected eyes met his. "Penny for them?"

"Oh, just the sale." On a hunch, he asked her the same

question he'd asked his uncle. "Does the name Hershman mean anything to you?"

She put down her eyeliner brush. "Why?"

"Oh, a Sara Hershman's coming tonight. Oliver didn't seem to know the name."

"The old liar. He knows it well enough. Simon used to say they were the only people who saw which way the business was going."

"What happened to them?"

"They were wiped out by none other than our own David Moore. Something about a forged painting. Years ago, of course, before the war. That vulgar Carl Bleigen took over."

"Would this Hershman woman work for Bleigen?" If so, it would be as well to double-check the bank draft. Bleigen's Fine Art Holdings had none too savory a reputation.

"It's more likely she works for Moore, if she's buying paintings. Bleigen's just the money man these days."

Realizing this was the first time Cicely had spoken of David Moore in his presence, Mark wondered how far to press the advantage. She must be feeling mellow indeed to speak of him so calmly; Oliver enjoyed describing the tirades that used to greet any mention of him. But she forestalled him by pushing aside her cosmetics and peering carefully at her completed makeup.

"What time is it, dear?"

"Quarter to six." Knowing what was coming, he downed the rest of his whisky, feeling the familiar sense of expectation, excitement, self-contempt.

"Then we needn't hurry, need we?"

The rest was a ritual between them. Obediently, Mark adjusted the venetian blinds to fill the room with soft evening light. The robe slipped from Cicely's shoulders, revealing small breasts, still firm, but she remained seated at the dressing table while Mark undressed, hung his clothes on the back of a chair, and lay in the center of the wide bed. Closing his eyes, he felt the familiar arousal, a function of the quiet warm room, the unseen but vividly sensed presence of the woman just a few feet away.

He could hear the crackle of her robe as she stepped out of it, the lightness of her footfall. Half opening his eyes, he saw her standing over him, wearing only a tiny pair of briefs.

"Hmmm. Very inviting," she said.

"Come down here." His voice was thick, despite himself.

"I'll ruin my face."

"No, you won't."

"*And* my hair," she went on, ignoring him. "No, I'll let you enjoy yourself now. It'll be my turn after the party."

Kneeling by the edge of the bed, she ran her fingers across his stomach, pausing just above the hairline. Her nails teased at his skin, threatening always to move just a few inches lower. . . .

"Go on." She was whispering now. "And tell me who you're thinking about."

23

In front of the hotel mirror, Sara admired herself, though even as she arranged the long skirts of the evening dress she knew it was neither she nor the dress that deserved admiration but the stout lady in the Oxford Street store who looked her over critically in the fitting room and said kindly, "Well, we *do* have a little problem, don't we, dear?"

Two hours of fitting and three hundred dollars had done a lot to ease "their" problem. As a first step, the lady ushered Sara to the foundation garment department where she wriggled into something called a "Torsolette," a tube of rubberized fabric that encased her from just below the breasts to halfway down the thighs, compressing her body into an approximation of the fashionable figure.

After that, the day improved. No longer restricted to outsizes, Sara could choose among the summer gowns that hung, rack on rack, like drooping butterflies. The green Empire line dress she finally chose flattered her outrageously, exposing her perfect breasts with a scooped neckline but disguising the rest in a cascade of skirts.

Delighted with the effect and urged by the shop assistant, whom she now regarded as a lifelong friend, Sara splurged thirty dollars more on a new hairdo that piled her black curls on top of her head in Napoleonic style and twenty more on a consultation with the store's beautician, a young woman of lacquered perfection who turned Sara to putty in her exquisitely manicured hands.

Absorbed in her reflection, Sara jumped as the phone rang. Her cab had arrived. After one last long look, she snatched up bag and wrap, fearful that the effect would fade before it could be admired.

Skirts rustling with every movement in the dry cool cabin of the taxi, she watched London drift by. Berkeley Square, with lovers strolling under the trees; a flower shop, its window streaming with water to make a rippling mystery of the roses grouped behind; men in evening dress helping beautiful women onto the curb. She was astonished when her cab pulled in by them and a doorman opened the door. Terrified, she gathered up her skirts and slipped out.

Three hours later she was giggling uncontrollably, champagne spilling from her glass to run in a trickling trickle down her forearm.

"Now come on," her companion said earnestly. "Do confess. You *are* an international swindler and art thief, aren't you?" The man, who resembled a large wading bird right down to gleaming spectacles, dropped his chin to look over them at her. "I do urge you to make a clean breast of it. It will go better with you when sentence is passed."

"No. Really," Sara said helplessly. "I'm not. I swear. If I was an international swindler and art thief, would I be out here, with all these people, where I can be seen?"

"My dear, the place is *teeming* with your confederates. It's a kind of convention." He buttonholed a passing waiter. "This chap, for instance. To you, a humble waiter. Yet in fact he is Arnold 'Basher' Pertwee, infamous second-story man, famed for his larceny of countless Landseer animal studies. It was he who whisked *Dignity and Impudence* from under the very noses of the Chelsea Dogs' Home Board of Trustees and purloined *Monarch of the Glen* from its proud place over the mantelpiece of well-known collector and international garter magnate Cyrus Elastic."

"Sir?" the waiter said wearily, beyond amusement.

"Not to worry, Basher. Your secret is safe with me. Just give me a couple of those"—adroitly he removed two glasses of champagne from the tray—"and you may make good your escape."

Struggling to keep her breath, Sara looked around the room and caught the eye of a young man watching her—a tall, dark

young man, perhaps in his early thirties, with thick black hair
and eyes which even across the room advertised their piercing
blueness. The phrase "Black Irish" fell into her mind, but he
might as easily be Spanish, Greek, or a quarter-breed American
Indian. There was something calculating in his look, as if he was
watching her, summing her up. On impulse, she grinned broadly
in his direction, then turned back to her friend with the fantastic
stories. But, lost without an audience, he had already adopted a
new group.

"Happy with your Bonnard?" She turned to find the dark
man behind her.

Flustered, she said, "Oh, yes. But it isn't mine."

"Well, I hope Mr. Moore is happy then. I'm Mark Turnbull.
For want of a better description, they call me the Deputy
Director."

"Oh." She fought down the impulse to say, Nice place you've
got here.

"We should talk about how you want the picture shipped.
Are you free tomorrow afternoon?"

"Yes." *Not so eager, dummy!* "Yes, I think so."

"Then let's have lunch. You're at the Connaught, aren't you.
Say twelve then?" He glanced over his shoulder and his smile
switched from affable to tightly professional. "Someone seems
to need me. See you tomorrow."

He wove through the crowded reception toward a group
dominated by a small woman with red hair in a brown velvet
dress. This was presumably the lady Sascha referred to so acidly
as "the redoubtable Cicely." She looked harmless enough,
leaning on the arm of a young man while three others
entertained her, but as Mark joined them her face briefly became
hard and she snapped something at him that the roar of
conversation drowned out.

The incident had not gone unnoticed by the group behind
her. "Ah, his master's voice," someone said mockingly.

Her entertainer of a few moments before sniggered. "No,
dear boy, his *mistress*'s voice, surely." And they leaned weakly
on one another, helpless with laughter.

So that was the situation; Sara found herself obscurely
depressed, though Mark Turnbull had made no particular
impression on her for good or ill. At the moment, her personal
emotional life extended only as far as David Moore.

The large clock over the saleroom door read a few minutes

after eleven. Five o'clock in New York. David never left the gallery before eight. Suddenly, Sara felt an urge to talk to him, to describe the day, the clothes, the sale, her lunch to come with Mark Turnbull. Now might even be the right time to confess the ambitions she had harbored all this time, the hatred that began to ebb even before the night in his apartment and now seemed only a distant memory.

Hurrying down the stairs, she felt like Cinderella fleeing from the ball.

The cameraman met her just as she reached the foot of the staircase. "Miss Hershman?" He was already pushing a bulb into the reflector on his flash, backing off, framing a shot.

"Yes, but what—" The blaze of the flash almost blinded her. Blobs of yellow light blotted out the man's face as she tried to focus on him.

"Thanks, Miss Hershman. Much obliged." By the time she reached the sidewalk, he was gone.

Puzzled, she took a cab back to the hotel.

Half an hour later, the switchboard connected her with New York.

"Mr. Moore? Uh, David? It's Sara."

There was a long pause. She wondered if they had put her onto an empty office.

"Hello, Sara," David said finally. His voice sounded impersonal.

"Hey, I got the Bonnard for you!"

"How high did it go?"

"Eighteen thousand. Way under the estimate."

The hoped-for praise didn't come. "Who else bid?"

"Oh, Agnew's, I think. But they weren't really trying."

"Did the two Cézannes go?"

"Yes." She rummaged in her purse for her notes and reviewed the bidding. The champagne seemed to be turning to vinegar in her stomach.

He made no comment on her summary. "Anyone interesting there?"

"No. Oh, well, a few people. That film star. The skinny one—Suzy Parker?" Angrily searching for barbs, she went on, "Mrs. Snow was there. I didn't talk to her, but she looked beautiful." Still no response. "Mark Turnbull is taking me to lunch tomorrow." The invitation was a talisman against his indifference.

"See if you can get him to tell you something about the rest of the Thornhill pictures. We might want to bid. And don't forget to see Gothard about paying for the Bonnard from our London funds. That's very important. Look, Sara, these calls cost money. Write before you go to Italy. 'Night now." The click in her ear was firm and final.

Hardly believing his peremptory dismissal, Sara sat with the phone to her ear until the operator asked if she had finished the call. The ebbing of her high spirits was almost physical, like the onset of freezing. Her body felt welded into her underclothes; the makeup clung greasily to her face.

Crawling onto the bed, she fell asleep in her underwear.

"Your tastes must be changing, Mark," Cicely Snow said tonelessly. The traffic light turned red as she raced through the intersection, and he glimpsed a strolling policeman look around as the tires squealed in protest. "I thought you liked them slimmer."

"Good grief, Cicely, I only talked to the girl." It was obviously inappropriate to mention tomorrow's lunch.

The next light she ignored was plainly red. Thank God the streets were almost deserted at this hour of the night. But it had obviously been a mistake to leave his car at her house and let himself be driven in the Corniche.

"I'm surprised you could think of anything to say with those vast bosoms staring at you." Hooking one hand in the front of her dress, she yanked, ripping it almost to the navel. Her exposed breasts looked white and bloodless in the pallid street lighting. "Don't you care for small tits any more? You know what they say—anything over a mouthful is wasted."

She giggled, a mindless and eerie sound that made his skin prickle. It was more than an argument now. He knew the signs of approaching hysteria.

"Perhaps we should stop and talk."

They were rocketing through some suburban avenue, trees flashing by, the road wet and glistening.

"Why? We can talk perfectly well like this."

"I think there's something wrong with the back tire."

"Nonsense."

"No. Can't you feel that drifting?"

From past experience, he knew that, of the few things that mattered to Cicely, this car was almost paramount. Grudgingly, she slowed down and pulled over to the curb.

With a slight weakness in his knees, Mark got out and peered at the rear of the car. After a minute, hoping Cicely had calmed down, he returned to the open window.

"No, it's all right—" He began, then jumped back as Cicely gunned the heavy car and roared up the long street. He watched until the taillights disappeared and it became obvious she was not coming back for him.

Two possibilities existed. He could wait half an hour, find a phone and call, begging forgiveness, pledging eternal devotion, and ask her to return for him. It wouldn't take long; right now, she was probably rehearsing the insults he would have to swallow before she agreed.

Or he could walk back toward the nearest main street in search of a cab.

The rain had begun again, a thin soaking drizzle that made him shiver as it went through his hair like cold, crawling insects. After a single wistful glance at the trees under which he might shelter until he made his call, he trotted back the way they had come, alert for the pumpkin light of a cruising cab.

It was almost an hour before one appeared, and he arrived home soaked to spend a restless, dream-filled night.

The next morning was no better when he opened the morning paper to see Sara Hershman's startled face staring out at him.

"There's a Mr. Turnbull to see you, Miss Hershman."

"Yes, ask him to wait, will you?"

Dropping the phone, Sara returned to the bathroom. Her reflection this morning mocked the perfection of last night. Face puffy and smeared with old makeup, intricate hairstyle crushed flat on one side, her mouth stale, her head aching, she barely recognized the apparition that confronted her when she woke at eleven after a sleep that only began at dawn.

Dragging on a shower cap, she let the water drum the tension from her neck and, as the headache faded, wriggled into her torsolette and a dress chosen almost at random. Her new compressed figure did wonders for a shift that had always looked like a tent, and courageously she cinched it with a belt, astonished to see a waist emerge. Nothing could be done for the hair; wrapping it with a scarf, she hurried downstairs.

Mark looked up from the paper and uncurled from the chair. She glimpsed the front page; under the picture of a girl in a swimsuit it announced BIG COMPETITION INSIDE, as if she were the prize.

"You look marvelous," he said diplomatically.

"Thanks. I feel awful. Champagne."

He handed her the paper. "You're in the news. Page five."

Sara turned to the page, blinked at the small picture of herself, wide-eyed, round-faced, the shot cropped to emphasize her cleavage, then with churning stomach read the story under the headlines ECHOES OF ART SUICIDE. It recapitulated all the details of her father's death.

"But how could they have got hold of all this?"

Mark shrugged, embarrassed. "Most of it is news to me. Perhaps someone just connected the names and did some research."

She knew he believed that even less than she did. The photographer last night had been waiting for her. She could feel the dammed-up weight of guilt and anger straining against the wall she had built against it. Her lip trembled, a prelude to tears.

"We'd better get going," he said, steering her to the door. "I expect you're hungry." At the thought of food, Sara nearly retched.

She hardly noticed the high spots of his quick guided tour—the Houses of Parliament, Buckingham Palace, the National Gallery. Victorian frontage succeeded Victorian frontage. Realizing that his diversions were a failure, Mark turned the car south of the Thames, threading through what had been London's dockland before war and decentralization left the warehouses derelict and the old houses fodder for urban renewal. In a landscape of old bombsites, softened by grass, they stopped at a tiny Elizabethan pub becalmed like a beached houseboat amid leveled acres rioting with wildflowers and weeds.

Beyond leaded glass windows, barges labored up the mud-colored river, supervised by shrieking gulls. Mark ordered two pints of beer as they waited for lunch. Sara sipped the bland warm brew, hardly tasting it.

"I'm afraid the service isn't much," he said. "Nothing happens quickly here."

She made an effort to be convivial. After all, the newspaper report said nothing that most people didn't know or couldn't discover with a little digging. Why fear the past? It was gone with its dead, wiped out like the buildings that once surrounded this tiny place.

"Not like New York," she said, glancing at the deserted acres around them. "In the States, they'd have cleared these ages ago and put up apartments." She felt nostalgic for her apartment, for the Italian restaurant opposite, the sculpture garden at the Museum of Modern Art where she took her lunch on sunny days.

Watching her abstracted face, Mark said, "Perhaps this trip wasn't a very good idea."

"Oh, no. Really. I was just thinking of another girl who works in the gallery." She explained about Fran: her strange obsession with filing her nails, and her relationship with Humboldt, the accountant, an affair consummated—she guessed, though there was never any evidence of it—in long silent evenings they shared locked in Fran's bedroom.

"I can't imagine what they get up to," Sara said musingly. "He goes in impeccably dressed, complete with attaché case, and comes out the same way, without a hair out of place."

"They probably trim each other's toenails," Mark suggested, and Sara smiled for the first time that day.

"You make Atropos seem a lot of fun," he went on.

"It is. David—uh, Mr. Moore—is a good man to work for. His instinct is incredible." She drank more of her beer. Perhaps it was only the body's need for an alcoholic hair of the dog that bit her last night, but she felt better already. Unsteadily, she put her elbows down hard on the edge of the table.

Too hard. The people who used the tomato ketchup bottle before them had left the cap resting lightly on top, and as her gesture shook the table, it toppled, the contents spilling out across the table and into her lap.

Staring at the oozing stain, Sara quailed from an avalanche of images as the frail barriers against the past strained and collapsed. The red pool...a body on the sidewalk, draped in canvas, blood spreading on the dusty concrete.... "You still my best girl, Sara?"

"Don't bother," Sara said harshly as the waiter hurried over with a wet cloth, but Mark took it and tried to sponge the worst of the stain from her dress.

"I said, 'Don't bother'!" At her angry order, he returned to his seat, watching her narrowly across the table. "Let me finish what I was saying about David Moore and his instinct for the market." Briefly, as if giving evidence in court, she sketched out the Sklar deal and his plans to exploit the new British financial situation with a mass assault on the London market, flooding it with his stock of Impressionist pictures.

Mark tried to calm the hysteria from her voice, but she ignored him. At the end of her recital, she left the table and stumbled out past the curious customers into the street. When Mark had hurriedly paid the bill and left the restaurant, there was no sign of her.

After hours of turning it over in his mind, Mark, later that afternoon, passed on to his uncle what Sara had told him.

"That's awfully interesting, my boy," Turnbull said thoughtfully. "You're sure this is authentic? Moore has a reputation for duplicity."

"You saw the papers. She has no reason to love Moore. I gather this has been on her mind for some time."

"I'll check it with some friends in the Treasury. Dashed unsporting of them not to let me know first, I must say."

"If it's true, how will we handle it?"

Turnbull glanced at Piper, still head of Old Masters, though stooped and gaunt from long service to the paintings he revered. "Norman?"

"Only one thing for it, I should think. Get together a big sale and hold it as soon as possible after the announcement."

Mark frowned. "Won't that rather cut the ground from under Moore?"

"Very likely." Piper was unperturbed, even gleeful. "The market can only absorb a small number of modern pictures at any one time."

"You aren't feeling qualms about the egregious Mr. Moore, are you, Mark?"

"I suppose not." He got up. "I've a few calls to make."

He rang the Connaught but Sara was not answering the phone. When he rang the next morning, she had checked out.

24

On the deck of the Channel steamer, Sara nursed her misery like a fretful baby.

England had chosen this week to produce one of its famous summers, the inspiration of Constable and Keats, the joy of Shakespeare. But Constable, Keats, and Shakespeare never experienced 88-degree heat on a jammed boat traveling lethargically between Dover and Calais with a cargo of holidaymakers.

With her plane bookings to Italy still three days in the future, Sara had no alternative but to take the first available means of leaving London, though the hotel's travel adviser made no bones about his distaste for ferries and trains. She stared him down and bought the tickets. Anything to get away from England.

From a yacht, with a drink in one's hand, the placid green Channel might have been idyllic, but the steamer, overflowing with sweating tourists, chugged along in a cloud of its own stink, a queasy combination of oil, sweat, suntan lotion, busy lavatories, and sausage rolls. Sara endured it belowdecks for an hour, then hauled her luggage on deck and squeezed into a seat as close as possible to the rail. Despite squealing children and aggressive newcomers, she refused to give up an inch of it.

At Calais, the stampede of passengers for the trains left her far behind, struggling with her bags and searching desperately for a porter. The few she found glared indifferently as she tried to communicate in signs and her few words of French. She finally found her compartment, only to discover her seat occupied, like all the rest, by boys in shorts and heavy boots, their rucksack's overflowing from the rack above.

"That's my seat!" she said angrily, waving her reservation slip. They ignored her, grinning insolently into her flushed face. One said something in German and the others laughed.

Latecomers clogged the corridors, phlegmatically perching on their luggage. The only available space was at the very end of the car, between the door and the lavatory. Throwing down her cases, Sara slumped on top of them and cried with impotent fury as the train shuddered into motion.

The journey was hell. A dozen times each hour, she hauled herself upright to let people through one of the two doors, interruptions she came almost to welcome as a means of stretching her aching legs. The rubber corset tightened minute by minute like an instrument of torture, but there was no room to remove it. A man came along the train selling sandwiches from a wooden tray. She bought a couple and choked them down, though the dry bread and rubbery cheese stuck in her chest.

Europe became a series of grim vistas glimpsed through dirty windows: industrial suburbs seen through a pall of factory smoke; flat swampy fields with ponds that glistened with a coating of oil. Only when an occasional castle appeared on the high ground above the towns did she realize they had passed into Germany, a judgment confirmed when the man with the tray returned, this time offering fat red sausages. Ravenous—it was nearly eight o'clock, though still light outside—Sara ate four, washing them down with tasteless brown fluid, probably coffee but perhaps tea or even soup.

Two of the Germans left her compartment at Strasbourg and she squeezed in, defiantly occupying the one seat they grudgingly made available to her—the drafty one, nearest the door.

She was glad of this when, waking in the night she felt ill and barely made it to the toilet before emptying her stomach in a series of retching convulsions. The water with which she washed out her mouth tasted brackish, like blood. It was as if something inside her had given way.

Lurching drunkenly, the train danced through the night. She was helpless, a microbe in its gut, pushed along by its muscular contractions. Half falling into the corridor, she stared through the window at an impossible vista of mountain peaks, jagged against a sky of midnight blue. Everywhere, hills fell away from the train in rolling meadows spotted with black groves of pine trees. Glinting like steel, a river wound through the valley, miles below.

Empty and dizzy, she fell into her seat and slept, her mouth open, snoring quietly.

Except for the debris of their occupancy—orange peels, tattered German newspapers, cigarette butts—the hikers had disappeared when she woke. When the window in the compartment refused to open, she hauled up the one in the corridor and let the soft dusty air of Italy pour in.

She loved the place at first sight. Sheets spread out to dry on trees beside the line fluttered like the wings of white birds; olive trees twisted their limbs in exquisite parody of the Crucifixion; a ruined church against the skyline was pure Piranesi. This country created art as a matter of course, like eating or excreting. Leaning on the dusty window ledge, she drank it in.

The respite was brief. At Perugia, where she had to change trains, there were even larger crowds than at Calais and fewer porters. She finally caught the local train to Castel d'Oco with only a minute to spare, to find the insolent Germans replaced by jolly but equally well established Italians who, however, cheerfully made room. She could only endure ten minutes before retreating as the lady in the corner produced a large salami which wept oil and pungently exuded garlic. For the rest of the trip, she sat miserably in the toilet, periodically heaving on an empty stomach.

At two in the afternoon, she found herself alone on the red dirt platform at Castel d'Oco station, the sun starting prickles of sweat all over her body. Abandoning her bags, she explored the cool darkness of the only visible building, a large waiting room with a ticket office, its wicket tight shut.

"Is anyone here?"

The man who wandered out of the shed halfway down the platform was stooped and battered by the years like an old pot pounded flat for scrap. He took her ticket without comment and turned to go.

"Can you help me? Do you speak English?"

He looked blank.

"Signor Valerii? Villa . . . uh, Villa Zurlini? Antonio Valerii?"

"*Ah. Il Professore!*" His face lit up, lips peeling back from toothless gums. She tried to stem the flow of incomprehensible Italian, then grabbed him by the arm and led him through the waiting room to the road outside. It was as empty as the station itself. She looked down the hill, to where a small town huddled.

"Villa Zurlini?"

"*No, no.*" Shaking his head vehemently, he pointed across the valley toward a fleck of white halfway up a hill capped with cypresses like a line of black brush strokes. "*Ecco.*"

"Taxi?" she asked hopefully. It looked like miles.

"No taxi. *Non fumare.*"

"Telephone?"

He shrugged, gesturing down the road, the game obviously losing its novelty. Glimpsing her bags baking in the sun, Sara peeled off a few thousand lire, thrust them in his hand, and pointed to the luggage. Resignedly, he picked up the bags and tottered toward his hut. Sara had ceased to care what became of them.

The sky had no color. It was just an absence of coolness, an excess of light. Within a few yards she was sweating all over, and at the bottom of the hill her clothes were stuck to her and the rubber Torsolette squirmed on her hips and thighs. As the street narrowed between high brown houses, all seemingly without windows, she zigzagged from shade to shade, the sun her pursuer.

Nobody stirred on the streets. The town was empty, its fountain dry, grit and yellowing scraps of paper heaped in the basin. A dog slunk by, drifting from shadow to shadow, watching her narrowly.

A scatter of rusted tin signs for beer and cigarettes announced a café, but its wooden door was locked. Rattling and shouting brought nobody.

Feeling ill again, Sara oriented herself on the far hillside and took a road almost identical to that from the station, winding again between the same indifferent frontages until the town thinned again into vineyards. She toiled up the dusty road, oblivious of blistered feet and the rolling nausea inside.

After what seemed hours, someone else came down the road—a large man, wearing an apron and carrying the flat leather holder she had only seen in old paintings, the traditional bag used by carpenters and masons since biblical times to hold their tools. Stopping a few yards away, he watched her, not unkindly, but with the indifference she expected of a donkey or a bull.

"Villa Zurlini?" her voice was almost a croak.

Now that she had stopped walking, the last energy drained from her legs. She knelt hard on the road, stones jabbing into her knees. As she fell, she heard the pounding of his feet, the heavy positive tread of the warrior, and waited to be carried off.

Despite his size, Cristaldo had the peasant's natural gentleness with sick things. He laid Sara on the bed as carefully as if she were a newborn lamb.

"I don't understand," Valerii said impatiently, tossing the papers from Sara's handbag onto the bureau. "She is this helper of David Moore whom he asked me to mind for the summer. What is she doing here, three days early?" A gesture of irritation took in her fluttering eyelids, flushed face, and sweat-soaked and dirty clothing. "And like this, so . . . so . . ."

"Ugly?" Paola Farnese said. "*Everything* can't be beautiful, *cara mia.*" Briskly winding the handle that drew wooden shutters over the windows, she waved Cristaldo out of the doorway.

"Go on, Cristaldo. You've done very well, but I can take care of her now."

"She will die?" His voice had the rasp of the stone dust that covered his face and sprinkled gray in his hair.

"Certainly not. You do not kill women so easily. Now off you go."

Bowing slightly, a lingering vestige of the formal manners taught him by his mother, a tiny birdlike woman of indomitable will who had set her heart on his entering the church, he crept away. The ghost of that gentility never failed to amuse Paola, like the thought of his enormous frame crammed into a soutane and celluloid collar.

Valerii paced the room restlessly. "I don't understand."

"Tonino, enough! Everyone changes their plans, and you know what Americans are like. Now, she must have come by train, so please send Carlo to the station for her luggage. And ask Maria to bring hot water and towels. Go, go!"

Rolling up her sleeves, Paola undressed Sara—no easy task. Peeling off the sweat-soaked dress, she caught sight of the rubber undergarment and raised her eyebrows. Did people really wear such things? Hooking her fingers under the top edge, she peeled it down, grimacing with effort.

Maria came in just as she rolled it off her legs. "*Madonna mia.*" For a moment she thought the maid would cross herself.

With a wet towel, Paola sponged gently at the flushed face, smoothing the tendrils of wet hair back from Sara's forehead, cooling those points on the chin, wrists, and behind the ears where the blood runs closest to the surface. When she turned to wet the towel again, Maria had, discreet as always, left her alone.

Five minutes later, Valerii strode in, head held high in best tragic style. At such times he bore an uncanny resemblance to a twenties matinee idol, a comparison she never dared mention to him. The closer he came to seventy, the more sensitive Tonino was to any reference to people no longer living.

"The luggage is on its way. Do you think we should cable David?"

"Wait until tomorrow."

"Yes, I suppose you are right." For the first time, he saw that Sara was naked. "Oh, la!"

"Not to your taste at all, I'm afraid."

Critically, he examined the sleeping girl. "These Americans—how can they do it to themselves? It is the hamburgers, you know. And the popcorn."

"You're too critical." Her hands continued to sponge. Already Sara looked less flushed. "The young are always beautiful."

"Then I give her to you, my dear." Valerii laid his hand briefly and companionably on her head. "Just remember, David Moore is one of my oldest friends."

Paola stopped sponging to look up. "Have I ever embarrassed you?"

"I should not have mentioned it. Forgive me. Now—"

"You must work. Good. Do so. I will be busy here."

Sara really slept now, breasts rising and falling regularly. Paola laid the towel on the edge of the enamel bowl.

Something in the sprawl of her body, the ingenuousness of the relaxed thighs and soft bent arms, touched the familiar chord and she felt herself begin to tremble. Delicately, she put one hand on Sara's breast, her small palm hardly covering the swelling nipple. Under her fingers there was an answering urgency, the tiny twitch of erection. As if burned, she snatched her hand away.

Spreading a cotton comforter over the sleeping girl, she went into the salon. Tonino was nowhere in sight. Already he would be immersed in the books that filled his study, ferreting for insights in the debris of the sixteenth century, insights that David Moore bought for thousands of dollars.

It was too hot for the terrace, but the cool of the marble-floored salon chilled her blood. Even the Carracci madonna looked more disapproving than usual, the infant turning a particularly cold eye as Paola morosely mixed a stiff vodka tonic and let her mind wander to the girl sleeping next door.

25

Tic . . . tic. A pause. *Tic tic tic.* A clatter of metal on stone. Then again *tic tic tic tic.*

Grudgingly Sara opened her eyes and wondered why the room was blindingly white: white walls, a ceiling of white plaster. A hospital? Carefully she sat up, the comforter falling from her breasts before she realized she was naked under it. Gathering it around her, she sat gingerly on the edge of the bed and tried to remember.

The floor was white too: marble, pale and translucent, veined with blue and green. Her foot almost recoiled from its imagined cold, but as it touched she welcomed the coolness. The room felt hot and dry—or perhaps it was her own skin?

The ticking noise came from outside the shuttered window, and, squinting between the slats, she saw a sunny patio and beyond it vineyards. A few yards away, at the edge of the terrace, a huge man chipped with a chisel at a wall, the wooden mallet forcing the blade across the stone. Something about his large arms and absorbed look was familiar.

At the other end of the terrace, under an apricot tree, two people were eating. Breakfast? Lunch? Sara had lost all sense of time, though her stomach rumbled as the man, who had the theatrical profile and flowing white hair of an actor, cut a slice from a peach and popped it in his mouth.

For a moment she mistook the woman with him for a boy. Small, flat-chested, with cropped hair, wearing a plain white

215

shirt and slacks, she might have been an urchin of the kind Sara had seen playing in every Italian street. Only the unmistakable delicacy of her gestures and the classic perfection of her features betrayed her sex and her breeding.

Suddenly feeling dizzy, Sara flopped back onto the bed, head spinning. With what remained of her strength she wriggled under the coverlet and rang the tiny bell on the bedside table.

A moment later the woman hurried in. "But my dear! You are up. Back into bed, please."

Sara let her rearrange the pillows and straighten the comforter. "I'm sorry. I have no idea how I got here. Is this Villa Zurlini?"

The woman smiled. "For a sick lady you did quite well. Yes, this is Villa Zurlini and I am Paola Farnese."

"Madam Farnese...." Something Sascha had said came back to her. "Contessa...."

"Paola is fine."

"I'm awfully sorry to have put you to this trouble. I got sick on the train and—"

"You are sick still, my little friend. Sunstroke, I think, and a little germ of the stomach. If you get worse I will call a doctor, but to tell you the truth our local *medico* is more likely to worsen a disease than cure it."

The voice chattered on and Sara lay back, at peace for the first time in a week. David, Mark Turnbull, and the rest disappeared from her mind, and she drifted to sleep even before Paola finished tidying the room.

When she woke again the room was dark, but slits of golden light came through the blind. This time the bell brought the maid, a squat, swarthy southern Italian in the all-purpose peasant uniform of black dress, black stockings, black scarf.

"Signorina?"

"Is there a toilet? Uh, *lavabo?*"

The maid's smile animated her dour face. She opened a small door which Sara had mistaken for a closet. A small bathroom lay beyond.

"*Grazie*. And I wonder if I could—um, food? *Mangare?*"

Miming that she should stay where she was, the maid disappeared, to return with Paola.

"Do you feel well enough to eat? Perhaps some juice, then, and a biscuit. But be careful."

The biscuits and orange juice stayed down five minutes. Whatever Sara had caught on the train was still with her.

The days dissolved into a seamless stretch of lazy time, woven of sleep and reading and desultory talk with Paola. She finally met Valerii, whose matinee idol pose proved only skin deep. Villa Zurlini, Sara discovered, belonged to Paola, the descendant of a family who had owned the land for generations. When Valerii moved from Paris to settle down in Tuscany he first rented the house for a summer, then a further year, until they slipped into a comfortable cohabitation that, as far as Sara could see, was entirely asexual. Paola's own sexual preferences were quite plain, and for the first time in her life Sara learned to be at ease with someone who enjoyed her own sex for more than friendship.

The couple would sit on the terrace for hours, gossiping about Castel d'Oco and their life there, but like all exiles they hungered for a glimpse of the outside world and Sara found her memory stretched to give them news of American politics, fashions, scandals.

A few weeks after she arrived, Sara was awakened by Paola alone with her breakfast on a tray. A sprig of wild thyme lay beside the coffee cup. Sara sniffed the delicious scent, half dust, half flowers.

"Tonino is off on another of his trips. I thought we might sneak out. Do you feel well enough?"

"Yes! When? Now?" She was halfway out of bed before Paola stopped her.

"Plenty of time, *cara*. Eat your breakfast."

Sara filled her mouth with biscuit. Weeks of fasting had considerably diminished her appetite and, from the way her nightdress swam on her, her figure. Sharing their diet of salads, grilled meat, fruit, and endless cups of bitter coffee was paring her down to the slimness of her host and hostess, though she realized that much of her hunger had been psychological.

"Where did Tonino go?"

"Firenze, then Roma. He spends his life in the basements of old ladies." She wrinkled her nose. "I went with him a few times, but never again. Dust, and the smell of cats! Now, do you feel ready for Castel d'Oco?"

On the terrace Sara paused by the stone relief that Cristaldo, her rescuer, was carving in the villa wall. Two thirds of a large landscape had emerged from the stone, the detail so intricate that it seemed impossible that anything as clumsy as a chisel could have cut it.

"When will he finish?"

"Cristaldo has other work, unfortunately. He only does this when he can. Perhaps next week, or the week after; nothing happens quickly here. Would you like to meet him? We could go to his workshop, if you like."

Sara remembered the ghost touch of those arms, cradling her like a baby. "Is it far?"

"Just on the other side of the village. You are ready? Then we will go."

Even on shaky legs the walk down the dusty road was paradise for Sara. Workers in the vineyards straightened up respectfully as they passed, Paola waving regally, stopping now and then to chat with the men closest to the road. One gave her a bunch of tiny green grapes, as perfect as marble. Tasting one, Sara grimaced at the bitterness. Paola smiled. "For wine, they should not be sweet." Taking the bunch, she handed them back and gave Sara a consoling pat on the cheek. She was surprised to find that the intimacy of the gesture, which a month ago would have made her shy, now seemed perfectly natural.

Castel d'Oco at least looked alive this morning, unlike her last visit. A few women shuffled along the streets, and shops of sorts were set up in the main square. A radio blared from the café, and as they passed a man stepped out into the sun; his beige suit, the coat draped casually over his shoulders, and his hat and sunglasses belonged to a city dweller, though the men behind him were obviously workmen. Seeing Paola they faded back into the shadows of the café, but he bowed courteously, taking off his hat.

"Contessa."

She ignored him. As they rounded the corner she said angrily, "The local *tombarolo*. A tomb robber. There are many Etruscan ruins around here, and Ruggiero has looted most of them. Tonino has tried to trap him often but he is very clever. Ah, here we are."

She pushed open a ramshackle set of wooden doors and they were in a small courtyard. Cristaldo looked up from his chipping, pushed back a battered set of goggles, and bowed respectfully.

Sara saw what Paola meant about Cristaldo's "other work." The yard was scattered with marble tombstones, some surmounted by weeping angels or soft feminine Christs. Italians loved a good funeral.

"He is a good workman," Paola murmured, running her

finger over a plump cherub. "Not an artist—he has no imagination at all. But he can copy anything, even after studying it only once. Like a big bird who can mimic other songs."

As Paola slipped into Italian, Sara looked round the yard. There was something timeless about the place. She could be standing in the house of Michelangelo or Raphael: stone chippings, wooden slats supporting half-carved blocks of marble, newly carved slabs leaning in the shade, and over all a smell of sun and dust.

Paolo called to her. "Sara, can you drink some more coffee? Cristaldo has invited us in."

Sara's eyes took a few moments to adjust to the darkness. Finally she made out the simplest possible room—a place to eat and sleep. Butane tanks fed a tiny stove, and on the other side was a narrow bed, neatly made. Cristaldo pulled out the two chairs from the wooden table and brewed coffee in a tiny aluminum espresso machine.

Over the bed half a dozen figures supplied the room's only decoration. Seeing her interest, he took down one of them and placed it shyly on the table.

The terra-cotta figure stood about a foot high, and though one arm and a large part of the draped skirt were broken off she recognized instantly the work of a master. The girl with her sly smile, gesturing for the watcher to follow, was so full of life that the relative crudity of the modeling and the ravages of age that pitted the surface did little to dull its vitality.

"It's beautiful. What is it, Etruscan?"

"The original, yes," Paola said. "If there *was* an original. Sometimes he combines two or three fragments."

"You mean *Cristaldo* did it? But it looks so real."

"I told you, he is a brilliant mimic. And he knows all the *tombarolo* tricks. The pieces missing, the cracks, the aging; they bury things in dung heaps, you know, then in earth, to fill up the cracks. It's lucky he is honest. Ruggiero has tried often to make him work for him, but he refuses."

In awe, Sara ran her hand over the piece. It seemed incredible that this was not at least two thousand years old.

Cristaldo murmured something. "Well, you have won a heart," Paola said, sounding slightly annoyed. "He wants to give it to you. It's impossible, of course."

"Of course," Sara said wistfully, wondering how much Paola's jealousy played in the decision. She only caught part of the explanation Paola gave him, but his disappointment was obvious. Sara tried to make up for it at the door. Taking his hand, so huge and calloused that it might have been a leather gauntlet, she said, "You were very kind to pick me up on the road. I might have died without you." She looked at Paola. "Does he understand?"

"I think you make yourself very clear." Her tone was brittle, and before Sara could follow she was halfway across the yard, her back stiff and angry.

The walk back to the villa was hard work. Twice, Sara's legs began to tremble with exhaustion, but she forced herself on, ignoring Paola's sidewise glances. They went the last few yards arm in arm, Sara leaning gratefully on her companion.

Inside, she flopped into one of the salon's deep chairs, letting the marble draw the heat from her aching legs.

"This house is fabulous," she said, watching the valley, hazy in the afternoon heat.

"There has been a house here since before Roman times," Paola said. "First some Etruscan palace. Then the villa of a provincial official of Caesar, then one of Charlemagne's men, then a Borgia, a Bourbon, and finally a judge who let it almost collapse." She shrugged. "We have added some things, but it is wrong to change such places."

"I can't think of anything that could be improved."

"You have not been here in winter. This marble is like a tomb. And the pipes freeze. *Virgine!* Then you would not find it so . . . what is your word? Fabulous." She stretched. "The sun is not so bad now. I will sunbathe for a while. You would like?"

"I don't have a bathing suit."

"So bourgeoise! We are alone. Who will see?" She wandered off, unbuttoning her blouse. As she left the room Sara glimpsed thin shoulders and a straight boyish back.

Nervously Sara undressed in her bathroom, rehearsing possible excuses—a sick headache, her period. But good diet and exercise had done a great deal for her figure. She was plump, certainly, but only slightly, in the waist and thighs. She would always be stocky, but a certain biblical voluptuousness was now evident in her shoulders and breasts.

Paola lay face down on a heavy green towel, the shadow pattern of the apricot boughs spattering her naked body. Less nervous now, Sara slipped out of her robe and lay down beside her. The cool air, mixed with patches of sun, descended like a drug and she drifted off to sleep.

When she woke up, Paola was propped on her elbow, watching her. To her surprise Sara found she wasn't embarrassed. Stretching and sitting up, she said, "What time is it?"

"About four. Time for a shower and a drink?"

"Tremendous."

As Paola scrambled up, boyishly agile, Sara saw that her body was quite hairless. It was impossible not to stare at the surprising smoothness between her thighs.

Miming astonished innocence, Paola placed one hand coyly in front, another over small pointed breasts.

"I didn't mean—" Sara said in confusion.

"In this heat it's much more comfortable. You should try it."

Sara stared in distaste at her tangled bush, suddenly very obvious. "There's so much, though."

"Anything is possible, my pigeon. Leave it to me." She strolled away, wrapping the towel around her hips.

When Sara came back to her room the bathroom door was open and the shower running. As she emerged, dripping, Paola came in, dressed, with two tall glasses, tinkling with ice. A long pair of barber's scissors lay on the tray beside them, as well as a straight razor and a shaving brush.

"You're not afraid, are you?"

"No, of course not." The vodka in the drink helped. She swallowed some more. "How do we do it?"

Paola pushed her gently back onto the bed, taking the glass from her hand. The towel disappeared and she felt a small cool hand on her stomach, just below her navel.

"Don't worry. I'll be very careful."

Cold metal on her skin made her start, but the calm hands continued their work, snipping, brushing away....

"Hmmm, not too bad. No, don't sit up. You look like a chicken before it is singed."

Glass rang on the marble floor. A hot wet cloth was placed on her thighs.

"Just for the softening. Open just a little ... a little more." A brush loaded with foam frothed, rubbed. Her body no longer under her control, she let herself drift into the gray and unreal area of erotic fantasies. It wasn't really happening. It was just a dream. Soon she would reach down there with her hand....

222   *John Baxter*

The delicious foamy warmth and wetness made her thighs tremble, straddle. Her hips pushed forward against the soft, delicate friction.

"Not so *anxious*, darling." Paola's voice, no longer light and playful, was a husky murmur.

The razor began scraping on the skin of her stomach and worked carefully lower. Lower still, and fingers parted the delicate folds. Sara knew she was swimming with desire. Her nipples felt enormous, her breasts swollen.

Hours of pleasure. Centuries.

"Almost done. Ah, yes. Very pretty. *Bellissima*." Another brushing touch aroused her and, with every nerve unbuffered, sent a tingling sensation through thighs and stomach. Her body took over completely now. Every part of her longed for that delicious friction, and her legs spread wider, one pulled up onto the bed, the other stretched out, toes scrabbling in ecstasy on the cool stone. The toes began to tremble. Calves. Thighs. Hips. Then the spasms shook her furiously, her head thrashing on the bedcover, fingers clawing, the sounds of her pleasure skittering around the room.

After minutes she raised herself on her elbow. Paola, flushed, knelt on the floor between her legs, her cheek on her thigh.

Squirming across the bed, Sara grabbed the coverlet and pulled it around her. They watched each other over the landscape of white linen, nervous and appraising.

Sara often tried to rationalize her affair with Paola and failed each time. She knew without any self-examination that she was not what the sociologists called so glibly a lesbian. Men appealed to her as much as ever, and even while making love with Paola her thoughts were often of their bodies, not hers. But her sexual appetite, like Paola's, was large and omnivorous; she recognized and acknowledged in herself a capacity to achieve sexual satisfaction in almost any way. Browsing through books on Roman life on Valerii's shelves, she found her senses aroused by stories of Roman women coupling with dogs, asses, with scores of men at one time.

Paola shared her greed for satisfaction. Sara soon realized this affair was one of a series with impressionable young women: students of Valerii's; willing girls sent by friends for "a summer in the sun"; when times were thin, a village girl willing to pay with her services for an undemanding job as maid.

The boldness of her sexuality made Paola an amusing companion, audacious, frank, and specific in her demands. The afternoons they spent in bed, Valerii considerably restricting himself to the lower floor of the villa until cocktail time, were not only pleasant. For Sara, they represented her first really useful education. She even acquired a rudimentary grasp of Italian.

"Paola, don't you like men—for bed, I mean?"

"I don't like them at all. I've tolerated them sometimes. To be a contessa, there must be a conte, no?"

"How did you please him?"

"The usual way. And some unusual ones. He was strange, my husband. Let's not talk of this, Sara."

"How? Tell me."

"Sara—"

"I'm only trying to learn. You like to teach me things. Tell me about how to please men and I'll do that thing you like with both fingers. See, I'll put one in now and just touch—"

"Enough! *Basta*. All right. But the little game first. Then we will talk about this unsavory subject."

But her satisfaction at the hands and mouth of Paola never equaled what she had felt with David Moore. The thought of him jabbed like a rotten tooth, but living day to day made it unnecessary to think for too long about the problem he represented. By now he would know she had betrayed him, and one day there would be a call, a letter, solving the problem once and for all.

Wandering one evening into Tonino's study, she browsed among the paintings leaning around the wall while Valerii scribbled at his desk, the leonine head marred by spectacles balanced on his nose.

"I had a letter from David today," he said, without looking up.

Sara had a flash of pain, a sense of falling. She grasped a heavy frame with both hands to steady herself.

"What did he say?"

"He sends his regards and hopes you are well. He asks when you will return."

For the first time in weeks Sara looked at the sunset. It was closer to blue-gray than pink. Mist gathered like smoke and the cypresses were blurred to silhouettes. Autumn.

"It will have to be soon, won't it?"

"*Cara,* you are welcome to stay here as long as you like. But you must find it dull. Your life is in America."

Although his eyes were still on his papers, she knew Valerii was not looking at them. For everything there is a season, including Paola's love affairs. In his quiet way Valerii was giving her notice.

"I could go at the end of the week," she said quickly. "If you can lend me enough money for the fare."

Conscious he had gone too far, Valerii rose quickly and, pushing his glasses on top of his head, put his hands on Sara's shoulders. She leaned against him as she had leaned against her father when he picked her up as a child.

"You've been very kind to me, Tonino. You and Paola. I would never ... I mean, Paola and I—"

He gravely laid a finger on her lips. "There is nothing to be said. My house is your house. Now be kind enough to tell that dragon in the kitchen that dinner had better be ready in twenty minutes or she will be back washing clothes for a living."

Wandering back upstairs, Sara was conscious for the first time of a chill in the marble under her feet. Images of New York returned with increasing vividness. The real world was rolling toward her like a wave.

The next day, matters came abruptly to a head.

Just after lunch there was a raucous hooting outside and a gleaming red Fiat Innocenti roared up the road from the village. An impeccably shod foot emerged.

"Sascha!"

Halfway out of the car, Sascha Beauclair stared in surprise at the beautiful young woman in the green dress and bare feet.

"Sara? Unbelievable!" His glance slid over her shoulder, and she knew Paola was coming down the steps behind her. Ideas connected in Sascha's mind, and the corner of his mouth curled. Leaning forward to brush her cheek with a peck, he murmured "Welcome to the club, petal"; then Paola was on top of them.

Before dinner, Sascha and Sara took their drinks onto the terrace to watch the sunset.

"I thought you'd be agog for news of home but you haven't asked me a thing. Paola must have addled your brains."

"That's cruel."

"My pet, she has bemused a large number of young women, some of them personally known to me. You mustn't ask me to be gentle about that aristocratic cannibal. What *is* wrong with you, if not a surfeit of sex?"

It was time. She put down her glass on the balustrade. "I did something in London." In fits and starts she told him everything. "So you see, I can't go back to the gallery."

Sascha had stared at her during the recitation. Now he grinned, delightedly.

"My dear! Talk about still waters. It has to be the greatest story of revenge since *The White Devil*. No, better—*The Prince*. Pure Machiavelli!"

"What's so funny about David Moore losing a million? And Arthur Sklar."

"Sklar was ecstatic, pet! He died richer than he had ever hoped. His paintings went for more than three million!"

"But the Snow sale—"

"Just forced the price up, sweetheart. What did you expect? Once a big saleroom like Snow's set the trend, everyone else followed. Every millionaire and film star in the world wants his own Renoir. We had Edward G. Robinson on the phone, *begging* us to take his money."

It made no sense. David had been so insistent that she tell nobody. Seeing her confusion, Sascha put one hand around her shoulder.

"Let me guess. You and our David had a little . . . encounter, should I call it? Before you left New York. Correct? Yes, I can see from your face. You went to London in a highly emotional state, with two conflicting ideas in your head—loyalty to our worthy employer and loyalty to your father." He paused. "Now comes the speculation. Did something happen in London to tip that balance, to make you spill the beans to Snow's?"

Sara frowned. "No. It was just a chance remark." Suddenly a number of things coalesced in her mind: the photographer who just happened to be in the right place, David's terse manner on the phone. . . .

Sascha's smirk was triumphant. "Bingo! I think that David, in the vulgar phrase, set you up. He *wanted* this information to reach Snow's. Then they could do the work and take the risks. When the market was well and truly bubbling, he'd step in and clean up."

Through the mixture of anger, humiliation, and embarrassment Sara remembered what David had said to her the day he took her to meet Sklar. *I owe him everything. Remember that when you're inclined to make judgments.*

She bolted from beside Sascha, not wanting him to see her tears. Locking herself in her room at the villa she alternately wept and raged, tearing in fury at her pillow, then collapsing in tearful helplessness in which images of bloody retribution warred with a cringing low desire to forget everything, crawl back to David's bed, and be loved.

Next day she went with Sascha for a long walk through the vineyards. He was helpful, compassionate, even affectionate—she should have suspected something, she realized later, but her mental state made rational thought almost impossible.

"If it's any consolation, petal, you aren't the first lady to be screwed—literally and figuratively—by our boss. There are stories that he played around with Cicely Snow in the old days. She certainly has a low opinion of him now. In point of fact she hates his guts. As do we all."

Stopping in surprise, Sara said, "I thought you liked him."

"I have to work like everyone else, sweetie, and Atropos has a reputation. But there's only room for one man in that business. I went to Carl Bleigen with a proposition once. He turned me down flat; told me if it was any good, Moore would have thought of it." His voice was waspish with hurt pride.

"Did you ever ask David for his backing?"

"I wouldn't give him the satisfaction. No, I'm just waiting for Moore to come unstuck. He doesn't know it yet, but that toad Bleigen has been doing some dirty little business of his own. One of these days, Atropos will blow up in his face, and I want to be there to watch."

They stopped to look out over the vineyards, apparently deserted until the occasional picker stood up from the backbreaking crouch in which they all worked, trimming the low vines.

"What do you think I should do, Sascha?" There seemed no longer anything to hold onto; occasionally, through the misery, waves of pure panic swept over her. All the patterns of her life, the webs of security on which she relied for balance and sanity, were snarled, twisted, even torn apart.

"You *could* go back to Atropos as if nothing had happened," he mused.

"No!" In her torment of last night, that proposition was the first to go. To let him get away with this was insupportable, impossible.

"Well, I did have one thought," Sascha said quietly. "Exactly who owns House of Hershman?"

Sara frowned, trying to remember. "Bleigen runs it, and my mother draws an income, but I think it's held in trust for me. But of course Bleigen holds my father's note. Why?"

"It's a bit complicated." He sat on a flat stone at the top of the slope that ran down into Castel d'Oco. With the stiff black cypresses along the skyline behind him he could have been a satyr pausing briefly to survey his hunting ground. "Did you know Ted Augustus is dying?"

"Yes." She remembered that awkward naked figure in the Greenwich Village loft, and the tiny oil of the Macy's parade that still hung in her room in New York.

"He might be dead now, for all I know. There's some kind of trust that's supposed to protect his work afterward, but if Bleigen gets a chance to overthrow it, he will; Augustus looks like a gold mine."

Manipulating the market in an artist's work after his death was almost a tradition in the art trade. By putting the paintings out to an "independent" valuer who was in on the fraud, one could reduce the book value of the work to almost nothing, then sell the paintings off at these rock-bottom prices to another confederate, who would reoffer them at the true price and split the profits. With the art world so small and incestuous that dealers often served on the boards of major galleries, and auction houses acted as advisers to the museums and pension funds who were their largest customers, opportunities for larceny were unlimited.

"Have you talked to Bleigen about this?"

"He approached *me*. He's got it all worked out. Between us, we could put the skids under Mr. Moore."

"What's in it for you?"

"Money. But cash isn't much use to me. I need my own place. A gallery"—he looked at Sara—"or an auction house."

"You don't mean Hershman's, surely? It's a dump."

"Yes, sweetheart, but the name's good. With a firm base in the market and some help from Bleigen, we could do a lot."

"We?"

"You have an equity. I'd need that to counterbalance Bleigen's share. And I think you have the makings of a dealer. We could be a hell of a team."

Sara mulled it over. Taking advantage of David Moore would pay him back effectively for the humiliations of London and for the death of her father. There was Ted Augustus, of course—but what would he care? She would see that his family had something; there was enough in the Augustus hoard to make them all rich.

But she could see one glaring flaw in Sascha's scheme. "Won't this take money? Bleigen won't give us Hershman's unless we can pick up my father's note. Have you got any capital?"

Sascha became abstracted. "Not enough. You?"

"A few thousand. How much would we need?"

"More than that, petal. About twenty or thirty thousand would give us something to start with. I could go to a couple of banks...." He sighed as the impossibility of finding even that much descended on him. "Oh, well. It was just a thought."

Sara had a jab of inspiration. (Later, thinking over that decision on the hill above Castel d'Oco, she wondered whose idea it had been. Did Sascha lead her to it, step by step, so subtly that she never realized how shrewdly her thoughts were being guided? But by then the matter was academic.) "When do you have to leave?"

"Friday. Why?"

"I've got an idea, but I'll need a few days. Can you stay until Monday?"

"Longer, if you like. There's a nice lad in the village I might call on again."

Walking back to the villa, she felt absolutely cool, committed to a course of action so clear that side paths and obstacles no longer existed. David had declared war on the Hershmans; the Hershmans would fight back. And when he was beaten, when he showed true contrition for what he had done—but that was a long way in the future, that happy ending which she naïvely assumed would take no more than an extended hand and a smile, and she put it out of her mind. For the moment, there were plans to make.

26

By night, Sara expected Cristaldo's yard to be a miniature of the cemetery for which its figures were intended, but instead it had a childish purity. The angels and pious virgins might have been marzipan figures for a wedding cake.

A wedge of light shone from the open door to his room. She went in.

He was drawing, face bent almost to the surface of the table in concentration. The lamplight shining through his beard lit the young face underneath. With a start, Sara realized he was hardly more than thirty.

"Signorina!" Jumping up, he looked behind her for Paola.

"I thought I'd come and see you myself. Is that all right?"

He stared at her, confused. If his neighbors ever found out....

"Do you mind if I sit down?"

Good manners overcame his nervousness. "Of course. Yes. A glass of wine."

He poured wine into enamel mugs, the same black-red stuff on which Valerii thrived but which she and Paola found acid and unpleasant. She sipped politely.

"I couldn't stop thinking about the lady you showed me. Could I see her again?"

Her eyes went to the shelf above the bed. There were four figures—a grave panel, with a grieving woman, veil held over her bowed head; a dog, its legs missing but the torso as agile in clay as any living animal; a warrior's head in a chested helmet, the face still smudged with "original" painting; and the lady with the secret smile.

"Of course." Carefully, Cristaldo placed the figure on the table and gathered together the papers on which he had been working.

"What are you drawing?"

He tried to snatch the papers away from under her fingers, but one remained, caught under the heavy terra-cotta figure. It was a nude, sketched from imagination but recognizably Sara. His anatomy was as skillful as she had imagined it would be.

She looked up to find him watching her, his face stricken. Dropping the sheet to the table, she took his hand, heavy and hard with its calluses, and placed it on her breast. In the warm room, perfume seemed to fill her head, the light silk dress evaporate on her body.

He was clumsy, awkward, and she had to lead him like a young animal, with firm, hard movements. As they toppled to the bed, she put one hand in his tangled hair and pulled his face down to hers, pressing a thumb into the corner of his mouth and kissing him savagely, feeding off the thick lips. Slipping a breast from her dress, she guided his hand to it, wincing as the rough skin abraded her like sandpaper.

He was totally hers. Squirming from under him, she pushed him back on the bed and straddled his hips, her fingers unbuttoning his trousers. The penis, gorged and tight, caught awkwardly in the cloth but she eased it free, then wriggled forward to squeeze it inside her, a long slow impalement of pleasure. Breasts bouncing, the heels of her sandals jabbing him like spurs, she rode him.

In the frenzy of orgasm, her eyes swung wildly around the room and caught those of the Etruscan warrior, face fixed in glee and hatred. It was to him that she gave herself, hands reaching down to fondle his heavy muscled thighs beneath her.

She left the house an hour later, the figure of the priestess heavy under her arm.

After dinner that night, she went to Paola's room.

"Can you lend me some money?"

Paola looked up from paring her nails. "What do you want with money?"

"I have to take a trip. How much is a hundred dollars?"

"About a hundred and fifty thousand lire. But where do you want to go? I could drive you, or Sascha." Recognizing the set expression on Sara's face, she opened the top drawer of her bureau and took out a roll of notes.

"Here is two hundred thousand. *Now* can I know where you are going?"

"What's the name of that auction room in Paris? The big one."

"Le Druout? You're going to *Paris?* Sara, why?"

"I'll be back before Friday. Tell Sascha I'll leave his car at the station."

Dropping her scissors, Paola reached for the house phone. "I don't know what this is about, but you must tell Tonino." She stared until Sara avoided her eye. "Yes?"

"All right." She had been foolish to hope the confrontation could be avoided. He mustn't talk her out of it. *Mustn't.*

Later, Sara remembered that evening as among the worst of her life. The three of them argued back and forth for hours, while Cristaldo's figure smirked from the table as if the arguments merely confirmed her sardonic opinion of mankind.

"And you expect me to be your accomplice in this fraud?" Surging up out of his chair, Valerii paced the room. "It's theft. Criminal! To take advantage of Cristaldo, that innocent—"

"He's no innocent," Sara said angrily. "As for the fraud, you've told me a dozen times how many fakes are hanging in big galleries, unsuspected by the owners. *You* know they're forgeries, yet you let them stay there."

"That is a different matter!"

"Why? Either you are absolutely honest, or you sell people what they want to buy. Cristaldo isn't naïve about his work. He knows what it's worth; Ruggerio has offered him thousands for it. He offered all of them to me, to do what I wanted with them."

"No doubt your offer was more attractive than Ruggiero's," Valerii said sarcastically. "For myself, I prefer a professional criminal to an amateur whore." He picked up the phone. "I am going to call the police."

"It wouldn't do any good. If you do, I'll just tell them you put me up to it."

"They would never believe it!"

"Some would. Mud sticks."

"David Moore—"

"David Moore has done worse things in his time," Sara said tightly. "If I learned from anyone, it was from him." She stood up. "Call the police if you like. I'm going to bed."

Getting to her bedroom was harder than she expected. The floors seemed to tilt, and she banged hard into the doorjamb before collapsing onto the bed.

She was crying, face covered by her hand, when Paola came into the room.

"I understand, Sara. Sascha explained—about David. I know why you are doing this thing."

"Do you?" Sara said. "I don't know. Sometimes I just seem to be . . . carried away. Things . . . things—"

"*Reste calma, bambina.* Tonino and I knew this would happen sooner or later." She bent close to Sara's ear. "I will tell you a secret that even Tonino does not know. Already some of the figures have been sold—by Cristaldo's mother, that pious old hypocrite." She mopped Sara's tears with a corner of the sheet. "Nobody will stop you, though you must be careful."

"But Tonino—"

"Do not worry about Tonino. He goes on one of his trips next week. I'll go with him. There will be time to talk." She stood up and went to the door. In the light from the hall, Sara saw the thin, sad smile on her face. "The smell of dust, and cats! The things I do for you, little bird." She closed the door softly.

The alarm woke her just before dawn. Wrapping her robe around her against the morning chill, Sara brewed coffee in the large empty kitchen and ate some apricots. Once welcoming, almost her home, the villa now felt like a ruin. A rat scuttling across the floor would not have surprised her. Hurrying back to her room, she started to pack.

The bottom bureau drawer revealed clothing so odd she hardly recognized it. A lurid pink shift, faded under the arms from perspiration, and a rubber tube as tough and unyielding as the sloughed skin of a snake. Leaving them there, she gathered up the new silks and fragile leathers which filled only one small Gucci bag and slung it in the back of Sascha's Innocenti beside the carefully wrapped Etruscan figure. She had a sense of leaving behind more than the villa.

From her terrace, Paola watched Sara squeeze into the Fiat and waved, but there was no answering gesture, only the clatter of the car's acceleration into the softening darkness, a noise that woke every dog and rooster in miles. There was winter in the air, hard and cold. She shivered and went inside.

Sara barely caught the first train at Castel d'Oco. The women on their way to market, vegetables and salamis wrapped up in their shawls, stared at the girl in the long sheepskin coat and high boots, wondering at the fixed passivity of her face as she watched the autumn landscape, a panorama of hills burned back to the stubble, of orchards sunk in the first mists of winter.

At Milan, there was time for coffee and a roll before she caught the express. She slept until the French border, then watched the country outside mellow from Italy's high drama to the bourgeois placidity of the Riviera. By evening, she was in Paris, at the Gare du Nord, and an hour later a surly concierge checked her into a small hotel in the Latin Quarter, with what sounded like a convention of students meeting in the café two floors below her room.

The phone book listed a number of names under Commissaire-Priseurs. Seven didn't answer; it was almost 8 P.M. But on the eighth call she got a cranky late worker who, at her insistence, directed her to an M. Alekan in Neuilly.

"'Allo. Alekan." The voice was abrupt, curt.

Sara rummaged in her schoolgirl French. "*M. Alekan, je m'appelle Sara Hershman. Je suis* . . . uh—"

"Speak English if you wish, mademoiselle." He was coolly contemptuous of her ignorance.

"M. Alekan, I understand you undertake sales at auction in the Hôtel Druout."

"I have an office for business, mademoiselle. If you wish to call tomorrow after ten, I will attempt to deal with your inquiry."

"This is a matter of importance. Something of considerable value. An antiquity."

"Surely it can wait until tomorrow?"

"I've just come from Italy. It's very urgent that this be dealt with as soon as possible."

There was a long irritated pause.

"I'm at the Hôtel"—she glanced around for a name, finally seeing it upside down on a towel—"the Hôtel de l'Europe. It's in—"

"I know it. Rue de l'Harpe. Very well, Miss Hershman. Would an hour be satisfactory?"

Sara expected a stooped old man with a nutcracker face out of Daumier, but Jacques Alekan was suave, fortyish, impeccable in his London-tailored three-piece suit and voile shirt. He warmed noticeably at his first sight of Sara, if not of her poky hotel room.

"Now, mademoiselle, how may I assist you?"

"I want to sell something quickly. For cash."

"All sales at the Druout are for cash. How quickly?"

"Tomorrow, if possible. *Is* it possible?"

He frowned. "I *do* have a sale tomorrow, but it is not usual to include items so late. Each lot must be passed by the Companie des Commissaire-Priseurs and registered for tax purposes." He tented his fingers judiciously. "Perhaps you do not understand our methods here. The Companie is a private firm with a monopoly of selling by auction in Paris. There are seventy registered Commissaire-Priseurs with the right to hold sales at the Druout. The government supervises us and levies a heavy tax on all sales. They also insist we offer a thirty-year guarantee on anything sold. If an object is proved to be false or stolen"—he fixed her with a particularly searching look on these words—"we must refund the purchase price in full. You can see why we are not inclined to make quick decisions."

Sara knew most of this; at Atropos she had made a thorough study of auction methods in most European countries. The French system, noted for its unwieldiness, was already being circumvented by shrewd foreign companies which held auctions in Switzerland and Monaco with French dealers particularly in mind. There were even rumors that Sotheby's proposed to set up a Monaco office in association with a Monte Carlo firm, as they had done already in Zurich. But for the moment, the confused French system suited her purposes; ill-organized, riddled with loopholes, it was the ideal place to dispose of any dubious item.

"I don't think this will cause any doubts, Monsieur." Gently she unwrapped the parcel and placed Cristaldo's figure on the table.

His interest was immediate. Gently handling it, he looked it over carefully for a full minute.

"It's Etruscan, is it not?"

"Yes. A grave figure, excavated in Tuscany."

"By whom, may I ask?"

"No. However, it *is* mine; I can assure you of that."

"Assurances—you will forgive me, mademoiselle—are not

enough. I must have proof. A provenance of some sort. An expert appraisal."

"If we are talking about experts, let me mention a few. Antonio Valerii, for instance."

He put the figure down and stared at her. "Signor *Valerii* has authenticated this piece?"

"I have been his house guest for the past three months."

Alekan smiled thinly. "I can hardly produce your personal relationship with Signore Valerii, whatever it may be, for the satisfaction of committee. If he has supplied some written evidence. . . ."

Sara played her trump card. Before she left New York, David Moore had written a letter of introduction on Atropos notepaper. She handed it to him.

Alekan read the letter and put it down on the table in confusion. "I confess that I am at a loss, mademoiselle. Such a valuable object—why should either Signore Valerii or Mr. Moore wish to dispose of it in this way?"

"I didn't say they did. If it were theirs, you might reasonably suspect me to be a thief. But I've told you that the piece is mine. I merely offer evidence of my good character and professional standing. If you're concerned about the figure's authenticity, I'll gladly sign an affidavit absolving you of all responsibility in the sale."

Alekan looked relieved. "That would certainly be of assistance." For the first time, he was treating the sale as a possibility, and calculating the potential profit. "If you would allow me to draw up the necessary documents, we could meet tomorrow morning."

Whatever Sara expected of the Hôtel Druout, it was not the elephantine structure just off the smart Boulevard Haussmann, its nondescript frontage plastered with posters for the day's sales, ranging through antiques, jewels, stamps, and furniture to household goods and machine tools.

Inside the main entrance, porters struggled in a large courtyard to empty huge vans of the day's goods—everything from a massive Victorian wardrobe to crates of toilet rolls. Passing through the melee, she climbed a staircase and joined the line of people waiting for the clock to strike 10 A.M. As it did so, the guard barring the door stepped adroitly aside and they surged in, to be swallowed up in the maze of corridors and

rooms that made up the Druout. In return for a hefty tip, a
porter directed her to Salle Two.

Everywhere, porters in black denim trimmed with red braid
dragged flat-bottomed cane panniers across the splintered
wooden floors, dumping them in heaps by the doors of various
salerooms. Sara peered curiously into one basket and found a
tarnished mesh evening purse with the clasp broken, a roll of
tattered posters, a paper bag containing a jigsaw puzzle, and a
rusted piece of metal that looked vaguely familiar. She was
holding it up to examine it more closely when a tiny man in a
heavy coat grabbed it—"*Pardon, mam'selle*"—he was reassem-
bling half a suit of medieval armor; she had been holding the
elbow guard.

Not all the goods were junk. Persian carpets hung on the
walls, and behind the rostrum she recognized three Renaissance
drawings. Raphael? Tiepolo? Or fakes? Since the Druout
published no catalogues, one had to guess or accept the seller's
assurances.

Alekan strolled in, saw her and came over. From the inside
pocket of his gray suit he took a folded paper. Sara puzzled it
out, then signed. She had gone so far that a mere piece of false
witness hardly mattered. If Alekan remained unconvinced, he
covered it very well. His doubts, she noticed, had not prevented
him from taking a healthy commission.

"I don't see the figure in here," she said.

"I've transferred it to another room—number four. A
colleague is handling the matter for us. If you want to see the
sale, I suggest you come along in a few minutes. It is better we do
not arrive together."

The sale in Salle Two was just beginning, buyers crowding in.
One of the new arrivals pushed against Sara and a furtive hand
groped her thigh. Recalling that this was an infamous feature of
the Druout, where half the audiences were traditionally there for
reasons other than buying, she planted her heel firmly on an
instep. The hand disappeared abruptly.

Sara watched the sale for a moment, trying to gauge its
pattern, but the system was incomprehensible to an outsider.
Bids were not so much discreet as invinsible, and the crowd took
little interest in what went on at the rostrum. Nevertheless, the
prices gabbled by the auctioneer were more than respectable,
and the porters were kept busy scribbling receipts and dragging
panniers out of the way. After a few minutes, she squeezed out of
the crush and found Salle Four.

Except for the higher value of the goods, this room was much the same as Two. The chairs, half of them occupied, held bored, clerkish men showing little enthusiasm for the sale; a few obvious *clochards*, who had clearly come in to escape the drafty streets, showed more interest than the dealers who occupied the front rows. Had Alekan been a good choice, she wondered? Nobody here looked as if he could afford a cup of coffee, let alone a valuable antiquity.

But people entered and left the room constantly, and after ten minutes new arrivals of more obvious solvency—three men in camel's hair coats, one of them with a beautiful girl on his arm—drifted in at the back of the room. Pointedly ignoring one another, they glanced around the room like strangers isolated under a tree during a rainstorm. Clearly their arrival had not gone unnoticed by the other dealers, some of whom craned around to stare.

Then a porter plunked her figure down on the table.

For an instant, Sara felt cold and sick. Perhaps there was still time to stop it. But bidding had begun. Hurriedly, she went out into the corridor, leaning against the wall to steady herself. A moment later, the three men and the girl walked by, trailing the expensive scent of cigars and perfume.

She beat Alekan back to the hotel by only ten minutes. He seemed disconsolate.

"Two hundred thousand! For a piece like that. *C'est rien*."

"How much is that in dollars?"

"About . . . oh, fifty thousand dollars. Less tax and commission, you understand. For you, about forty-three thousand dollars. I will have a check made out immediately."

"For cash, please. And certified."

"Naturally." He stood up. "The dealer who bought the piece was most interested to know if there might be others."

"No." She put the rest of Cristaldo's collection out of her mind. He had been exploited enough.

"A pity. But if by chance some should come to light, I would be glad to handle them for you."

"As I said, Mr. Alekan, that is the only piece. I'm sorry."

Next day, she took her new fortune and went shopping on the Champs Élysées.

Her new figure solved most of the problems that had faced her in London a few months ago. French couturiers regularly designed for women built on the voluptuous continental scale, and by midafternoon her wardrobe had trebled.

Conscious for the first time of the need to create an impression, she bought shrewdly, choosing dresses that emphasized her dramatic coloring, her look of almost animal ferocity at moments of passion or excitement. One shopgirl quailed in astonishment as she slipped into a changing room and found Sara in a deep blue evening dress baring her teeth at herself in the mirror. Blushing, Sara paid quickly for the dress and left the shop.

About five, footsore and tired, she chose the smartest bar in sight, the Closerie des Lilas, and marched in. The early drinkers, male and female, eyed her with varying degrees of interest, but Sara's attention was entirely on the ranked bottles behind the bar. Trusting to instinct, she pointed to a tall bottle with a brown label. "*Là.*"

The barman raised his eyebrows. "*Sambuca, mam'selle. Certainement.*"

She sipped the liqueur, sickly sweet and tasting of aniseed. But some water made it palatable, even refreshing. She filed the name away in her new mental index under "Drinks" and wondered about her next move.

27

Moore and Bleigen were holding the annual general meeting of Fine Art Holdings, the company they shared. It was, as usual, a nervous and unproductive event, observed in the interests of a superficial harmony by two protagonists who cordially hated one another.

Age had accentuated the froglike cast of Carl Bleigen's features, the flesh flowing down off his cheekbones as it had already drooped from his chest and arms. He pooled in his deep chair like a toy figure stuffed with beans, gravity drawing his bulk deep into the seat.

"Business good, Carl?" David discovered long ago that these meetings, kept to four or five a year, became bearable only if he maintained an absolute detachment.

"I get by." The familiar gravedigger's smile rendered his face more toadlike. "We're getting good figures at Hershman's, and the print side is cleaning up." Lately, FAH, at Bleigen's insistence, had diversified into high-class reproductions of Old Masters, printed photographically on canvas and touched up in oils by hand; these saccharine copies of Renoir and Rembrandt glowed in their chocolate-box colors from the walls of every cheap hairdresser's and dry cleaning shop in Manhattan, to David's acute distaste. He had been very sure his clients knew Atropos had nothing to do with that side of Fine Art Holdings.

"You seen the figures?" Bleigen asked, indicating the balance sheet.

David nodded. If Bleigen was skimming anything off the business, his accountants had not been able to figure out where. "They're acceptable."

"Better than that! I never thought there was so much money in that abstract stuff you're selling."

"It won't go on much longer. The market's peaking."

When Bleigen looked skeptical, suspecting David of setting him up for a drop in profits, he sketched in the background.

Throughout the last decade, European dealers in particular had dived into the burgeoning market in twentieth-century art, driving living artists to produce more work and ruthlessly exploiting the paintings of those no longer alive to protest.

Lithographs by Picasso, Matisse, Braque, and Chagall now fetched auction prices as high as those gained by original oils a few years ago. Editions now ran into the hundreds, rather than the traditional ten or twenty, and the new middle-class market, attracted by the promise that a signed Picasso etching was as good an investment as shares in AT&T or Coca-Cola, bought everything offered.

Forgeries were everywhere, and David, along with other perceptive dealers, was looking for a new area of investment in expectation of a spectacular collapse as the true nature of the rotten and inflated market became evident.

As David spoke, Bleigen nodded, toying with the knicknacks on his desk, a set of clear plastic cubes in which brightly colored beetles were locked forever, their carapaces glittering like jewels in the overhead light.

"Yeah," he said at the end. "Well, I guess you should know. Maybe we'd better offload some of that Augustus stuff."

The hair prickled at the back of David's neck. Bleigen's sleepy lack of interest was deceptive.

"I think Augustus will hold his value—like Pollock and de Kooning. He's in the Museum of Modern Art already."

"So are Picasso and them others you said were finished."

"Good Picasso *oils* and early lithographs aren't going to lose their value," David said irritatedly. "I'm talking about cheap lithograph editions, and the rejects they try to sell as his best work. Anyway, Augustus has put his work in trust. We couldn't sell it, even if we wanted to. And I don't."

"I hear he's pretty sick."

"Yes." On his last visit to the clinic in which Ted Augustus slipped daily deeper into coma, he had had time only to glimpse the recumbent, wasted figure before the nurse hustled him out. It was almost a year since he had last been able to paint. Now he could not walk. Soon speech would go as well. But death itself might take years. David said as much.

"Well, since you're executor of the will—"

"We've discussed this before. I won't be a party to defrauding Ted Augustus or his family. If you want me to put all this in writing—"

Bleigen put up a conciliatory palm. "Listen, it was just an idea. If you're sure the firm won't lose on this deal, I'll take your word. Can this fraud stuff."

"Over the next ten years, we stand to make more out of Ted's work than we could from all the quick sales now. Atropos has exclusive rights to sell paintings on behalf of the trust, and there's a good commission for every sale."

"OK, OK. I said I agree. Anything else you want to talk about?"

David left the office feeling uneasy. Every meeting with Bleigen disturbed him, but he sensed something different in the air this time, a new menace.

Back at Atropos, he paused for a moment in the empty main gallery, then went downstairs and opened the vault which took up thousands of square feet under the building. Along one wall, slotted into racks specially built for the purpose, the best of Ted Augustus's work awaited his death, every canvas wrapped in sacking, indexed, labeled, and valued—the panorama of one man's creative life.

In the fizzing white light of the fluorescents, the room had an air of surrealist menace, as if something more than inanimate canvas and paint lay swathed in the heavy fabric. A brief image came to him of Ted, himself cloth-wrapped, immobile, waiting for death in a silent room across the river.

This air-conditioned cul-de-sac was like an existential concept of hell. His instinct warned him that disaster threatened—that the paintings represented a part of that threat.

Turning out the light, he stood in the silent dark, listening.

28

London was a new city for Sara that spring, though she knew it was she who had changed.

A brief look of confusion passed over the face of the desk clerk at the Connaught as he compared this attractive new arrival with the distraught guest of a year ago. What a joke if he suspected her of being an imposter! But the British excel at refusing to accept the obvious.

"Glad to have you back with us, Miss Hershman," he said, handing the key to the porter. "Number Seven oh four."

As if her new appearance placed her in a higher category, her room was better than the one she occupied last time. It still looked out over the roofs of London, but this time they were Mayfair's elegant Georgian pediments: bronze domes green with age; black slate already powdered gray with the dust of the summer to come. Snow's was somewhere among them, but she couldn't pick it out.

Flopping down in a deep chair, she savored the psychological comfort of having come back at exactly the right time. Last autumn, after the break with Paola and the sale of Cristaldo's gift, she was still confused and vulnerable.

Her new fortune had given her a breathing space which she accepted gratefully, taking a villa outside Antibes at the cheap off-season rate and spending the winter in luxurious solitude. Cocooned in the old house, with the mistral rattling the dried vines of the bougainvillea on the stone walls, she read, planned, considered strategy for the conflict to come not only with David Moore but the auction establishment itself. When buds appeared again on the vine and the first tourists nosed up into the hills to camp, unasked, on the roadside opposite her house, she packed up and took the plane to London.

Her first week in the city passed in desultory shopping, theatergoing, and sightseeing, none of it undertaken with much interest. She felt like an actress in the wings, waiting for her cue to enter. It finally came at the start of the second week, taking her almost by surprise.

An ineradicable professional curiosity drew her to Bond Street, and to the galleries clustered around Sotheby's and, on the other side of Piccadilly, Christie's. Taking in an indifferent show of lithographs at one of them, she recognized a familiar face among the browsers.

Casually pausing to examine the picture next to him, she waited to be recognized.

Mark Turnbull scanned the attractive girl in the smart Italian clothes with appreciation, then wondered where he had seen her before. A second later, with considerable surprise, he connected her with the overweight Sara Hershman of last year's sale.

"Hello! What are you doing here?"

"Passing through. I've been in Italy."

The changes in her appearance had begun to achieve their full effect. "It obviously agreed with you. I wonder you could tear yourself away."

"I needed the rest."

"You came to the right place." They looked around the room, full of shabby dealers and bored browsers. "Not exactly a *Punch* luncheon, is it?" Glancing at his watch, he said, "Um, speaking of luncheon, I don't suppose—"

"If you hadn't asked me, I should have called someone and accused you of indecent overtures."

Their eyes met with a hint of conspiracy. "Ah, well, those can be arranged too, you know."

As they walked down Piccadilly, Sara said, "How's Mrs. Snow?" Mark, waving for a cab, pretended not to hear.

She asked again, over lunch. "Oh, fine," he said casually, looking down the wine list. "You never actually met, did you?"

"No. But I'd like to. Will you introduce us?"

If the wine waiter knew what was going on, he displayed indifference to it, staring over their heads while Mark gave the order. When he had gone, Mark said, "I'm not sure you two would get along."

Sara nibbled at a breadstick. "Why not? We like the same things."

After that lunch, there was never any doubt that Sara would spend some time in London. Their affair began a week later, in a discreet little hotel behind Langham Place, the faces of its staff worn smooth by decades of discretion. Demanding little of one another, Mark and Sara made love with a casual, almost friendly detachment, sensing that the true excitement of their liaison lay elsewhere.

"I never did compliment you on your performance last year," Mark said on their third meeting. "You fooled us completely. You know, for a day or two, I really believed all that about getting back at David Moore. I rang up the Connaught to console you, but of course you'd gone."

"It seemed the best thing," Sara said diplomatically. "The whole scheme really worked, did it?"

"Beautifully. Cicely was furious when your boss flooded the market with the Sklar collection after her sale had prepared the way. They thought interest in modern pictures was a minority thing, but of course there was money around that we'd never even suspected. Some of these continental dealers had been waiting for ten years to buy. Moore must be delighted."

"I suppose so. I haven't seen him since."

"Oh?" He sat up in bed. "Why not?"

"I'm thinking of going on my own. I still own part of my father's company. I'd like to revive House of Hershman. That's one reason why I'm here—to learn the auction business."

"I shouldn't have thought there was much we could teach *you!*"

"I'm more ignorant than you think. Could you make me into a good saleswoman?"

He grinned. "Perhaps." His weight descended gently onto her soft welcoming breasts. "With a little encouragement. . . ."

"Do you feel sufficiently encouraged to start teaching me?" Sara asked as they strolled through Regent's Park that afternoon. The trees, caught in the frenzy of the English spring, already seemed too gloriously in leaf, thick explosions of green.

"What is there to learn? People bring you things to sell. You sell them and deduct seven and half percent for your trouble."

"I hear you're going to start charging ten."

"Yes, that's on the cards. We'll be charging the buyer a fee soon too."

"What for?"

"Supply and demand, my sweet. All the big salerooms compete for good items, and the owners know it. You don't really think a man with a dozen masterpieces to sell is going to pay ten percent for the privilege? More like one percent these days, if he's charged anything at all. So if our customers want Rembrandts, they'll have to pay us to offer them. You watch—a ten percent buyers' premium will be a regular thing in a few years."

"I thought there was nothing to learn about the auction business."

Mark smiled. "Well, perhaps a few things."

As he became used to his role of tutor, Mark began to enjoy it, and the pace of her teaching quickened. His companionship gave her an invaluable entrée to the inner circles of London's art-dealing world, and his colleagues talked openly with her. In the Columbina Restaurant, around the corner from Christie's which its staff and that of the thirty or forty galleries clustered in the few blocks north of Jermyn Street used as a meeting place, she heard enough to understand—imperfectly at first, but with accelerating insight—the intricacies of the auction world.

She was even admitted to the holiest of London saleroom ceremonies, the Monday morning "Halling" of pictures at Carthew's, London's oldest and most respected auction house.

If they knew she had no business there, the doorman and other Carthew's employees in the foyer showed no sign of it as, nodding casually, Mark escorted her across the wide expanse of carpet, along a narrow corridor barred by a half door marked PRIVATE: STAFF ONLY and into the astonishing chaos she was beginning to take for granted behind the facades of the big salerooms.

If sellers could see back here, they would clutch their treasures and run for home.

Leaning in piles of a dozen or more against the walls, pictures filled the long corridor that sloped for almost a hundred yards to the service bay at the rear of the building. As vans lined up to unload a small fortune in fine art, the porters, as blasé as moving men, grabbed each crate as if it were worth five pounds rather than five thousand and piled it wherever it would fit in the confusion of the long hall.

At first from necessity but later to honor the tradition, Carthew's held their discussion of the month's new pictures in the corridor. To the trade, "Halling" at Carthew's was the ultimate test of authenticity; curators and dealers were known to consign their treasures to a basement on the raised eyebrow or dubious comments of a Carthew's jury.

As Sara and Mark moved through the banks of pictures, they passed half a dozen other men, some carrying coffee cups, others chatting quietly. At the top of the first slope in the corridor, where the floor leveled for a few yards, all of them joined another group already browsing among the canvases, occasionally tipping them out against their legs to look down at the surfaces.

All of them seemed perfectly at ease, gathered more to chat than to work—the office's least-busy clerks, loitering around the water cooler. Mark's arrival with Sara caused no particular stir, and the few glances were of appreciation, not resentment. As if their presence made the circle complete, there was a general laying aside of cups and conversations.

Charles Carthew, a tall man, still handsome in his fifties, but wearing half-glasses that gave him the look of an amused and quizzical examiner, took charge.

"Well, who's first today? Andrew, how about those drawings of yours?"

Andrew, young and pimply, hardly more than a schoolboy, was obviously new to the firm. With considerable nervousness, he displayed four framed pastel sketches of eighteenth-century pastoral scenes.

"I thought . . . Kobell?" he said of the first two. And, picking up the others, "These look like Bürkel to me."

Looking around the circle, Carthew said, "Any doubts?"

"Are you sure of the Kobells?" someone asked.

"Well, they came out of the Desperet sale originally. . . ."

"The 1865 one?" a fat man asked in a foreign accent. His tone suggested not quite doubt, just an unspoken knowledge.

"Yes. I thought that was fairly reliable."

The foreign man shrugged. Nobody else spoke.

His confidence undermined by the question, the boy looked nervously from face to face. "Perhaps I'd better have another look at them," he said at last, defeat in his voice.

"If you think that's necessary," Carthew said. He had taken no part in the discussion, but his comment ended it. Another canvas was hauled out and displayed.

Certain that the boy was right about the drawings and that the old hands had put pressure on him for their own reasons—seasoning? envy?—Sara saw "Halling" in a new light. More than the pictures were being tested here.

The new painting met with instant agreement around the circle. "Angeli, isn't it?"

Carthew made a note on his clipboard. "Right. Next?"

It went on like this for an hour. Picture after picture came out of the stacks, to be studied, argued over, and then either ignominiously rejected as too damaged, restored, or dubious to sell, or identified, given a suitable description for the catalogue, and "drawn off" into another room.

Carthew and his men knew their jobs; between them, they represented centuries of study, cataloguing, argument, and simple experience of pictures. Fine points of brushwork were offered as evidence of authenticity; most could even point out where a student had taken over from his teacher or a retoucher ruined the composition or coloring. It took decades of just looking at art—in galleries, museums, collections, and sales—to acquire the instinctive feel for style that no degree in Art History could ever inculcate.

But again and again, these experts had to admit defeat when a picture, though obviously painted by an artist of skill, went utterly unrecognized, to be entered lamely in the catalogue as "Flemish School, c.1700" or "Pupil of Boucher?" Like detectives, they needed clues to identify a work of art, and often the best clue of all, the artist's signature, had been painted out in restoration or cut off during reframing. Two hundred years ago, this had meant little to the owners; nobody in the family was likely to forget that the portrait over the fireplace was by Lely or Kneller. But families died out, records disappeared, and the paintings became indistinct blurs under centuries of grime and varnish.

Out of curiosity, Sara followed one painting as it was "drawn off" and porters with stencils and white paint marked the back with a code number, indicating the date of acceptance for sale, the category to which the work belonged, and the picture's own special coding which would allow it to be identified as long as Carthew's records survived.

The storage rooms had none of the corridor's confusion. Neat racks held the attributed paintings, whose newly stenciled codes would ease the task of the cataloguers as they got down to writing descriptions and choosing photographs to illustrate them. A few priceless items did not remain in this room but were carried into the sealed, air-conditioned vault at the far end reserved for Carthew's treasures. Its heavy red metal door opened twice that morning with a breath of cold air to swallow an exquisite Duccio and a Dürer, thudding shut after them with an admonitory boom.

Toward the end of the morning, with her feet aching and the whole group showing signs of strain, Sara watched two porters struggle down the hall with a canvas so horrific that even the fat man, so certain in his attributions all morning, seemed ashamed to display it.

"Good grief, Carl!" Carthew said, taking off his glasses to stare.

It was a nude, but one so voluptuous that only over the bar of a New Orleans brothel or in the private chambers of some Bourbon king would she have looked at home. Pink, proud, and ready for anything, she leaned against a tree, her thick soft body almost obscuring its trunk, while from the undergrowth a satyr regarded her nervously, wondering at his chances.

Even Mark was shaken. "What a bastard!" he murmured to Sara.

"Would that be Bastard the Younger or the Old Bastard?" someone asked facetiously, overhearing him. In the laughter that followed, Mark, straightfaced, took up the joke without a pause.

"Oh, Jean-Paul, of course. Old Philippe never went in for mythological subjects. Too shortsighted; did mainly self-portraits and pictures of goldfish."

"So you'd say Jean-Paul...er, Bâtarde, Mark?" Carthew asked.

"Indubitably."

"Anyone else?" The group was silent.

To Sara's astonishment, Carthew wrote the name down as carefully as any other attribution of the morning. A few months later, she saw the painting—"*Chloe and Satyr* by Jean-Paul Bâtarde"—in a sale of eighteenth and nineteenth-century masters. An Arab snapped it up for seventeen hundred pounds to hang in the backgammon room of his Kuwait palace. It was the end of Sara's illusions about the sanctity of sale catalogues.

There was obviously more to be learned than she imagined. She found an apartment, bought a typewriter and a basic collection of reference books, and settled down to some serious study. Catalogues and copies of trade magazines became her main reading, and the auctions of London an increasingly absorbing entertainment.

Mark's frequent absences from Snow's and his even more frequent assignations with Sara didn't go unnoticed either by his colleagues or by Cicely Snow.

"It's very irregular," Piper said to her after one of their quiet meetings, at which the aging but still alert head of Old Masters passed on to his employer all the gossip of the trade. Nothing in his tone betrayed the fact that Cicely's affair with Mark was as open a secret as this new liaison; on the surface, he spoke only of the effect such a relationship might have on Snow's prestige.

"I'm not sure it matters much, you know," Cicely said. She missed Mark's attention, but he could be an irritating lover; she was better served, at least for the moment, by the newest in a succession of young men chosen almost at random from those anxious to make their name and career in the art market.

If there was one thing she had learned from her active love life, it was that they all came back in the end. She was good; she knew that, and the knowledge buoyed her up in even the greatest despair. There was no gathering in London where she could not choose three men at random and be sure of being in bed with one of them that night. Mark would drift back to her, and when he did it would be a contrite, amenable Mark, anxious to do what he was told. He would also know more about Sara Hershman than anyone else, and that knowledge would give Cicely the power she wanted. She would watch, and wait—in many ways, that was half the fun.

Sara soon found that though fine art sales won the publicity, they represented only a fraction of the city's auctions. In shabby suburban halls she watched furniture and carpets sold as her grandfather sold them before the war—in an atmosphere of ribald backchat and raucous argument. She discovered Edward Barker and Son, who sold only cases of bristles from India and the Far East for the brush trade, and attended the noisy Monday morning sales at the Tea Brokers' Association in the same building on Upper Thames Street. Stone's Rooms for stuffed animals and birds, Stanley Gibbons for stamps... salerooms that sold only wine, cars, carpets, and just plain junk. She studied them all.

With Mark's help, she made contacts among the dealers and saleroom correspondents of the big newspapers, offering them discreet previews of her décolletage as they ran on about current scandals. But most of her time was spent prowling through the cellars of Snow's, learning her trade literally from the ground up. Soon she knew the porters by their first names and was equally friendly with Snow's staff of experts, all of them happy to show her around and to talk, if allowed, for hours on their specialties.

Time had made few inroads on Snow's air of gentlemanly absorption; in rebuilding, the architects had retained much of the old mansion's intricacy and its plethora of tiny rooms and half-hidden cupboards, seemingly inseparable from the auction trade. Guarnerius and Stradivarius violins still hung like hams in the cool darkness of understair cupboards—ideal, according to the experts, for air circulation and humidity. In the topmost room of the whole building, where a cage held the clicking, buzzing telephone-switching system, every spare inch was filled with antique musical instruments. Shawns and krumhorns lay mute in dusty corners, waiting for a sale that might take a year to put together.

Customers seemed no more anxious than Snow's itself to sell things quickly. A good sale of rare books or porcelain could take six months to assemble, yet the owners seldom complained. To buy or sell at Snow's or Sotheby's or Christie's conferred a cachet on the transaction, which was why prices at the big salerooms often topped those of antiques dealers. "I could spend a day shopping around Chelsea and Kensington," a dealer confided to her, "put everything I bought through Snow's, and make more than twenty percent on the deal."

After her first few months in London, Sara understood why. Buyers loved the glamour of the auction room, the excitement of bidding hard and winning over a crowded saleroom. Others enjoyed the hole-in-corner machinations of auction selling; the bidding codes, anonymous mail and phone offers, the game of hiding one's interest from fellow collectors.

But they paid for that glamour—paid in ways they seldom

suspected. Behind the suave facade of the saleroom lay
corruption, incompetence, and greed on a scale Sara had never
dreamed of.

Her suspicions were first aroused at a sale at one of the
smaller London auction rooms. The auctioneer, ignoring bids
from the back of the room, knocked down a silver salver at a
fraction of its value to a man whose smirk advertised his
satisfaction. Later, Sara saw buyer and auctioneer in close
consultation—and it was the auctioneer who carried off the
hurriedly wrapped parcel with the salver inside.

That evening, she passed on this story to Mark.

"You're surprised?" he said, smiling. "Why? It happens all the
time. I do it myself. All saleroom staff do."

"Well, yes, I *am* surprised. Snow's and the other companies
have such a reputation for honesty."

"They also have the worst salary scale of any business in
London. Do you know the income of the average auctioneer?
About three thousand pounds."

Eight thousand dollars? She thought of Mark's smart
apartment, his Austin Healey sports car, his Savile Row suits.
Eight thousand dollars would barely cover his bills for food and
wine.

"The top man in a department gets more," Mark went on,
"and he's paid a commission on sales. But a company only has so
many top men, and they don't leave until they're too senile to
carry on. We underlings have to feather our nests where we can."

The compendium of dirty tricks that Mark outlined for her in
the next hour was extensive, and it was clear he knew it
intimately, from experience.

Everyone in the saleroom had his opportunity for graft, from
the doorman up.

A dealer not wishing to show interest in a lot would ask the
doorman to bid for him. With the tip for this service would go
another tip, not of money but of information—news of an
undervalued picture at a bargain price or a piece of silver
wrongly described in the catalogue. The commissionaire at one
large London saleroom had recently retired with a water-color
collection worth thousands, acquired almost entirely from his
clients' advice.

Even the lowliest trainee, spending six months on the public
desk where people brought their family heirlooms in the hope of

discovering a treasure, could strike it rich, providing his eye was good and his nerves even better.

"I don't know," he would say as he turned over a classic Ming vase. "It *might* be worth fifty pounds."

"Is that all?" The owner would look disappointed. "My uncle told me it was quite valuable."

"Well, porcelain isn't really my line." Leaning forward, with a careful glance at his colleagues, he would go on. "But if I were you, I'd take it round to the Shantung Galleries up on Curzon Street. See Mr. Blegrave and mention my name." He would slip a card over the counter. "He's likely to give you much more than we could raise here."

And of course Mr. Blegrave *is* very generous, increasing the offer to one hundred, perhaps one hundred and fifty pounds, which sends the owner away with a song in his heart, unaware that Blegrave and his confederate on the saleroom desk will shortly split the ten thousand pounds their vase fetches at auction.

For the unimaginative, there was always simple theft; despite a security force led by a retired Scotland Yard man from the Antiques Squad, not even a dozen officers could cover every exit. And since everything on the premises was automatically insured, nobody looked too closely at those bulky handbags and bulging pockets.

Mark explained too the power of the catalogue staff, which had the job of describing items, supervising the photographs, and calculating the estimated value of each item. It was extraordinary how a valuable piece could seem less so if the description was unflattering, the picture taken from the wrong angle.

On a higher level, the department head and executives practiced their own genteel graft. Occasionally, a painting or sculpture, after having been "lost" and its owner paid off by the insurance company, turned up, renamed, reframed, and with a glowing provenance from a Carthew's or Snow's expert, at a saleroom in Paris or New York, where a commission agent sold it on behalf of "an anonymous collector"—the expert who "mislaid" it in the first place.

Remembering how David Moore let her destroy the fake Renoir rather than risk its being sold as authentic, Sara wondered if she had not been hasty in condemning him as entirely immoral. There were times when, by comparison with the sharks of London's fine art trade, he looked almost saintly.

Sara received weekly reminders of David in the letters and calls of Sascha Beauclair, now busily wheeling and dealing in New York with the help of the forty thousand dollars in seed money earned from the sale of Cristaldo's fake Etruscan piece.

Characteristically, Sascha's news was no news at all—just veiled hints of discussions with "our friend the frog" and of activities at Atropos, to which he had returned after Italy. Preferring not to know the details of his double-dealing, Sara didn't press him; duplicity came naturally to Sascha, but to her, the betrayal of David Moore was not made palatable merely because of its moral justification. Occasionally, she almost decided to pull out of Sascha's scheme, but her remoteness from New York and the danger of discussing it in letters deterred her. Gradually, the point of no return was reached and passed.

BOOK THREE

1962

29

The machine gave a querulous whine as it unrolled the cables that lowered Ted Augustus's mortal remains into the sandy California soil.

Feeling remote from the other mourners, David Moore stood motionless as the lacquered lid disappeared below the neatly cut edge of the grave. Among the fifteen people, there was no one he knew—nor anyone, he suspected, who had known Augustus intimately in life. What contempt Ted would have felt for the audience that watched him buried—the plump men in their polyester leisure suits and two-toned loafers and the women in their frilly hats, high-heeled shoes cutting neat holes in turf.

Like most California cemeteries, this one imitated Forest Lawn. There were the same terraced hillsides, with plaques set a few inches below grass level to facilitate mowing, the same mock antique church, in this case a concrete replica of St. James's, Piccadilly, with Grinling Gibbons's garlands reproduced in grained plastic around the altar. *Sheep May Safely Graze* had wound on a worn tape among the steel beams of the roof as the mourners drowsed through the droning absurdity of the service, calculated to offend no shade of religious or antireligious opinion. Wondering about the sheaf of white cards set in the rear of the pew in front, David found that a thrifty management, unable to resist a captive audience, encouraged the bereaved to fill in name, address, and phone number if they wished a salesman to call and discuss "pre-need provision." They even supplied a pencil.

Everything about the funeral would have horrified Ted. He remembered Ted's drawling, laconic comments on the intricate minuet of a cocktail party they had both been forced to attend at the Museum of Modern Art on the occasion of a "New York Artists" show in which he had two pictures. David wondered if Ted's presence, in spirit at least, at this, his last public appearance, accounted for the particular sourness he felt at the empty mouthing, the mechanized mourning, worn as thin as the hymn tape with prolonged use.

With a last pious phrase, the young minister turned from the grave as if expecting applause. Delighted to have it over, David put on his hat.

"Mr. Moore?"

He'd noticed the man in the group closest to the grave—overweight, balding, sweating in a vivid suit of overlapping blue and gray checks. A woman in cerise polyester trailed after him.

"Arnold Bessarabian." His handshake was as diffident as his voice. "Ted was my cousin-in-law. Er, that is, my wife's cousin."

"Pleased to meet you, Mr. Bessarabian. Mrs. Bessarabian. Ted's death was a great personal loss."

"Yeah, to us too, of course. Uh, Mr. Moore, I understand you're the executor of the will."

The vultures gather. "Well, I represent the trust Ted set up to look after his work. Actually, a firm of attorneys are the executors of record—Rotha, Lindgren and Durgnat. I'm sure they'll be in touch with all the relatives in time."

"We talked to them already. I guess you heard not all of us are happy about this trust thing."

"No, I hadn't," David lied. "Look Mr. Bessarabian, if you want to discuss this, I suggest we get out of the sun."

The foyer of the church offered the only shade in sight. Apparently it was a quiet day—no new funeral had moved into the pews they had so recently vacated.

"The thing is, Mr. Moore," Bessarabian said, "we can't seem to get any sense out of anyone about how much Ted actually left. Isn't that right, Berenice?"

Mrs. Bessarabian tried a disarming smile that her china-white dental work turned into a sharklike grin. "That girl friend of his won't even talk to us, and we tried Mr. Bleigen, but he said you were the only one who would know. It's really strange that Ted should be worth anything. He was always the black sheep, you know. Daddy just threw him out of the house after he came to live with us—" Conscious that she was betraying her assumed grief, she subsided. "Of course, we were all deeply shocked when we heard."

"I see where one of his paintings sold for twenty thousand," Bessarabian persisted. "How many did he leave exactly?"

"It's hard to tell. The studio was crowded with them, but they're not all completed. I have more than a hundred in the vault at our gallery, but there are others on loan, perhaps stored in places we know nothing about."

Bessarabian's smile became as sharkish as his wife's. "A hundred at twenty thousand dollars—"

"It isn't that easy," David said. "Ted's paintings are selling better now, but I believe they'll rise even more in the next few years. In five or ten years, he could be fetching twenty times these prices. You have to regard this as a long-term consideration. That's the beauty of the trust idea. As the paintings are sold, you'll all receive a portion of the profits—or so I understand from the attorneys."

"A portion, yeah," Bessarabian said sulkily. "About five percent, with most of the money going to that girl of his and the kid. Not even married."

"That was Ted's wish," David said, trying not to lose his temper. "And even five percent could be substantial, in time."

"I'm not sure I can wait that long. We've got expenses. I'm a talent representative. The business is expanding and you have to invest if you want to keep up."

David could visualize Bessarabian's idea of investment: sleek new premises with a French or English receptionist at the front desk, a new house, a Cadillac. In these few minutes, he had proved himself an inept negotiator—against the local competition, he must have to run very fast indeed to stay in the race at all.

"Mr. Bessarabian, even if the terms of the trust allowed me to sell any of Ted's paintings right now, I wouldn't do it. It's true there's a surge of interest in his work; that's usual when an artist dies. But if we flooded the market now, we'd destroy Ted as a commercial prospect for ten years, perhaps forever. There's a tiny market for modern art. Perhaps two hundred individuals and galleries in the world have the funds and the taste to invest in work like his. Rarity is what we sell in the art market, Mr. Bessarabian. It may be necessary to hang onto these paintings for ten years to realize their full value. Believe me, you'll be glad you did."

Neither of them liked being told they could not be rich overnight. David watched the gleam in their eyes turn to a glitter of resentment.

"I guess we can take this up with the attorneys," Bessarabian said grudgingly.

"Do that." Turning on his heel, David walked quickly toward the semicircle of asphalt on which he had left his car parked. The rented Buick stank of its newness, the odors of paint, metal, plastic, and gas heated to a choking miasma by the glaring sun. Savagely turning on the air conditioning full blast, he drove along the freeway with icy air stinging tears into his eyes.

You're getting old, Moore, he told himself. Maybe the mid-forties were a good time to stop and think about what he was doing. The flesh peddlers were wearing him down.

On impulse, he ignored the airport exit and drove back through Los Angeles until his way was barred by the flat bronzed surf of the beachfront, the water as blinding as a mirror in the afternoon sun. Turning north, he followed U.S. 1 until Los Angeles slipped behind and the cliffs and forests of Big Sur slid out of the dusk to bulk around him, cool, moist, and sunk in a blessed silence.

He stayed that night in a tiny motel in some unfashionable holiday town, bypassed by the swingers anxious to make it to Carmel and San Francisco but inhabited even now, in midweek, by families snatching a week away from the city. The calm thump of the surf put him to sleep that night, and children woke him in the morning with their laughter and the rattle of bucket and spade. For a moment, he remembered Brighton and the country he hadn't seen for almost twenty-five years.

The maid—probably the owner's daughter, because she dumped the tray down with good humor and refused his tip—brought breakfast, and David sat in bed, watching the pattern of light from the surf reflected through the venetian blinds onto the ceiling. Sipping his coffee, he took stock of his life.

Essentially, his career had created not a close-knit fabric but a tangle of loose endings. Except where death intervened, as with Simon Snow, Arthur Sklar, and now Ted Augustus, to snap a thread, his relationships with people remained as connected now as when he had tried to break away from them.

His mother, still living in England, dutifully acknowledged his quarterly checks, but otherwise stayed out of his life. Cicely Snow remained an ambiguous, taunting figure about whom his emotions continued confused and disturbing. Michael Gothard had agreed readily enough to be his London representative, but their relationship remained exclusively professional, as did his contact with Tonino Valerii. He had created a shield around himself in the early days, from behind which he could build his business safe from attack. Once there had been room behind it for friends and intimates; lately, however, its compass had shrunk until now only he existed within it, increasingly confined by its gleaming walls.

Only one person had come inside—Sara Hershman. And even that had been a trick, a brief touch of intimacy to dazzle her and bait the trap.

Sara returned often to his mind, even though it was more than a year since he had last seen her. She had never resigned, but from Sascha Beauclair he gathered she had no intention of returning to Atropos.

From Sascha, he received a gloating account of her Italian interlude, and Gothard kept him informed laconically of her activities in London, where she appeared to be the mistress of Snow's Mark Turnbull. More than once, he thought of writing her an apology, an explanation, but each time the cynicism of the trick played on her stopped him. At the time, Arthur Sklar's illness and the imminence of the Snow's sale blurred his judgment.

From their first meeting, David had suspected Sara's motives in wanting to work for him, and to turn that plan against her seemed like poetic justice. She had asked for it, and if you couldn't stand the heat you should stay out of the kitchen, but a moral itch remained that defied any amount of scratching.

More than by guilt and a sense of recrimination, he was troubled by the fact that their brief affair had not been entirely calculated. The visit to his apartment should not, in his original plan, have ended in bed, but merely in the entrusting of an important task, backed up by all the solemnity he could muster. She should have gone to London thinking of herself as a respected member of the Atropos staff, a confidential courier—not, as she finally went, in a haze of love and hero worship which made her subsequent humiliation all the more painful.

In his clearer moments, David knew why Sara appealed to him. He enjoyed her eagerness to learn, her willingness to be trained and to learn from what he taught her. And behind it all was that killer instinct, the skill in selling that only one man in a thousand possessed and one woman in ten thousand. Sometimes, if the idea were not so obviously ridiculous, he could have sworn he was in love with the girl.

David took a week over his reevaluation, loafing up the coast road to San Francisco, then farther north into Oregon, and finally leaving the car in Portland to fly back to New York. Now on his mental agenda were four or five pressing new items, some personal, some professional. The trip had given him time to reassess the art market as well as his own life, and there would be changes in both when he returned home.

He could not know how few of his new plans would ever be put into practice.

His new receptionist looked up brightly as he came through the door and dumped down his bag. Fran having astonishingly announced her forthcoming marriage to his accountant Humboldt a month before, her replacement, personally chosen by her and in many respects a duplicate, down to the beehive hairdo and predatory nails, was too new an addition for David even to have memorized her name.

"Ask Danny to take my bag upstairs will you . . . uh, dear?"

"Mr. Gothard called from London, Mr. Moore. He wants you to get back to him. I think it's urgent. And there's a gentleman." She waved toward the back gallery, where a thin figure in leather jacket and faded brown cotton trousers was browsing among the abstracts. David joined him.

"You wanted to see me?"

The man turned. "You David Moore?" He had the level stare of a man who looked carefully at anything before making up his mind about it. His blue eyes were surrounded by almost china whites, the color accentuated by a tan burned deep into the skin. Scars around his mouth were partly hidden by a drooping mustache. He might be forty, or perhaps it was the effect of a hard, dangerous life on a man ten years younger.

David nodded, and the other held out his hand. "Brian Jolson." There was a leather holdall at his feet. "Something I wanted to show you."

They went into his office, David wondering what kind of art he was going to be asked to buy. Jolson hadn't looked like an artist, but everything else pointed to it. The tiresome conversation was already mapped out in his mind, its evasions and half-helpful advice so familiar he had long ago ceased to be embarrassed by them.

But Jolson surprised him. The bag held something about the size of a cabbage, wrapped in cloth. David unwrapped a rough stone head and picked it up.

The stone was something like jade, something like granite—close-grained, a combination of brown and green specks, the surface highly polished to bring out the sheen of both. A thousand years of culture lay between the Monet on the wall behind him and this crude head, but they were united in their artistic vision. The man who carved this face did so with the skill and insight of a Picasso, a Bellini.

"Mayan?"

"Olmec. Same place, more or less, but a thousand years earlier."

"Mexico or Guatemala?"

"People down there don't make much of a distinction. The bandits kill you, the kids get rickets, they all die around forty whether it's Mexico or Honduras or Guatemala. Maybe a bit quicker in Honduras, I guess."

The neck was snapped off just below the chin. David fingered the edges.

"This is a new break."

"Until a month ago, it was probably on some idol down in El Peten."

That placed it in the high mountain country of Guatemala. David put the head back on the table and looked at the face. This man would have known about the bandits, the rickets, the early death, and cared hardly at all.

"It's beautiful."

Jolson seemed to relax. "You're the first man who didn't ask me what I wanted for it."

"I'm not sure I'm in the market. I don't deal in pre-Columbian pieces. Have you tried Gomez? And Cottafavi?"

"Gomez is out of town. Is Cottafavi a little guy who works out of a hotel suite up opposite the Metropolitan?"

"That's him. Not interested?"

"I could hardly get him to let it go. But he looked a bit too greedy for me. People tell me you're fairly honest."

David smiled at the "fairly." "I gather you're not just looking for a quick sale."

"You got it. Mr. Moore, I run a little charter flying service down in the Yucatan. Fly some tourists, fishermen, hunters, occasionally oil people and copper prospectors." He picked up the head and looked into its face. "This guy was sitting on a shelf in a foreman's office of a copper dig down in Los Soldados. He got it from a farmer. Gave him twenty dollars and a bundle of .American magazines. I think there are lots more down there. It looked to me like they oughta be worth more than twenty bucks and some old *Newsweeks*."

"Good pieces are really priceless," David said. "But you could start the bidding on this at around fifty thousand dollars. What did Cottafavi offer?"

"Ten."

"The price does tend to go down if you aren't a dealer and can't prove ownership."

"I can prove I bought it from a guy named Giannini in Arroyo Pesquero, for what that's worth."

"It's not worth a lot, I'm afraid. It probably didn't belong to him, legally. The Mexican and Guatemalan governments have laws about taking antiquities out of the country."

"I know all about the law, Mr. Moore," Jolson said sourly. "I also know what happens when these things get into the hands of museum officials down there who earn about twenty dollars a month, and museum guards who don't even get that much. You know as well as I do that half the Mayan and Olmec stuff in big American museums came from some crooked curator. I figure it's better off in the United States. It'll get here sooner or later; I'm just trying to cut out the middleman." He glanced up at the Monet. "I don't know—what's legal anyway? Did you buy that from the man who painted it, or from some dealer who got it for a couple of dollars when the old man needed to pay the rent?"

David felt the stirrings of a hunch. Most of his career was based on random events like this meeting, flashes that illuminated some new twist in the market. Impressionists had, as he predicted years ago, followed Old Masters into the rarefied price levels that made dealing a new impossibility, and soon major contemporary works would follow. Pre-Columbian art was a new growth area; already there were private collections and museums clamoring for good pieces.

He checked his watch: 6 P.M. In London, Gothard would be at his club or at dinner.

"Mr. Jolson, let's have a drink and we'll talk about this."

It was eight o'clock before David let Jolson out by the front door of the gallery. Back in his office, he took a special checkbook from his safe and, on an account whose existence Humboldt had carefully disguised beyond the probings of even Bleigen's ferreting auditors, wrote out a check for ten thousand dollars in favor of Brian Jolson. Slipping it into an envelope he addressed and stamped himself, he placed it carefully in the middle of the dozen letters laid on his desk for signature by the secretary. She would mail them tomorrow without noticing the addition.

Then he dialed London, standing alone in the dark office, listening to the phone ring thinly on the other side of the world.

"It's David, Michael. You've been trying to get me?"

"Yes—for a week." He sounded angry.

"I'm sorry. I took a few days off after Ted Augustus's funeral."

"It's Augustus I want to talk about, needless to say." His voice was heavily weighted with sarcasm. "You might have kept me informed, David."

"Informed of what?"

"The Augustus exhibition. What else?"

"Michael, slow down. What exhibition?" Except for a few works in private hands, the bulk of Ted's paintings lay in the vaults under his feet, legally frozen until the will was probated.

"David, please, no games. It's common knowledge you're behind this show. I've had a dozen people on the phone today alone, all customers of ours."

"I have no idea what you're talking about, Michael. What show?"

Gothard sighed. "The show of forty-three oils at the Greene gallery in Bond Street which opens tomorrow."

"You mean a loan exhibition?" There were few major Augustus works in museums and collections as yet, but it was just conceivable that some gallery might have rounded them up for a quick posthumous show.

"Not a loan exhibition," Gothard said. "Everything is for

sale. The prices start at twenty-five thousand dollars and go on from there. They'll sell them, too. Augustus's death has started a real boom."

"This is crazy, Michael. Do you have a catalogue there? Read some titles."

Still obviously skeptical, Gothard said, "There's four paintings from his Italian series: *Radicofane, St. Francis. . . .*"

"But they're in the vault here. Wait until I check." He unlocked the filing drawer of his desk and reached for the fat Augustus file. It wasn't there.

"Sorry, Michael," he said after a long pause. "I'll call you back."

The vault looked exactly as it had on his last visit, months before—the paintings, wrapped in sacking, lodged in their racks. Walking along the rows, he found the distinctive large canvases of the Italian series and checked the title cards stapled to the burlap. "*Radicofane.* 2.5 meters X 3 meters. Oil on canvas. 1953."

Hooking his fingers under the sewn seam, he pulled at the stitches. They came away easily and he peeled back the covering from a few square feet of the painting. For a long time, he stared at the blank unpainted canvas, then looked down the rows, knowing that they were all the same.

30.

"Didn't you tell me you owned one of these?" Mark asked.

Sara looked around the crowded gallery, which the usual mob of professional first-nighters filled with a deafening hubbub. Few seemed to be taking much notice of Ted Augustus's paintings, but the roster of guests—fashionable artists, a handful of politicians, the usual crop of expensive women, and one middle-league royal—guaranteed the exhibition's success. Already half a dozen paintings bore the tiny red sticker indicating a sale, and three more the half-disk showing the work was under consideration.

"Just a small oil of the Macy's parade. Augustus gave it to me the first time we met."

"In exchange for what, I won't ask."

"In exchange for nothing, Mark!" Sara snapped. "I don't think you believe in any sort of relationship not based on money or sex."

"No, I suppose not. Are there any? Not in this room, as far as I can see."

Looking around, Sara could only endorse his pessimistic view. The art world appeared at its worst on these occasions, its members circling like bantams in an intricate dance to establish precedence.

"Oh, I heard something interesting," Mark went on. "Your old friend David Moore is coming to London."

The blood drained from Sara's face. Luckily Mark was

looking the other way; he would have been astonished at the change, the sudden pallor that made her face into a death mask. She took a sudden gulp of her gin and tonic, coughed as the spirit burned her throat, and covered her confusion by burying her face in her handkerchief.

If Sara hoped to disguise her reaction, she failed. Mark missed her shock, but the rest was obvious enough. "For heaven's sake! I didn't think you disliked the man *that* much."

"I'd just rather not meet him, that's all."

Mark looked around the crowded room. "I expected to see him here tonight, to tell the truth, but from what I hear he won't get in until later in the week. Maybe then we can get some answers."

"Answers to what?"

"The questions about this show—what else? For the last six months, everyone interested in Augustus's work has been told there was none for sale. It was all supposed to be in trust. Now, suddenly, this. A real Moore coup, if you like. Yet he isn't here to savor it. Was there ever a trust?"

"I haven't worked for him for more than a year. How would I know?"

"Oh, somehow I expected you to have your finger on that sort of thing. You or Beauclair."

"What does Sascha have to do with it? You're just looking for conspiracies where none exist."

She was aware that his questions were flustering her—and aware as well that Mark saw her confusion.

"Who mentioned conspiracies? Unless—" He grinned suddenly. "Oh, I *see!* You and Beauclair. And, I suppose, Carl Bleigen? You put it over on David Moore, the three of you?" He laughed delightedly. Putting her drink down firmly on the nearest shelf, Sara stormed out, her face burning.

When she got home, the phone was ringing.

"Petal!" The familiar voice filled her with a sudden chill.

"Hello, Sascha. When did you get in?"

"I've just changed my mind. Is that so hard to understand?"

"Frankly, yes. It was your idea, let me remind you."

It was two hours later, and Sara's apartment, so calm normally, with its view over the tiny lighted park of Ladbroke Square, held an electric tension. Sascha prowled the living room, punctuating his conversation with a nervous examination of the small antiques Sara had collected over the last year. Each merely increased his sullen and hurt expression.

"My memory isn't quite that bad, Sascha. You know very well you dreamed it up. I knew nothing about the Augustus business until you told me."

Sascha put down a tiny Meissen figure with an angry click. "What does it matter who thought of it? I've committed us to working with Bleigen, in return for control of Hershman's. Doesn't that interest you? You're now the proprietor of your own saleroom."

"I thought Bleigen still held forty-eight percent."

"All right, *part* proprietor. But it's yours to run. Ours, anyway, if you're not going back on *that* part of the agreement as well."

"Sascha, I'd love to run Hershman's, and you know I can't do it without your help. But framing David Moore—"

"What happened to the Sara who complained so bitterly about Ted Augustus living on a pittance while Atropos took fifty percent?"

"I've learned a lot since then. Maybe David was right. I don't know. But anything's better than letting Augustus's work fall into the hands of a toad like Bleigen."

"A toad who's handing you hundreds of thousands of dollars."

"But for my father's death—which he may have caused—I'd own Hershman's anyway."

Sascha dropped wearily to the couch. "I don't know why we're even arguing about it. It's all done."

"Then undo it."

"Too late. I signed the papers before I left New York. You went into this with your eyes open, sweetheart. I might have thought it up, but you played along. And don't forget where the working capital came from. That scheme with the Etruscan piece was your own idea." As he lifted his glass in a mocking toast, she recognized the implied threat. "Cheers, partner. I'm going to make you rich, despite yourself."

Michael Gothard had waited for him at the Atropos offices in Jermyn Street. Feeling constricted, almost coffined by the pinched, low-ceilinged version of his own office in New York, David took the chair that offered a view through the main showroom to the traffic edging by outside.

"What's this all about, David? Are we selling these things or not? I've seen provenances on Atropos notepaper, letters signed by Sascha Beauclair authorizing the sale...." Nervousness seemed to increase the elasticity of his ample flesh. His multiple chins quivered as he talked.

David explained the plot, the details of which were clear enough once he found the paintings missing from the vault. "Bleigen wanted to sell the Augustus paintings while there was a demand after Ted's death. I refused, because I think they'll go higher. Carl didn't like this, so he removed the paintings from our vault, put them out for valuation to someone who would rate them at well under their real value, then shipped them over here to be sold. I suppose he assumes that, since they'll make far more than the valuation, the heirs will be too pleased to complain."

"He'd need someone on the outside."

"He had somebody—Sascha Beauclair." He paused, unwilling to state what now seemed obvious. "Sara Hershman was in on it too, it seems."

"Oh." Gothard took some time to digest this information. David wondered if he believed him; a reputation for deviousness encouraged skepticism in one's colleagues.

"In any event," David went on, "Bleigen claims I authorized the sale, as trustee of the estate. Which of course I have no right to do, under the terms of the trust."

"Surely that won't be hard to disprove. Wouldn't he need some signed authority from you?"

"Carl knows enough forgers to manufacture one. But if Sascha and Sara testify they heard me tell Bleigen it was OK, that would be enough. After all, we're partners, even though he takes no part in the business. We wouldn't necessarily put everything in writing."

"What about other papers? Agendas, correspondence? There must be *something* to back you up."

"Sascha cleared out the files before he left. It's just my word against theirs."

Gothard avoided David's eye. "What are you going to do now?" Suddenly the problem was his alone. It didn't surprise him.

"Stay here as long as it takes to clarify things."

At the door, Gothard avoided shaking hands, as if failure made David somehow unclean.

"This doesn't have anything to do with that newspaper piece about the Hershman girl, does it? You know I wasn't happy about fixing that. I'm no gossip columnist."

It was clearly time to pay off old scores. "It was necessary."

"I don't doubt that." His voice had an air of satisfaction. "But in my experience that sort of thing has a way of recoiling."

As David stepped out into the street, the door shut firmly behind him. By the next morning, Gothard would be sniffing around for a new job.

He walked toward Mayfair, his problems pushed from his mind by the changes he saw in the city. Not much of his London was left. They were reaming out the little alleys to accommodate the ever-growing traffic, uprooting old buildings to make way for skyscraping office blocks. The new city combined the worst of London with the worst of New York, and he was glad to find that the Connaught still remained unchanged on Church Street, a bastion against the twentieth century.

He had a corner room, overlooking a slice of Berkeley Square. A pile of catalogues and magazines lay unread on the table, the result of a conviction that he needed to get up to date on the London saleroom scene, even if, as it seemed, he no longer had a place in the business. He wondered if a gin and tonic would help him to get through the daunting heap, a decision postponed by the phone. He picked it up, unsuspecting.

"David? Cicely Snow."

A curving avenue of trees with drooping boughs . . . a colored engraving of a girl in wig and brocaded shoes . . . a smell of perfume and dust . . . a maid's impassive face . . . scent swirling in a bottle . . . the rattle of a cab on a rainy night. . . .

"Oh." His voice sounded thin, like a bad recording. "Hello."

They met the next day for drinks.

She had changed hardly at all. The red hair a trifle chemical, perhaps, but then look at his own thinning scalp. Her body was thicker inside the silk dress, but she moved with the same perky animation, all eagerness. The face showed a lot of living, but most of the changes were for the better. At his own age, more or less, she looked an effortless thirty-five.

"Cicely." He was surprised to find himself smiling. They touched lips casually, like cousins.

"Darling, do me a large favor. Don't say 'You haven't

changed' and I won't either. Let's just agree that twenty-five years is a long time."

"You're stealing all my conversation! What about 'A lot of water's gone under the bridge since then'? And those 'Whatever happened to' lines?"

"Pretend we're total strangers. At a bus stop." She looked around the crowded Connaught lounge. "Am I right for the one thirty-one to Fulham?"

He laughed, wondering how he could possibly do so after... well, after everything. Cautiously testing the air for some returning emotion, he found nothing there. This Cicely might have been an older sister, perhaps even the mother of the girl of 1939, serious where she was flirtatious, assured where she lacked sophistication. He felt the urge to ask this new Cicely for advice on handling the mercurial and impetuous younger version.

"I heard about Oliver Turnbull," he said, making conversation. Snow's Chairman had died, predictably of heart disease, a few months before.

"He couldn't live forever. And at the end I think he was tired of it all. Beating Simon was all he had really cared about, and of course that chance eluded him too."

"So now you're in charge."

"Officially, though really Mark, Oliver's nephew, runs things day to day." The waiter slid silently to their elbow with drinks. "Actually, my sweet, that's why I wanted to see you. How would you feel about coming back to Snow's?"

The crowded room seemed suddenly silent. Could such a bombshell have gone unremarked by the chattering drinkers?

"Back? To what, exactly?"

"Well, we're thinking of opening a New York office. Sotheby's and Christie's plan to do the same, but we want to beat them to it. I thought Atropos would be an ideal nucleus for it. What do you think? You'd have a position on the board and full autonomy, of course."

"I can't believe you're serious, Cicely. Haven't you heard about this Augustus business? There's every likelihood I'll face a huge lawsuit when I go back—even criminal proceedings."

"We know all about that." Her voice suggested no particular concern. "Bleigen is behind it; everyone knows that. If we make it worth his while, he'll drop the whole thing."

Suspecting that this was true, David wondered how long

Cicely had known about the scheme—what part, in fact, she may have played in its confection. There had always been a little madness in her, and a genius for hatred.

"It's been too many years since I worked in a saleroom, Cicely."

"We don't think that matters."

"Who is 'we,' exactly?"

"Michael Ballard, Shroeder, Wallenstein—they were all very keen when your name was mentioned."

If Cicely now ran the business and employed all of them, David was not surprised at their enthusiasm.

"I don't think I could become an organization man at this time of my life."

"We have lots of organization men, darling. That's our problem. Your value lies in different areas. We need your flair. Peter Wilson didn't build up Sotheby's by being an organization man."

It was a shrewd and flattering comparison. Sotheby's chairman had almost revolutionized the auction business, opening branches in Monte Carlo, in Geneva, even in Hong Kong. Sotheby's were into wine, stamps, houses, railroad cars—they sold the Diaghilev ballet costumes onstage at La Scala, as part of a sumptuous Milanese gala, yet their trade in low-priced art items had tapped the new middle-class collectors' market so that items under a hundred pounds accounted for almost all their income.

In fact, the comparison was a little *too* tempting. He was being set up.

"What about Turnbull? Surely he'd do well in New York. Sounds like an aggressive chap."

"He's too young."

"Simon was hardly any older when he took over the whole company."

"How did we get onto Simon?" Her hatred chilled the air between them. "That weakling, with his coughing and his little-boy eyes and his books. Jesus, his books!"

For a long moment, the ghost of Simon seemed to rise between them. David couldn't meet Cicely's eyes, so potent was his sense of disgust.

The waiter came with the check and she reached for it, but David snatched it first, signed the back, and handed it to the man.

"I knew you weren't happy with Simon," David said quietly when the waiter was gone, "but I never realized how much you hated him."

She accepted the charge without comment. "I should never have married him." Her voice was sullen. "I should have married you."

"Then I'd be dead now, like poor Simon. You're a killer, Cicely. You belong in another time. Renaissance women were like you: without scruples."

"That's cruel."

"We're cruel people. But I'm not cruel enough to rob Mark Turnbull just to satisfy your need for revenge. What's he done to you anyway? Walked out, like I did?" He stood up. "You *haven't* changed, you know."

Outside, the effect of a double gin on an empty stomach hit him. He was halfway across the road before he realized the cars weaving around him were trying to avoid running him down. Up Hay Hill lay Albemarle Street and Snow's, but, unable to face it so soon after leaving Cicely, he turned into Piccadilly and joined the rush-hour crowds oozing toward the railway station of Piccadilly Circus.

Above his head, the neon signs sizzled. It was raining lightly, turning the dust on the sidewalks to a gritty paste. Veering out of the crowd, he almost fell over the beggar kneeling on the pavement, bent double over a harmonica on which he wheezed an unrecognizable tune, formless and reiterative as an Indian chant. His body sheltered from the rain a crudely chalked drawing of a yellow sunrise over acid green hills. Underneath, neatly lettered, was the word VETERAN.

Rocking slightly on his feet, David fumbled for money. This was art for you. Ted Augustus would have loved this man, seen an echo of himself in that pose, that message—hunched over his sunset, desperate for understanding but frightened to accept it. There were coins and notes in David's hand now, and he scattered them before the man like an obeisance.

31

It took less courage than Sara imagined to call on David Moore, and she was unprepared for the sudden loss of nerve that overcame her in the lobby of the Connaught as the desk clerk directed her to the bar, where, he assured her, Mr. Moore had been sitting for the last hour.

He sat alone in a corner, reading what looked like a legal document and sipping occasionally from the drink at his elbow. The three years that had created a new Sara Hershman had left few marks on him. From the doorway, she catalogued the familiar features, placing them one by one on the image held in her mind. Perhaps the hair at the temples was a little grayer, the frown lines slightly deeper—though that might be a result of the papers he scanned with such absorption.

Now or never, Sara thought. Palms slippery with perspiration, she launched herself on the crowded bar like a small boat into choppy seas.

"Hello."

"Oh, hello, Sara."

What had she expected? A clap of thunder? A cold stare before the eyes dropped again to the papers? Her prepared scenarios did not include his slightly weary smile and the gesture to the chair beside him. Gratefully, she sank into it just as her knees went weak.

"Drink?"

"Please. Sambuca and ice."

He raised his eyebrows and looked around for a waiter. "Where did you pick that up?"

"Paris. The bottle looked nice."

He glanced at his own drink. "I never thought to use the bottle as a guide. Anyway, gin bottles look like they should hold kerosene."

She clung to the subject like a life preserver. "It was a choice between Sambuca and that stuff in the long bottle with the flowers in it."

"Alpini Fiori. Mmmm. I always wondered if you ate the flowers when the booze was gone."

"I don't know." The conversation receded like a sudden tide, leaving her high and dry, her mind a blank.

"Well, I can talk liquor all night," David said, "but I don't suppose that's why you came. How did you know I was here, incidentally?"

"You booked *me* in here—remember?"

"Oh. Yes. I forgot."

Sensing that the conversation could slide into a recital of recriminations, she said quickly, "David, I didn't come here to drag up what happened last time. I think I know why you did it. I can understand—"

Glancing over her shoulder, David saw the couple at the next table prick up their ears, sensing confidences. "I'm not sure we should discuss this here. Have you had dinner?"

"No. But I'm not hungry."

He stood up. "Then we'd better walk."

The last commuters were gone from Mayfair, leaving the streets to late-afternoon strollers like themselves. Even Hyde Park had fewer pedestrians than usual. As they stopped to let a few late riders canter by on the dusty track nicknamed Rotten Row, the smell of dust, horses, and the soft damp of the evening filled the air with a thick, almost choking scent. Sara felt dizzy with it.

They talked—later, Sara could never remember the subjects. She did recall talking about the Augustus business, stumbling through an explanation, a sort of apology, before David quieted her with a look—not of anger or surprise but of concern.

"It doesn't matter, you know."

"But—"

"Sssh. How is Tonino? I meant to see him this trip but I won't be able to manage now."

She told him about Italy—about Tonino, Paola, and Mark, then took refuge in the present, detailing her experience in London's auction world and her delight in a growing knowledge of the trade she intended to pursue now that Hershman's was finally hers.

As they moved deeper into the park, their talk became a screen against the real issues between them. They were almost in Kensington now, and she could see the low stone buildings of the Palace that marked the farthest border of the public park. A shiver reminded her it was dusk, and as if her recognition was a signal, the lamps sprang on, hanging yellow, like jack-o'-lanterns, in the trees.

"We've come a long way," she said. "I'm almost home." She could see the roof of her house through the trees. "Would you like to see it?"

They stood in the hall without turning on the lights. Sara never remembered who began the kiss, but later it seemed to her that no other act could have resolved the tensions of that evening. It was as if for two years she had waited for nothing else.

"That's nice," David said as they moved apart. "Are you going to take me to bed?"

A long, drowsy time later, Sara said, "Can I ask you something?"

"What?"

"Back in New York, did you go to bed with me just because of the Sklar thing?"

"No."

She snuggled up to him contentedly. "I didn't think you did—not deep down."

"I must say you're very trusting. In the circumstances, isn't it more likely that I'd lie?"

"I don't think so. You don't believe in letting people down easy. Why break the rule of a lifetime?"

"Maybe I'm getting old."

Her hand slid down to grasp him gently but firmly. "I don't think so."

"That doesn't prove anything."

"It does, you know. I may be inexperienced, but I can tell if—" She meant to go on to say, "If I'm loved," but paused, hooked on the admission like a thorn. Later, she wondered at the pattern of her life and David's had she spoken the three words. Instead she finished lamely, "If someone means it."

"I never do anything I don't mean."

"What about turning down Cicely Snow's offer? You didn't do that because you disliked her?"

"No." He made an effort to explain the malaise he experienced at the thought of returning to a life of buying and selling. Had it ever been enjoyable, he wondered? Or was it always a tool to get back at Simon or to prove his superiority to Bleigen and the rest of the New York sharks? He felt almost grateful to Bleigen for taking matters out of his hands.

"You're just depressed," Sara said positively. "Once you get back to New York, you'll feel differently. You wouldn't let Bleigen take Atropos away from you—not after all the work you put into it. And I'll help. I'll talk to Sascha. . . ." She yawned.

Within a few minutes, she was deep asleep. Carefully disengaging himself, David dressed in the dark and slipped out of the room. Pausing in the doorway, he admired for the last time the profile on the pillow, the pale face outlined against a cloud of hair, then firmly shut the door.

"But he wouldn't just disappear, Sascha!"

Pausing with a spoonful of vichyssoise halfway to his lips, Sascha said, "*I* certainly would, if I had as much to run from as David Moore. The Augustus heirs think he milked them of millions. I'd find a hole and pull it in over my head. Incidentally, aren't you going to eat that avocado? If not, I suggest you send it back or we'll wait all afternoon for our main course."

"No, I don't want it." She poured a third glass of wine from the bottle cooling in the ice bucket beside the table.

Sascha looked at her keenly. "I'm beginning to put two and two together. You and Moore didn't . . ."

Sara glared at him and his smirk became more pronounced.

"Well, really! Some people."

"It's none of your business, Sascha."

"Agreed. But Hershman's is—a fact that I now have in writing." They had just come from a long session with the lawyers at which the precise relationship between herself, the House of Hershman, and Sascha Beauclair had been eternalized in thirty sheets of legal linen paper. As General Manager, with a hefty share of the profits and guaranteed representation on the board, Sascha stood to make as much out of the revitalized firm as did Sara. This lunch was intended to celebrate the agreement, but by now the idea was as sour to Sara as the feeling in her stomach.

She had never dreamed David would leave her like that, to have her wake in an empty bed and a cold, deserted apartment. She called the Connaught, but he must have returned there immediately and checked out. She searched the apartment but found no note, no sign that their lovemaking had been more than a dream. Two days later, news of the suits brought against him by the Bessarabians and other heirs to the Augustus estate reached the London papers, and David became technically a fugitive, since process servers had been unsuccessful in locating him to deliver their subpoenas. Atropos, its assets impounded, its doors locked and sealed, was closed down. David Moore might never have existed.

Sara had no head for alcohol. It pandered to the dark side of her character, as marijuana freed the playful and companionable part of her nature. Anger, resentment, fear, and a sense of loss flitted through her brain like evils liberated from the Pandora's box of her adolescent misery. She found her love for David overshadowed by a cold resentment.

"If you're so keen to make your first million," she said, "we had better get on with it. What do we need?"

"Ah, that's better." Sascha beamed. "Well, premises, for a start. I suppose we could use the old place on Eleventh Street—"

"No. It's not worth starting at all unless we start fresh. There must be space to rent."

"It'll cost us."

"What about our capital?"

"All gone. Lawyers cost money, dear."

"Can Bleigen help?"

"Much as I appreciate Carl's help," Sascha said carefully, "I'd rather not get in too deep to him. A place to sell will be top of my list when I go back. Second, staff."

"Hire some to start with, but we'll train the rest ourselves. Sotheby's are starting their own school. It makes sense for us to do the same. I want Hershman people, not retreads from Parke-Bernet."

From Sascha's irritated look, Sara guessed he had already promised jobs to the gaggle of ex-lovers and current admirers that clustered around him in New York. But he didn't protest, a fact she should have seen as ominous.

"All right. Last and not least, something to sell."

"I'll look after that. Just find us a place to sell it in."

Wondering why Sascha was smiling at her, she looked down to see the wine bottle in her hand. It was tilted above her glass but nothing came out. Clearly she had emptied it as she talked.

"I'll look after it," she repeated. The empty bottle rattled back into the bucket with a noise that made the nearest diners turn and stare. Sara glared at them until they looked away in well-bred astonishment.

"This promises to be quite a partnership," Sascha said.

32

"If you're really ready to start buying," Mark said one afternoon, as they dressed in the cramped hot room of the hotel in Hallam Street that they reserved for the assignations, "I've got a few interesting items for you."

Wriggling into her dress, Sara sat on the edge of the bed to buckle her sandals. The window, half open, admitted the sound of shuffling feet from the pavement, two floors below.

"At Snow's?"

"Dear me, no. A little close to home, I should have thought. No use giving Cicely all our secrets. I was thinking of Carthew's, actually. I have a few friends there."

Three days later, they met for coffee in another of their hideaways. Mark had the typed manuscript of a Carthew's auction catalogue.

Sara leafed through it. "Porcelain?"

"Forget about that—the experts have it sewn up. Turn to the back."

Twentieth-century pottery took up the last half-dozen pages of the catalogue. She scanned the photographs of heavily decorated De Morgan and Moorcroft vases, once the white elephants of parish jumble sales, now sought after by collectors, then turned with relief to four pages of bleakly modern stoneware by Bernard Leach, Shoji Hamada, and their followers.

Sara knew a little about Hamada, the greatest of all modern

Japanese potters. Leach studied under him in Japan, then returned to Cornwall to open his own studio and carry on the tradition of simple, elegant pottery. The work of both men, mainly plates, jugs, and pots glazed in plain earth colors and decorated with ideograms or childlike sketches of birds, grass and flowers, had an ageless simplicity that improved with acquaintance.

"Feel like plunging a little on these?" Mark asked, pointing to the Hamadas.

Sara turned to the estimated prices at the back of the catalogue. Though kept low to encourage buyers, they were a fair indication of what the items were worth. None of the Leach or Hamada items were listed at less than eight hundred pounds, which meant they might go as high as a thousand each.

"They're not worth it, Mark. I'd have to get at least a fifty percent markup to make them profitable, and there just isn't that much interest in the States."

Mark smiled, "Let's go and have a word, shall we?"

The ceramics department of Carthew's, its shelves piled with pots and plates, each heap flagged with scraps of paper indicating the sale for which it was intended, was as unglamorous as she expected. For the two men working at a scarred wooden table, peering at the marks on a large collection of Coalport figures, the arrival of Mark and Sara was a welcome diversion.

"I was interested in these Hamadas," Mark said. "Could I have a look?"

One man took down a cardboard box and set the Hamadas on the table: two tall jugs, one decorated with leaping fish, the other with ears of wheat; a large platter in green and gray, with an ideogram at its center; and two square brown vases, exquisitely proportioned but undecorated except for their creamy oatmeal glaze.

"I noticed these weren't signed," Mark said, picking up the square vases.

"Hamada doesn't always sign, but the old boy who's selling them got them direct, I'm told."

"Still," Mark said dubiously. Opening the catalogue, he read, "'A Fine Pair of Stoneware Bottle Vases by Shoji Hamada.' That's pretty positive."

To Sara, it was like watching a conversation in code, where the information exchanged bears no relationship to the form of words. Studying the vases, the man said, "Well, come to think of it...."

With a pencil taken from behind the ear, he amended the catalogue copy to read, "A Pair of Stoneware Bottle Vases, Japanese, in the Style of Hamada," and initialed it. Striking out the estimate "£600–£800," he wrote in "£80–£100."

"Happen to know who's taking this sale?" Mark asked.

"I am, actually."

"Oh. Well, see you later, then."

"What was all that about?" Sara asked as they left the building.

"Just come along on the seventeenth, and bring your check book."

It was all absurdly easy.

Two days before the sale, Sara dropped by to view the Hamadas. Both the tall jars and the plate were on view, pored over and examined by dealers, but of the bottle vases there was no sign. Before she had a chance to ask a porter about them, someone beat her to it.

"Oh, dunno, sir," the porter said. "Half a tick. I'll check up."

He returned five minutes later.

"Sorry, sir. They're upstairs." Conspiratorially, he dropped his voice. "Bit of a question about 'em, I hear."

The dealer needed no further encouragement to cross them out of his catalogue, and by lunchtime word would have gone around the trade that they were "dodgy," "wrong," not worth bidding on.

At the sale, the "real" Hamadas went quickly for figures well over the estimates, but the enthusiastic auctioneer cooled visibly as he put up the small vases.

"Pair of stoneware jars, style of Hamada. Begin at ten pounds?" Sara bought the pair for fifty pounds—a profit, she estimated, of at least fifteen hundred.

Mark made it clear that the vases were just for practice, to accustom her to the system. For people of his standing, there were other more sophisticated means of lining their pockets. As the summer waned and the auction business picked up, he took her on occasional weekend trips to the country sales which still offered the best chance of a real bargain.

At one such sale, in Bath, Sara learned how the biggest profits were made.

Sara looked forward to the Bath trip, with its promise of a weekend in one of England's most beautiful old cities and a big house sale on Saturday afternoon. As they drove in Mark's sports car through the green lanes, sun flickering through the trees overhead, a wave of well-being swept over her.

Sold for taxes after the death of the last of a long line of county aristocracy, the house had a reputation for richness and good taste. From the hundreds of chairs set up in the old banqueting hall, the auctioneers obviously expected a good crowd, and there were already dozens of cars parked on the gravel when Sara and Mark arrived.

Picking up a catalogue at the door, they strolled through the main foyer with the other early arrivals, then stopped by a group of old photographs the proud vendors had pinned to the oak paneling of the hall.

They belonged to another England. Lines of maids in floor-sweeping black dresses and crisp linen aprons stood along the wall as the lady of the manor inspected them. Horsemen assembled on the front lawn for a stirrup cup before the morning's hunt. And at massive banquets in this same room fifty starched shirtfronts and an equal number of beaded Mainbocher and Worth bodices turned toward the camera, the fixed faces above them beaming with bonhomie, brandy, and overeating.

A final picture puzzled Sara. It showed the hall and morning room floors covered in deep white drifts, like feathers. Not carpet; it was obvious that this Jacobean plank floor, fastened with pegs centuries ago, had never been sullied by nails or underfelt.

"Rose petals," Mark explained. "Rather than have them fall and clutter up the garden, they had every bloom cut and strewn around the house. You were supposed to walk on them. The oil in the petals was good for the floor." He looked around speculatively. "Tells you something about the people who owned this place, doesn't it? They obviously spent money as if it was going out of style. I wonder how much of this stuff is genuine?"

He was right to be dubious. Hardly an item fulfilled the description of the catalogue. Successive generations, determined to keep up appearances in the face of rising income tax and living expenses, had quietly gutted the house, replacing true antiques with copies. Only the reputation remained. Sara wondered if the auctioneers knew.

As they took their seats at the back of the room, a tiny man with neat hands and feet and a gleaming hairless head strolled down the aisle. He was so much like some small animal that Sara expected him to pause and preen imaginary whiskers.

"Didn't expect to see you here, Mark." His voice matched his appearance, quiet and whispery.

"Oh, just a whim, you know. Sara, Anthony Carisbrooke of Margrave Galleries. Sara Hershman. Anything here to interest you, Anthony? That picture over the fireplace, for instance?"

Soot had built up so thickly on the woman's portrait that it was hard to make out more than a tilted low-lit face and a turban, once presumably red but now a rusty black. Sara remembered Mark pausing before it and putting a small tick beside the description in the catalogue, "*Head of a Woman with Turban*. Copley Fielding."

"I knew you'd spot it," Carisbrooke said with a sigh.

"I'm just a tourist, old boy. Don't worry about us."

Carisbrooke beamed. "Glad to hear it. Of course, we'll look after you. At the Beaufort after supper this evening?"

When he returned to his seat, Mark winked at her. "How does it feel to be a criminal?"

"Who, me?"

"Both of us. Not to mention Anthony and half a dozen chaps I could name. We're now members of a ring at this particular sale."

"For that picture?" At the last moment, she stopped herself from pointing at it.

"It's by Delacroix. I suspected it, but Anthony's the expert."

She consulted the catalogue. "Then who's Copley Fielding?"

"A minor English painter. Friend of Delacroix. They visited one another a lot, and I suppose Delacroix left this behind. Might have been a gift to Fielding, but Fielding couldn't have painted it in a million years. I bet Anthony went puce when he saw it."

The sale went briskly. To an outsider, the buyers would appear keen collectors of good English furniture who picked up some low-cost items to beautify their homes, when, in fact, a handful of Kensington and Chelsea antique dealers were buying up a few thousand pounds' worth of fakes for later sale to gullible tourists at vastly inflated prices. The Delacroix aroused no interest other than Carisbrooke's and went to him for eighty pounds.

Mark and Sara ate a leisurely dinner at a little restaurant overlooking the Avon, strolled under the poplar trees through the sleepy streets with their houses of honey-colored stone, and around nine o'clock knocked at the door of room 78 at the Beaufort, the large, modern, and ugly hotel that most commercial visitors to Bath used as a base.

Carisbrooke opened the door. Seven men Sara recognized from the sale rose automatically as she came in, but there were no introductions, a delicate recognition of the fact that this was an illegal gathering.

Sara wasn't sure what she expected of the ring—vulgar vests, big cigars, diamonds on fat fingers, and blondes draped over the furniture? Instead, here were pillars of the art establishment, some of them council members of the official body set up to police the auction trade and stamp out practices like the ring.

"We were just starting," Carisbrooke said. "Some sherry?" As they poured a glass of Tio Pepe each, Carisbrooke took out a petit point case, removed a pair of frail gold spectacles, and put them on.

"Mmmm, to begin at the beginning, Lot Seven," he said, shuffling through a sheaf of auction bills. "That's the Cuthbert Silver bottle. We paid fifty pounds. Anyone like to claim it?"

"I'll have it for seventy," one man said.

"I daresay," Carisbrooke said dryly, "but a hundred's more like it, don't you agree, gentlemen?"

"All right, a hundred," the man said with a smile. Sara knew it was worth at least three times that.

"No more? Right. One hundred." Carisbrooke made a note on the bill and went to the next.

With half an hour, all seventeen items bought by the ring were sold off to its members, including the Delacroix, which Carisbrooke himself "claimed" for two thousand pounds.

Mark settled comfortably into the society of these men, unconsciously imitating their talk, their sprawl, the easy unspoken communication of raised eyebrow and half smile. Sometimes, Sara longed for the directness of the auction trade as she had grown up to know it. These men never shouted bids, stood up to contest angrily a decision they thought to be unfair, or betrayed by look or word their interest, let alone admiration, for the things they bought.

Once, Mark might have been an exception to the bloodless norm of the London saleroom scene, but in two years Sara had seen him change. Free of Cicely Snow's influence, and responding to the comfortable sexuality which Sara fed him in judiciously rationed doses, he resembled more and more his uncle, whose porcine presence had dominated Snow's during Sara's first months in London. Occasionally, a mannerism brought back the memory of Oliver Turnbull with startling vividness; Mark was even developing an incipient paunch, and had taken to leaving permanently undone the two lower buttons on his waistcoat instead of the customary one.

Watching these calm, complacent men, Sara thought of New York, of David Moore, and of a satisfaction unfelt since the evening when they last made love—a night every detail of which she could summon up with undiminshed vividness.

But it did no good to brood. David was gone, and she had work to do.

Anthony Carisbrooke readjusted the spectacles that threatened to slip onto the end of his mouselike nose.

"Quite satisfactory, I think," he said, adding up the bills. "Now, gentlemen, if I could have your payments."

Soon there was more than five thousand pounds in notes in a neat pile on the table. Obviously expecting such an end to the day, all had come with cash.

For Carisbrooke, this meant another flurry of calculation. "For the seventeen lots, we paid . . . uh, five hundred and eleven pounds." Taking that amount from the heap, he pocketed it, reimbursing himself for the money he had spent on the ring's behalf. "That leaves four thousand eight hundred and eleven pounds to be shared out nine ways." He scribbled quickly. "I make that five hundred and thirty-four pounds each. Would someone like to check my figures?"

Sara watched in amazement as each of the men, including Mark, took their share of the cash. More than a thousand dollars to Mark alone, just for doing and saying nothing! No wonder some dealers with tiny shops managed to live in style.

Then she remembered the family who owned these things and who put them on the market in the hope of raising money to pay taxes and save their house. The ring had defrauded them of at least a quarter of the sale's entire value.

Gathering up their purchases, four of the men left to catch the last London train while Carisbrooke, Mark, and two others, all staying overnight in Bath, settled back for what Sara assumed would be shop-talk. She was quite wrong. As soon as the door closed on the four, there was a new electricity in the room.

"Have you got a buyer for the Delacroix?" Mark asked.

"I thought you weren't interested."

"Well, I'm not, especially. But I know someone who might be. Care to put it up again?"

Carisbrooke glanced at the other two men. "Gentlemen?" They were obviously eager; this was what they had waited for.

Taking out the bill again, Carisbrooke made another note. "Very well, the last bid was two thousand. Anyone claim it?"

"Two five," Mark said.

Slowly, between sips of sherry and the sort of banter Sara remembered from her grandfather's pinochle sessions when she was a little girl, the price climbed to five thousand two hundred. Mark took out his wallet and calmly counted out the whole sum in twenty-pound notes: obviously the visit to the bank earlier in the day "for some pin money" had been a subterfuge.

"But it's crazy!" she said as they walked back to their hotel, the Delacroix under Mark's arm. "You could have had it for less than a hundred pounds, but you ended up paying more than five thousand."

"You're not thinking," he chided. "If I had bid against the ring, they would have been forced to bid too, if only as revenge. God knows how high we would have gone. Perhaps to five thousand. Perhaps even higher."

"But that's what you paid anyway."

"Don't forget the knockout money: I *actually* paid about three and a half thousand for the picture. If it's handled carefully and I put it through Snow's, it could go as high as eight."

"Isn't that illegal, selling through your own company?"

Mark caught the mockery in her voice and smiled. "We seem sunk in illegality today." Putting his arm around her shoulders, he savored the softness of her upper breast through the light cotton of her dress. "Yes, it's not done to sell through your own firm, but there are ways. I know a dozen dealers who do nothing but go to sales like this, buy at the knockout, then put their buys up for sale at a saleroom. We pay a standard four percent commission for any business they bring in, but if I offer them eight, they'll fall over themselves."

"So it's been a good day," Sara said as they came to their hotel.

"Indeed it has." As they waited for the elevator, his hand wandered lower on her breast, to the polite astonishment of the operator who chose that moment to open the door. "And I have high hopes for the night."

For another year, throughout 1963, the pattern of Sara's life remained a shadow of Mark's, echoing her reliance on him professionally and emotionally. During the week, she attended sales, buying carefully at the low prices her increasing skill permitted. Weekends were spent with Mark, sometimes at sales but more often on trips out of the country; her French improved in line with her understanding of the Continental auction scene and its intricate, rule-bound structure, which made London a mecca for European dealers.

Taking stock after that year, she found that the real value of her holdings was almost fifty thousand pounds, but acquired for a fraction of that. Proudly she showed her accounting to Mark over lunch at the Colombina.

"Oh, *you* got that Lowry. I had an eye on that myself."

"Would you like to have it?"

He looked up, surprised. "That's very kind—and uncharacteristic, if I may say so."

"Call it a good-bye present."

"Ah." He took a large mouthful of his wine. "The victim felt no pain, and died instantly."

"We always agreed, Mark—"

"Yes, we did. But you must allow me the vice of a few romantic notions. Would I be indiscreet in asking the name of my successor?"

"There isn't one. I'm going back to the States. Sascha's found premises for the company, and I've got enough material for a season of sales." She put her hand on top of his. "You've been very kind, Mark."

He carefully extracted his hand. "No kinder than you, Sara. I'm privileged to have had the opportunity to view the property, as it were. I'd like to make an offer, but the reserve's too high." Standing up, he took the bill. "I think I'll forego my customary liqueur. Take care."

She watched him step out into St. James's Street, carefully

crossing to the sunny side, as usual.

Franco came to clear the table. "Signor Turnbull will not have dessert?"

"No, Franco. But you can bring me a Sambuca. A double, please."

She had planned to carry off the moving with the same coolness she had shown at lunch, but her empty apartment, with its furnishings carefully chosen from Snow's No Salable Value room and the more perishable items from Harrod's, just a half a mile away, cracked her frail resolve. Her whole life in London seemed to have been delivered, intact, by the same green vans that brought the weekly groceries, the smoked salmon, the paté, and the Scotch beef; she should be able to send it back as easily, but the objects clung, tore, refused to be abandoned. She cried a lot, but by the end of the evening she was packed and gone.

Hearing the news, Cicely Snow allowed herself a little smile, then dialed the number she knew by heart.

"Mark, I'm so awfully sorry! Could you bear some company? Do come round—just for a drink."

There was a single tear in her eye as she hung up the phone. Catching it on a fingernail she examined it critically. How odd. For a moment there, she had almost convinced herself that she felt sorry for the man.

33

Standing before the frontage of Lilywhite and Van Nuys, Sara admitted to herself that she was impressed.

The architect hired in the 1910s to decorate the facade of New York's most distinguished auction house specialized in the New Baroque. He had already set the windows of the Yacht Club in the sterncastles of stone galleons, and welcomed students of the New York Institute of Dramatic Art with a portico copied from the proscenium of London's Drury Lane Theatre. A saleroom's awkward marriage of commerce and art posed problems, but he solved them brilliantly.

On one side of the wide door, at the top of an imposing flight of steps, a heavily incised relief showed Art, in the person of a brawny young man with mallet and chisel raised, contemplating Beauty, a seminude lady, back chastely turned to the street.

Above this couple, a tier of sculptures and canvases—presumably the morning's work—flowed subtly into a frieze of popular classics like the Venus de Milo, the *Mona Lisa*, and *September Morn* that spanned the doorway, to cascade down on the other side where the symbolic figure of the Dealer, a toga-draped sage with a compass in his hand, took delivery of them on behalf of the art lovers massed supplicatingly at his feet, arms upraised.

Significantly, money figured nowhere in the composition. Lilywhite and Van Nuys had liked to give the impression that profit was the furthest thing from its mind.

291

"Sascha, you're a genius! Can we get the lease?"

"Are you sure we want it?" he asked, looking around.

The street had declined since the great days when New York's carriage trade patronized its plush establishments. Now, the flashing bulbs of sex shops advertised 25-cent peep shows in a garish frieze along the other side of the street, and the pedestrians, sullen and black, shouldered past the two uptown dudes with as little interest as they showed in the street itself.

"It's too good to pass up," Sara said, leading Sascha up the steps. Yellow sheets of newspaper and the debris of years had jammed the central revolving door, but they squeezed in through a side entrance to find themselves in an echoing hall, its marble floor disfigured by the marks of showcases. Naked light bulbs shone on dirt, disuse, and ruin.

"It *was* a cut-rate carpet warehouse," Sascha said. "Before that, a five-and-dime, then an unemployment office, a job printer's, and God knows what else. The floors upstairs are a mess, and the roof!"

"That doesn't matter. We've got the money. What about the lease?"

"We can have it for peanuts if we don't ask for repairs."

"Then we won't ask. Better get the lawyers onto it. We might be able to move in by spring."

The cab taking them back to her temporary office drove up Madison. Sara's eyes, almost against her will, were drawn to the windows of the Atropos gallery, still blank. In more than a year, there had been no news of David Moore, though rumors circulated freely: he was a suicide, unidentified in some foreign morgue; he had changed his name and fled to Italy, South America, Africa; he was still in England . . . you could take your pick.

Following her eyes, Sascha said, "Qualms?"

"No. Not really. I suppose it has to be done."

"It does indeed, my sweet. And so far Carl has stuck to his side of the bargain. We're doing all right, and don't you forget it."

Sara nodded. Ever since she returned to America, the question of David Moore had been pushed to the back of her mind by the struggle to revive the House of Hershman, a move resented by her potential competitors and actively opposed by salerooms and dealers alike, none of whom cared for an auction house run by a woman, least of all a woman just over thirty.

But some slick magazine dubbed her "a devious Venus" after a particularly intricate series of negotiations over a furniture collection she had earmarked for one of her first sales, and the label somehow made her, if not acceptable, at least fashionable. For the first time, she was aware of having supporters in the auction community, though her enemies still outnumbered them.

She had entered the business at exactly the right time. Antiques shops were springing up everywhere, selling an appalling mixture of faked "bygones," genuine collectors' items and plain junk. Within the next few years "Antique Fairs" would fill armories, cow palaces and sports centers all over the country, and most drive-in movies would have a Saturday morning flea market where junkmen and amateur dealers sold the week's pickings from the back of their vans.

The public would buy anything whose authenticity was assured by a familiar signature, desperate for the reassurance of age and a guarantee that their purchase was resalable at a profit. "Lalique" or "Daum" on a piece of twenties glass, "Gallé" on an inlaid table, "Preiss" on a figure of ivory and bronze, even "Coca-Cola" on a tin tray catapulted a piece from a mere knickknack to the status of an antique, dealers riding roughshod over the traditional definition of "antique" as anything more than a hundred years old. Naturally, forgers would soon be at work fabricating the sought-after signatures where they did not exist.

Anything produced by the famous or fashionably artistic would find a buyer somewhere. In London, Christie's solemnly offered for sale an intricate glass and gold reliquary containing a flake of dried skin and tendon which the owner claimed, with letters and learned analysis, to be the penis of Napoleon Bonaparte, while at Sotheby's a small tin labeled, in three languages, "Produced by Piero Manzoni: Artist's Shit," drew bids up to four hundred pounds before being bought in as not having reached its reserve. Sara calculated that this made the contents of the tin more valuable than gold.

A clever forger could sell his work quite openly as forgeries and get high prices, providing he had a flair for publicity. For years, Elmyr de Hory, comfortably settled in his Ibiza villa, had produced impeccable copies of modern masters for gallery owners all over the world, none of whom probed too deeply into the provenance of these apparently authentic Matisses, Picassos and Dufys. When his own bombast and the writings of his friend Clifford Irving exposed the fact, the forgeries continued to sell, even when the bold signature was not *Picasso* but *Elmyr*. De Hory's self-aggrandizement had made him a collectible celebrity in his own right, and he was soon being forged in turn.

The range of collectibles expanded daily. Sara discovered there was even a brisk underground trade in casts taken from the erect penises of film and rock stars. More in amusement than interest, she mentioned this to Sascha, who showed no surprise.

"A friend of mine has quite a few of those."

"But what does she do with them?"

He smirked. "Not 'she,' heart—'he.' And as for their use ... well, to quote Rudy in *The Sheik*, '*Mon Dieu*, are you not woman enough to know?'"

There were more serious aberrations in the auction world. An Englishman auctioned off his own insurance policy. If the buyer kept up the payments, he would benefit by half a million when the man died. What was the next step, she wondered? "Personal service contracts" sold at auction? And then slavery, the oldest industry to employ the auction system, with bodies on the block going to the highest bidder?

She fought back such negative thoughts. If they wanted it, then she would sell it. Hershman's would hold at least one sale a day, and two or even three if the goods justified it. Learning from Sotheby's, she had a vintage wine sale lined up and others devoted to antique erotic postcards, a collection of classic violins, and some of the last remaining eighteenth-century French furniture outside of public collections. Her agents in California were already looking for premises to open a Hershman's West.

But, perhaps best of all, she had Bobby D'Antoni.

They had met at one of Manhattan's interchangeable parties, a milling crowd of mismatched urbanites jammed into a switching room for the telephone exchange; the fashion that season was for subterranean celebrations, with receptions and launchings conducted in IRT tunnels, excavations, sub-basements—everywhere but the sewers.

Separated from her escort and wedged into a corner by one of the city's most tedious art journalists, she paid more attention to the conversation going on behind her.

"You name it," the tall boy with the mop of hair was bawling drunkenly at a bored girl in a Jackie Kennedy-style hairdo with nothing much under it. "Change the world. Change people. Make money. Spend money. I can write you a program to rob a bank, corner the grain market, switch all the traffic in N'York from right hand side to left. Hell, there's a program to create the world in five days—who needs seven?"

To emphasize his omnipotence he waved his arm carelessly over his head, splashing his drink all over the girl's pink pastel dress. She retreated, mopping, with an eintirely Kennedy-like curse.

"Then how come my telephone bill is always wrong?" Sara said over his shoulder.

He swung around unsteadily and looked down at her. A foot of height separated them. "People. People push the wrong buttons. The hardware's only as good as the people. Who are you anyway?"

"Sara Hershman. How about you?"

He fumbled for a card, producing one with someone's telephone number already written on the back.

ROBERT D'ANTONI

Systems Analyst
Paladar Industries

"I see." She handed it back. "You Italian?"

"Sure. You Jewish?"

"No prizes for guessing that."

He had begun to take in her appearance, and in particular the deep neckline of her dress. "We should stick together. I mean, racial minorities—"

"You mean, 'Your place or mine?'"

"I could tell you all about computers." His eager drunken grin looked odd on the Sicilian bandit face.

"You won't believe this, but I'm really interested."

Outside, snow sifted down like powdered sugar from a five-o'clock sky. In a few days, Christmas. Where to this time? Not Momma and all that bickering. Not Sascha, with those camp parties. Working alone in the penthouse? At least it was quiet, and with enough booze on Christmas Eve you could disconnect the phone and sleep the clock around.

She watched for a cab as cars skated along the jammed streets in an inch of slush. "We didn't really decide, did we?"

"What?" The cold had hit him hard. His tall frame drooped.

"Your place or mine."

"Have to be yours. I got thrown out."

"Why?" A cab swung towards her. They climbed in.

"Company folded. No bread."

Great! "Central Park West," she told the driver. Before they reached Columbus Circle, her companion was asleep. Good picking, Hershman.

Leaving him slumped in the living room with a couple of head-clearing Alka-Seltzers, she took a shower to wash off the grime of the party. She came out of the bathroom mopping her hair with a corner of her enveloping towel to find him in bed, bare hairy chest on the pillow.

"You were supposed to be in bad shape."

"Warmth brings me around. Like those Siberian fish."

"I'm the same with chicken soup. Look, I really meant it about computers."

"Sure. I'll talk computers until they come out your ears." He folded back the bedclothes. Resignedly she dropped the towel and climbed in.

His hands dived for her body but she fended them off, finally reaching under the covers and giving his penis an abrupt deflating tweak.

"Ouch!"

"Computers. I'm listening."

"You're kidding!"

"No."

"Listen, how can I concentrate when you're . . ." He pointed to her bare breasts; she pulled up the sheet to cover them, snuggling down like a little girl about to hear a bedtime story.

"Ten minutes on computers, then ten minutes of whatever you like."

"Whatever I like?" His look was lewdly skeptical.

"Sure. What are you into? Garter belts? Black stockings? Leather? I've got a crazy pair of boots that come almost up to my ass. We can do it straight or French or Italian—"

"OK, OK!" he said hurriedly. "Now the first thing you've got to remember about computers . . ."

He talked for half an hour the first time, a tribute to his natural enthusiasm for his subject; later he showed equal enthusiasm for lovemaking. On Christmas Day, with an influence Sara was not sure even she could have wielded, he had an ex-colleague opening up the offices of a Brooklyn construction company to explain just how a big computer worked in practice. In the New Year, she bought a small Honeywell layout for Hershman's and filed away for future use some of Bobby's more intriguing suggestions about computers and the auction business.

And also in the New Year, Carl Bleigen rang up. He was ready to push finally on the lawsuits against David Moore.

"You really think this is necessary?" she asked.

"We've talked about it before. Yes. Essential."

"But what's the point? Nobody knows where David is. Atropos is dead. Doesn't that satisfy you?"

"No."

"What would?"

He laughed, a scratchy rasping on the phone. She wondered if the rumors of cancer were true. On the few occasions when he appeared in public these days, the comic frog looked more like a withered amphibian, choking in an alien environment.

Sickness would explain a great deal, including his fanatical hatred of David Moore. Sklar was dead, and safe from his resentment, but David remained—the man who robbed him of half his business, who outsmarted him to set up one of the most successful of all art dealerships. Who would remember Carl Bleigen after his death? A few accountants and attorneys—men paid to remember.

But Moore, even on the run, retained a charisma and a reputation for honesty and skill even this scandal did not seriously mar. Bleigen hated David as the toad hates the dragonfly. Lurking in the mud with quivering tongue, he waited for that glittering shape to draw close enough. Then he would drag it down.

"That's not your concern, miss. Just do what has to be done and you won't have any trouble. Sascha will explain."

34

The young auctioneer could remember feeling frightened before. His first day at Harrow, for instance, when he faced the skeptical and self-assured gaze of the seniors, on whose approval his whole comfortable existence would depend.

And the summer evening he made love to his first girl, a moment whose romance was not enhanced by the fact that it happened on a railway embankment and was observed with interest, he later found, by three other students out for a walk.

Nor had it been easy to face the interrogation that preceded his appointment to a cadetship at Snow and Son. Little remained of his composure or confidence after a selection panel led by Mrs. Snow remorselessly examined every aspect of his family, education, and ambitions. The memory of that morning still filled him with horror. Putting her head on one side, Cicely Snow would smile and, just as he smiled automatically in return, transfix him with a question that probed the precise point of his weakness.

"Forgive me for mentioning it, Jeremy, but I noticed that you stumbled over a few words just then. You don't have a tendency to stutter, do you?"

He defied anyone to construct a coherent sentence after that. He sat, opening and closing his mouth like a goldfish, until old Debenham came to his rescue.

Until now, that interview had looked like the low point of his life; today, when he took his first sale, promised to surpass it.

Huntley was looking at him pointedly over the desk. Desperately, he tried to recall what had been said.

"I didn't get the last one, sir. Lartigue, was it?"

Huntley, who had been through it all a thousand times before, said patiently, "Larigue. L-A-R-I-G-U-E. A buy bid. Lot Eighty-nine."

Paging hurriedly through his specially prepared auctioneer's catalogue with the pages of the regular catalogue interleaved with blank folio sheets, leaving wide margins for his vital notations, he found Lot 89.

Next to the figure 200—the reserve, below which the owner of this particular lot was not prepared to sell—he wrote *Larigue* and the symbol indicating that M. Larigue (or whoever masqueraded behind this name) had entered a buy bid, authorizing Snow's to top any other offers. Below the name, he ruled two lines, wrote *Larigue* on the first in expectation of his purchasing the lot, but left the second blank for the name of the nearest underbidder.

"Well, that's the lot, my boy," Huntley said. "It's nearly ten thirty. You'd better run along. Good luck." His dry hand contrasted with the sweaty palm that grasped it.

The tiny Commission Room suddenly felt more welcoming than what awaited him outside. In eighteen months at Snow's, this was the first time he had been admitted, and unless he handled another sale it was unlikely he would be allowed in here again.

The Com. Box was tucked away at the back of the building in what had once been the catalogue sale office; with its windows blanked out in thick white paint and its door triple-locked, it became the nerve center into which the most secret information of the auction house was fed—the phone and mail bids of buyers all over the world, the true value of the goods sold, and the probable price they would fetch all came through the three phones on Huntley's desk. So did the dealers' bidding codes thought up to fool their opponents, and the confidential reports Snow's occasionally commissioned on a work they suspected to be a fake or stolen.

Sensing the familiar unwillingness to leave, Huntley propelled the young man gently toward the door and locked it after him.

At the end of the corridor, Jeremy saw the crowded saleroom and heard the murmur of his first audience. At that point, his nerve almost failed entirely, but with a deep breath held all the way to the rostrum, he made it.

The two clerks standing at the table below the rostrum looked up at him expectantly. He stared back, puzzled, until one said wearily, "Anything for us, old boy?" Recovering his wits, Jeremy leafed to page one of his catalogue. Having just come from the Commission Room, he alone knew which lots were withdrawn, and whether any dealers would be bidding with a code that the clerks should know about, since part of their job was to spot bids he might miss.

"Seven, nineteen, and forty-four are out," he said hurriedly. "Mr. Devine will be bidding for Agnew's and a private client as well—with the catalogue if it's Agnew's, with his head for the other."

The clerks noted this down phlegmatically in their own catalogues, already as heavily decorated with notations as his own. Dealers often left bids directly with them, so throughout the sale the auctioneer would juggle with bids from the audience and his own clerks, as well as those phoned in or mailed.

Few people attending a sale realized how fragmented the staff of a saleroom could be. The auctioneer worked essentially for his department, preparing the catalogue and taking the sale, then collecting a special commission on top of his salary if he was lucky enough to be head of his particular section.

Clerks, on the other hand, ranked much lower in the pecking order of the company. Usually employed first as minor helpers or porters, they could rise to become administrators, but the glamorous world of the experts and auctioneers would always remain closed to them. Like most salerooms, Snow's recruited its prospective auctioneers from the best public schools and the minor aristocracy, confident of finding there the blend of sophistication and artistic education on which an auctioneer based his work.

Most recruits knew little about art or antiques when they entered the company; as vacancies occurred in the various departments, trainees were appointed to them, whether they found the subject interesting or not. Outsiders were always astonished at how readily an untrained cadet became intimate with the finer points of silver or eighteenth century portraiture under the benign despotism of a saleroom training scheme. They didn't realize that, if a new boy failed to show aptitude, he was quietly asked to leave.

This knowledge contributed to Jeremy's nervousness as the clock at the back of the room remorselessly reached ten thirty. Closing his eyes to the rows of expectant faces below him, he glanced down at his catalogue and plunged into the sale.

"Good morning, ladies and gentlemen. The following lots have been withdrawn...."

For a while, it looked as if everything would be all right.

The first five lots went quickly. Without reserves, and with no phone or mail bids, he could sell to the highest bidder in the room. He hardly looked at the porters as, with the ease of long experience, they sought out each item, picking it up if it was portable and standing by if it wasn't. "Lot Eight" would bring an instant call from somewhere behind him: "Showing over here, sir." But every few lots, he checked that the description matched the object, remembering a horror story of an apprentice who turned over two pages of his catalogue at once and didn't notice until twenty lots had been sold with the wrong reserves.

His own nightmare began at Lot 25. Glancing sideways at the picture as the porters placed it on the easel, he wondered what people could find to like in a Dutch flower piece apparently identical with a thousand other pictures of chrysanthemums.

But five mail bids were recorded, the clerk caught his eye to indicate that he would also be bidding, and at the last minute Huntley hurried from the Com. Box and whispered that an American dealer also wished to bid by phone. A clerk stationed himself on a phone behind the rostrum and Jeremy, his stomach a fist of nerves, launched into the bidding.

"Lot Twenty-five. The flower piece by Vroom. I must start at—" Hurriedly, he reviewed the mail bids, ranging from £300 to £650, noted the reserve of £600 and Snow's private estimate of £1000. "Two hundred pounds?"

He skimmed the rows of indifferent faces for a glance, a wave, anything. Nobody moved. All right, they were waiting to see how the bidding went. No point in offering £200 if you could have it for £50. It was up to the auctioneer now to push the price upward, always staying within the structure laid out in the catalogue.

He started by inventing bids, taking them off the wall. Seeing imaginary catalogues waved at the back of the room, he said, "Two hundred is bid. Two fifty? Thank you, sir." This to a startled man who had wandered in to look over tomorrow's sale. "Two fifty. Do I hear three hundred? Three hundred is bid...."

Behind him, he could hear the clerk transmitting the bids to his client on the phone, a disturbing murmur that did nothing to ease his nervousness.

At three hundred, he remembered to glance at the clerk's desk. The clerk nodded without looking up, indicating that his client had authorized him to go to three hundred and fifty.

"Three hundred and fifty at the desk. Three hundred and fifty. Against you all in the room." Bidding now against his own clerk, he pushed the price in fifty-pound stages to six hundred, when the clerk shook his head, indicating that he had reached his limit. The phone bidder also dropped out.

This was the danger area. The technique sounded simple enough. Lead the bidding up to the reserve price with invented bids if necessary, let someone in the room carry it over the reserve, then sell as soon as interest seemed likely to flag. The art in selling by auction—and the senior partners of Snow's were masters of it—was to coax up the price without outbidding either the customers or the client.

Occasionally, a saleroom was forced to admit, humiliatingly, to a client that their auctioneer, in his heated confusion between real bids and false, had managed to outbid the room. In that situation, he could only knock down the lot to one of the fictitious "buy in" names allocated to each sale and pray that the underbidder, if approached quickly after the sale, would take the piece off their hands.

Every good salesman turned into a schizophrenic on the rostrum, his mind divided between real bids and false. Most reminded themselves of the personality currently in charge by an imperceptible rhythmic movement from foot to foot, so that fake bids were called with the weight on the left, real bids accepted on the right, where the clerk's table, with its stream of authentic bids, provided a useful reminder.

The young auctioneer fell into a similar rhythm now, swaying slightly as the tempo increased and more bids led the price safely over the reserve.

"Eight hundred and fifty pounds is bid," he said with relief, scanning the room for any last-minute offers. Some bidders waited until this moment, then slipped in to whip a piece infuriatingly from under the noses of their colleagues. But nobody moved today.

His mind already running through the checklist of things to do—since the client was an outsider, unknown to him, send the

clerk down with a card to get his name and address; put down
the name of the underbidder; don't forget to note the price—he
made the last announcement absently.

"All done at eight hundred and fifty pounds?" He raised his
hand to bring the gavel down.

"Wait just a moment!"

Someone strode up the center aisle to peer at the painting.
There was an incredulous hush over the room.

Turning to the crowd, Mark Turnbull said, "This painting's a
fake!"

The auctioneer gaped, his gavel poised. "What?"

"It's fake. I tell you, it's a fake."

The auctioneer stared at the painting as if the answer lay
there, then looked at Mark in mute appeal.

Turnbull shook his head and held up one hand to bring the
sale to a halt.

"OK, relax everybody. We'll stop here for a while." The
"customers"—all students in Snow's cadet training program for
auctioneers—relaxed visibly. These weekly practice sales, at
which all would eventually take their place on the rostrum where
a crestfallen Jeremy now stood, were quite a strain. The objects
on sale might be from stock and the clerks and porters trainees
too, but senior staff members like Turnbull watched every
movement, deciding who would be offered permanent jobs at
the end of the course.

"You need to have your wits about you more than that,
Jeremy," Turnbull said. "I know it's hard to keep track of bids
when they come that quickly, but never forget that *people* are
making the bids, and you never know with people. Once or twice
a year, you'll get someone standing up to claim that some lot is a
fake, or stolen from him, or selling at too low a price.
Occasionally, you even get someone wanting to make a speech
about the Wrath to Come. You have to learn how to deal with
them all."

"But how *can* you deal with something like calling the picture
a fake?"

"Get the porter to throw him out," someone suggested from
the back of the room.

Mark turned quickly. "And lose a good customer? Maybe
he's an expert and the picture *is* a fake. But he could be a dealer
who's angry that he didn't get the lot, or a client who didn't make
the reserve high enough. Sometimes it's worse. A few years ago

at . . . well, I won't say where, but at one of our friends down the road—"

He waved in the direction of Mayfair, and there was a murmur of laughter at the expectation of hearing something discreditable about a competitor.

"A certain titled gentleman," Mark went on, "arrived for a sale, sat in the front row, and bought the first eleven lots at top prices. As he got ready to bid for the twelfth, two men in white coats came in and dragged him away, kicking and screaming, to the sanatorium where he'd been locked up for the last three months." Mark looked up at the rostrum. "How would you have handled that?"

"Suicide?" Jeremy suggested glumly.

"Our colleague didn't have your death wish. He just turned to the front of the catalogue, announced that lots One through Eleven would be offered again, and went on as if nothing had happened." Mark looked around the assembled group. "And there's a lesson in what happened next. Every picture sold, and for *more* than they fetched from the old boy a few minutes before. What does that suggest to you?"

"Theater," said a girl in the front row. Mark bestowed a smile on her.

"Exactly. Don't ever forget that an auction is only half business—the rest is theater. If you get a crowd excited, whether it's by high prices or some unexpected event in the room, like a film star turning up or a couple of dealers arguing over who made the last bid, prices will rise. It's been shown again and again."

Walking down the aisle, Mark turned to face the rostrum once more. "So let's see you handle this situation now. The last bid is Eight fifty, you're about to knock it down, and I yell"—his voice rose to an angry shout—"that's a fake!"

His gavel hovering, Jeremy looked down, realizing for the first time how the rostrum gave him a commanding position, like a priest in the pulpit. Exploiting it, he peered at Mark with an expression of polite inquiry.

"I beg your pardon, sir. Are you bidding?"

"No, I am not bidding. Not for that fake!"

"Well, if you aren't bidding, I must ask you to sit down. You're interrupting the proceedings."

"But I tell you the picture's a fake. You're selling it under false pretenses."

"Oh, I don't really think so, sir." His pitying smile took the whole crowd into his confidence. "Another nut," it seemed to say. "If it comes to that, I'm less certain of you than of the painting."

In the general laughter that followed, he caught the eye of the successful buyer in the front row. "I take it, sir, that your bid still stands?"

The man had no time to consider any alternative. "Well . . . er, yes."

"Then it's yours, for eight hundred and fifty pounds." The gavel cracked smartly, the auctioneer turned over the page, the porters placed the next item on the easel, and with a surge of interest that was almost palpable the sale moved on.

As Mark slipped back into his seat, a porter whispered, "Could you see Mrs. Snow, sir? In her office?"

Trust Cicely. "Doesn't she know I'm taking a training session?"

"Very important apparently, sir."

"All right."

He wondered what bee she had in her bonnet this time. Lately, Cicely's unconventional behavior verged occasionally on the manic, and Mark wasn't the only person on Snow's board to speculate about an enforced early retirement for the good of the firm. But palace revolutions took time, when control of the company was divided between four or five individuals. Mark watched and held his peace. The time would come soon enough.

Nodding to her secretary, he went into the inner sanctum.

"Oh, hello, sweet." The engaging youthful smile remained, but not much else of Cicely's girlish style. Middle age had hardened her, emphasizing the foxy eyes, the small predatory teeth.

"I was in a practice session."

"I know. Sorry. I wanted you to see this." She pointed to the small terra-cotta figure of a woman on the desk.

"Mmmm, very nice. What is it? Etruscan?"

"Supposedly. Kukulides wants us to sell it for him."

"Should do well, then, coming from a collection like his."

"I'm not so sure. It could be wrong."

"A fake? Well, no way to tell, is there?" Although experts could date organic remains with carbon analysis, a similar system for stone, metal, and clay eluded them.

"There could be," Cicely said. "At Cambridge, they're working on something called thermoluminescence that can date ceramics. I've asked them to have a look at it."

She handed him a letter with some invoices attached. It was from the owner, asking Snow's to arrange the sale. The invoice he noticed first was for its original purchase in the Hôtel Druout in Paris eight years ago, in 1958.

"The provenance is quite interesting," Cicely said, "particularly to you, Mark."

35

"Sara? For pity's sake, love, you've got to get me out of here! I just got beaten up."

In the New York office, Sara was dealing with the afternoon's mail, though it was almost midnight. "Darling, how awful! How did it happen?"

She listened for a few seconds, amending a memo and putting it back in the tray for retyping.

"That's impossible," she said at last. "I need you out there. Have you seen a doctor?"

Sitting on the lavatory in his rented Hollywood apartment and speaking on the bathroom phone that seemed to come as a standard fitting in Los Angeles, Sascha dabbed at his cut lip. "Not yet."

"Then do. The best man. Charge it to the firm."

"They tore out some of my hair!"

Sara sighed. "Then have some more put in. We'll pay. Actually, I'm glad you called, Sascha. How are things going?"

"Sara, I was nearly killed!"

"I know, pet. Maybe talking shop will take your mind off it."

"I've written you about everything," he said reluctantly. "They still haven't finished the air conditioning, and the carpet had to go back—the color was awful. But it should be ready on time. Have you decided what to open with?"

"The Battaglia drawings, I suppose."

"Oh, so you've come around to my way of thinking." She was irked by the satisfaction in his voice.

"Yes." There was no point in discussing it. "Sascha, go see a doctor. And don't take those kind of chances again. You're valuable to us. Look, I'm leaving for Dallas tomorrow. Give me a call on Friday. *Ciao.*"

In the bronze marbled mirror, Sascha contemplated the ruin of his face. Turning it from side to side under the unforgiving overhead light, he charted the bruises that already puffed out his cheek, and probed with his tongue the cut on his upper lip where a tooth had all but ripped through the skin. Worst of all, he examined the tiny dribbles of blood from his forehead where the little shits had ripped out dozens of the precious hairs transplanted so expensively and painfully from his armpits the previous winter.

The man looking back at him had no more shields to erect against the world. He was forty-one, overweight, his pasty face dissipated, with the beginning of jowls along the jawline.

Of course, he could embark on the rigorous regime of the movie people: no liquor, no candy, no boys. Mornings in the sauna or the gym, lunches of carrots and wheat germ. But nothing in his past prepared him for the onset of asceticism in middle age.

Sara could afford to be generous; she had not been abandoned. Men clamored for her as energetically as they pursued the precious objects she sold. She even had her own millionaire—Austin Catton, a lanky Texan with enough beef to feed all of Africa and enough oil to fly it there and back. Sara led him about like a little boy, using his private jet as a runabout and bullying him into adding to an already magnificent art collection, destined in time for the Dallas Gallery.

It wouldn't matter what happened to a woman like Sara. She would land on her feet. But what about Sascha Beauclair? Could they really blame him if he found other means to make his life bearable?

Wandering into the living room, he poured a glass of Niersteiner from the chilled bottle in the refrigerator. The lighted pool at the back of the apartment building glowed an evil green. He watched two other tenants swimming, their pale hairless bodies hardly disturbing the water.

*   *   *

"No advance on two hundred and seventy-five thousand
dollars...?"

Sara peered out into the vast hall, wondering if she looked as
anonymous to them as they did to her. A lighting system suitable
for anything from grand opera to a full-scale revival of
Oklahoma! bathed the whole stage in such brilliance that the
audience faded into a shadowy blur from which bids
materialized like messages from the hereafter.

Reverberations of her last words still fluttered around the
hall, and she paused until the last echoes died. There was no
other sound. It was nice to know that even Texans could be awed
by the mystery of a great sale.

"At two hundred and seventy-five thousand dollars..." She
paused dramatically, then brought down the gavel hard. "Sold,
to Mr. Austin Crane Catton."

She had been warned about the electronic rewiring of the
rostrum, but not even Austin's proud description prepared her
for what followed.

As the gavel made contact, its sound, amplified and
reamplified, filled the hall with a barrage like hailstones on a tin
roof.

High over the stage, an electronic board, a distant and
gigantic cousin of those which translated bids into foreign
currency at New York and London sales, erupted with five-color
fireworks, a waving Confederate flag, and a strutting parade of
majorettes that marched across the fifty-foot display to the
sound of "The Yellow Rose of Texas."

At that instant, the hall itself filled with the same tune, blared
by a brass band which double-timed from the distant recesses of
the lobby, trailing a squad of majorettes as precise and
mechanical in their movements as the electric troupe overhead.
Men with the huge red faces and bulging shoulders of farmers
stood on their seats, threw their Stetsons in the air, and howled,
and in the front row Austin sat content, arms folded like a little
boy around his secret delight.

Sara couldn't help herself. She giggled hysterically, turning
away from the rostrum so that nobody would see. She found
herself facing the object of all this celebration—a small Sisley
oil, hardly bigger than a large magazine, for which her current
lover had just paid more than a quarter of a million dollars.

She had a brief moment to feel satisfaction that the price had gone so high. The difference between Austin's purchase price and the estimated value of the painting went to whatever charity this event supported—Sara had done so many such auctions that the causes blurred into one—but since the Sisley came from her own stock, Hershman's stood to make thirty thousand dollars on this one sale alone. And people wondered why auctioneers gave their services free in the cause of charity.

It took five minutes for the pandemonium to cease. In that time, half a dozen sexy girls in cowboy outfits, indistinguishable from the strutting majorettes now disappearing through the double doors at the back of the hall, carried off the Sisley and its easel. Sara turned back to the crowd.

As she did so, the glare of light concentrated itself into a single spot, pinning her like a butterfly on a card. A hush settled over the crowd, and she let it build, waiting for the right moment to look up from her catalogue.

"Now, ladies and gentlemen, the high point of the evening: the item you've all been waiting for. Number Twenty-three in your catalogues. A rare opportunity, to benefit our cause tonight and to acquire an attractive investment. No words of mine can enhance the qualities of this lot—it speaks eloquently for itself."

She pointed dramatically to stage right, and the spot swung abruptly from the rostrum, leaving her in total darkness.

Audiences reduced to murmurous silence by a great work of art were familiar to Sara, but the awed hush that fell now over this crowd had no comparison. Flashbulbs flared like silent cries of delight.

The Aberdeen Angus bull, a natural aristocrat, stood four-square, with a look of bored disdain, its coat gleaming, its polished hooves buried in the gold carpet of the stage. Taking a cue from this calmness, its handler, squeezed for the evening into a dinner suit but refusing to give up that symbol of Texan masculinity, his high leather boots, stared off into the distance as he led the animal forward.

What Stubbs or Lawrence could have done for this scene, Sara thought, as she got down to the business of coaxing her audience into paying more for this animal than for the average Rembrandt.

Two hours later, she sank back gratefully into the deep black leather cushions of Austin's Lincoln Continental, savoring the peace after the cacophony of the celebration party which still roared in his penthouse suite and would do so until dawn.

He was upset that she left so early, and more so that she would not stay the night, but worst hurt of all that she had again turned down his proposal of marriage. Austin had the calm, good-natured power of the bull she had sold so profitably a few hours before, but who wanted that placidity every day of one's life?

"You happy with the way it went?" Dave Pendleton asked from the other end of the seat. The car was so cavernous that she had almost forgotten his presence.

"Mmmm, best yet, I think. More than a million and a half gross. That should do a lot of good for Multiple Sclerosis."

"Cancer."

"Oh. Yes. Multiple Sclerosis was last month, in Houston."

"A million and a half gross—how much net?"

She opened her eyes and glanced at him. "You'll have to ask Austin Catton about that."

"I did. He said it warn't none uh mah business."

She smiled at the imitation. "Well, not for publication—"

He held up his hand in an "I swear" gesture.

"At current market rates, the paintings are worth about half a million. Don't ask me about the bull."

"How much will Hershman's make out of that?"

"Ain't none uh yuh business," she drawled.

"Off the record?"

"Not even off the record. Dave, most of the paintings belonged to clients who left them with us, to sell whenever there seemed a chance of good prices. They get the money; we only take a commission—and not a very big commission at that. A few we owned outright, I'll admit. We're not dealers, but sometimes a customer wants cash so urgently that we make a deal. We take a lot of studio sales as well. When a painter or collector dies, the family sells us the contents of his house for a lump sum. We sort it out, annotate it, and feed the paintings into the market over a few years to keep the prices high. So who knows how much we made tonight? The accountants will take weeks to sort it out."

There was enough truth in this statement to satisfy Pendleton, though Sara suspected that back at the offices of *Time*, for whom he was writing her profile, better figures would be available. Sometimes Hershman's soaring profits embarrassed her, but the public thrived on news of huge sales and record prices—if others could speculate in the art market, so could they.

Wheeling through the airport gates, the car slid by the brightly lit passenger terminal, out to the smaller hangars of the private owners—dozens of them, since this was Texas, after all.

Sara had flown in Austin's Gulfstream often, and the spacious cabin, adapted into a single long room furnished like a lounge, was almost home to her. The steward stood as usual at the open door.

"Good evening, Miss Hershman."

"Hello, Paul. Paul, this is Mr. Pendleton of *Time* magazine. You'd better watch what you say."

"I'll certainly be careful, miss." He smiled. "I'll bring drinks before we take off."

The plane rose so smoothly into the night sky that the glasses hardly trembled in their hands. Sara looked down as the city wheeled under her, skyscrapers probing like fingers into the sky, then pulled the curtains. She had had enough of Texas for one day.

"What's that you drink?" Pendleton asked.

"Sambuca. Have a taste."

He sipped from her glass and grimaced. "Awfully sweet."

"I suppose so." She wondered if she even liked the stuff any more. "It has associations," she went on, explaining about Paris and the Closerie des Lilas, with its row of bottles. "This all comes under the heading of colorful background, I suppose."

"Sort of." He didn't look up from his notes. "We can go on to something more meaty if you like. I thought you might be tired."

"If I fall asleep, you'll know you've lost me."

Expecting an eager college journalism graduate, she had not been prepared for the shaggy, balding, and untidy Pendleton, with his bitten nails and watery gray eyes. He reminded her of an old dog, poised between an active life of guardianship and honorable retirement to a rug before the fire. But as his questions probed and pried, she realized that much of the appearance was protective coloration. Pendleton knew his business and had done his homework.

"OK," he said. "The future of Hershman's." He looked up expectantly.

"Well, Hershman's West, of course. We'll be opening in L. A. in September, with any luck. That's a major breakthrough for the whole business—we'll be the first big saleroom on the West Coast."

"You think there's enough business there?"

"Sure of it. For a year, we've been running Heirloom Days all over the country, sending our experts to all the state capitals. We work with the museums usually; people bring in their valuables and we appraise them. If they want to sell, we put them through Hershman's. By far the largest amount of worthwhile material has come from California and Oregon. And there's money there as well. A lot of collectors are in the movies. If they won't come to New York, we'll go to them."

"You really think that market's reliable? Half the time, the whole state is in recession, and the movie business isn't exactly steady work."

"We don't rely on big buyers alone. I must have told you that more than half what we sell goes for less than four hundred dollars an item. The culture's changing. Once, only collectors and dealers bought antiques; now everyone does it, just as people who once had their clothes made now buy them off the rack. Transpose that to furniture, paintings, books, cars, and houses and you've got the auction business. All we do is arbitrate between the people who want to buy and those who have something to sell."

She noticed he hadn't written any of this down, but then it was familiar ground.

"And you don't manipulate the trade at all?" Pendleton asked.

"How could we?"

Unfolding a sheet of paper which she recognized as Hershman's monthly newsletter to art investors, he read, "The sale of an ivory inlaid violin bow by François Tourte for twenty-five thousand pounds in London last month highlights the growing trade in these items. With good examples still available in the two-thousand- to twenty-thousand-dollar range, collectors already possessing a musical or woodwork interest could benefit from diversifying into this promising area."

"Well, it's true. They sell. Not only to collectors but to musicians. They'll pay almost as much for the bow as the violin."

He leafed through the rest of the newsletter. "What's a Senna Kelim?"

"Rug. Oriental."

"To go with the camel saddles, I suppose. I see you recommend them as a good buy at anything up to a thousand dollars."

"Why not? Some people like camel saddles. We had a sale last month of nothing but barbed wire—foot-long pieces of barbed wire. A man paid four hundred dollars for one rare example. Who am I to criticize his concept of beauty? If I had to choose between a Modigliani and that bull I sold tonight, I'd take the Modigliani, but who else would?"

"Traditionally, salerooms have specialized in fine art, though."

"No, not at all. One of Christie's earliest sales was a field of unmown hay. Until the First World War, Sotheby's specialized in books—not just valuable first editions but whole collections. They even sold off publishers' remainders for a while, and they're reviving that again, I hear. My own grandfather started by selling furniture on Eleventh Street."

"OK, OK." Belatedly, she realized Pendleton had set her up for this outburst. He was checking her, like a newly wired machine, to make sure all her earlier answers had not been invented on the spur of the moment. "Which reminds me—how do you feel about us mentioning your father's death?"

Another area where he obviously sensed her hedging. "Does it matter how he died?"

"Everything matters. But I'll try to steer around it, if you like. And then there's David Moore."

She frowned and swirled the ice cubes in her glass. "We've been over that."

"It still doesn't make a lot of sense."

"Did you talk to Carl Bleigen?"

"To his lawyers. Nothing to say."

"Well, then."

"Off the record, do you really believe he ripped off Ted Augustus?"

"There's plenty of evidence," Sara said lamely.

"Mainly from Sascha Beauclair, who now works for you and Bleigen."

"The paintings *were* sold; you can't deny that."

"No, but who sold them? According to some people I've talked to, Moore intended to hang onto them until Augustus built up a bigger reputation. It wasn't his style to dump them like that, especially with the market about to slump."

Sara remembered that period of the early sixties, less than five years ago, as did every dealer in fine art. In retrospect, it was inevitable that the boom in abstract art would collapse.

Made greedy by the huge prices paid for anything by a major modern, unscrupulous dealers, particularly in Paris and Cologne, fed the market with a flood of second-rate canvases, lithographs printed in thousands, and a number of outright fakes, knowing that spectators who missed the Impressionist boom would be anxious to cash in on this latest gold rush.

New York critics and collectors retaliated with an ingenious campaign on behalf of local artists, pushing Lichtenstein, Warhol and Augustus as natural successors to Pollock, Rothko and Johns. European collectors fell for it, paying higher and higher prices while the dealers scoured art schools for new talent and the already established artists shoveled out more and more work. Some London salerooms literally cleared out the studios for the more popular artists, sending up two of their brawniest clerks to fill a van with canvases. A reclusive elder artist, most of whose work was fueled on gin, resisted the attempt to make him rich until the experts from Carthew's arrived with two cases of his favorite liquor. It was not until they arrived back in London with a heap of new work that it was discovered none were signed. Undeterred, the saleroom had a large rubber stamp made of his signature and slapped it on every piece before selling them at record prices.

David Moore had known that one puff of wind would topple this house of cards. It came in the form of a sharp economic recession on the Continent. Stocks tumbled, and collectors, desperate for ready cash, dumped their paintings on an already overloaded market. Not only the new moderns but masters like Picasso, Braque and Chagall saw the value of their work fall overnight. Incredulous collectors found themselves able to pick up formerly priceless prints for a song, and canvases for a fraction of the estimated price.

Since then, the market had corrected and purged itself. Augustus, as Moore predicted, now stood with the other masters of American modernism, to the satisfaction of collectors who had bought his work at the London sale for bargain rates.

"I can't speak for David Moore," Sara said. "Everyone makes mistakes. He might have thought he could get away with it."

"There's talk he was framed." He smiled. "If that's what you call it when it's done to an art dealer."

"You'd better ask him about it yourself."

"I will."

"If you can find him."

"Oh, we found him, all right. One of our researchers tracked him down."

Sara felt suddenly cold. "Where?"

"Central America. He's in partnership with a man named Jolson, dealing in pre-Columbian art. A man named Freyer in New York is their agent. I gather they do fairly well." He smiled. "In case you're thinking of getting him extradited, I don't think the Mexicans will play ball."

Paul came out of the cabin.

"We're coming into Kennedy, Miss Hershman. Sir. Buckle up, if you will."

Sara groped for her safety belt, fumbling with the cold metal. Pendleton, she saw, was watching her carefully.

36

Sara woke in sudden panic, swimming away from her dream toward the surface of consciousness, miles above the pit where something chased her, whickering and howling.

Mouth dry and heart pounding, she lay there, still trembling. That whickering hiss remained, filling the room. Then a shadow swept over the drapes as the helicopter from Kennedy turned above her penthouse on its way to the landing area on top of the Pan Am building on 44th Street, and she relaxed.

As the sweat dried on her body, she wondered what brought on a dream like that. Nightmares troubled her rarely, most often when she was ill. This one, out of the blue, seemed to presage something. But what? Conscious again of events slipping away from her, uncontrolled, she rolled out of bed and put on a robe.

Sleep was impossible anyway. She could never stay long in bed past 8 A.M., unless with a lover, and even then she usually slipped away around nine to make coffee and read the papers. Sitting now at the long glass table beside the window that offered a panorama of morning New York, she drank the day's first cup and scanned the headlines without reading them.

Something was happening that the headlines did not reflect. It was out there, where she couldn't see. Impatiently draining her cup, she went back into the bedroom, determined to get down to her office at the saleroom where there was at least a semblance of order.

Then the phone rang. Her unlisted number. She picked it up cautiously.

"Sara? It's Mark. Did I wake you up?"

For a few seconds, she wondered if this was one of Sascha's jokes. She hadn't seen Mark Turnbull since she left London, five years ago.

"Mark? Is it really you? Where are you?"

"New York. I just got in. We need to talk."

"What about?"

"Nothing we can discuss on the phone, love. Look, I'm at the Algonquin. Can you meet me over here?"

"How about lunch?"

"I'd rather it was now. Is that very inconvenient?"

"No, of course not. Give me half an hour to get dressed."

Driving the few blocks to the hotel, she wondered what Mark was doing here. As far as she knew, he seldom came to New York, leaving Snow's American work to a local representative. The conviction grew that his arrival and her presentiments were connected.

Mark looked much as he had five years before. Perhaps slightly heavier, but as well dressed and assured as ever. Ankle crossed on knee, he was reading the *New York Times* with a look of polite incredulity that changed to a smile as Sara came into the lounge.

They kissed chastely.

"Mark, you should have written. I'd have given a party for you. There's a million people I'd like you to meet."

"It's a lovely idea, but I'm not here for long, and the fewer people I see, the better. How's business?"

"Not bad. Very good, actually, But why don't you want . . . ?"

A waiter put down a bowl of nuts and a gin and tonic on the table.

"Would you like a drink? Oh, of course, I keep forgetting it's morning here. For me it's already about two in the afternoon."

She let him take his first sip, then said, "Mark let's forget all the intrigue. What's this about?"

In answer, he put an airline bag on the table between them. As he unzipped it, she saw an object wrapped in paper. He tore away a corner and she recognized, with a chill, what it contained.

"Where did you get it?" she asked, worrying away more of the paper to be sure it was the figure Cristaldo had given her and which she had sold at the Druout.

"Someone brought it in to Snow's to sell—almost a year ago

now. Cicely had it tested and found out it was a fake. I sneaked it away from the vault when she wasn't looking. Did you know it was fake when you sold it?"

"Yes." There seemed no point in explaining the circumstances.

"Well"—Mark leaned back—"I'm afraid it's put you in an awkward position, Sara."

"If Cicely wants to make an issue of it, I can just say I sold it in good faith."

"Yes, that's true. But there's more." From under the figure he produced a thick file of papers. Inside, Sara found photostats, copies of letters, computer printouts, all with the House of Hershman emblem. Some were even annotated in her hand.

"Cicely has a little scheme to put you out of business. Or rather, to take over your business for herself. As you see, someone in your organization has given her a lot of help. Some of that material is quite damaging."

Every auction house balances on the knive edge of legality, shading the tax laws to aid its clients, avoiding customs duty where it can, ignoring the rules on importing and exporting art from countries like Italy which have strict legislation to prevent the loss of national masterpieces, manipulating and inflating prices to keep the market buoyant. The dossier in her hand detailed a dozen such infringements.

"This could put me in jail," Sara said quietly.

"It won't come to that. She just wants the business. Sotheby's and Christie's are moving in on the American side, and she wants her own local affiliate. It would all be quite legally done. A merger, a stock issue—you'd do very well out of it."

"And if I don't want to sell?"

"I don't think she admits to that possibility. I must say she has a point."

"Is that how she told you to present it to me?"

Mark looked away, his face stiff. "She doesn't know I'm here. I thought you deserved a warning—for old time's sake, if you like."

His sincerity was obvious. Feeling ashamed, Sara said, "I'm sorry, Mark. It's all been a shock. I need to think this out. How long can you stay?"

"A few weeks, I suppose. Cicely thinks I'm on a buying trip in Europe. There are people who will cover for me."

As they stood in the lobby while the doorman signaled for

Sara's car, Mark said casually, "What do you hear about David Moore?"

She stared at him. "Why?"

"Obvious reason, I should have thought. I always rated you two as a team, whatever your differences."

"He's in Mexico. I just heard yesterday, as a matter of fact."

"Are you still harrying him with those silly lawsuits?"

"It isn't just me. Carl Bleigen deals with all that."

"Ah, yes, Bleigen. I can see how he would find someone like Moore intolerable. But I'm surprised at you helping him."

"You don't know business over here, Mark. It's a jungle."

"Even in jungles, there are good animals as well as bad." He pecked her again on the cheek. "Give me a call if you want to talk some more."

The usual weekday traffic clogged the streets. Wedged into the mass of fuming, hooting cars, Sara was forced to think about Mark's words.

David hadn't entered her mind in months, yet today seemed full of memories—and fears. Far from dissipating her sense of impending danger, Mark's arrival had added to it. Almost as if another mind were in control, she turned up Madison toward the one reliable source of information about David.

Max Freyer's gallery combined the best qualities of boutique and museum, with a touch of the smart hairdresser's thrown in. The carpet was ankle-deep, the chairs comfortable, the side tables strewn with the latest copies of Paris *Vogue, Burda, The Connoisseur*. Mozart tinkled on the Muzak. Here and there, almost as decorations, Freyer placed the Aztec and Mayan artifacts that earned part of his annual half million turnover, though like most dealers in pre-Columbian art his main sales were to galleries and collectors who asked no questions and did business in private.

"I want to see Mr. Freyer," she told a receptionist suspicious of so early a visitor. "It's Sara Hershman."

Short, bald, and Hungarian, Freyer erupted from his office. "Sara, darling!"

They had met perhaps twice, but the art business thrives on spurious affection.

"I need to get in touch with David Moore," she said without preamble.

Freyer looked perplexed. "*The* David Moore?" He shrugged. "Of course, I've *met* him, but—"

"Don't kid a kidder, Max." A few phone calls on her return to New York last night had revealed that most pre-Columbian dealers knew about David's operation. With some twisting of arms, they had filled her in on the gossip. "That turquoise mask last year? The Manché stones? That temple you tried to sell the Met, the one they made you give back to the Guatemalans? The Toltec—"

Nervously, Freyer glanced around for unseen eavesdroppers. "Come in back."

With the door closed, he relaxed.

"Suppose I do know where Moore is. Why should I tell you? You're the one who put out all that paper on him."

"You'll just have to trust me."

"Write a letter. I'll see he gets it."

"This is personal. And urgent. A phone number at least. Please!"

Freyer deliberated, then scribbled a number on a pad. "Don't say you got it from me. That Hemingway pal of his would put a knife in my ribs."

"Thanks, Max. I owe you."

Waving a hand, Freyer said, "Nothing. Anyway, to tell you the truth, I don't think I'm giving you much. I've been ringing them for a week. No answer."

Sara felt a crawl of fear. "Is that usual?"

Freyer shrugged. "They go off on trips sometimes. But usually David tells me before he goes. Lately, that Jolson has been running with some pretty tough characters. People get killed down there. Not just the *esteleros*, the grave robbers. Americans as well."

Outside, on the street, Sara stared at the number and knew instinctively that her fears had substance.

Mark didn't seem surprised to find her telephoning him from the Algonquin lobby. When she came into his suite, he was sitting in front of the TV, feet on the coffee table, bemusedly watching *Tom and Jerry*.

"*Now* you need a drink, right?" Automatically he reached for the phone and called room service. "Still drinking that Sambuca stuff?"

When it arrived, she drank half the glass without tasting it, then began prowling around the room. Mark watched her with amusement.

"Did you find out who's giving Cicely her information?"

"What? Oh, it's Sascha. I knew that as soon as I saw the printouts. Nobody else has access to those."

"So it's not Cicely on your mind, I take it."

"Of course it is." She stopped pacing. "No. Oh, I don't know, Mark."

"Then it must be Moore."

"I just went to see his agent. He doesn't know where he is. I wish I knew why I feel this ridiculous—" She stuck on the word "premonition," then, angry at the irrationality that seemed to have overtaken her, put her glass down firmly on the table. "I have to talk to Sascha." Whatever her feelings about David, the survival of Hershman's was paramount.

"Isn't he in Los Angeles?"

"I can get the midday flight. Will you stay here until I call you? It'll be sometime tonight. Unless you want to come?"

"I burn too easily. Just let me know what you've decided to do about Cicely." He smiled, crookedly. "And give my best to David Moore."

37

A week before, David Moore and Brian Jolson had flown into
Puerto Alvarado. Pelicans flopped awkwardly into the air as
Brian banked the plane toward the rutted gray paddock of the
local airstrip. How many planes came this far out into the
Yucatan, David wondered? Perhaps three or four a year. The
field showed it. Only a few places were actually cleared of grass,
and puddles from the last rainstorm spotted the rest. But,
unconcerned, Brian steered for a flat place and, with a shower of
black mud that spattered the windshield, brought the plane
bumping to a halt.

From a few yards away, a goat regarded them resentfully.

"Welcome to Puerto Alvarado," Brian said, pushing open
the door. "Tropical paradise of the Yucatan Peninsula."

"I don't know why I wasted all that time in Acapulco."

Sooner or later, this tiny fishing village would be eaten whole
by the tourist industry like hundreds of its fellows along the
Caribbean coast, but for the moment its isolation and the
poverty of its people kept developers at bay. Jungle still crowded
in a green wall right up to the roadside and cascaded from the
black rock cliffs of the tiny offshore islands floating like galleons
at anchor in the bay.

Though it was 10 A.M., the place still wore the crisp wet
freshness of morning. David sniffed the air and felt glad to be
alive.

A man in faded whites, wearing a drooping straw hat, ambled

toward them from the corrugated iron shed that was the only airport building.

"Diego Saura," Brian said shortly. "David Moore."

"With much pleasure, señor." Saura regarded David searchingly as they shook hands.

"Equally." His ear for Spanish was now good enough to sense the tension in Saura's voice. Brian's contacts lived dangerously, slipping through the gaps between Guatemalan laws and Mexican and dealing with men not above slitting a throat to get what they wanted.

Like most of them, Saura had been a *chiclero*, harvesting the raw material for chewing gum in the forests for a few cents a day. His fortunes had improved since then, but acting as an *estelero* for Brian did little for his appearance; one ear was almost entirely missing and when he spoke he revealed teeth as battered and broken as his face. Three of the front ones were replaced by what looked like copies made of aluminum.

A battered American car, crudely converted into a pickup by slicing out the rear seat and trunk with a cutting torch, stood on the road outside the field. Heavy metal implements rattled deafeningly in the back as they jounced along the rutted back road.

"Our man is expecting you," Saura said. "I told him only that you were dealers from up north. He knows you as Señor Ford and Señor Westinghouse." He grinned at his joke, revealing the aluminum teeth in their full glory.

"And you think he has something to sell?" Jolson asked.

"That I must leave to you. Much was found in this area once, but the museum has been closed for years. It may all have gone." David wondered if he imagined the guarded tone of Saura's words. He glanced at Brian but saw only the eagerness that came over his partner when they were on the scent of a new find.

As a partner Brian had enough good qualities to outweigh his recklessness. Sometimes David lectured him on the value of detachment, of caution, then remembered himself at that age, eager for every advantage, unconcerned with who he outmaneuvered if it meant getting the piece he wanted.

After three years they had settled into a comfortable routine. Brian did the flying, made the contacts, and kept his ear to the ground while apparently continuing to work as a charter pilot. David, working from their base at Ciudad del Carmen near the border between Mexico and Guatemala, researched the finds, wrote up provenances, and handled the intricate financial details of trading semilegally with collectors and museums in the United States and Europe, to which he made frequent surreptitious trips, confident that the process servers would find it hard to track him down. The system worked; he was now richer and more at peace than at any time since he left England almost thirty years ago.

Or perhaps it was just middle age catching up with him. They lived pleasantly enough in their big house on the slopes of the coastal range. The food was good, the wine even better, and any luxury not available in Mexico City could be flown in from the States—including women, whom Brian encountered in all sorts of odd places and to whom he handed out holiday invitations with a generous hand. The most amazingly heterogeneous collection of ladies thought the buccaneering art trade attractive, and at times David found himself overwhelmed by their geniality.

He had also begun to write. A diary begun when he came to Mexico was now a short book, detailing the intricacies and the larcenies of the art-dealing business and his own career. One of these days he would try it on a New York publisher.

Saura pulled the car into the side of the road as it widened to show signs of more frequent use. "It is better that we are not seen together. Take the car and leave it at the field when you go. It will not be touched." David could believe that anybody interfering with Saura's possessions knew what to expect.

"There have no doubt been expenses," Brian said, reaching for his shirt pocket and taking out a wad of folded peso notes.

Saura grinned again. "Good luck, Señor Ford, Señor Westinghouse. Go with God."

With a clashing of gears Brian got the car moving. Turning the curve they saw the road dip down into a miserable village huddling by a beach of black sand. Bedraggled huts of sheet metal and adobe straggled unevenly along the three or four main streets. Thin children played in the puddles and gaunt dogs snapped at their wheels as they jolted into the center of Puerto Alvarado, where occasional two- or three-story buildings did their best to dominate muddy plazas. Most, predictably, were churches, though a vast pile built in imitation of Mexico City imperial architecture was obviously the town hall. It showed no signs of occupation.

"This place has a museum?" David asked, disbelieving.

"Sure. Used to be a status symbol, like a waterworks and a technical college. Also gives jobs for the wardheelers and the local governor's relations. The pumping station never works, of course, the technical college is usually burned down in the first riots, and the museum is never open, but salaries get paid anyway."

Another empty square was filled this time along one side with a flat blank building devoid of ornament, its facade blinded by shutters. They parked in front on the fringe of shattered and uneven paving. A sign, almost obliterated by decades of sun and rain, identified it as the MUSEO ETNOGRAFICA E CULTURALE. The gray weathered doors were firmly shut.

A few minutes' hammering brought the reluctant squeal of bolts from inside. One of the fattest men David had ever seen, an obese giant so huge that only a slice of his vast belly was revealed by the open door, glared at them.

"Closed." His voice was a ridiculous eunuch squeak.

Reaching for his pocket, Brian rustled notes energetically and kept up a barrage of complaints, demands, threats, and wheedling requests until they were reluctantly admitted.

They stood in a hall of church dimensions, its paved floor scattered with dusty glass cases, some of them leaning drunkenly or collapsed on wormy legs. A mezzanine ran around the upper levels, reached by a staircase so encrusted with bird droppings and other organic debris that it seemed carpeted. It creaked ominously as the fat man put his feet on it. In the shadows invisible creatures scuttled and, high above, a bird beat tiredly around in the dark, looking for escape.

Dr. Lancanja, the director of the museum, might himself have been trapped here like the bird. A pale bespectacled little man in a blue suit almost green with age and spotted with food stains, he quivered visibly at every movement, as if ready to evade a blow.

Guessing David to be the senior partner, he took his hand. "Señor Ford?"

"With great pleasure, doctor," David said, holding the thin hand gently. "May I present my colleague, Señor Westinghouse."

"Angelo—chairs." Too big to squeeze into the director's office, the giant handed two dusty kitchen chairs through the doorway as if feeding food to animals.

Lancanja's deprecatory gesture at the confusion of the office had a touch of prewar gallantry. "As you see, we are presently closed for recataloguing, and the regular staff are busy elsewhere. Angelo normally looks after the building—a night watchman. You have had a chance to examine our treasures?"

David thought of the moldering displays downstairs. "There are many fine pieces."

"Yes. Thank you. But, as you know, competition is now fierce. We do not have much money for necessary improvements." He glanced around at the ruin of the office: the dusty files, obviously untouched for years, the bottles heaped just out of sight in a wastepaper basket, the scraps of bone and carved stone with numbers lettered on them in Indian ink, reminders of a systematic regime now long in the past.

"You bring us to our reason for coming here, Señor," Brian said smoothly. "We understand you may be disposing of certain items."

"It is possible," Lancanja said uncertainly, disconcerted by Brian's bypassing of the amenities. David could almost feel his eagerness for news of the world outside.

"We are prepared to pay cash for any interesting material," Brian pressed.

With obvious reluctance Lancanja took a cardboard box from his desk. Brian poked briefly among the scraps of pottery and jade. "Señor, these are just shreds. I had hoped for something better." In leaning forward, he had revealed the wad of notes in his pocket. Lancanja licked his lips.

"I've read of some Nebaj pieces found here some years ago," David said. "Might these be for sale?"

"Perhaps." He disappeared into the gloom outside the door, returning five minutes later with his clothes mantled in dust, holding what looked like three heavy green tiles. David took them with care, even reverence.

Once these slabs of green jade had decorated the throne of a Mayan king, so close to a god that his people accepted with utter faith his pronouncement that only with living blood could the sun be made to rise and warm the land each day. He was here still, on the tiles, a squat naked figure in profile, hook-nosed, heavy-eyed, and dissolute, on his head a spectacular mask made from the skin of a jaguar, waist and wrists circled with elaborate jewelry of gold and jade. Below him his subjects cowered, rank on rank, abased, faces in the dirt before the god-king.

Brian affected a detached interest. "I think we would be

interested in these. Perhaps twenty thousand pesos?"

With a weary smile Lancanja rummaged among the papers on his desk and took out a familiar dog-eared volume. Sotheby's *Auction Prices Current* reached the remotest areas in the world these days. David had seen *esteleros* in the depths of Guatemala produce it, and with the same smirk. Next to the .45 pistol it was the great leveler.

"You are as well informed as I might have expected, señor," Brian said. "In that case, let me increase my offer to sixty thousand pesos." Even at this price, less than four thousand American dollars, they were a bargain, and when they settled for sixty-five thousand pesos a few minutes later, David knew they would turn a profit of more than three hundred percent on the plaques.

As Brian counted out the money, David's eyes wandered around the office. It wasn't all dusty, he noticed. In the corner lay a pile of heavy digging equipment—shovels, a pick, and three machetes, edges sharp but the back of the blades and the handles gluey with mashed vegetable matter. There was also a pair of high boots, covered in dried red mud.

He wondered if he should draw Brian's attention to the heap, his instinct jabbing him with warnings of some latent violence and evil in the objects. Then the other man followed his gaze briefly, and David saw the same conclusion in his eyes.

"I see you have been digging, señor," he said. "Are there still ruins in the area?"

Lancanja's eyes became shifty. "Ah, the tools. No, sadly, we needed only to clear vines from around the back of the building. If only there was still work to be done here." He shrugged. "It has been a great pleasure to meet you, gentlemen." Courteously he shook hands with both of them. "Señor Ford, Señor Westinghouse." He permitted himself a small joke. "My regards to your colleague, Señor Chevrolet."

They waited at the bottom of the stairs for the lumbering Angelo to open the door. As he fumbled with the locks, Brian said, "What did you think about that gear?"

"I didn't notice any vines around the back of this building."

"And you don't find red mud down here. Only up on the altoplano." He patted the wad of notes in his pocket and eyed Angelo speculatively. "Do you suppose Gary Cooper here would like to open his own ice-cream shop?"

As they converged on the huge man, David tried to suppress

the sense of danger that made the building seem more of a mausoleum than ever. He noticed that the bird no longer fluttered up by the ceiling.

38

"Evening, Miss Hershman," the doorman at Hershman West said with surprise. "When did you get in?"

"Just a while back, Bill." The yellow light of late afternoon brought out the bronze of the building's frontage. It seemed warmed to life. "Everyone gone home?"

"Mr. Beauclair hasn't come out yet."

Taking the elevator to the third floor, she bypassed the galleries and went straight to her own office. She spent too little time here to know the place well. It took five minutes of fiddling with the international dialing codes before she heard the phone ring distantly in David Moore's Mexican home. Even before the first *brr-brr,* she knew there would be no answer, but she waited for five minutes before hanging up. Next she called the airport, then put down the phone and pushed the button that would, she hoped, bring Sascha.

He came in, plainly astonished. "What on earth! I thought you were in New York."

"Some things I had to do. Sit down."

For the first time in years she took in Sascha Beauclair as a man rather than a colleague—an aging homosexual whose double-breasted Bill Blass jacket and silk cravat could not disguise the ravages of age. Pink scalp gleamed through the carefully teased remnant of his hair transplant, and there was powder on the puffy cheeks.

"How are things, Sascha?"

333

"Oh, not so bad. Some union's been wretched about the trucking entrance but I'll sort that out. Your friend D'Antoni—and where did you find *him*, incidentally?—installed your computer last week. I suppose it works; at least all the lights go on when you push the button." Noticing Sara's peculiar stillness, he stopped talking.

"Mark flew in this morning. He had some news for me. About Cicely."

"Oh." Fear played momentarily across Sascha's face, then cunning, and finally a weariness that made the pouches under his eyes and the lines at the corners of his mouth lengthen visibly.

"You can't blame a person for trying," he said at last.

"Not a bad try either. You might still win."

He shook his head. "Not me personally, heart. Cicely will squeeze me out when she can. I was just a convenient source of information."

"Sascha, if you needed money—"

"It isn't *just* money—it never is just money. No, I suppose I wanted, just once, to run something for myself. I'm really no better off with you than I was with David—just a glorified busboy. Cicely seemed to offer some real influence." He shrugged. "I gather this will not be forthcoming."

For the first time, she was sorry for Sascha. With each year the cost of his particular needs rose more steeply, the rough trade along Hollywood Boulevard upping its prices as they checked out his car, his clothes, his apartment, but most of all his need. If only he were the domestic type, he might have settled comfortably with some young man in Malibu. But, like Sara, he was too much the hunter, ruined for domesticity by a life in the art world where everything went to the quick and the hungry.

"What next?"

"Cicely will put the squeeze on," he said. "Or is that what Mark came to do?"

"He's on my side."

"Maybe he just thinks he is. Cicely can turn your brain inside out if she wants." He stood up. "Suddenly I feel like the heel I no doubt am. Perhaps I'll go for a drive and buy myself a friend. It will relieve you of the painful necessity of firing me officially." He paused at the door. "What do you hear about our old friend David?"

"He's down in Mexico someplace."

"Ever thought of taking a holiday, petal? I'm sure your Mr. Catton has a plane over here that you could use." He touched the swollen side of his face. "Don't end up like me, having to take the kind of friendship you can afford."

After he had left the office, Sara waited for only a few minutes before taking Sascha's advice.

39

Sara wasn't sure what she expected of David's Mexican headquarters. Something tumbledown perhaps, a tired pile of adobe bricks subsiding gradually into the clay.

In fact, the partners had taken over the country hacienda of a Belize plutocrat ousted in one of the biennial shifts of power. Built in California style, the house spread along a low hilltop in a scatter of low-pitched tiled roofs, the windows appearing to look out under the brim of a slanted hat, cautious and discreet.

A chain-link fence ten feet high ran along the road, but she found the gate open and drove in. The house's sandstone patio, its walls festooned with wisteria, was more welcoming, and the front door, though closed, was not locked. She went in.

Beyond the terrace of stone steps, the sprawling living room curved out of sight. Vivid rugs littered the floor, the only furnishing that could compete with the building's architectural splendor. Fifty people could lose themselves in the room, and it was only one of a dozen. Guest suite opened onto guest suite, bathroom onto dressing room onto patio, and most had at least one door leading to the tiled edge of the wide green swimming pool.

Nobody seemed to have cleaned house for a week or two, but there were signs everywhere of recent occupation: newspapers a few days old, cigarette ash in the ashtrays, a refrigerator well stocked with food.

At the back of the house she found two wooden buildings,

both locked. Through the cracks in the doors she saw a small
truck, splashed with mud, and crates that could hold antiquities
ready for shipment to the States. Why would they leave such
valuable items unguarded? It made no sense.

One room in the house was a kind of office. She pored over
the maps spread on the table, tracing the fine pencil lines that
might be trails.

It became clear the two men were on a trip—a trip from
which they had expected to return long before this.

Sara hardly noticed the light ebb into dusk.

A storm was coming. The air was restless with the imminence
of approaching thunder. Yellow light from outside fell softly on
the faces of Mayan and Mixtec and Olmec sculpture, making the
masks seem alive, alert, the patterns on the rugs weave, curve
within curve hypnotically.

Prickly and nervous, she went into David's study, sniffing the
scent of books and paint and wood as one might a lover's
bathrobe during his long absence.

The diaries stood along an upper shelf; six plain-bound
books. She opened the first and found herself reading a
description in his neat hand of a day in London more than forty
years ago: crowds on Hampstead Heath enjoying a warm Bank
Holiday Monday; fairs and squealing kids and a boy with his
mother toiling up the slippery grass slope toward the pavilion on
top that gave a panorama of all London, spread out almost to
the sea.

An hour's reading later, she found the first reference to
herself.

The storm broke as she read, but she hardly looked up as the
thunder cracked and lightning glared blue-white on the masks,
impassive above her head.

At eight, she closed the last of the books in which David,
before he left on the last trip, had carefully recorded the details
of his visit to the museum in Puerto Alvarado, and reached for
the phone. The police in Mexico City, initially unhelpful, were
finally persuaded to take an interest in the fate of David and
Brian.

40

David shifted back into the temple to escape from the worst of the rain. His leg twinged agonizingly at every movement, but by keeping his side almost stiff and dragging himself across the floor with elbow and knee he could reach the farthest corner, where vines and vegetation still bound the stones together as tightly as when they were put there centuries ago.

Wedging himself painfully into the shadows, he wondered for the first time if he would be the only fugitive from the storm. Nasty to find a snake or one of those hairy spiders the size of a dinner plate already in residence. But he was learning about the jungle after three days up here. Rain didn't keep the predators indoors, it just gave them the extra camouflage they needed to get on with the daily business of eating and being eaten. Rain pelting on the leaves covered the sound of their approach if they were large. It also brought out worms and bugs, as well as the burrowing animals who lived on them. Only the birds lost out. With their natural food, the iridescent flying things of the jungle airspace, grounded, they sat disconsolately in the trees, fluffing out their plumage and squawking derisively at the feasting below.

On the first day, a similar rainstorm encouraged the men who shot him to make one of their expeditions against the temple. But they climbed very badly, and David heard them when they were still halfway up the pyramid.

Crawling out onto the ledge next to the altar, he glimpsed a man toiling up the overgrown stone steps through the gray haze of the downpour and rolled off one of the large stones gathered on the edge for this purpose.

The builders had made this pyramid for rolling. His stone followed the same path as the thousands of bodies that had been flung from this same place, then went bounding off into the rain. Beyond his wildest hopes it hit one man full in the chest as he rose to try a shot. Then there were two shapes tumbling down into the jungle. A couple of shots cut through the creepers above him, but there were no more expeditions that day, nor the day after. Perhaps they expected the jaguars or the snakes to dispose of him on their behalf.

Well, they had something there. David gave himself perhaps one more day before the jungle predators crept up and found him too weak to fight them off.

Looking out from the temple down into the choked courtyard and then at the matching temple a quarter of a mile away, he could fool himself that this was an inhabited place, that sooner or later someone would happen by and rescue him.

But Queen Elizabeth the First was still ruler of England when the last people lived here, and it was less than three months since old Lancanja found it again by accident. The chances of rescue were remote to the point of absurdity. As the weight of this realization crushed down on him, he forced himself into the daily ritual of counting his blessings.

Blessings? A dismal group to be included under that heading. He was alive, at least. Not like poor Brian, his head blown off in the first minute that they stepped into the clearing and stared around in awe at the twin pyramids cloaked in valances of vivid green. The body had surged back against him and the mules shied, squealing, as blood spattered them. David had lowered Brian gently to the path, conscious only of astonishment.

Lancanja was dead too. Poor old Lancanja, with his outsized tropical gear, made for the man he had been twenty years ago, and his ideas, almost as much out of date, of winning his way back into the circle of the world's great archaeologists.

When finally they had winkled news of his find out of the lumbering Angelo, Lancanja had been willing, even eager to tell them all about it, even to show the photographs taken after his accidental discovery a few months before and to produce, shyly at first but then with the passion only collectors know, the few samples brought back from the trip: a stone mask still covered with its original painted human skin; exquisite jade carvings, miraculously intact; and, most incredible of all, a life-sized skull of solid rock crystal, the spatter of fractures and imperfections within its temples flaring like the ghost of thought.

They decided on a deal both simple and mutually beneficial. David and Brian would get the stuff out, catalogue it and prepare it, in return for the right to sell whatever the Mexican government did not want to keep. Lancanja got the credit, the pictures in the press, the right to read papers to learned societies and have himself interviewd by the *New York Times*.

David and Brian had exchanged a glance as he rambled on about his dreams of glory. At the first mention of a major find, the vultures would descend. Some bureaucrat would steal his credit, and the greedy chain of curators and conservators between here and Mexico City would skim off the best pieces while the rest found its way onto the international market.

Brian had other plans, with which David reluctantly agreed. Freyer was eager for new material and confident of his ability to place it with museums that would keep their mouths shut. Lancanja would be persuaded—Brian just looked evasive when David pressed him for details—to give them exclusive rights to dispose of anything they found. In return, he would have a fair share of the profits and the right—in time—to release details of his find to the world.

The plan made David uneasy, and that unease had grown as Brian became more eager for the loot and indifferent to how they got it. That eagerness had finally interfered with his judgment, neutralizing the instincts that should have warned him of the trap. Now he had the whole hoard. The jungle city was his mausoleum, with all eternity to count the treasure.

After the first shots, Lancanja seemed hardly to believe what had happened. There was a kind of maniacal courage in the way he walked into the clearing, arms outstretched as if in brotherhood to the dozen men in ragged clothes heaping firewood around one of the steles. The first volley of shots from the jungle on the far side of the courtyard blew him reeling across the stones and killed Brian, who was just behind him.

Trailing behind Angelo and the mules, David had had a moment to think. Angelo, bulking stolidly in the middle of the path, seemed indifferent to the shots, and those in the first volley came nowhere near him. A double-cross? Angelo might have tipped off the tomb robbers.... But there was no time for speculation. David dived sideways into the jungle beside the path just as the riflemen came out of the wall of green and aimed in his direction. The slam of the shot in his leg came an instant before the head-high brush swallowed him up.

He slithered and scrambled through the matted vines until, miraculously, a sharp black edge of volcanic rock barked his knee. Another, slightly above his head, offered a handhold and he hauled himself up, hidden in the creepers that cascaded down off the ruin. He was high above the courtyard before they glimpsed him, and seconds later, the tiny temple with its hook-nosed god on top became his shelter, to be shared with the white roots of the vines and the jittering spider monkeys.

He wondered how the looting was going on down below. Badly, judging by the glimpses he snatched of their work. Artifacts undisturbed for centuries by weather and an insistent ecology didn't give up easily. The giant steles, basalt slabs twenty feet high decorated on every face with reliefs, needed cranes and tractors to be moved, and the *esteleros* had neither. To create something a collector or curator might buy, they sliced off the reliefs with saws or broke the whole block into fragments by building fires all around and dousing the surface of the red-hot stone with cold water, usually ruining the block completely.

They hoped for jade, gold and jewels, but such treasures were hidden in places only an expert could spot. In killing Lancanja they had destroyed all hope of finding such caches, though David suspected he was sitting on such a hoard right now; the flagstones behind the altar showed signs of having been recently disturbed, probably by Lancanja on his first trip.

His leg twinged again, agonizingly. Hunger made the pain worse, though he knew another day would bring numbness and inevitable death. The irony of dying in the midst of treasure amused him, though not enough to laugh.

He lapsed into a doze then, waking to find rain pattering again on the vines and veiling the opening into the temple. At first, he took the pop-popping sound for particularly heavy drops landing on a large leaf, but then a shout—more like a scream—floated up to him. Dragging himself to the door he stared out, wondering if the bandits were trying one last attempt on his hiding place. It was almost ten seconds before he really believed the large blue helicopter hovering a quarter of a mile away, and the sodden militiamen fanning out across the courtyard.

41

Sara spent a lot of time by the pool during the weeks David stayed in the hospital. She welcomed the time to think, though the respite produced nothing conclusive—just a strengthening of the sense of dislocation that followed Cicely Snow's attempt to take over the firm.

Of this plan, she heard little. Lacking any direct orders to leave, Sascha seemed to have stayed on, but obeying whose orders Sara wasn't sure. Mark Turnbull remained in New York. They had a brief telephone conversation, but since he showed no inclination to leave immediately she left that situation also in abeyance.

This was the surprising aspect of her time in Mexico—the way it suddenly made Hershman's, in fact the whole auction business, less urgent, even uninteresting. What had she been fighting for all these years?

She did not realize at the time that this was a mere interval, a pause in the action before the drama reached its final disastrous climax.

They brought David home one morning, two bored ambulance drivers insisting that he remain on a stretcher until safely installed in his bedroom. Rather than fuss, Sara confined her greeting to a wave and waited by the pool until they had gone and the newly employed maid had given the room yet another quick examination to see it contained everything the invalid could need.

While she waited, the postman clattered up in his ancient station wagon with the mail. There was one fat official letter for her.

About an hour later, while she still sat beside the pool, a shuffling footstep and the dull tap of a cane sounded behind her.

"You shouldn't be up," she said, not looking at him.

"It's boring in there, I need the sun." He took the chaise longue beside her, first sitting on the edge, then hauling himself awkwardly onto his back. The bad leg stuck out ridiculously, still strapped in its light splint and noticeably thinner than the other.

"Hurt still?"

"A bit. I walk like a drunken sailor, too."

"The doctors said you always will."

"Should do a lot for my image. Perhaps I could get someone to lean on permanently, like those dowagers at Parke-Bernet. Always a new 'nephew' to help them around the private views. Must save them a fortune in canes." He looked over at Sara with a grin. "I don't suppose you'd like the job?"

"Maybe."

He looked better than the last time she had seen him, and greatly improved from the sallow, thin, hallucinating creature they brought down from the altoplano slung under a helicopter. Even from where she had stood when they slid him into the ambulance, the stink of his gangrenous leg had soiled the air.

Now his hair was recognizably paler than his face; before there had only been a paper mask from throat to hairline. More pain showed in the lines around his mouth and eyes, but they were just echoes of suffering. The old alertness, the sense of banked energy, was returning almost as she watched.

"Who's the girl?"

"Her name's Conchita. You're going to need someone around the house for a while."

"I suppose so. Funny how we never needed a maid before, when Brian was here. All those girls who just loved to cook and do the washing-up—I never understood it." For the first time he saw the papers in Sara's hand. "Mail?"

"From Cicely Snow's lawyers, about the company."

"What's happening?"

"About what I expected. She's got it all planned. Sascha as general manager, me as vice-president. Carl Bleigen is in there too someplace."

David, reading through the papers, smiled. "That man! I don't suppose there's any twist to the market he can't make money on. He'll outlive all of us, and when he's ninety they'll give him a testimonial as a pioneer of the business. If I'd stuck with him, I'd probably be a millionaire now. Or in jail."

"He never forgave you for stealing Arthur Sklar, did he?"

"I'm a hard man to forgive, apparently." He read the rest of the papers. "Looks like you wouldn't be too badly off if you signed."

"As long as I kept out of Cicely's way. She wants me clipping coupons for the rest of my life."

"There are worse ways of earning a living." Sitting up straighter, he looked around the view from the patio. The slow green slope of the fields ran down into a valley brimming with haze in the sun. Except for the slow movement of clouds, solid and white as stone, the world was at absolute peace. "You don't think you could get used to this?"

She paused so long that David thought she didn't mean to answer. At last she said, "That could be anything from an idle conversational remark to a proposal of marriage."

"Yes. Yes, it could."

A touch of breeze rattled the stiff white papers of Cicely's agreement where he had placed it on the tiles by the pool. They shifted an inch this way and that, like a crab feeling for a way of escape.

"Are *you* going to stay?" she asked.

"At least until the leg heals. And I've got some writing to finish. I'll have to decide what to do with all the stuff Brian and I accumulated, too." He glanced over at her, slightly amused. "Maybe you could get rid of it for me."

"You're not serious!"

"Never more so. This was Brian's business—I just paid the bills—but under our agreement the survivor owns everything."

"But it's worth a million! *More* than a million."

"You can owe me."

Sara lay back, knowing he was offering her the capital and the credentials to get back into the game, to fight Cicely if she chose.

"You'd like me to refuse, wouldn't you?" she said.

"I'm not sure. Maybe. We could enjoy ourselves down here. Good food, good weather." He straightened up painfully. "But I wouldn't be sorry to see Cicely stopped. If she can be stopped."

"You don't think I can handle her?"

"I suppose there's only one way to find out."

Watching her face, David sat back, half listening, as the breeze carried the papers toward the edge of the pool. Rattling, they edged to the tiled lip and fell in. Soon he drifted off to sleep.

42

"I want her out," Cicely Snow said quietly. "Now. *Immediately.*"

"Yes, I do see that," the lawyer said patiently. He had put on his tinted glasses ten minutes into the conference, allegedly because the morning light through the boardroom windows of Hershman West hurt his eyes, but Sascha, watching from the other side of the room, recognized a defensive mechanism when he saw it and sided with the man. Working with Cicely, one needed every piece of armor one could lay one's hands on.

"Has she actually signed the papers we sent her?" Sascha asked, knowing the answer already.

"Her attorney says there are minor problems," the lawyer said. "She might be holding out for more money, I suppose."

"If that's the case, she has quite the wrong idea," Cicely snapped. "If she won't agree amicably, we have other ways of gaining control."

"I'd hesitate to try anything like that except as a last resort," the lawyer said worriedly. "Pressure tactics, in my experience—"

"Then get on to her lawyers and tell them that if we have no answer by the end of the week, the information at our disposal will be released to the police."

"I'm sure you don't mean that, Mrs. Snow. It would be most inadvisable, as I've said before."

"Whatever methods we use, I want this cleared up." Her face went icy calm. Was she just obsessed, Sascha wondered, or quite mad? He'd heard something about her father being gaga when he died.

"If there's nothing else, Mrs. Snow?" the lawyer said.

"No. Get out, both of you."

Leaving the room, Sascha glanced back once at the small figure at the head of the conference table in the slanting morning light. Distance smoothed out the masklike face, taut after too many facelifts, disguised the thinning birdlike wrists, the too-teased, too-tinted hair. She looked like a mad little girl, filled with the obsessive hatred of the innocent abused.

His phone rang as he came back to his office. God knows where his secretary had gone. Later, her absence seemed one of the most crucial details of his life. He answered it himself.

"House of Hershman?" a girl queried. "Mr. Edward Argento calling."

The name rang a bell. An agent. Handling showbiz people, some rock stars.... Something clicked in Sascha's mind, the report a few weeks ago of someone dying.

Ten minutes later he put down the phone and arranged the notes scribbled as they talked. He had the sale of the century right here in his hands. The big *big* one. His hand reached automatically to call the boardroom, then stopped as he thought of that small quiet figure. She would learn—very quickly—that he was no busboy to be ordered out.

His secretary wandered back to her desk. "Petal," he called, "have we got a number for Sara Hershman?"

43

"He's like family," Eddie Argento said. For emphasis, he placed on Sara's thigh a hand tanned the color of pigskin. "I mean, brothers: that close."

Sara nodded as the hand massaged lightly, savoring the silk and the flesh underneath.

Like back projection in a movie, the Pacific Coastal Highway unwound in front of them: cloudless blue sky, water the color of aquamarine, foam white as lace frothing perfectly on the pebbles of the beaches. A gull swooped low over them, squawked on cue, and disappeared.

"It's pretty down here," she said. Argento glanced around once over his sunglasses before accelerating to overtake a truck whining toward Los Angeles.

"Yeah. I guess." From what she had learned of Argento in the last three weeks, he was like most attorneys in finding beauty only in small print and percentages.

The hills of the Sierra unrolled like wrinkled horsehide, tumbling to the ocean. Above, three miles away, on the highest ridge, the jagged shape of a building broke the skyline.

"Is that it?"

"Yeah." A large sign around the next bend confirmed her guess. LA PALOMA NEXT EXIT. Another hundred yards, and an enormous billboard with garish caricatures of—she guessed— Clark Gable and Jean Harlow twenty feet high announced SEE LA PALOMA HOLIDAY HOME OF THE STARS. Their grin and half the message were obliterated by a crudely painted diagonal streamer—CLOSED.

Swinging the car onto a black macadamed parking lot, Argento drove past the weathered wooden ticket office. By the heavy cyclone fence, six of the open buses that had once taken tourists up the winding mile of road to the house moldered in the sun, tires flat, woodwork dried and split.

Only two things looked fresh in this decay, the intercom box bolted to the gatepost and the sign a few feet farther down the fence. NO ADMITTANCE. SAVAGE GUARD DOGS.

Argento punched the phone buttons and snarled into the speaker. With a click, the gate latch opened and they drove up the hill.

"I backed them when they wanted to buy this place, you know that?" Argento's voice was contemptuous of his gullibility. "It looked like a good deal, taxwise. But look at it!"

His wave took in the parched hillside, gouged by erosion, and the occasional signs of roadside care, long since seared to death in the California sun. The road in particular had suffered from years of neglect. More than once, she felt the car lurch as the tires dug into unsupported asphalt, bedded only on shifting rubble. On either side the road fell away in saw-tooth erosion ridges; a careless driver could find himself in a lot of trouble.

There had been a Spanish farmstead here on the highest ridge of the coastal hills since the eighteenth century. By 1900, successive landowners had adapted and expanded the original adobe and tile hacienda of Casa Paloma into a sprawling mansion, the weekend retreat of a prosperous San Francisco family who motored down most Fridays with a few guests for a little riding and hunting.

One such guest on a weekend just before the First World War was Jameson Aldous—Jameson Aldous the Third, as he liked to be called—then just feeling his oats as heir to the second-largest newspaper chain in America.

With the casual confidence of a man with sixty million dollars in the bank, he bought the ranch and in ten years turned it into the ultimate showplace for his fortune, his friends, and his collections.

Buying was life to Aldous. At the peak of his collecting career, between the world wars, he accounted for ten percent of all the art sales in Europe and the United States. Agents combed Europe for paintings, bronzes, furniture, and paneling and in time for whole houses, churches, and palaces that could be shipped to La Paloma. Art treasures by the boatload were hauled up the narrow coast road and through the gates of the hilltop citadel, where builders labored almost incessantly, creating new galleries, guest houses, kitchens, and servants' quarters—all to accommodate Aldous's possessions and the people summoned from all over the world to admire them.

The greed for collecting never outran Aldous's imagination, but it did tax and finally destroy his fortune. When he died, bidding at Sotheby's in Bond Street for the Bernini naiad that proved to be his last purchase, he was hopelessly in debt, his holdings mortgaged to support the vast white elephant of La Paloma.

Accountants took more than two years to unravel the intricate financial puzzle he had created. Single-handedly, Aldous had raised market prices in a dozen areas of art, ranging from antique armor to Renaissance wood carving, but his holdings would realize their purchase price only if doled out piece by piece over decades. To dump them on the market would destroy their value as surely as if they had been burned. Despondent creditors handed the house and its contents over to the California government to be run as a museum.

For twenty years La Paloma remained a weekend tourist spot for San Francisco. The public dawdled along the Neapolitan colonnades and the Gothic clerestories, tossed their paper cups into the marble pools, and scratched initials and obscenities across the plump buttocks of Florentine *putti*.

As the building began to deteriorate in the spectacular fashion of stately homes everywhere, the administrators turned first in vain to the legislature, then to public appeal, then finally, in a desperate bid, offered the house for sale to anyone prepared to maintain it. Their astonishment was as extreme as their distaste when they found a tenant prepared to put down the necessary millions.

No pop group estimated the public taste in the late sixties quite so precisely as Beast. Its capering lead singer, Nick Fargo, face grotesquely painted, body almost naked in a succession of bizarre and androgynous sequined costumes, became the single most potent emblem of youthful rebellion and formed, with his mistress (and lead bass player) Epiphany Phillips, the most emulated and admired couple of the decade. Their thin, painted faces, paired in sexuality, summarized exactly the fashionable

blurring of sexual and social distinctions and encouraged a rash
of "'Phany and Fargo" jokes, costumes, and songs.

Beast could use La Paloma. Even its remoteness suited them.
Of all the pop groups to retire into a citadel against fans and
fame, they would be the most isolated, the most immune from
interference.

The vast spaces of La Paloma offered room to record their
albums, space to throw their legendary parties, isolation to live
in any fashion they chose, free of social or legal interference. One
of its largest rooms even gave Fargo room to display his own
personal collection, an inexplicable but overwhelming accumulation of art deco glass, one of the best in the world.

It was among the Lalique and Daum and Sabino that the
ranger found Fargo when, curious that a week's mail and
groceries had not been collected from the drop-off point by the
main gate, he had driven up the winding path to find the
Doberman guard dogs, mad with hunger, flinging themselves
against the wire of the fence.

Shooting them, he broke in. Fargo, emaciated, catatonic,
blue with exposure and malnutrition, lay on the floor of his
gallery, the victim of a drug overdose which would have killed a
man less habituated to every form of hallucinogen. His body
seemed almost transparent as he lay, barely breathing, in the
carpet of light from his shelves of glass.

Upstairs, Epiphany Phillips and the three remaining
members of the group, together with four groupies who shared
the house, were jumbled, naked and putrescent, on and around a
bed that had once belonged to Marie Antoinette. Five more
bodies were scattered through the house, all victims of the same
exotic drug.

As the group's primary legal adviser, Argento controlled the
estate. He wasted no time in disposing of this white elephant of a
property and its grisly history. With the dead hardly buried, he
was contacting the top auction houses, angling for a deal. Sara
endured his fondling, his broad invitations to bed, but strung
him along with sufficient skill until he agreed that La Paloma
and its contents should go under the hammer through the House
of Hershman.

All they needed now was Fargo's power of attorney—
presumably no problem, with Fargo his dearest childhood
friend.

La Paloma's frontage had a barbaric simplicity. Broad steps

looted from some Venetian palazzo led grandly to an arch that
belonged on a cathedral; its saints looked down grimly as
Argento yanked at a bellpull, then pounded on the metal-
studded wooden door.

The noise finally brought a shaggy young man in a red T-shirt
stenciled MUSIC SECURITY.

"Where's Felix?" Argento demanded.

The boy waved vaguely at the staircase leading to the upper
floor. Sara saw other rooms opening off the foyer. In the main
ballroom, now cluttered with recording equipment, musical
instruments, and music stands, someone on a synthesizer
noodled to himself in the gloom, running over a fragment of
Bach until the music became as meaningless as a muscular tic.

"Jesus, you got to do everything yourself," Argento grunted.
"Get Felix. *Now.* I'll be with Nick. How is he?"

"OK, I guess."

"You *guess?* I told you he was never to be left alone. Is
someone with him now?"

The man shrugged. Grabbing his arm, Argento spun him
around and propelled him toward the stairs. "Get up there,
asshole! Find Felix and find him *fast.* If anything's happened to
Nick, I'll—" But the boy was already halfway up the staircase.
Argento and Sara followed.

Everywhere, antiques cluttered the walls, the hallways, the
stairs. Statues leaned, dust-mantled, in niches; tapestries sagged
on the walls, Boule, Sheraton, Ming, Canova crowded in on her.
She was surrounded by the loot of the world.

Two more men in red T-shirts waited for them at the top of
the stairs.

"Felix, what's going on here? I told you never to leave him
alone."

Felix, pot-bellied and balding, scratched his stomach. "He's
asleep. I don't think he's slept since . . . hell, I just thought we
oughta leave him be. He's in shit shape, man."

"Yeah, well, that's too bad. I got some papers I need signed.
Better get something."

The master bedroom was built for an emperor. A small
apartment could have been contained in its space, a car parked
on top of the canopied bed. Bedding and mattress had been
removed, and Sara realized that it was in here that . . . She
caught the faint lingering scent of corruption.

Nick Fargo lay curled in a sheet on a French antique chaise,

laid like a sacrifice before the majesty of the view, a twenty-mile
sweep of the Pacific coast.

Grabbing him by the shoulder, Argento hauled him upright.
The bleary bearded face that stared at them was a clumsy
caricature of the features that had filled a thousand concert
halls, whipped millions into a frenzy.

"Nick. Nick, baby," Argento wheedled. The voice lacked any
trace of feeling. "C'mon, wake up." He looked over his shoulder.
"Felix."

Felix came into the room with a small black leather bag.

"What's he on?" Argento snapped.

"A few downers, maybe. Bit of hash. Mostly, he's tired."

"He can sleep all he likes when I'm gone."

"Yeah. Right." He opened the bag.

Small bottles, professionally labeled, and a range of
hypodermics filled it. Sara watched hypnotized as Felix
skillfully drew colorless liquid from an ampoule, tested the
syringe by jetting a tiny needle into the air, then pulled Fargo's
limp arm from under the sheet.

"Christ!" Even Argento was briefly appalled. Bruised blue
tracks ran up the veins from wrist to elbow. The other arm was
as bad.

Grabbing the sheet, Argento yanked it, spilling Fargo onto
the floor. He lay on his side, moving his arms feebly, like a
swimmer falling deeper into the cold grasp of drowning.

"In the ass?"

Felix shook his head. "Too slow." Taking Fargo's head in his
left hand he pulled the mouth open, peeled back the lower lip,
and carefully injected him in the gums. Sara, nauseated, looked
away, but Argento watched carefully as it was done.

Ten minutes later, Fargo could sit up. Blearily, without
comment, he signed the papers that gave Sara the right to sell La
Paloma, house and contents. For a moment Sara met his eyes.
They held nothing but the farseeing glazed stare of the dead.

Outside the room, she paused by one of the embrasured
windows, staring at the ocean and regaining her breath. She felt
poisoned.

"Well, it's all yours, honey." Argento came up behind her,
one hand companionably on her hip, and held the folded paper
before her eyes. She took it.

"All mine, less eighty-five percent," she said.

"Yeah." Argento smiled as he contemplated the possible profit on the deal. "You really think this junk will fetch ten million?"

"I'll know better when I've looked it over. Mind if I do that now?"

Argento frowned. "Well, I kinda hoped you'd come on down to L. A."

She put her hand on his arm and squeezed with enough warmth to convey her interest. "Let me take a rain check, Eddie. I mean, business—"

"Yeah. I guess." A prospect of millions from the sale of what a month ago had looked like his largest liability did much to allay his disappointment. "Later, huh?"

"I'll give you a call."

After he had departed, whistling, down the main staircase, Sara stood in silence, letting the castle impose its reality on the sham of its last occupancy.

She saw caballeros in high-heeled boots escort their ladies along these halls, and Jameson Aldous, gawky, greedy, chivy incurious guests from room to room, overwhelming them with the sheer volume of his treasures, some so new he hardly recognized them himself.

In the vast refectory, at a table long enough to seat a hundred, Hollywood stars had breakfasted before swimming in the marble pools or riding along the circular mile-long grape arbor, built twelve feet high so that riders could enjoy the shade. Above them, the grapes must have dangled invitingly, but Aldous, disliking his castle's past history as a farm, forbade the eating of any fruit grown on the estate. While fruit was shipped in from San Francisco, on the hilltop peaches and oranges grew ripe, fat, then rotted and fell to the ground.

For hours, Sara wandered through drawing and dining rooms, libraries, bedrooms, parlors, billiard and card rooms, boudoirs, suites, and cinemas. Sleeping here must have been an experience as alarming as it was impressive. Aldous thought nothing of using paneling from a French medieval chapel, so that saints looked down disapprovingly on lovers coupling in the canopied beds.

Feeling along a carved mahogany cornice, Sara sensed it move under her hand. A tiny door opened onto a narrow flight of stairs leading up to . . . what? She guessed the octagonal tower suite where Aldous had slept like a Moorish prince, his empire on view all around. Behind a reliquary in another room she found signs of a more common human frailty—an ancient bottle of whiskey, half empty, the shoulders thick with dust.

What was it all worth?

She had guessed at ten million, but that was just a figure pulled out of the air. Aldous's accountants had despaired of selling everything and thus flooding the market. But it was an infinitely larger market now, and one so greedy for antiques that buyers would crowd in just for the chance to view these treasures, most of which had not been seen for twenty years.

In Aldous's day, perhaps a dozen men collected medieval tapestries like those hanging in half the rooms of La Paloma; now, every gallery in the world would compete for them, not to mention a hundred collectors. The same went for furniture, porcelain, carpets, silver, and the building itself. La Paloma was a living embodiment of the saleroom rule, "Wait long enough and you'll turn a profit on anything."

At last, ascending long narrow staircases, galleries, and bare cement access hatches that exposed the modern bones of the skeleton on which Aldous had built his treasure house, she found herself on the roof, with a view of the Santa Lucia range on one side, with the Sierras behind, and on the other the crawling blue-green Pacific.

Higher still, a hawk climbed, to hover in the air, then wheel and skate in a tightening spiral toward the sun—higher and higher, until Sara lost it in the light.

44

From the upper terrace of Los Angeles Airport, Mark Turnbull watched the 747 crawl into line for takeoff. Ten minutes later, as it smoked into the air, he went to a phone booth and punched out a number.

"The coast's clear."

"You're quite sure?" Sara asked.

"I even waited until it was in the air. It wouldn't surprise me if she had jumped out on the runway."

"You're a treasure. Sure you won't stay?"

"I want to be in London when she hears you've covered Bleigen's note. That's worth a dozen transatlantic trips."

"And you're sure you can handle her?"

"For a day or two. That should give you enough time. Look, I'd better get onto my flight or there'll be some awkward questions when she gets back." Cicely was stopping off in New York for a day, so Mark would beat her home; she should never know about his trip to warn Sara.

"You're a pet. Take care."

Hanging up, Sara turned back to the crowded office, where eight young men were chattering in a language that might be Abyssinian but which she recognized from Bobby D'Antoni's tutoring as one of the computer languages. They looked unkempt and downbeat, but between them they constituted a notable concentration of computer expertise. She tapped on the desk for quiet.

"Listen, guys. I know this is easy for you, but we're in the dark. Just how are things going?"

"For this kind of deal, pretty good," D'Antoni said. "It would help if we could do business by daylight. . . ."

"I explained the need for secrecy."

"Yeah. Well, we're doing fine anyway. All the gear is leased and we're ready to put it in any time you like. There are also a few bills." He handed her a thick bundle. With the comfort of a swelling bank balance fed by the sale of David's pre-Columbian collection, she confidently passed them to Sascha.

As he riffled through them, his eyebrows rose until, had he had much hair, they would have disappeared into it.

"How long will it take to set up everything?" Sara asked.

"A couple of months."

"Incredible," Sascha said from across the room. "I would have said a year to catalogue a sale this big."

"Sure," Sara said. "To catalogue, check, write up descriptions, design and print a catalogue, mail it, and get it distributed—at least that long. But with a computer . . ."

There was nothing new in the idea of computers in a saleroom. Everyone was using them in some capacity or other, from the automated boards that translated bids into all the international currencies to the billing and invoicing systems now commonplace in the big auction houses.

Others had tried to go further in automating the art business. Fifteen New York museums and the National in Washington had formed the Museum Computer Network; when complete, it would give the location, value, and condition of every major art item in the world, whether in public or private hands. The authorities were dithering about putting this ambitious scheme into full working order, but as soon as she read about it, Sara saw an application to Hershman's. All she had needed was computer expertise and capital. Now she had both, plus the ideal sale to exploit them.

Luckily, Jameson Aldous's exhaustive catalogue of his holdings still existed. Transferred to magnetic tape, it provided the heart of the sale. D'Antoni's programmers broke the collection down into categories—silver, paintings, furniture, jewelry, and the rest—then a horde of out-of-work university students stirred up by the indefatigable Bobby moved in to photograph and number every item in the building. The number-crunching computer engulfed all this information in a day.

To examine an item in the sale, a buyer had only to dial the Paloma machine on his own terminal and punch out a lot number. If his credit were already established, a photo and a full description of the item would be on its way to him by telex and wirephoto within minutes; someone unknown to the computer received an itemized account for the service. Bids were accepted in all major credit cards, or bank drafts, the whole transaction handled by the machine. At Bobby's urging, Sara briefly considered conducting the whole auction by computer from cataloguing to delivery, but the chance to lead a sale personally against the backdrop of La Paloma proved too seductive. The choicest items in each class were reserved for personal buyers at a special five-day sale at La Paloma itself.

Later, she wondered if that decision alone led to the disaster. Or was it, as David suggested, that they were all fated in time to come together at La Paloma in that holocaust?

45

"OK. Let's move it."

With a grunt, the six men took the strain, and the stone coffer, half a ton of porphyry, rose shakily from the ground. They tottered off with it down the path to the front lawn of La Paloma, where the pennants on the candy-striped marquee snapped in the Pacific breeze.

That had been the last of the stone items spread around the marble reflecting pool. The Canovas and mock Michelangelos left behind only stained disks on the otherwise flawless white stone. It was the same inside the house. For a week, teams of men had been hauling out anything that could conceivably be sold. They were like ants at a picnic, carrying not crumbs or grains of sugar but Barbizon oils, Sheffield plate, Regency furniture, medieval medals—the accumulated loot of the millennium.

A waiter came onto the terrace and put down a tray with a single bottle, a jug of water, and a bowl of ice.

"Thanks, Luis. How is it going?"

"Quite well, Miss Hershman. The caterers are low on champagne but they can cope."

She poured a drink. It seemed a century since she drank this first, but she still remembered her hand trembling, the dryness of elation and fear in her mouth. As she raised the glass, ice chimed and she saw in it her own inverted image, a twisted imp in red.

The dress was a calculated striving for effect. Only a few

women could carry off the deep crimson that hints at the red of poinsettia and hibiscus, but Sara was one of them. She seemed to walk in flames, like an empress or a saint; this might be the sale of the century but it was also the sale of her life, and she was determined that nobody would forget it.

Conversation buzzed audibly from the lawn four stories below where her guests milled—a thousand of the world's most prominent collectors, dealers, and artists, flown in and royally entertained to give her the audience she needed. Shortly she would sweep down the main staircase of La Paloma and out onto the front steps that made such an effective dais for the rostrum. No matter how often she rehearsed that moment, it retained its special magic.

Finishing her drink, she stepped through the French doors into what had been a long salon housing Aldous's collection of eighteenth-century furniture but which now served as command post for the sale.

Five switchboards took up a large part of the space, their operators frantically punching figures into the computer terminals on their desks.

"Silver. Yes, sir." One girl smiled up at Sara and expertly tapped out a lot number. The screen lit up with description, value, and current bidding. "Lot Seven-oh-two-two. We have a reserve of ten thousand dollars on that. Last bid eight. Yes. Up to eleven-five. I'll enter that. And your code number? Thank you. Please confirm by telex, as usual." She waited, listening. "I'm sorry. Furniture is another operator. I'll transfer you."

At the other end of the room, Sascha, phone jammed to his ear, the other hand signing, checking, making notes, kept the sale in precarious balance. Cupping a hand over the mouthpiece he grimaced at her.

"How's it going?" she asked.

"Could be worse. Has everyone arrived?"

"Most of them, I think."

She went to the corner window and looked down on the forecourt where a hundred expensive cars gleamed in the sun. As she watched, two more, a Rolls-Royce Corniche and a Mercedes long enough to act as a hearse, emerged from behind the building and were shown to their places by two of the corps of attentive ushers.

Reluctantly, Sara had decided not to depend on the crumbling main road to the house, on which at least one heavy van had already come to grief, almost toppling off into a ravine. The service road running around the hill to the back of the house was in reasonable condition, and it was up this that guests were directed. They missed the spectacular switchback ride with its views of the Pacific, but the panorama from the terrace below her more than made up for it, especially when waiters immediately pressed into every hand an iced glass of Dom Perignon.

"I can't see anyone on the highway," Sara said to Sascha when she returned. "We can start on time, I think." Opening the glass doors that led to the unoccupied south wing of the house, she said, "I'm going out to get some peace."

"Want some company? I'm bored with this."

"Be bored afterward."

These rooms had been the first to be cleared. Squares of darker green marked the faded walls where pictures had protected them from the sunlight, and in the corners of the rooms scraps of paper, cloth, and dust added their seal of disuse.

This salon joined another in a long L, and as she turned the corner she found herself no longer alone. A man in a black suit, leaning on a cane, stood looking out at the view of coast and mountains.

"David!" She grabbed him like a child running to her father, then had to steady him as his injured leg weakened under him.

"Careful, I'm still an invalid."

"I didn't know you were coming. You insisted you wouldn't."

"And miss the sale of the century?"

"You've been reading the papers again. You know that rots the brain."

"I had to do something. It's been too quiet down there with only Conchita for company. When are you coming back?"

"Oh, David, I don't know." She waved at the scene below: the marquee, the strolling guests on the lawn, the blue Pacific. "I've never enjoyed myself so much in my life."

David was silent. He had seen too many sales to find them glamorous, and this one, with its appalling richness, seemed less sale than circus, a chance for dealers and collectors to show off their money, mistresses, and, most of all, their greed. Buying here would demonstrate not taste or investment skill but sheer wealth and acquisitiveness.

"It reminds me of a sale I went to once," he said. "A bit like this one. A country house. A marquee. . . ."

He seemed mesmerized by the memory. "It was winter, so they had heaters in the tent. Big gas things. We were sweating. About halfway through the sale, I noticed that the auctioneer was scratching his head. Then the man in front of me started as well. I even felt a little itchy myself. I looked down at my hand, and there on the back was a tiny spider. One of those red ones, the size of a pinhead."

"Money spiders," Sara said.

"Yes. The heat brings them out." He pointed at the milling group, weaving in their intricate pattern of recognition and speculation. "That's us, Sara." She knew he meant the crowd. The money spiders.

At that moment, Sara realized this would be her last sale. Let Cicely have the company. It didn't matter. She couldn't know how strangely that resolution would finally be achieved.

"I'd better go down," she said. Afterward, there would be time to tell him. "Are you coming?"

"Not just yet. I'm enjoying the view." But he knew his presence would make it less of her triumph.

So as Sara made her way through the front doors of La Paloma and the crowd broke into spontaneous applause, as the cameras of the photographers flashed and the TV cameras whirred, David was the only one to see the large white Lincoln pull up in the deserted parking lot at the foot of the hill. The driver got out and stood irresolutely in front of the heavy wire gate with its NO ADMITTANCE sign.

"What's the trouble?" Cicely Snow said, winding down the back window. The wave of heat made the skin of her face seem tight. She felt stifled.

"The gate's locked, ma'am." He pushed back his cap to scratch his head. Ridiculous to expect more from a yokel hired in the nearest town to drive her up here. She turned to the other man beside her. "Can't you do anything?"

The deputy sheriff looked wearily. "Lady, I'm just here to serve a writ on your behalf. Transportation is usually provided."

She looked around the parking lot for another entrance; from where they were parked, the entrance to the service road, a hundred yards further up the highway, was invisible. "We just have to get through that gate."

Baffled, the driver climbed back into his seat. "I don't see no way to get up there, lady."

Cicely pointed to the crowd assembled on the top of the hill, clearly visible in the sun.

"*They* got up there, didn't they?"

"Well, I guess so."

"Then we'll just have to break down the gate. It's imperative I arrive before the sale begins."

The deputy sheriff was horrified. "That's forcible entry!"

"I don't care. They can send the bill to me." Slapping the driver on the shoulder, she said, "Get on with it."

Reluctantly, he put the car into drive and eased it forward against the wire. The hinges were old. Metal parted with a squeal and they trundled in over the remains of the gate.

"Surprising what you can do when you try," Cicely said with satisfaction. "Now let's get up there."

David followed the whole incident from the terrace, at first unaware of what was to happen, then helpless to stop it.

Almost as wide as the road, the car clung uncertainly to the first curve. Then, the wheels digging deeply into the rotten asphalt, it accelerated up the hill to the next zigzag. Here, the whole road had been undermined by the rains, so that only a shell of asphalt and gravel remained.

The driver almost made it. But as the rear tires dug in to accelerate away, the whole ledge crumbled. For a second, the car hovered, its wheels spinning; then it tipped into the ravine, balanced for a moment on the knife edge of an eroded ridge, and rolled over three times before stopping with a crash against a tree.

Before the dust settled, David had begun to limp toward the terrace.

Oblivious of what had happened, Sara stood on the rostrum and acknowledged the applause of the crowd. As it faded, she opened her catalogue.

By design, the first day included most of the bizarre and rare items that attract novelty interest and give the papers good copy. Lot One stood on the table beside her, an intricate cage less than a foot high containing two tiny mechanical birds.

"A Swiss Gold and Enamel Singing Bird Cage. Late eighteenth century. Can we start at three thousand dollars?"

For a moment, the whole marquee was still. Perhaps it was the oddity of the location, the sheer improbablity of the object

for sale, or the effect of champagne and sun on the crowd. Then
a young porter darted forward, pushed a panel on the base of the
cage, and a scratchy tweeting filled the tent.

The grin of delight on the face of a dour old dealer in the front
row told Sara that everything would be all right.

"Now do I hear three thousand dollars?" she asked with a
smile. The man in the front row raised his glass. "You do indeed,
Miss Hershman."

The sale of the century was on, and in the chatter of bids
nobody heard the ambulance siren at the bottom of the hill.

Sara, in the blur of emotions running through her, could not
identify the one that was making her cry.

People flocked to La Paloma from all over the world, lining
up for hours to climb the hill, squeeze into the marquee, and bid,
often wildly, for any souvenir of the event. Prices mushroomed,
skyrocketed—you could sell anything. By the end of the five
days, the exhausted team of auctioneers were getting hundreds
of dollars for brooms and buckets from the castle closets, some
still bearing labels from the local supermarkets where they had
been bought.

Once or twice a day, they might be lucky enough to see Sara
Hershman herself as she ascended the rostrum to be filmed by
the camera crews who followed the crowds to the castle.

Her regular staff looked on sardonically at these "guest
appearances," but she sensed their affection. None of them, she
realized, resented the general opinion that this was her sale—not
even Sascha who, relaxed for the first time in years, took the
whole event as a welcome holiday and basked in the admiration
and interest of the more prestigious customers. Watching the
smiles of "her people," Sara realized the fight was over. The
legend of La Paloma would become the legend of Sara
Hershman as well.

On the last day, she gratefully got into her car and drove
down to the tiny town on the coast, savoring the peace of the
evening, the satisfaction of the sale's conclusion.

Half a mile past the turnoff to La Paloma, a car passed her
going in the opposite direction—a heavy gleaming car that
looked vaguely familiar. Putting it down to exhaustion she
dawdled into town, unaware that La Paloma's most dramatic
hour was yet to come.

46

Only the dead owned the castle now—except for one madman.

The beam of his flashlight, a paranoid extension of his own sight, slid from corner to corner. Somewhere, he knew, They were watching him.

Sensing his unprotected back, he whirled, scanning the gloom, but saw only the bare walls of the huge hall, distant as sky.

"Eddie?" A whisper in the dark, unanswered.

Probing the warm dark silence, his beam crept up the walls and paused.

Though a velour of grime coated the ceiling's intricate coffering and carving, it remained exquisite, a formal garden on whose sky he walked like a spider. Moving forward, fascinated, craning to see more, he tumbled headlong into a shattering trap of wire and glass. The torch spun from his hand, to fall with its beam fixed on the ceiling, pinning one gilded rose in a needle of light.

The dope numbed the pain in his slashed hands to a satisfying tingle. Grabbing the flashlight, he studied the chandelier, lowered from the roof for safety. A tulip-shaped funnel of egg-shell glass enclosed each of the hundred candles, though a dozen funnels lay in bloody shards.

Kneeling, he scrabbled for matches in his pocket and lit a candle, using its flame to touch off others. Yellow light bloomed, but They were invisible still.

Ignoring the splinters of glass in his hands and forearms, he grabbed the dusty rope and heaved. Rocking and rattling, the chandelier climbed toward the ceiling.

Higher. Higher. Shadows thinned and faded, but it was still only halfway to the ceiling. Arms too tired to haul any more, he hung onto the rope and backed away, bare heels feeling for a purchase on the splintered boards of the floor.

Eighty feet above, the chandelier hit the ceiling with a crash. Burning candles and broken glass showered down.

Brought from some Spanish monastery half a century ago and untouched since, the ceiling, once solid cedar, had dried, then rotted in the desiccated mountain air. Riddled with woodworm, it needed only one flame to set it ablaze. Fire rushed along the beams, the heat bursting sealed cavities in which the dust of fifty years' patient nibbling was stored. The dust gushed out, caught fire, and blazed.

The man watched fire spring from beam to beam, crawl down rotted tapestries that drooped like oozing lava as the fire ate their worn threads. Squatting contentedly against the wall, he admired the shifting patterns of light as, eating through the decorative ceiling, the flames attacked the beams of the roof itself.

47

After a week, Sara knew the staff at the small hospital so well that they admitted her without comment. David sat where she usually found him, in the corridor outside the private room they had given Cicely Snow.

She sat down beside him. "Any change?"

"She woke for a little while today, but there's obviously brain damage. They don't think she'll ever really come round."

"Is it worth waiting then?" She tried to sound gentle.

"I keep asking myself that. I suppose not. Put it down to guilt."

"What are you guilty of? You might as well blame me. If I'd signed those papers as she asked—"

"It goes back farther than that, Sara. Cicely and I declared war when we were younger than you."

A nurse came out of the room and smiled briefly at them. "She's on the drip feed now. I don't think there's much point in waiting any more tonight."

David stood, levering himself upright with his cane. "You'll call me if there's any change?"

"Yes."

Taking his arm, Sara walked with him to the parking lot. The night was warm, almost scented. In the darkness, the surf thumped regularly like the slow lashing of a giant tail.

"Are you finished up there now?" he asked as she opened the car.

"As of this afternoon. Nothing left but the marquee, and I even had some offers for that."

"What about the house?"

"Nobody was *that* crazy. What would they do with it?" She started up the engine. "But do you mind if we drive up there for a while? Bobby's pulling out the computer and I said I'd drop in."

"Providing we can have shrimp afterward."

"A deal."

They cruised along the coast highway, dawdling past the beaches to savor the gleam of the afterglow on a tranquil surf, hardly more than a foaming ripple as it rolled in. Kids laughed and splashed in the shadows; dogs chased sticks they could hardly see.

With no more tourists, the guard on the lower gate was reduced to two. They waved Sara through without comment.

Silhouetted against the afterglow, the long hulking shape of La Paloma might have been the Ark, broken-backed on Ararat.

"I never realized till now just how desolate the place is," David said as they got out of the car. "It tells you something about Aldous, doesn't it? To put his castle up here, as far away from people as he could. Collectors!"

Thinking of the low companionable hacienda at Ciudad de Carmen, Sara silently agreed, wondering when and how to broach the subject of what happened next to them.

Bobby was almost finished loading his gear. Jumping into the cabin of the truck, he said, "I'll get this back to the warehouse and have them bill you."

"No matter what it cost, it was cheap," Sara said. "Tell them I might be in the market for some of this gear, if they give me a good price."

"Jew," he said amiably, grinning through his mustache.

"Spik."

"Yeah. But with class. You said so yourself." Then, seeing in David's presence the shape of things to come, he blew her a kiss. "I'll be in touch."

As the motor caught, he leaned out again. "Don't lock up until he's left."

"Who?"

But he was gone with the revving of the heavy engine.

Puzzled, Sara walked around the corner of the marquee and looked into the old bus parking lot. The car parked there was the one that had passed her on the highway. She recognized it now; it belonged to Eddie Argento. She had a sudden premonition.

The main doors of the house gaped, tied back for easy access to the larger pieces of furniture. She went into the dark, eyes searching the shadows.

Upstairs, a rattling thump echoed through the building, stirring sounds everywhere. She became aware of a flickering yellow light seeping into the hall.

Now the glow lit the hall almost as brightly as candlelight. Watching the flickering light crawl on the walls, she knew what caused it.

"Sara, are you all right?"

David stood in the door, silhouetted against the dusk. Sara ran up the curving staircase. Halfway, the smell of burning hit her, and at the top there was enough heat to make her perspire. She stopped at the door to the main hall, shielding her face.

The whole roof was a canopy of flame from which burning debris rained constantly to the floor, a pattering background to the rushing roar of the flames. In a hundred places the floorboards were on fire, and Nick Fargo staggered among them, giggling. His hair was already crisping with the heat and his clothes smoked, hovering at the edge of combustion. As Sara watched, a fragment of burning wood fluttered to his shoulder and the whole back of his jacket flamed yellow.

In an instant he became a pillar of flame, jerking into motion to run in a crazy zigzag down the hall toward its far end where smoke coiled and billowed, as impenetrable as black velvet. She saw him briefly, a glowing ghost in the smoke, then nothing more.

David was behind her, dragging her away. Her eyebrows were scorched, her dress yellowed by the heat. They ran down the stairs and into the air, icy after the inferno of the hall. Looking up, she saw flames burst through the upper windows and a tiny hole appear in the main roof, spurting sparks.

Hauling her to their car, David pushed her in.

She could only stare through the back window as he struggled with his stiff leg to start the car. "God, the fire brigade, the police—"

"Not much use now," David said. The car jerked into motion. "We'll call them, but it won't do any good."

"It was Fargo. He was in the hall. Burning...."

The guards at the gate had already rung for the fire brigade;

they heard a distant melancholy whine as David drove across the highway and onto the beach. Stumbling out, he looked up the hill to watch La Paloma, now alight from end to end. A good end for poor Nick Fargo; for the whole place, if it came to that. Aldous would not have wanted it to live on as a ruin.

He followed Sara down to the water's edge, where she stood ankle deep in the bloody froth that the fire made of the surf.

"You're getting wet feet."

"Mmmm." She leaned against him softly. "I am just so very very tired, David."

They sat down on the sand. Though the house burned behind them, they took no notice as the night carried them away, farther and farther with each wave from the world of the buyers and the bought.